A
Green
Place
For
DYING

R. J. HARLICK

A
Green
Place
For
DYING

A Meg Harris Mystery

DUNDURN
TORONTO

Editor: Allister Thompson/Sylvia McConnell
Design: Jennifer Scott
Printer: Webcom

Library and Archives Canada Cataloguing in Publication

Harlick, R. J., 1946-
        A green place for dying / R.J. Harlick.

(A Meg Harris mystery)
ISBN 978-1-926607-24-5

I. Title. II. Series: Harlick, R. J., 1946- . Meg Harris mystery.

PS8615.A74G74 2011   C813'.6   C2011-900554-9

1   2   3   4   5   16   15   14   13   12

We acknowledge the support of the **Canada Council for the Arts** and the **Ontario Arts Council** for our publishing program. We also acknowledge the financial support of the **Government of Canada** through the **Canada Book Fund** and **Livres Canada Books**, and the **Government of Ontario** through the **Ontario Book Publishing Tax Credit** and the **Ontario Media Development Corporation**.

Printed and bound in Canada.
www.dundurn.com

Dundurn	Gazelle Book Services Limited	Dundurn
3 Church Street, Suite 500	White Cross Mills	2250 Military Road
Toronto, Ontario, Canada	High Town, Lancaster, England	Tonawanda, NY
M5E 1M2	LA1 4XS	U.S.A. 14150

To Jim

The Meg Harris Mysteries

Death's Golden Whisper
Red Ice for a Shroud
The River Runs Orange
Arctic Blue Death

Grandmother Moon
You know all women from birth to death
We seek your knowledge
We seek your strength
Some are STARS up there with you
Some are STARS on Mother Earth
Grandmother, lighten our path in the dark
Creator, keep our sisters safe from harm
Maa duu? Mussi Cho

— Kukdookaa

Reprinted from the website of the
Native Women's Association of Canada

CHAPTER ONE

A loon called from across the lake in the hushed stillness of the rising moon. Its silvery path rippled across the water to where we sat on a grassy knoll. Skirting the ridge of the distant shore, the blinking lights of a passing plane wrenched me momentarily back to this century.

Above the rhythmic beating of a solitary drum, I could hear the uneasy breathing of the other women and the girls as we sat cross-legged, holding hands, waiting for the ceremony to begin. I glanced around the circle at their faces partially revealed in the pale glow of the crackling fire. Most had their eyes downcast, lost in their own thoughts. One or two met my gaze before dropping their eyes back to the ground. I dropped mine too.

On my right I felt the comforting warmth of Teht'aa's hand in my own, while on my left, my neighbour's hand seemed forebodingly cold. I tried to put life into it with a gentle squeeze, but the hand remained indifferent.

My feet were growing numb. I wanted to stretch out my legs but was afraid to disrupt the silence. I didn't want to remind the others of my presence. After all, I, Meg Harris, an escapee from Toronto, was the outsider, the stranger in this sacred circle of Algonquin women. No, not entirely Algonquin.

The two women sitting across from me in the circle were Cree from a James Bay reserve a thousand kilometres or more due north from where we were sitting on the shore of Lake Nigig in the Migiskan Anishinabeg First Nations Reserve. The two women were sisters. The younger, prettier one in a blowsy sort of way, was Becky's mother. She was gripping her sister's hand as if her life depended on it. And perhaps it did.

The limp hand resting in mine belonged to the other outsider, although technically she wasn't, since she was married to an Algonquin and lived on the reserve. In fact, she probably made more effort to follow the traditional ways than any other woman on the reserve, apart from the elders. She was Marie-Claude, the French-Canadian mother of Fleur.

I squeezed her lifeless hand again more as a show of support than anything else. She was obviously numb with worry. I certainly would be, given the situation.

A sudden spark of flame at the far end of the circle lit up the broad, wizened face of the elder leading tonight's ceremony. Although her official name was Elizabeth Amik, she preferred to use her spirit name, Summer Grass Woman. Many, out of respect for her position as an esteemed elder, called her Kòkomis Elizabeth or Grandmother Elizabeth.

She bent over the almost flat ceramic bowl resting on the ground in front of her and ignited its contents, which judging by the scent was dried cedar. She fanned the flame with a slender white-tipped eagle feather until it disappeared, leaving a glimmer of burning embers.

With the smoke swirling upwards into the night, she raised the bowl heavenward. Chanting in Algonquin, she offered the smudge to the four directions of the medicine wheel; east, south, west, and north. She set it back down on the ground beside her medicine bundle, a disparate collection of items sacred to her, both natural and man-made. These were laid out on a piece of felt.

Apart from the red, yellow, white, and black flags marking the four corners of the felt, the predominant colour of her regalia was green. Like the items, this colour was sacred to her. This she'd explained to me on my first visit to her healing wigwam, a visit Teht'aa had suggested during one of my particularly low moments after breaking up with her father.

Summer Grass Woman had gone on to tell me that the smooth piece of jade had been found by her long dead husband near his family's traditional trapline. The piece of lime green checked cotton came from the baptismal dress of her first granddaughter, and the palm leaf, she'd pointed out with a soft chuckle, had been brought back by a favourite niece from the land of the Maya in Mexico. She said it reminded her of her friend, a Mayan elder she'd met at one of the annual Circle of All Nations gatherings. And of course there was the sheath of dried summer grass kept in place by a leather tie intricately decorated with dark green beads. Even the felt was green, a rich emerald.

Pleading that the pain of her arthritis kept her from coming to us as tradition required, she asked instead that we come to her for our ritual cleansing. One by one, we unscrambled our cramped legs and stamped our feet to get the circulation moving. Then each of us in turn walked over to her in a clockwise direction, which she, as its elder, had established when we first entered the circle.

Since making my home at Three Deer Point, the wilderness property I'd inherited from my Great-aunt Agatha, I'd attended enough smudging ceremonies to become sufficiently familiar with the etiquette. During the first one I attended, I'd started walking in the wrong direction before Eric, its elder, hurriedly corrected me. It had been a dark, moonless night. The mood had been warlike and boastful, unlike tonight's sombre tone. It had been a ceremony meant to embolden rather than to seek guidance, the intention of tonight's ceremony.

As I became more involved in the neighbouring Migiskan community, initially because of Eric, who in addition to being my then friend and lover was the reserve's band chief, and since because many community members had become my friends, I'd had the honour of attending many more. But even though I enjoyed the ceremonies and found they imbued me with a sense of inner peace, no matter how fleeting, I couldn't quite rid myself of the feeling that I would always be an outsider wistfully watching from the sidelines.

Summer Grass Woman smiled as I approached her. "Good. You come. Grandmother Moon help you," she said in her soft, measured old woman's voice.

Although I didn't believe it, I did what politeness dictated and smiled in return.

She gently fanned the smoke around me with her feather while I performed the hand motions of the ritual washing. My nostrils twitched with the cleansing scent of the smouldering cedar. And as was often the case, I felt the beginnings of an inner quietness, a settling of my jittery nerves. I wondered if the smudge was having the same effect on the two mothers, for surely their nerves were jangling.

Although Teht'aa occasionally attended these monthly ceremonies to honour Grandmother Moon, this was the first one I'd been invited to. Grandmother Moon was considered a powerful teacher for women, since she controlled many aspects of a woman's life. It was believed that she provided women with a special connection to the grandmothers who had passed into the spirit world. Her teachings would help them become better mothers in their sacred role as life-givers.

But being better mothers wasn't the purpose of tonight's ceremony. It was to seek Grandmother Moon's guidance and insight on quite a different matter.

Fleur and Becky, the daughters of Marie-Claude and the woman from James Bay, were missing. They had vanished without a trace sometime in mid-July, a little over a month and a half ago. Nothing had been heard or seen of them since. Tonight the two mothers were seeking a sign from Grandmother Moon that their daughters were safe and would return home soon.

CHAPTER TWO

After we resumed our places in the ceremonial circle, Summer Grass Woman began chanting. Teht'aa had told me little other than to bring a red tie of tobacco and a small bottle of water. They rested on the ground at my feet where I'd seen the others place theirs.

I felt the coolness of the rising breeze on my face, a welcome respite from the late summer heat we'd been experiencing. The trees behind me rustled with its energy. The moon had risen higher. Its stark silvery light now completely flooded the circle.

A girl threw some branches onto the fire. The faces of the women and girls glowed with its renewed energy. Most kept their eyes closed, but the old woman sitting next to the elder noticed my gaze and smiled and nodded as if welcoming me to their special ceremony. I smiled back, closed my eyes and tried to relax.

The elder's chanting was soft and strangely hypnotic against the steady beat of the drum. I found myself swaying with its rhythm as it reverberated through my body and into my mind. And from the way Teht'aa's hand moved with mine, it seemed she was also swaying.

So too was Marie-Claude. Her hand had taken on life, warmth. Perhaps the ceremony was already achieving its purpose.

I thought of the two missing girls. I knew Fleur, but I didn't know Becky. In fact, I'd never heard her name mentioned until it was linked to Fleur's. It had cropped up a good month after word started spreading around the reserve that Marie-Claude had been unable to reach her eldest daughter at her brother's Ottawa apartment, where the eighteen-year-old was supposed to be staying. Apparently at the end of the school year in June, Fleur had gone to the nation's capital to look for a summer job.

Her parents had waited a week, hoping their daughter had been sidetracked by a visit to friends and would eventually show up at her uncle's. But when the girl didn't appear, her father contacted the Ottawa police. In the month and a half since, the police had discovered nothing other than she'd been last seen with this girl Becky, who had also disappeared.

The community was in a heightened state of worry, afraid this girl with the shining eyes would never be seen in their community again. One of the top graduating students this year from the Migiskan High School, she'd been crowned Miss Algonquin at the annual pow-wow, not only for her ripening beauty but also for her scholastic achievements. With her easy, friendly manner, her quick wit and intelligence, many felt she was one of the most promising teenagers to graduate in a number of years. The question on everyone's lips was why had she run away?

A sudden edginess in the drumming brought me

back to the moment. I felt a blackness, an uneasiness as goosebumps crawled over my skin. *Something's wrong...* I opened my eyes.

But no one else acted as if they'd felt the chill. Their eyes remain closed, their swaying calm as the elder's chants continued to float on the breeze. Then I realized the moon was gone. A cloud had extinguished its light. But even as I took note of this, the cloud drifted onward and the moon's brilliance returned to bathe our circle.

I closed my eyes and immersed myself back in the chanting. Switching to English, Summer Grass Woman spoke of the moon-cycle and every woman's destiny to be a sacred life-giver. She spoke of how the moon time was a time of power, a time to give life. It was not only a time for renewal but also a time to relax and take it easy. And it was a time of reflection.

"It also time for cleansing," she said. "But first we make a path to the spirits."

With help from the girl sitting beside her, who I now realized was Marie-Claude's middle daughter, Moineau, the old woman painfully raised herself from the ground, smoothed out the creases in her skirt and slowly limped to the fire. Chanting once again in Algonquin, she loosened a small deerskin pouch, extracted some tobacco, and threw it onto the fire. It flared with renewed life.

When she resumed her place, the rest of the circle one by one approached the fire with their offering. Some sang quietly to themselves, others muttered prayers. While I emptied my red tie of tobacco into the flames, I offered my own silent prayer for a safe and healthy return for the two girls.

The night breeze brought the distinctive sound of a car from across the lake. I listened to it until it merged with the night rustlings.

"We make offering to Grandmother Moon," Summer Grass Woman said.

She motioned to Neige, Marie-Claude's youngest daughter, to walk a birchbark container around the circle. As the eleven-year-old passed by, each woman, including the older girls who'd reached puberty, emptied their bottle of water into the container. Many of the older women, some with their eyes glistening, patted the hesitant water carrier or gave her a sympathetic smile. When she reached her mother, the tears she'd been trying desperately to contain started flowing. Her hands shook so much, she almost spilled the water.

"Be strong, my little one," her mother whispered in French as she added her portion to the others. "It is your duty to your sister."

A younger, shyer version of Fleur, with the same satiny, dark mahogany hair and amber-brown eyes, Neige didn't project the easy confidence of her eldest sister. Although she'd inherited her colouring from her father, she was slim like her mother, with the same dancer-like grace. Fleur, on the other hand, had all the right curves, some emphasized more than others, of a young, nubile female eager to experience what life had to offer.

"*Oui,* maman," Neige whispered. Closing her eyes, she breathed in deeply, moved her shoulders back and lifted her head.

When she offered the container to me, its contents didn't jiggle quite so much, and although her eyes still glistened, the tears had stopped. I patted her on the arm and tried to ease her worry by telling her that her sister was all right and would be home soon.

As Marie-Claude's daughter continued along the circle, I heard the sound of a car again, this time closer. It was coming down the road towards us. I noticed others were also glancing in the direction of the sound.

Neige placed the birchbark bowl on the ground in front of Summer Grass Woman, who fanned the smudge over the water with her eagle feather. The speed of the drum picked up. She held the bowl up to the moon. The water glinted in the moonlight. She began chanting in a high-pitched voice. Many voices joined her, including Marie-Claude's. Together the drum and her voice reached a crescendo. For a second they hovered then abruptly stopped. The silence was deafening.

I let out the breath I'd been holding and felt the tension drain. As one, we absorbed the stillness. I didn't know how many minutes had passed before I felt a presence pass over me. I looked up in time to see an owl silently floating through the moonlight. It vanished into the trees.

I heard the crunch of tires as the car slowed to a stop. A door clicked open then closed. Annoyance creased the elder's face as she turned her head towards the noise. I knew that a sacred ceremony was to be respected, that no one was allowed to interrupt it.

For several uneasy seconds Summer Grass Woman continued to stare in the car's direction, as if trying to discern who lurked within the forest's shadow. Then, grimly pursing her lips, she turned back to the ceremony.

"Grandmother Moon make the water clean. We give first water to Mother Earth." She sprinkled some of it onto the ground. "Moon water is ready."

She gave the container back to Neige, who walked once more around the circle. This time each woman dipped her bottle into the moon water and extracted some. As the girl brought it to me, I raised a questioning eyebrow to Teht'aa.

"It's medicine water," she whispered. "Suppose to make you strong."

I filled my bottle, screwed the top back on tightly, and placed it by my feet.

As I did so, someone cleared their throat gruffly behind me. I tensed. This had to be a man. Surely they weren't allowed to watch this sacred ceremony intended only for women. I could sense that I wasn't the only one who'd grown nervous. The relaxed harmony was gone, replaced by a restless fidgeting.

"Come, Sarah," Summer Grass Woman said. "Join the circle."

The short, stocky figure of Patrolman Sarah Smith, a recent recruit to the Migiskan Police Department and its only female officer, strode into the moonlight. Out of respect for the elder, she'd removed her police cap to reveal her short-cropped dark hair. If I hadn't known better, I would've thought she was a man from the way she held herself. But perhaps it was the Kevlar vest cinching in her breasts that gave her the barrel-like masculine look.

Embarrassed, the young policewoman, daughter of one of the band council members, started to apologize, but the elder hushed her, saying, "You late. But you come. It good."

Summer Grass Woman fanned the smudge over the young woman as she performed the ritual washing. Then she ordered Sarah to sit.

A couple of women moved to create a space in the circle. Sarah sat down cross-legged and took a deep breath as if trying to calm her nerves.

Summer Grass Woman continued, "Harmony come back to the circle."

The drumming, which had stopped, started up again and was joined by the old woman's soft chanting. I closed my eyes and tried to recapture the lost peace, but it was difficult. I was too worried by the sudden presence of this police officer. Marie-Claude gripped my hand as if she were drowning.

Finally, after several long minutes, Summer Grass Woman, said, "Sarah, tell us message from Grandmother Moon."

Marie-Claude sucked in her breath while her fingernails dug deeper into my hand.

The cop glanced nervously around then cleared her throat and in her husky voice said, "Sorry for the interruption, Kòkomis Elizabeth, but I … ah … I'm not sure if it's a message from Grandmother Moon, but Chief Decontie wants to see Marie-Claude and Mrs. Wapachee."

"It good Will respect Grandmother Moon. He send you and not a man." Summer Grass Woman paused. "Do they find the girls?"

Patrolman Smith fiddled with her hat resting on her knee. "I don't know, Kòkomis Elizabeth. The chief just said he wanted to see them as soon as possible. I'd like to take them with me now." She paused. "If it's okay with you."

The elder lifted her face to the moonlight and stared at the cool white orb almost as if she were seeking direction from Grandmother Moon. A bank of cloud approached. Its tentacles spread across the moon's face until the mass blocked the light and plunged us into darkness.

With a deep sigh, Summer Grass Woman dropped her gaze. "Grandmother Moon tell us."

She turned to the two mothers. "Marie-Claude and Dorothy, go." Not bothering to hide the sadness in her voice, she continued. "Grandmother Moon say be strong."

Marie-Claude's breathing quickened, as she dropped my hand and struggled to get up. I helped her, telling her that everything would be okay, that the police chief just wanted to give them an update. But I didn't believe it. And I could see that neither did she. Like her youngest daughter, she straightened her shoulders and slowly left the circle with her head held high.

An hour later we learned that a body of a young native woman had been found.

CHAPTER
THREE

The community was on edge while we waited for Marie-Claude and her husband, Jeff, to return from the medical examiner's office in Gatineau where the dead girl had been taken. This morning, over six hours ago, they'd set off with Becky's mother and aunt and the Migiskan police chief on the two-hour drive to learn if the body was one of their missing daughters. Nothing had been heard from them since.

To help allay Marie-Claude's fears at leaving her remaining daughters alone, I'd offered to sit with them until her return. I'd brought Sergei, my standard poodle, as a distraction. But neither his friendly licks nor his spurts of playful energy were successful in banishing the girls' tears. It took the grandmotherly touch of Summer Grass Woman to stop the flow. She even managed to coax weak smiles from each of them.

To escape the hot August sun, we'd retreated to the shade of a birch grove in the back corner of the Lightbodys' large property, where Marie-Claude and her children had built a traditional Algonquin camp. Wanting to help her daughters connect with their heritage, she'd first erected a birchbark wigwam complete with firepit and sleeping platforms among the birch overlooking a beaver pond. She'd since added a sweat lodge and a workshop for craft making and had come to view the camp as a retreat from the pressures of modern life.

Once the tears had dried, Summer Grass Woman cajoled the girls into making birchbark baskets. Surrounded with rolls of supple bark, pliant willow branches for rims, and spruce roots for stitching, the girls became so absorbed in their basket making that their fears for their missing sister were all but forgotten. Several of their friends joined us, along with their mothers.

As dragonflies flitted across the pond and the wind rustled the leaves, we toiled in the sun-dappled shade. Some were more skilled than others, namely me. My basket had a decided tilt, which immediately relegated it to berry picking, not water holding. A heron landed in the swampy shallows on the far side of the pond and proceeded to fish, undisturbed by our presence. A beaver headed out from its lodge towards a tangle of severed birch saplings. Unfortunately, Sergei spied its silent movement through the water and stood up. The beaver submerged with a loud slap of its tail and the heron took off with an angry squawk.

Drawing on the heron and the beaver, Summer Grass Woman filled our minds with the old stories. She'd almost reached the end of a tale about how the hare received his white winter coat when the sound of an engine punctuated the late afternoon peace. As the two girls exchanged worried glances, Summer Grass Woman nodded at me as if to say the time had come.

We stopped working. In anticipation, some placed their partially completed baskets on the ground. But none of us made a move to go to the front of the house, to where the Lightbodys would be getting out of the police chief's SUV. We wanted to remain ignorant for as long as possible, for in ignorance there was hope.

We did keep our eyes focused on the path that led through the birch towards the house. Although the trees blocked any view of the two-storey building, I could just make out the glint of sun on one of the back windows. For a moment I worried that Marie-Claude might not know where to find us, then I remembered it had been her suggestion that we retreat to this traditional oasis of peace.

But as the minutes ticked by and they didn't appear, I began to assume the worst, that the dead girl was Fleur. The other women exchanged worried glances while the elder held the two girls tightly and kissed them gently on their heads, their eyes brimming with tears.

I decided to seek out the Lightbodys. Maybe they wanted to break the bad news to the girls alone without an audience. However, when I reached the house, instead of finding Decontie's Explorer with the Migiskan Police Department insignia stamped on the doors, I saw parked in the driveway a massive black Harley-Davidson motor-cycle with a lot of blinding chrome.

For a second I tensed, thinking the bike belonged to Eric. I didn't want to face him. Even though we'd broken up a little over a year ago, too much had been left unsaid. Twice Eric had tried to reopen the door, but I wanted it kept firmly shut. So I avoided him, which wasn't difficult.

He seemed to be spending more time away on Grand Council of First Nations business than looking after the affairs of his community.

The bike, however, couldn't belong to Eric. It was just too biker-ish, with its elongated front wheel, tooled leather high-back saddle, and long handlebar fringes that flicked in the breeze. Besides, the condition of this bike was considerably more immaculate than the dusty condition Eric's was usually in.

When I turned around to search for the owner, I found him standing directly behind me.

"Oh! You startled me," I said, stepping back.

Reflective aviator sunglasses stared unsmilingly back at me. A white puckered scar streaked out from under the right sunglass lens and down the man's heavily tanned cheek to a reddish-brown goatee. His light brown hair was flat and sweaty where his helmet had clamped it against his head, and ended in a thin rat-tail braid tossed over his shoulder. He wore black leather chaps over faded black jeans and scuffed black biker boots. A black leather vest covered in a variety of patches hung loosely over a black T-shirt with the arms ripped off. I tried not to notice the tattoos covering his arms, one in particular of a set of projecting boobs that put my meagre ones to shame. Emblazoned across the shirt's front were the words *"Les Diables Noirs,"* the Black Devils, with a suitable rendition of a snarling devil's face etched in red. Although his stance was just as menacing, his physique didn't fit the towering, bulging muscle, protruding stomach image I had of a biker. Rather, he was thin yet compact and coiled as if ready to spring.

"Where's Marie-Claude?" he spat out in *joual*, a nasal, colloquial French that sounded like a duck quacking to my untrained ear.

I glanced down the Lightbodys' long dusty drive towards the main road, hoping to see them or someone else passing by. "She's not here," I replied in my school-learned French. "May I tell her who's dropped by when she returns?"

He spat something in reply.

Although I'd learned some *joual*, it eluded me for the most part, especially when spoken in a rapid-fire slur.

"Sorry, could you repeat that more slowly."

"Have they found Fleur?" This time he spoke English, but with a strong accent.

I hesitated. I had no idea who this man was. I didn't feel comfortable passing on information about the missing girl. For all I knew, given his unsavoury appearance, he could even be involved in her disappearance.

I was about to tell him to return later, when Neige and Moineau ran up and wrapped their arms around him, crying, "*Oncle, Oncle!*"

So he was their uncle. Why hadn't he said so, rather than leaving me squirming with apprehension?

When he finished greeting his nieces, he turned back to me and removed his sunglasses. A black patch covered the eye with the radiating scar, while the other eye bore Marie-Claude's faded blue colour, except in his case it projected a challenging glint and not the resignation I was used to seeing in his sister's eyes.

"You gonna tell me about Fleur?"

Moineau must've sensed my continuing hesitation, for she said, "*Oncle* J.P. was helping maman look for Fleur."

Not only was Moineau, like her younger sister, tall and slim like her mother, but she had the same pale eyes, although grey rather than blue, and her hair was a light brown instead of the rich mahogany of her sisters. Though she looked out at the world with the growing brashness of a fifteen-year-old, I sensed an underlying wariness that reminded me of Fleur. It was almost as if they couldn't quite give you their complete and unwavering trust.

Turning back to her uncle, she switched to French, "Maman and papa are in Gatineau. The police have … have found … a —" She stopped, unable to continue.

I finished for her. "Unfortunately, the body of a young woman has been found. Marie-Claude and Jeff have gone to see if it's Fleur. We're praying that it isn't."

At that moment Chief Decontie's vehicle turned into the driveway.

CHAPTER
FOUR

As the police vehicle crunched to a stop beside us, I tried to interpret the Lightbodys' expressions through the back side window. But the solemn stillness of both parents gave no hint. Even the police chief's acne-scarred face remained obliquely impassive. But I did notice that they were alone. The mother and aunt of the other missing girl were not with them.

The two girls ran up as their parents climbed out of the SUV. Marie-Claude's brother, however, remained standing by his bike. His hand gripped a Nazi-like helmet almost as if he were planning a fast getaway. By now Summer Grass Woman, the other women, and their daughters had joined us. They stood clumped together in nervous silence, a safe distance from the biker.

Jeff and Marie-Claude also ignored J.P., although I thought I caught Marie-Claude glance quickly at her brother before returning her gaze to her daughters.

Will Decontie frowned at the biker but made no attempt to acknowledge the man's presence. With his uniform jacket hanging open and matching navy pants sagging under the weight of his overhanging stomach, Will looked disheveled after the long drive, an appearance that wasn't entirely unusual for the police chief. He was often challenged in maintaining an orderly, cop-like demeanour.

Like Will, Marie-Claude's thin cotton skirt and sleeveless blouse were also rumpled, her wavy, white-blonde tresses in need of a comb. But I'd never known her to pay much attention to her appearance. Nonetheless, the fine delicacy of her features invariably shone through.

Her husband, on the other hand, in his pressed khakis and crisp button-down shirt with the sleeves partially rolled up, could've stepped out of a Brooks Brothers catalogue. But this was standard. I'd never seen him with so much as a shirttail hanging out. I guessed it was his way of reminding us of his importance in the community. A chartered accountant, he was the reserve's financial manager.

He and Marie-Claude had met while at the Université de Montréal, she in anthropological studies and he in economics. It was love at first sight, Marie-Claude had confided in me. She'd fallen for his animal magnetism that spoke of his warrior ancestry, her words, not mine. I couldn't sense it myself. But through the eyes of love, one could see anything.

Afraid of the answer, none of us were prepared to ask the question. Instead we stood silently waiting for one of them to speak up. Finally Will removed his cap and shook his head sadly.

I felt more than heard a collective moan. I was about to offer my condolences when Jeff spoke up. "Thanks to the Creator, the girl wasn't our Fleur. But ..." He ran his fingers through his thick black hair and sighed deeply. "It was Becky. Our hearts are with Dorothy."

Although everyone visibly relaxed, I could sense a sheepishness in their expressions of sympathy for the dead girl's mother and aunt. Summer Grass Woman even offered to hold a smudging ceremony in Becky's memory. None of us, though, asked how she'd died, an accident or murder. We knew that if Becky had been killed, it would not bode well for Fleur, something the Lightbodys would not want to dwell on. Instead they probably wanted to quietly rejoice in the hope that their daughter lived.

Then, as if noticing his brother-in-law for the first time, Jeff called out, "Christ! What are you doing here? You know you're not welcome in my house."

Marie-Claude clutched her husband's arm. "*S'il te plait, mon marie.* I asked him to come. I thought he might be able to help find Fleur."

Jeff turned his anger on his wife. "What can he do that the police can't?"

"I … I thought he might be able to ask around the biker community. Maybe they know something."

"What?" He glared down at his wife, who was at least a foot shorter and eighty pounds lighter. "Woman, you shame our daughter." Marie-Claude cringed backwards. "You think our daughter is into drugs, is a prostitute?"

"*Non*, no I don't.…"

"That's the only world this scum knows." He advanced towards his brother-in-law. "Get out of here."

J.P. stood his ground with his legs planted, ready for action, while the threatening devil on his T-shirt sneered through his crossed arms.

The policeman placed his bulk between the two men. "Now, son, I think it best you leave. These good people are upset enough without adding more wood to the fire."

J.P. remained rooted, his goatee jutting out defiantly.

"*S'il te plait, petit frère*," Marie-Claude pleaded. "It's best you leave. I will call you."

The biker continued glaring at his brother-in-law, then strapped on his helmet, kicked his motorcycle into action with a violent thrust of his boot, and powered out of the Lightbodys' drive and onto the main road in a spray of gravel.

As the bike's roar faded, Jeff spoke up. "Marie-Claude, I don't want you involving your brother, okay?"

She remained silent as she bit her bottom lip.

"Do you hear?"

"*Oui*," she whispered, crumpling her skirt in her hands.

"This is our affair and nobody else's, you understand?"

Marie-Claude nodded numbly, while the rest of us squirmed.

"Papa," Neige said. "Is Fleur okay?"

He tugged at one of her pigtails. "I hope so, little one. I dearly hope so." He placed a protective arm around each of his daughters. "Let's go inside."

But before he did, he turned back to us. "Kòkomis Elizabeth, Meg, and the rest of you, I want to thank you ladies for looking after my girls. *Meegwich*."

With Marie-Claude straggling behind them, they disappeared inside their house with a solid click of the front door.

The rest of us didn't move, unsure whether we should rejoice that the body didn't belong to Fleur or be more worried now that death had intervened.

Summer Grass Woman spoke up. "It is their time to be alone. Come. We go."

The old woman trudged down the dusty drive. She was joined by one of the women and her daughter, while the rest of the girls' friends and their mothers dispersed in their trucks and ATVs.

I stayed behind. I wanted to learn more. I nabbed the police chief as he was climbing back into his vehicle.

"Will, I hope you don't mind my asking, but how did Becky die? Was it a natural death?"

He sighed. "It'll be on the news soon enough, so I can tell you. She was murdered."

"How?"

"I think it best to see what the Sûreté du Québec release to the media, but let's just say it wasn't a nice death or a quick one."

"Does that mean she was also raped?"

"Wait for the press release," he replied.

"How dreadful for her mother."

"For sure. Never easy having a child murdered. I gather Becky was her only one."

"Do you think Fleur might have been with her when she was killed?"

"It's possible. We know they were seen together in Ottawa shortly before the two of them disappeared."

"Are they concerned that Fleur might have been killed at the same time?"

"I don't suppose I'm speaking out of turn if I say that the SQ are looking into the possibility. In fact, they have police dogs combing the woods right now."

"I guess because the Quebec provincial police are involved, it means Becky's body was found on the Quebec side of the river and not in Ottawa."

"Yup. A couple of birdwatchers found her by a beaver swamp near the northern border of Gatineau Park, a good thirty kilometres from downtown."

"Kind of an isolated place. What in the world would she be doing there?"

"Your guess is as good as mine."

A flicker of movement caught my eye, and I turned to see Marie-Claude staring at us from a side window. I thought I saw tears on her cheeks before she let the curtain fall back into place.

I shuddered to think of the unrelenting seesaw of worry and hope the Lightbodys must be on.

As if reading my own thoughts, Will said glumly, "All we can do is pray that Fleur wasn't with Becky when she died."

CHAPTER FIVE

The community didn't have long to wait. Within a day, the Quebec police told Chief Decontie that the dogs had failed to discover another body. Moreover, their forensic investigators had found no evidence that put Fleur at the crime scene. They finished by saying they were no longer treating Fleur as a possible murder victim. Rather, they were dropping her case altogether and tossing it back across the provincial boundary to the Ottawa police, where she'd gone missing in the first place.

I'd overheard this while sitting in the shadow of the front counter of the Migiskan police station.

"And we know what that means." Will's deep baritone came from the other side of the counter, where he was standing with his back to me. "The Ottawa cops are going to do piss-all, like they've been doing all along." He thumped his fist on a desk to emphasize the point.

I'd dropped by the small brick building to complain, and not for the first time, about hunters from the reserve killing either a moose or a deer on my property. While out hiking this morning, Sergei had sniffed out the kill site.

A set of ATV tracks leading directly back to the reserve identified the culprits.

"One fuckin' day," the police chief fumed. "That's all the time the SQ spent searching. Said the dogs and investigators were needed elsewhere. Said they were confident Fleur wasn't with Becky at the time of the murder. How in the hell do they know if they only spent one fuckin' day?"

Normally a roll-with-the-punches sort of man, this was the angriest I'd ever seen him. And I could tell from the stunned expressions on the faces of Sergeant Sam Whiteduck and Ellie Tenasco, the MPD clerk, that they were equally shocked.

"The bastards didn't even spend a day. It was more like a bloody afternoon. Christ, the crime scene was a fuckin' forest, not some goddamn city street."

I wasn't sure if he knew I was eavesdropping. I debated announcing my presence but figured I might learn more if I kept my mouth shut.

"Now calm down, Chief. They probably had their reasons for cutting it short," Sam said. A tall, thin reed of a man with a bristling brush-cut that accentuated the length of his narrow face, the sergeant was Decontie's second-in-command.

"Christ. They didn't want to spend any more money on a fuckin' Indian. That's their only reason. I even offered them some men. It wouldn't have cost them a dime. But they said it was outside our jurisdiction."

"Yeah, but Chief, maybe the Ottawa cops have new evidence that places Fleur elsewhere," Sam suggested.

"Not bloody likely. Nope, the only evidence is no evidence after an afternoon's search of the crime scene."

"Did the SQ say when Becky was killed?"

"A little over five weeks ago. That puts it at about a week after the girls were last seen."

"And the only thing we got that says they were together is that witness statement." Although Sam's eyes drifted in my direction, he made no sign to suggest he'd seen me. "That's right, eh, Chief?"

"Yeah, the woman at the Anishinabeg Welcome Centre."

Sam tried again. "You know, Chief, a lot can happen in a week. Maybe the SQ is right. Maybe Fleur wasn't with Becky when she died."

Decontie stared hard at his subordinate then sighed. "Yeah, you're right, son. I just got a little carried away. Christ, that frog made me angry. He knows my French ain't too hot, but he wouldn't speak English."

The police chief reached across the desk and helped himself from the tin of sugar-coated bannock, replenished daily by Ellie to feed his sweet tooth and those of other members of the seven-man police force.

"Do you want me to talk to him?" Sam offered.

Will wiped the sugar off his mouth with the back of his hand. "Nope, I understood enough. I don't think you'll learn anything more from that bastard. But you're right, in one week the two girls could've easily gone their separate ways, that is, if they were together in the first place. Christ, it's not as if they were friends. They'd only just met. But they went missing at the same time, so their disappearances gotta be connected."

"Yeah, you got that right, Chief." Sam nodded. "So what do we do now?"

"Becky's murder makes me very nervous. Remember it

was less than a year ago that another young Cree woman was found dead along Highway 5."

"But wasn't that a lot closer to Gatineau?"

"Yeah, but two native girls murdered within a year is too much of a coincidence for my liking. I hate to say it, but it reduces the odds of finding Fleur alive."

"Weren't two other women, also native, killed a few years back?" Sam asked.

"Yeah, you're right. I'd forgotten about them, except they weren't in the same area. Still, their bodies were found on the Quebec side too."

"How was Becky killed, boss? Maybe they were all killed the same way."

"I don't know about the others, but Becky was killed by multiple stab wounds. The coroner thinks the murderer downed her by throwing a knife into her back but didn't kill her outright. Then, almost as if he was wound-up by his failure, he stabbed her multiple times in the chest. And you know, Sam, something else has me worried." Will paused to chew on another piece of bannock. "The coroner found some strange markings on Becky's wrists and ankles."

"Like she was being kept a prisoner before she died, eh?"

Will grunted. "And if they kidnapped her, they could have taken Fleur too."

"But surely this should be enough to get the Ottawa and Quebec police doing all they can to find her," I piped up, forgetting that I was trying to pretend I wasn't there.

Will whisked around as the other two pairs of eyes focused on me. Sam smiled surreptitiously as his eyes met mine.

"Meg, sorry, I didn't realize you were there," Will said. "I guess you must've heard me mouthing off. What can we do for you?"

"I have another hunter complaint, but that can wait." I stood up and approached the counter. "Sorry for listening in, but like everyone else, I'm worried too. Are you saying that neither police force is going to do anything more about finding Fleur?"

"Like I said, the SQ are washing their hands of the case, insisting she ain't their missing persons file. Christ, I hate these jurisdictional problems. And the Ottawa police mouth the words that they're gonna put renewed effort into the case, but from the outset they've classified Fleur's disappearance as a runaway, which means they do nothing."

"But Fleur isn't the kind of girl to run away. She was all excited when I talked to her in the spring about starting her nursing studies this fall in Montreal. I didn't get the impression it was something she would readily give up by running away."

"Yeah, trouble is she didn't go to her uncle's place like she was supposed to," Will said.

"Does anyone know why not?"

"Nope. Apparently she really likes her uncle and stayed at his apartment downtown last year."

"I'm assuming this uncle isn't the biker who turned up yesterday."

Will grunted. "I tell ya, if he hadn't been Marie-Claude's brother, I would've run him off the rez so fast. Last thing we need are bikers roaming our community. We have enough problems with drugs without help from outside. Nope, the Ottawa brother is considerably more upstanding. He's a professor at Carleton University."

"Have the Ottawa police been able to determine where she did go?"

"According to the woman at the Welcome Centre, she moved in with this Becky, a girl she'd only just met. The Ottawa police also have a witness at the apartment building where Becky lived saying he saw her with a native girl that fits Fleur's description."

"But she never told her parents?"

"Nope. The last time they had any communication with Fleur was in Somerset when they put her on the Ottawa bus. The Ottawa police were able to determine that she was living in Ottawa a good three weeks before her disappearance. Yet during that time she made no attempt to get in touch with her parents or her uncle. So I hate to say it, but it does show the signs of a runaway." He paused and ran his hand through his short black hair. "Christ, *I* even thought she was a runaway."

"But you don't think so any more."

"To tell you the truth, Meg, I don't know what to think. But at this point it doesn't matter. Becky's murder changes everything."

"But if you think the people that killed Becky might also have Fleur, surely the Ottawa police would come to the same conclusion and ramp up their investigation."

"So you'd think." He shook his head.

"So what are we going to do, Chief?" Sam asked.

"The first place to start is with the crime scene. I want to satisfy myself that Fleur wasn't with Becky when she died. But doing an official search is outside our jurisdiction. So

I'm gonna propose the Lightbodys launch a private citizen's search. No rule that says they can't as long as they have the property owner's approval. Since it's government-owned Crown land, that shouldn't be a problem. Then we're gonna volunteer ourselves to make sure it's done right."

"And what about the Ottawa side?" I asked.

"I'm gonna do my damnedest to get the Ottawa police off their butts and onto the streets, pursuing all possible leads. We've gotta find that girl." He paused. "If it's not already too late."

CHAPTER SIX

"Thank God, Decontie has finally gotten off his butt and is doing something about Fleur." Teht'aa shifted her gaze to me from the road zipping by in front of us.

Her annoyance did little to mar the model-like beauty of her high cheek-boned features. In fact, a hot-blooded male would probably be drawn to her inflamed looks like a moth.

Teht'aa was a result of a teenage pregnancy when Eric was playing hockey out west. Her mother, wanting nothing more to do with the young man who seemed more intent on living in the white man's world than his own, returned to her northern Dené reserve, where she died shortly after their child was born. Eric never knew. It took twenty-two years for him to discover that he had a daughter. Teht'aa had been living with him on and off ever since.

"Watch out!" I cried as another sharp curve fast approached.

She flicked her eyes back to the road and manoeuvred Eric's Grand Cherokee as expertly through this turn as she had the other twists of this narrow two-lane highway that clung to the ragged shoreline of the Gatineau

River. Carless herself, Teht'aa was taking advantage of her father's absence. Apparently he'd been on a big canoe trip up in the Northwest Territories before going to Vancouver for some GCFN meetings. But according to his itinerary, he would finally be coming home today. His flight wouldn't land until early afternoon, too late for him to join the search, which was just as well. There was no way I could've spent ten minutes with him, let alone a couple of hours cooped up in a car.

We were driving southbound on Hwy 105, known as the "Killer Highway" for its high incidence of traffic deaths. As if to reinforce this reputation, a car shot out of a driveway in front of us. Teht'aa braked, narrowly missing the rear bumper as the compact car veered into the opposite lane.

"That stupid idiot didn't even look," Teht'aa cursed.

"You could slow down," I hazarded, releasing my grip on the dashboard. I supposed she was being heavier on the gas pedal than usual in her haste to get to the search site.

She shot me an annoyed glance but did slow down … a bit.

In addition to ourselves, we were transporting Wendy and her husband George, part of the overflow who couldn't get seats on the two buses chartered to carry people to the location where Becky's body had been found. We'd left the reserve as the sun lit up the spire of Migiskan's All Saints Church and had been on the road for the past hour and a half.

"Yup, Will just sat on his fat butt eating bannock," Wendy quipped from the backseat before popping another Timbit into her mouth. Her plump, junk-food-fed figure made me wonder who was calling whom fat. It also suggested she was more at home in front of a TV than spending a day tramping through the bush. I wondered how long she would last.

Like us, they hadn't hesitated to join the search for one of their own. In fact, so many people had turned up at dawn at the Council Hall that the Lightbodys had to scramble to find additional transportation, which was why Teht'aa and I were in Eric's Jeep.

It had taken the Lightbodys the better part of a week to organize the search for their missing daughter. In addition to Decontie's support, they were also using a volunteer organization specializing in such searches. The main hold-up had been the Quebec government, which had at first turned down their request to conduct the search on Crown land. But after it made headline news, a bureaucrat had reluctantly given his approval with the proviso that it be conducted under the oversight of the provincial police.

Decontie had laughed. "Serves the SQ right," he'd said. But he wasn't expecting more than a nominal presence on their part, nothing for us to be concerned about.

"But surely Will would've done something when her mother reported her missing," I now asked. I'd been in the Far North when her parents raised the alarm.

"Nada, zip, nothing," Wendy answered. "He told Marie-Claude she wasn't his problem. Since she'd gone missing in Ottawa, it was up to the Ottawa police to find her."

"I suppose in a way he's right. Ottawa is outside his jurisdiction."

"Yeah, but she's a member of our community. He

coulda made the Ottawa police do something, eh? Instead he done nothing. He left it up to Jeff and Marie-Claude to try and get their butts moving."

I was sorry to hear this. I'd always respected the police chief and felt he did the best he could to maintain the peace and security of the thousand or so residents of the remote Quebec community.

"At least he's doing something now," I said.

"Almost two months later, when it could very well be too late," Teht'aa shot back.

"Jeez, I tell ya, this search is sure making me real nervous, eh?" Wendy said. "I figure it's bad news if we find something belonging to Fleur. And I sure don't wanna be the one to find her body."

"I couldn't agree with you more," I replied. "Still, I think it has to be done. Hopefully we won't find anything, and we can all breath easier knowing she wasn't with Becky when she was killed."

"I sure hope you're right," Wendy sighed. "What a shame. Such a good kid. She never gets into trouble, not like a lotta kids on the rez. Mind you, Jeff's pretty strict, so she probably doesn't get much chance to get up to any mischief."

"I think she manages to do her bit," Teht'aa chuckled. "I came across her and Pete Smith's boy smoking pot in the woods behind the Rec Centre. And from the guilty expressions on their faces, I wasn't sure what else they'd been up to."

George laughed. "Yeah, I figured she weren't such an angel when I caught her with Eddy Tenasco at the pow-wow. Things were sure hot and heavy. She'd been drinking too, something I know Jeff sure don't like."

Wendy answered. "I tell ya, I was kinda surprised he

let her go to Ottawa on her own like that. But maybe Marie-Claude convinced him it'd be okay. After all, Fleur was gonna stay with her brother, the professor."

"Except she didn't," I said. "Anyone got any ideas why not?"

"Nope, it don't make sense," Wendy replied. "And it don't make sense she ran away. Jeez, I sure hope she's okay."

"I think we'd all second that," I said.

A sudden chill seemed to fill the car as each of us lapsed into our own separate silence, afraid of where further discussion might lead us. The sun that had started the morning with such promise had vanished. Clouds heavy with moisture filled the sky, and the first drops of rain were splattering the windshield.

"Oh crap, I didn't bring my rain jacket," Wendy wailed. "Or rubber boots."

"You ain't gonna melt, honey," was George's flippant retort. "There's too much of ya." He followed this with a loud guffaw and a resounding slap on her thigh. In contrast to his wife's lush flesh, George was stringbean thin, his face gaunt and bronzed from years of guiding wealthy fishermen and hunters.

"Now stop that, George," Wendy said, trying to sound annoyed, but she couldn't quite hide from her voice the pleasure of being loved.

Thankfully, the rain had slowed to a drizzle by the time we drove into Parking Lot 48 on the northeast side of Gatineau Park. I say thankfully, for in my rush to leave, I'd also forgotten my rain gear.

A couple of SQ cops were leaning up against their cruiser, paying little attention to the few people who'd preceded us. I didn't expect to see the bulk of the searchers for another twenty minutes or so. We'd breezed past one of the buses and left the other one in the Council Hall parking lot waiting for a searcher who suddenly remembered she'd forgotten to turn off her stove.

A man wearing a fluorescent lime green vest approached us and identified himself as a member of Ottawa Valley Search and Rescue. After taking down our names on his clipboard, he told us to help ourselves to the hot coffee and donuts being doled out from the back of a nearby van.

As the four of us walked to join the others crowded around the van, I pointed at the surrounding crush of trees and underbrush. "No wonder Will was so annoyed at the SQ for not spending more time. It would've been next to impossible to do a thorough search in only a few hours."

"Yeah, but do you think a bunch of amateurs can do any better?" Teht'aa said.

"I'm sure these search guys are going to tell us what to do," Wendy added. She stopped to zip up her jacket. "Brrr … it's cold. It sure don't feel like September, eh?"

"At least the rain has stopped." I zipped up my fleece jacket and stuck my freezing hands into my pockets. I'd forgotten my gloves too.

"I tell you, if the missing girl were white, these cops would be crawling all over the place." Teht'aa glanced in my direction. "No reflection on you, Meg."

I didn't reply. Teht'aa never expected me to. A native activist, she often threw out these one-liners as if testing my own biases. Often her opinions were just a little too militant and one-sided for my liking, but in this case, I was inclined to agree. I'd had my own first-hand experience with the blinkers cops wore when dealing with natives.

At that point, Will Decontie arrived in his police vehicle with Jeff sitting beside him in the front and Marie-Claude sitting forlornly by herself in the back seat.

CHAPTER
SEVEN

A short while later, Teht'aa and I found ourselves in a line of nine people strung out in front of an impossibly dense section of forest. The underbrush was so thick, I could barely see my trail shoes, let alone the surrounding ground. Little wonder Will had been so angry at the minimal time the SQ had spent combing these woods.

Through the trees behind us, I could just make out a distant flicker of yellow police tape marking where Becky's body had been found. But none of us had been allowed near the crime scene. In fact, the search and rescue organization had strung another line of tape further out to dissuade the more curious, including myself, from being tempted to check it out.

At Will's instigation, their more experienced volunteers were going to redo this area allegedly searched by the Quebec police, including the shore of the beaver pond where Becky had been killed. Statistically this area closest to the crime scene was supposed to have the greatest likelihood of containing evidence. Will wanted to use proven skills to find whatever the SQ might have missed. For the same reason, he'd also insisted that the SAR people bring some divers to dredge the beaver pond, which the SQ also claimed had been done.

We amateurs had been split into ten teams that were assigned specific areas of bush radiating out from the crime scene. Our section started in a low, muddy area a good couple of hundred metres' walk from the parking lot and seemed to stretch up an incline through a forest of mostly spruce and poplar.

We each held the long stick we'd been asked to bring, in my case a ski pole. Tehta'aa had brought the smooth maple branch once used by her grandfather as a walking stick. We were waiting for the search to begin, while our leader, Francine, an SAR volunteer, who appeared more flustered than in control, carried on an intense conversation on her walkie-talkie.

I could see Wendy chatting away with her husband in the neighbouring line. I hadn't seen Marie-Claude or her husband on any of the teams. Just as well, in case they discovered what none of us wanted to find, their daughter's body. But I did see her brother J.P. join Wendy's group at the last minute amidst nervous stares and raised eyebrows at his biker leathers. However, when he'd identified himself as Fleur's uncle, everyone relaxed. I did wonder what would happen when his brother-in-law discovered his presence.

"All right, people," yelled our leader, replacing her walkie-talkie in her backpack. "I want you to keep your line. Walk very slowly and look only at the ground in front of you. Use your stick to move aside anything blocking your view of the ground."

"What about them trees? I don't got my chainsaw to cut 'em down," someone shouted amidst nervous laughter from other members of our line.

"As you've already been told, walk around them and resume your place in the line," Francine replied rather testily. "But if it's an evergreen, carefully check the ground under the branches. I want to remind you that the second you see anything suspicious, stop and call out to let me know. And everyone else, the minute you hear the shout, you stop too. I don't want anyone going ahead, okay?" She ran her eyes along the line as if daring us to challenge her, then yelled, "Okay, let's go."

As one, we started advancing slowly forward, using our sticks to move the underbrush aside. But within seconds our line became an undulating wave. The many trees and saplings made it impossible to maintain the same pace. At one point I found myself held up by a fallen branch that refused to move when I jabbed at it with my pole. When I finally dislodged it and looked up, Teht'aa and my other neighbour were a metre or more ahead.

"Okay, everyone," Francine shouted. "Those in front stop and wait for the others to catch up."

I inched my way forward, slashing aside a leafy clump of saplings in an attempt to see the ground.

"Hey, I think I found something," a woman called out.

I tensed as everyone else fell silent.

"Stop," Francine shouted as she raced to where a heavy-set woman with thick braids flopping onto her large bosom reached under a spruce bough to pick something up.

"Don't touch it!" shrieked Francine. "Just leave it where you found it."

The woman froze as a greyish-white object fell from her hands.

Francine knelt and examined the object and surrounding ground closely. Finally she stood up and without bothering to hide her irritation, said, "It's a rabbit's skull. Okay everyone. Let's start up again."

The chatter resumed. I even heard laughter, no doubt from the relief of knowing that the item had nothing to do with Fleur.

And so it continued for the next couple of hours. Whenever there was a sighting, everyone grew very quiet. We shuffled nervously while Francine checked it out and smiled with relief when she declared it of no interest. I felt like we were dodging bullets and prayed that none would point at Fleur.

As lunchtime approached, my hands were numb from the cold and my aching back and feet were seeking a much-needed rest. I could tell others were also feeling sore and tired. But though we'd so far found nothing, the mood wasn't one of dejection or disappointment. Instead I felt a growing sense of hopeful optimism.

One of the grandmothers, who'd held us up on several occasions, sat down on a rock and declared she wasn't going any further until she had some food in her. Before Francine could intercede, others also sat down. When the frazzled woman muttered, "I guess it's lunchtime," the rest of us joined them. "Don't lose your place in the line," Francine admonished. But few paid attention. We clumped around the few outcroppings of rocks to avoid sitting on the wet ground.

I found myself sharing a somewhat flattened but very

hard piece of granite with Teht'aa and a woman I didn't know who'd joined our line late.

"Jeez," the stranger said, brushing a strand of henna-dyed hair from her deeply seamed face. "I didn't know we were supposed to bring food."

"Here, have some of mine." I thrust the plastic bag I'd just removed from my pack towards her. "I made an extra sandwich."

Her leopard-spotted fleece jacket hung loosely on her bony frame, and her jeans were soaked a good way up from her ankles. She shivered. "Are you sure?"

"I'm sure." I held up another bag. "I've got plenty."

"Thanks." Without further comment, she delved into the sandwich and was finished before Teht'aa and I had started ours.

"Here, have a cookie, I've got lots." I thrust another bag towards her. "By the way, my name is Meg Harris, and this is my friend Teht'aa Tootootis."

I waited for her to introduce herself, and when she didn't, I asked, "What brings you to the search? Did you know Fleur?"

Ignoring my question, she looked at Teht'aa and said, "Dené, eh? I'm Gwich'in. Name's Claire. Guess we come from the same neck of the woods, eh?"

"I suppose, if you can call a thousand kilometres close," Teht'aa replied. "I'm from Fort Simpson in the Northwest Territories. You must be from somewhere in the Yukon?"

The woman lit up a cigarette before replying. "Yup, Old Crow. I guess a job brought you south, eh? Like me. That or a man." Her chortling was quickly cut off by a bout of hoarse coughing.

"A man, actually," Teht'aa replied. "My father. He's band chief of the Migiskan Anishinabeg."

"Oh." The woman blew out a stream of smoke and eyed Eric's daughter thoughtfully. "That's the same reserve as the missing girl, eh?"

She reached inside her purse and brought out a slim plastic bottle containing a clear liquid. The glint in her eyes suggested it was more than water. I tensed as she uncapped the bottle and took a long swig, but I couldn't stop my mouth from watering in hope.

"Keeps the old bod warm, eh? Want some?" She offered the bottle to Teht'aa but not to me. Teht'aa declined, while I cleared my throat and said, "Ah, if you …"

She jerked her head around and gave me a long perusal before handing the bottle over. I knew I shouldn't. I'd been good since my fall from grace in the Arctic, but I was cold too, and tired.

I didn't dare glance at Teht'aa as I brought the bottle to my lips. I knew she'd be angry. Since Eric was no longer a part of my life, she'd taken over his role as my watchdog. She never ordered alcohol when we went out or served it when I visited, even though I knew she liked her beer. She'd even gone so far as to check my cupboards when she thought I wasn't looking to ensure I wasn't harbouring a stray bottle of liquor.

But I didn't care. The burning liquid warming up my insides felt good, very good. Vodka, my old standby, along with a bit of 7Up, a sweetness I usually didn't like. But hey, beggars couldn't be choosers. Just what I needed to get me through the afternoon. I took another swig and passed the bottle back to the woman.

I repeated my question. "Why are you here? Do you know Fleur?"

She turned her bloodshot gaze back to me, except she didn't quite look me in the eye. "Yeah, she came to the Centre a couple of times."

I was trying to figure out which centre, then I realized. "You're talking about the Anishinabeg Welcome Centre in Ottawa, aren't you?"

"Yup. Police already talked to me, so I can't tell you much more than I already told them." She passed me back the bottle.

Ignoring Teht'aa's angry scowl, I deliberately took a long, lingering sip. "So you're the one who saw her with Becky?"

"Yup, I saw her with that slut, but that's gotta be a couple of months ago. That how long she been gone?"

"More or less," Teht'aa replied. "Why did you call Becky a slut?"

"That's what she was," the woman snorted before taking another drag on her cigarette. "Turned tricks in the Market. Some john musta killed her."

Teht'aa and I exchanged startled glances.

"Surely you're not suggesting that Fleur was a prostitute, too?" I asked, not bothering to hide the incredulity in my voice. It certainly didn't fit with my fresh-faced, girl-next-door image of Fleur.

"I dunno if she was in the game or not. Just saw her hanging out with that hooker, that's all. But ya know what they say about birds of a feather hanging out together."

As she passed me back the almost empty bottle, she gave me a knowing look, which left me wondering whether she was referring to the two young women, or us.

"Princess. She thought she was a goddamn princess," Claire continued. "Had no time for the likes of us."

She tipped up the bottle and drained it, leaving Teht'aa and me completely mystified by her strange comment.

CHAPTER EIGHT

The woman's vodka had warmed me up nicely. I was ready to take on whatever the afternoon's tramp through the woods would bring. Even the drizzle starting up again didn't bother me.

As we returned to our places in the line, Teht'aa cast me a reproving frown. "Why did you drink that booze? You know what it does to you."

"Yeah, it makes me feel really good, that's what it does," I shot back and stomped forward but was immediately chastised by Francine for starting before the others.

I grudgingly returned to my spot beside my watchdog, but as I did so I couldn't help but notice the woman from the Welcome Centre uncapping another plastic bottle. This one appeared to be full. I was tempted, really tempted to change places with the man standing beside her, but I resisted. Teht'aa was right. I'd had enough vodka. I didn't need any more.

We trudged forward, slashing the dense underbrush with our sticks. Within minutes mine bumped against something that glimmered gold when I bent down to investigate. I was about to push the weeds aside to get a better look, when Francine shrieked, "Don't touch!"

I'd forgotten.

She rushed over and almost toppled me in her haste to move me away from the object. I felt my head spin as I raised myself upright. Boy, I sure couldn't drink like I used to.

She carefully moved the foliage aside to reveal a shoe with a spike heel and crisscrossed straps made from gold leather. Although the shoe was covered in dirt, the leather still had the sheen of newness.

I heard her catch her breath at the same time as I caught mine.

"Do you think it belongs to Fleur?" I asked.

"I have no idea," she said, "but it certainly doesn't belong here. And the condition of the leather suggests it's only been here a few months at the most. It certainly hasn't overwintered."

She took out a camera and snapped several pictures before picking up the shoe with her latex gloves and inserting it into a large Ziploc bag. She marked the location with a red marker.

All eyes were glued to the bag as Francine slipped it into her pack. The hopeful optimism I'd sensed earlier had gone, as were the smiles and chatter.

Another wave of dizziness caused me to bump against Teht'aa as I resumed my place in the line.

"See, I told you not to drink," she said. "You can't handle it."

"Yes, I can," I snapped back. "I don't need you to tell me what to do."

"Of course you do. You have a drinking problem. You shouldn't be drinking anything, not even a sip."

"Look, I've got it under control. A couple of sips won't hurt me."

"Yeah, sure. Look at what those few sips have done to you. You can't even stand up straight."

I glanced over at Claire. There was no way I wanted to spend the rest of the afternoon listening to Teht'aa's harping. I ran over to the man, a stranger, standing beside her.

"Do you mind changing places with me?" I asked.

For a second he appeared about to refuse, but then his eyes widened with interest at the sight of the gorgeous woman he'd be walking beside. Brandishing his version of a lady-killer grin, he swaggered over to Teht'aa, while the Welcome Centre woman snorted, "Ain't that just like a man." She passed me her bottle.

To hell with Teht'aa. I can drink as much as I want to. I knew what I was thinking was wrong, but I was too far gone by that point. I took a long swig and passed it back. "Thanks, but that's probably enough. I'd hate to drink up your supply."

"No problem. I came prepared." She winked con-spiratorially, one drinker to another, which annoyed me. I wasn't a drinker, not any more.

At a yell from Francine, our line plodded forward.

I stumbled but caught myself with my ski pole. "Damn rock," I muttered. "Shouldn't get in my way." I kicked at it and almost lost my balance again.

Claire snorted and passed me the bottle. "Here, have another."

I hesitated. I didn't need any more. But the rain had started back up, and I could do with a little warmth. I tipped the bottle up and took a long, searing sip. I could almost feel Teht'aa's disapproval boring into my back, but I refused to turn around and look at her.

We continued trudging forward in our ragged line. For the umpteenth time, I slashed at a miniature spruce then another, then at several poplar saplings, at a clump of purple flowers followed by more weeds. I played footsie with a maple tree that refused to budge and a few metres later did it again with another. This was getting boring, very boring. I drained another good measure of Claire's vodka.

Rain trickled down my neck. My hands were numb, my feet soggy. I brushed away drops dribbling from my nose. I tried to figure out how much further we had to walk, but I couldn't see beyond the barrier of trunks.

My foot suddenly caught on a rock, and I went sprawling onto the wet ground. It felt good to lie down and rest.

"You okay, Meg?" Claire asked.

"Hmmm … hmm. Guess I better get up, eh?" I laughed as I thrashed around in the wet leaves trying to get a purchase.

"Here, let me help." Claire grabbed my arm but lost her balance too and fell next to me.

Both of us lay giggling on the ground amidst cries of "Stop!" from our exasperated leader.

I heard footsteps thrashing through the vegetation towards me. They stopped next to my head.

"Get up! You're making a fool of yourself," Teht'aa hissed.

Her hands reached under my armpits. She yanked me upwards. I tried to resist, but she was stronger and pulled me to my feet. She whirled me around, and I found myself teetering back and forth in front of her glare.

"We're leaving now." She grabbed my arm and started pulling me away from the line.

"I'm not going anywhere with you," I muttered through clenched teeth as I tried to free my hand from her grip.

We struggled until I finally broke free. I rubbed my arm. Behind me I could hear Claire's drunken laughter.

"Leave me alone," I said. "You're not my mother or my sister."

"But I'm your friend and I'm worried about you."

Her anger had vanished. Instead she looked at me with the same caring compassion that I used to see reflected in her father's eyes, a reminder I couldn't deal with right now.

"I didn't ask you to worry about me. So please, leave me alone."

I spun around and almost lost my balance. But I hung in, pretending everything was okay. Once the whirlies settled, I stomped off. As much as I wanted to help find Fleur, my need to get away from Eric's daughter took over. With as much concentration as I could muster, I managed to weave my way through the trees without a collision or tripping over deadfall. I didn't stop until I could no longer hear Claire's hoarse laughter.

I'd reached the top of a deep river gorge that cut a precipitous swath through the grey granite. I dropped my pack to the ground and sat down on a rock ledge overlooking a fast-moving river. I waited for Teht'aa to arrive. I figured there was no way she would leave me alone. Her father wouldn't have. He had viewed curing my drinking as one of his missions in life. And he had succeeded, but now he was no longer around. So it didn't matter any more, did it?

I was mesmerized watching the water sluice over the rocks far below. I could feel its pull drawing me downward. I tried to imagine what it would feel like floating on the fast smoothness and wondered how long it would it take for me to reach the chute further downstream. Would I fall through the mist into a crystal clear pool, or would I hit rocks?

I could feel myself leaning further forward. The smooth racing green far below looked so enticing. I could get lost in its crystal coolness.

Without warning, I was jerked backwards away from the edge.

"You shouldn't get so close," a voice said. "You could fall."

I turned around to find myself staring into Marie-Claude's worried face.

I burped. "Whoops, sorry."

I placed my hand on the ground to steady myself. It slipped. I started to fall backwards. Next I knew I was being dragged from the edge as my head bumped over the hard granite.

"You're drunk, aren't you?" Marie-Claude said without expressing any of Teht'aa's disgust.

I gingerly sat up and massaged my sore head. I was now a good couple of metres from the drop-off. As I tried to tame the whirlies whizzing around my head, I nodded guiltily, feeling very embarrassed. "I'm sorry you had to find me like this. Please realize I don't mean any disrespect to you or your daughter."

"I'd heard you had a drinking problem." Marie Claude dropped to the uneven lichen-covered rock at the canyon's edge. "But I thought you'd stopped."

While doing my best to avoid looking directly into her eyes, I mumbled something about being able to stop any time. I glanced around in case Teht'aa had arrived in time to see my shameful behaviour. The forest was eerily empty but for a blue jay high on a pine branch squawking at our intrusion. A sudden gust of wind and rain sent a phalanx of dead needles hurtling to the ground. Several jabbed me. I brushed a clump of soggy hair from my eyes.

I debated telling Marie-Claude about the shoe I'd found but decided it would be better if Will raised it with her. Although Fleur didn't seem the kind of girl to wear such a sexy shoe, I didn't want to cause her mother unnecessary worry before she actually had it in her hands. Only then would we know for certain whether it belonged to Fleur.

The spectre of her missing daughter hung heavily between us. Feeling incapable of providing any false encouragement, I lapsed into silence, as did she. Above the noise of the river, I could hear the slow, steady rhythm of her breathing along with an occasional sigh. I was feeling decidedly damp and cold. Marie-Claude, I'd noticed, had come fully equipped with the appropriate rain gear, although her jacket was open, the front of her sweatshirt wet. My dizziness was starting to fade. I was beginning to feel a little more normal, but I was shivering. I sneezed.

"*Mon dieu*, you will be sick," she whispered. "Here, take this. I don't need it."

She started to remove her jacket.

I hastily stopped her. "Please, I'm fine. My clothes are mostly synthetic. They'll dry quickly."

She smiled fleetingly then turned her gaze back to the gorge. "Pretty, isn't it?"

"A little too pretty and too hypnotic. Watch yourself," I warned.

She nodded absently and turned her attention back to the chasm.

I assumed that we were close to the parking lot, but when I glanced around at the surrounding forest, I didn't see or hear anything suggesting it was nearby. In fact, there was no sign of a trail, not even an indentation through the carpet of dead pine needles.

"How did you get here?" I asked.

A wisp of blonde hair trickled out from under her hood. When she didn't respond, I thought she hadn't heard me. But before I could repeat the question, she raised her head. Instead of looking at me, she stared across at the line of pine on the other side of the gorge.

"I walked," was her soft reply.

"Sorry, I didn't phrase that very well. What I meant to ask was whether you knew the way back to the parking lot."

She turned around and pointed vaguely in a direction behind my back. As she did so, I noticed that her eyes were red from crying.

"Are you okay?" I asked hastily, feeling guilty that I was putting my troubles before hers.

She nodded listlessly and returned her gaze to the tumbling river below.

"Why are you here? Wouldn't it be better to wait in the parking lot?"

She shook her head as the tears started spilling from her eyes. She whispered something.

"I'm sorry, I didn't hear you."

The anguish that washed over her face sent a chill down my spine. I leaned forward to catch her answer.

"My fault ... all my fault."

She turned her focus back to the river. As she did, she seemed to lean closer to the precipice.

"Please come away. You're making me nervous." I readied myself to grab her as she had done with me.

At that moment an arm reached over my head and held her.

"Come, Marie-Claude, we have to go back to the car," her husband ordered.

I scrambled to get out of the way as he pulled her from the edge. Without acknowledging my presence, he gripped her arm and propelled her in front of him. Only then did I see the vague trail through the pine. I followed a discreet distance behind.

After they were safely away from the river, he released his hold on his wife and wiped his hand on his jeans, as if removing dirt. But when his hand passed close to my face, it had looked pristine to me.

CHAPTER NINE

Not once during the twenty-minute hike to the parking lot did I see Jeff comfort his wife, despite her obvious distress. Instead he remained several paces behind her as she walked haltingly with her back hunched, her head bowed more like a woman of eighty than one closer to forty. He didn't even offer a helping hand when she stumbled and almost fell. And he completely ignored my presence. Nor did he give me a glance when he hustled Marie-Claude into the backseat of the police chief's SUV and clicked the door shut.

It was as if the scene above the river had never happened, as if he didn't want to admit what we'd both witnessed. Instinct told me that Marie-Claude's near fall into the gorge hadn't been caused by an accidental loss of balance, but by a death wish.

When I called out to ask how she was doing, he continued to ignore me, although he did acknowledge me with a scowl as he climbed into the other side of the vehicle. He slammed the door with a resounding thud that caused people milling near the buses to glance over.

The police chief must've also heard the sound, for

he broke away from the command post where he'd been talking to the SAR commander and strode over to his vehicle. After several minutes of conversation through the partially open back door, he closed it again, his face set in grim determination.

"Is she okay?" I called out as I walked up to him.

"Jeff says she's fine, but she didn't look good to me. I'm gonna get Patrolman Smith to drive her home. Marie-Claude shouldn't have come. This has been too hard on her."

I agreed but hesitated revealing what had just taken place at the gorge. If Jeff hadn't told him, then perhaps I shouldn't either. Instead I suggested, "I can go back with her, if Jeff wants to stay."

"You don't mind?"

"Nope. I'm wet and cold and don't feel like hanging around here any longer."

I didn't want to tell him that there was no way I was going to return in the same car as Teht'aa. She'd either sit there in stony, reproving silence or give me a lecture.

He stuck his head back through the open door, but within seconds he closed it again. "Jeff says he'd better stay with her. But I don't see any reason why you can't go with them. You might as well get in the car, while I go get Sarah."

I saw his nostrils twitch and his lips firm in disapproval as his hand reached inside his pocket. He pulled out a handful of candy mints. "You better chew on these. You smell like my jail on a Saturday night."

Without another word, he headed off in search of the young policewoman.

Shit. Now I had Will mad at me. But at least he hadn't given me a lecture.

I knew my bladder wouldn't last the long drive back to Migiskan, so I headed off to the porta-potty. But by the time I returned, the MPD SUV was gone.

Damn, now I'd have to go with Teht'aa. Unless ... I glanced over to the entrance of the parking lot, where Will was engrossed in a conversation with one of the SQ cops. He would probably drive Sarah's police cruiser home. I'd beg a ride with him.

I was feeling decidedly fragile. My head ached and I trembled from head to foot from the dampness and the cold. It was nothing that another nip of vodka couldn't remedy. But I wasn't going to go there. Besides, my supplier was still in the bush. So I helped myself to a steaming cup of coffee and a donut and retreated to a nearby picnic table to wait for Will.

The rain, thank God, had stopped and the sun was trying to squeeze through the clouds. But the wind had risen and was whipping the forest canopy into a frenetic uproar. Leaves and pine needles swirled around me. I zipped my fleece up to my chin and stuck my hands in my pockets. I watched a gust grab one end of the command post tent, but a couple of people managed to catch it before it toppled over.

With more people emerging from the forest, it looked as if the search was winding down. Although I didn't see anyone from my team, I did see Marie-Claude's biker brother sauntering over to the coffee van, creating a wave as people hastened to get out of his path. I wanted to leave before Teht'aa made an appearance, but felt I couldn't interrupt Will's conversation, which didn't appear to be going well. Both men stood with their feet spread, arms crossed and their chins jutting out in an up-yours stance. I did, however, notice the MPD cruiser that Sarah must've driven. Will probably wouldn't mind if I waited for him there. I popped one of his breath mints into my mouth and headed over to the car.

The coffee had helped to clear my mind, but it hadn't done enough to prevent me from colliding with Marie-Claude's brother as I strode towards the cruiser.

"*Câlisse!* Watch where you're going!" he snarled in French. Then perhaps remembering me from his sister's house, he switched to English, "Sorry, my problem."

"No, it was my fault. I wasn't watching where I was going."

He waved away my excuse with a dismissive flick of his hand. "You friend of my sister, *non?*"

"Yes, I am."

"You seen her today, talked to her?"

"For a few minutes," I answered warily.

"How she doing? That bastard won't let me near her."

"She's going through a tough time."

"She always have tough time with that *maudit chien sale.*"

I tried to ignore the biker leathers, the tattoos covering his neck, and the jagged scar streaking from under the black eye patch. Instead I concentrated on his uncovered eye, which seemed to be pouring out genuine sympathy and concern for a loved sister.

I decided to tell him what I'd witnessed and finished by saying, "I don't know whether she meant to kill herself or whether she was just feeling faint. But she's blaming herself for something. I think it's her daughter's disappearance."

"More like the fault of that *maudit bâtard*."

"You think Jeff is responsible?"

"*Tabernac*, he keeps them in a prison. Won't let Fleur go on a date. She's a young girl. She like boys. She want to be with them, but that bastard won't let her."

"Maybe he's worried about her getting involved with the wrong crowd."

"On a fuckin' reserve?"

"Believe it or not, there is a gang of kids heavily into drugs. Maybe Jeff wants to keep her away from them?"

He spat on the ground. "You gotta cut kids loose. Let 'em find their way. Fleur is a good kid. She know to stay outta trouble."

"Maybe going to Ottawa was just a little too much freedom, particularly if she'd led as sheltered a life as you're suggesting. I talked to a woman today from Ottawa. She saw Fleur just before she disappeared. She seemed to think that Fleur had become a prostitute."

He spat again. "No fuckin' way. I tell ya, she a good Catholic girl. I know whores. Fleur ain't no whore." He craned his neck around. "Show me the woman? I make her tell the truth."

He pulled at his knuckles as if preparing for a fight. Although I felt Claire was brash enough to handle him, I wasn't about to inflict him on her. Fortunately the arrival of the SQ policeman saved me.

"Your kind isn't wanted here," the cop said in French and began herding J.P. towards his bike.

"But he's the brother of the missing girl," I called out. "He wants to find her as much as we do."

"Yeah, more like he had a hand in her disappearance,

ain't that right, bro? Bet if we dig deep enough, we'll find your brothers' shit all over this case."

J.P. gave a philosophical Gallic shrug as if to say, "*C'est la vie*," clamped his Nazi helmet onto his head, and kicked his bike into action. We all watched his bike, with its streamers flying horizontally, roar out of the parking lot and onto the main road. I sensed a collective sigh of relief at its departure.

Decontie, his brow furrowed, his lips compressed into a thin line, walked towards me.

"What's up? You don't look too happy." From the corner of my eye I could see Teht'aa sipping coffee at the command post.

"I'm not. The SQ are closing their case on Fleur. Or more correctly, they aren't going to open one."

"Why not?"

"Simple. No evidence was found that places her in the province of Quebec after her disappearance."

"What about the shoe I found?"

"Jeff's certain it doesn't belong to his daughter."

"But surely that's good news, isn't it?"

"Don't get me wrong, it is, but we need the SQ looking into her case. Just because nothing of hers was found here, it doesn't rule out the possibility that she's somewhere else in Gatineau. But they refuse to do any kind of a follow-up."

I watched Teht'aa throw her empty cup into a garbage can and signal Wendy and her husband to go to the Jeep. She started walking towards Will and me. It was too late to hide behind his bulk. Her eyes were already riveted on me.

"What about Becky's case? The shoes could belong to her."

"True, and they said they were gonna run them by her mother, but if she doesn't recognize them, they can't be ruled out without forensics having a go at them, and that ain't gonna happen any time soon. According to the sergeant, Major Crimes is up to its eyeballs in a high-profile case."

"But surely solving Becky's murder is just as important?"

"Hrmph. What's the rush? She's just another murdered native woman. Her case can be handled anytime."

Will had reached his limit. I'd never heard him voice such cynicism.

"But they must be doing something. That SQ cop mentioned the possibility of bikers being involved."

"Who knows? He wouldn't discuss the case with me. Becky's Cree and not from the Migiskan reserve, he said. Therefore she ain't none of my business. That bastard. If he wasn't a fellow cop, I'd take him on." He shoved his police cap further back on his head. "But if there is a prostitution angle to this, then biker gangs could very well be involved. In Quebec, they have their fingers pretty much into anything illegal, drugs, prostitution, arms dealing, you name it."

"I guess not finding any evidence for Fleur also means the Ottawa police won't ramp up their case either?" I said.

He formed his fingers into a gun and fired at me. "Dead on, but I'm gonna see what I can do to get it moving."

At that point, Teht'aa arrived. Pursing her lips, she said, "You coming with me? I'm leaving now."

Before I had a chance to come up with a good answer, Will intervened. "If you don't mind, Teht'aa, I'm going to take Meg with me. There's something I want to discuss with her, okay?"

As she walked away without so much as a goodbye, I gave Will my grateful thanks.

He smiled sheepishly. "I could tell that woman was on a mission. I figured you didn't want to listen to her go on about the evils of drink. I tell you nothing is worse than a reformed addict, even if her addiction was drugs and not alcohol. Besides, I figure you know what you're doing. Today was a minor setback. I don't see you going back down that road again."

He paused as if not sure he should go on. Then he continued, "That's what I believe ... and so does Eric...."

He paused again and looked me straight in the eye. "You know, he still thinks highly of you."

CHAPTER
TEN

I felt like I'd been punched in the stomach. How dare Eric discuss me with Will, with anyone. What went on between us was our own private affair. I breathed deeply. I didn't know how to respond. A red squirrel scolding from a nearby branch expressed my sentiments exactly. But I knew I couldn't lash out at Will. He was only Eric's unwitting messenger.

I took another deep breath before turning back. "Well, he has a funny way of showing it. If Eric thinks so highly of me, why hasn't he called?"

Clearly embarrassed, Will removed his police cap and ran his fingers through his bristly brush-cut. "I guess I opened my big mouth, eh?"

"Sorry, I didn't mean to put you in the middle, but it upsets me having Eric talk about me behind my back."

"Look, Meg, I know I'm not one to speak, after all I'm not exactly batting a thousand when it comes to relationships with women."

He had a point. He was currently on his third marriage, and according to Teht'aa, it was floundering.

He shuffled his feet then looked me straight in the

eye. "But if I could offer some words of advice. It's time for the both of you to stop the bullshit. The two of you have backed yourselves into your high and mighty corners and refuse to budge. Sure, you probably have good reasons for waiting for him to make the first move, the same way he's convinced it's up to you.

"But I tell you, life's too short. Who knows what will happen tomorrow? So Meg, if you truly love the guy, which I believe you do, pick up that goddamn phone when you get home and call him, okay?"

I felt myself reeling. "But *he* doesn't love me, otherwise he would've called by now. After all, it's a year and one month since we broke up."

"Oh, Meg, cut the crap. Of course he loves you. What in the hell do you think he's been bending my ear about since you kicked his butt out of your house?"

"I didn't kick him out of my house. He left of his own accord."

"Yeah, but not without some pushing by you."

I tried to hold back the tears. I didn't want to cry in front of Eric's best friend. But I could feel them beginning to trickle down my cheeks.

"I don't know what to do, Will. I'm scared to death of marriage. And Eric gave every indication that it was the only kind of relationship he wanted with me."

"Are you sure? Have you talked it out with him?"

That sweltering summer night a little more than a year ago, when Eric had asked me to marry him, was seared in my brain. His offer had been so unexpected and sudden that it had freaked me out. As my stomach twisted with fear and dread, I'd stood there like a zombie, unable to speak or move. Seeing my hesitation, he'd accused me of refusing to marry him because he was native. As I tripped over a plausible explanation, terrified of revealing the real reason, he'd slammed my bedroom door and raced down the stairs and out of my life. We'd shared nothing but icy politeness since.

I shook my head. "No…." I hesitated. "I'm afraid to."

"Come here, Meg, you need a hug."

Will folded me against the barrel of his chest and gently patted me on the head. It felt good, so very good. It had been a long time since a man had held me.

"I know you've got problems," he continued. "That's why you drink. But Christ, we've all got them. There's nothing for you to be afraid of. Eric is one hell of an understanding guy. Besides, you're not the same scared woman who arrived in our neck of the woods I don't know how many years go. I think you're a lot happier in your own skin now, aren't you?"

He gave me a final squeeze then released me.

I wiped the tears from my face and looked up into his almost puppy dog eyes, hardly the kind one would expect in a cop. I wasn't sure if I could agree with him. Life hadn't seemed too hot lately … not since Eric had exited my life. But I wasn't going to admit this. Will would only turn around and tell Eric.

"Promise me, you'll call him, okay?" Will said.

"Un-hun," I muttered. I had no intention of doing so.

Why should I be the one to span the gulf? Eric could do it just as easily as me. I glanced back up at Will. His expression of hope had changed to skepticism.

"Don't be so quick to reject it, Meg. At least think about it."

"But why should I be the one to make the first call? If you're giving Eric the same advice, why hasn't he called me?"

Chuckling, Will shook his head. "Because he's a lot more stubborn than you are."

I smiled inwardly. That he was. I remember the time he was teaching me to paddle whitewater. I was having difficulty grasping the proper paddling techniques. I wanted to give up, but Eric kept badgering me until finally the light bulb went on and I found myself doing prys and draws like a pro.

"Okay, I'll think about it."

But if I did go back with Eric, the truth about my brother would eventually have to come out. And what would Eric think of me then? I knew I wouldn't be able to face the disgust in eyes that had once held love. At least now it was plain ordinary indifference. Yes, I would think about it, but I knew the answer would have to be no. Better to have parted on a misunderstanding than to be spurned because of the terrible mistake I'd made almost thirty years ago.

A sudden horn blast jarred me out of my thoughts. I found myself at bumper level with one of the buses while the driver waved frantically at Will and me to get out of the way. We hastily jumped to one side as the bus slid by with the passengers' curious stares firmly fixed on the two of us. Some even had the glint of gossip in their eyes. Most likely tongues would begin wagging the minute they got back to the reserve. I doubted Will's hug, as innocent as it was, would help his floundering marriage. And it would only serve to widen the gap between Eric and me. But that was okay.

On the drive home, Will had no further opportunity to chastise me. Thank God. With the cruiser
crammed with others from the reserve, the discussion
focused on the search and its failure to find anything
belonging to Fleur. Needless to say, they viewed this as
good news. I followed the chief's lead and kept the bad
news to myself.

As we wended our way back along the highway, I
played with a piece of quartz I'd noticed in the parking
lot. Its sparkle had caught my attention as I was getting
into the cruiser. Close examination revealed the sparkle
came from a thin thread of what could very well be gold.

It reminded me of the quartz I'd found on Whispers
Island when a mining company had wanted to develop a
gold mine directly across from my cottage on Echo Lake.
Worried that the mine would destroy our northern paradise,
Eric and I had joined forces to fight its development. That
was the first time I'd had anything to do with the Migiskan
band chief. Afterward, our relationship had grown, sometimes bumpily, until I'd felt he had become my other half.
He was like an old shoe, comfortable and safe. And I'd
loved him. Oh, how I had loved him. I still did.

I glanced at Will's profile as he concentrated on the
quirks of the road. Maybe he was right. Maybe I should
be the one to break the logjam. Maybe I *should* call Eric.
And maybe, just maybe, I could keep my dirty little secret
to myself.

I fingered the rock again. It felt warm and comforting, like Eric. In fact, he kept a stone similar to this one in
the amulet he wore around his neck. I tucked it into my
inside pocket and sighed.

No. I couldn't pretend my brother's death had never happened. It wouldn't be fair to Eric. If we were to get back together, it would be for the long haul, regardless of whether we married or not. He would want an open and honest relationship. As would I. Maybe he would be able to forgive me, but if I had never been able to forgive myself, how could I expect him to?

CHAPTER
ELEVEN

Although I'd summoned up the courage to call Eric when I got home, I ended up convincing myself I was too tired after spending all day in the bush. He probably wouldn't be in any state either for a serious discussion after his long day in airports and the long-haul flight from Vancouver. Besides, the headache reverberating through my brain was preventing me from concentrating on anything other than the necessities of life.

All I could manage was cooking up a basic meal, my usual Kraft Dinner smothered in homemade chili sauce, a local farmer's, not mine. I wouldn't know where to begin to make the scrumptious tomato sauce. Dinner was eaten on the sofa in front of the TV, where I flaked out for another couple of hours before retreating to bed. I wasn't even up to joining Sergei in his evening walk. I just clicked open the door and shooed him outside.

In the morning, after a surprisingly solid night's sleep, my resolve was somewhat emboldened, but after dialing Eric's number, I chickened out and slammed the receiver down. I decided a brisk morning walk would do wonders for settling my jangling nerves, so I rounded up reluctant Sergei, who'd been happily asleep on his bed in the kitchen, and spent the next couple of hours rambling the trail through Aunt Aggie's once prosperous sugar bush. I even tackled the steep incline up to the Lookout, a granite outcrop overlooking my rambling nineteenth-century cottage and the lake beyond.

I tried to spy Eric amongst a group of people at the end of a dock, which was all I could see of the Forgotten Bay Hunting and Fishing Camp at the far end of the bay. But without binoculars it was impossible to distinguish one tiny figure from another. I plunked myself down on the edge of the outcrop and pondered the rest of the view of Echo Lake, while Sergei, intent on searching out enticing smells, rummaged through the underbrush behind me.

Across the lake, an aluminum boat from the Fishing Camp carved a line through the flat water towards one of the good fishing spots near Whispers Island, while above a bald eagle circled perhaps in hopes of nabbing one of their fish. The gap in the island's old growth white pine forest, where loggers had cut a number of the ancient giants before being stopped, was starkly visible and would be for another hundred years or more, until they succumbed to the forces of nature.

For me this scar was a constant reminder of what can happen when man's greed takes over with little respect for Mother Earth or the people that honour her. Thankfully, the island was no longer in danger. Several years ago its new owner had passed its guardianship on to the Migiskan Anishinabeg with the proviso that they kept the forest intact. Nonetheless, a faction within the community had clamoured to take advantage of the wealth the harvesting of the mature pines would bring.

Fortunately, Eric succeeded in convincing them that preserving the ancient trees was more important than money. He'd emphasized that it was the last undisturbed forest left in their ninety-square-kilometre territory where they could walk trails their ancestors had walked, camp under a forest canopy their ancestors had camped under, and pay homage to the same trees their ancestors had revered. As one of the last remaining links to the old ways, it should be kept sacred.

Since then a traditional Algonquin camp had been set up as a learning centre to reacquaint band members with their ancient culture and as a retreat when modern life became too hectic. At various times, an elder would take up residence in one of the birchbark wigwams and serve either as a teacher of traditional Algonquin ways or as a listening ear for life's burdens.

It was to this camp, to the hearth of Summer Grass Woman, that I'd fled during one particularly low moment a few months after the break up with Eric, when the bottle had beckoned strongly. The previous day I'd happened on Eric chuckling his all too familiar chuckle in the company of a gorgeous, twenty-pounds-lighter and twenty-years-younger woman. The tranquillity of the island and the elder's sensible calm had managed to quell the shouting demons, and I'd left feeling sufficiently fortified to resist the alcoholic's urge. I had remained so for the most part, except for one or two or maybe three slip-ups ... like yesterday. Maybe I should visit the island again.

But no, surely a simple phone call to Eric would be enough....

Hell, who was I kidding? It would only unleash more demons.

Through the trees I could make out a glint of morning sun on the back windows of my cottage, while the roof of the turret with its crowning Canada goose weather vane rose above their height. I'd fallen in love with its Victorian eccentricity on my first visit as a child, when I'd come with my family to spend a couple of weeks with Great-aunt Agatha. Over the years she and I had developed an enduring friendship. One of our special times together would be to retreat from the hot summer sun to the shade of the deep wrap-around verandah, where she, rocking back and forth on her bentwood rocker and holding a crystal tumbler of single malt, would regale me with tales of my Harris ancestors, mainly Great-grandpa Joe, her father and the architect of Three Deer Point. Although she never told me the source of the name, I suspected it came from my great-grandfather's successful hunt of three deer depicted in an old photo hanging in the living room. The "point," of course, comes from the long finger-like granite peninsula upon which the cottage stands.

Though I hadn't immediately taken up residence after she'd bequeathed it to me, it wasn't because of lack of desire. My husband Gareth had hated it, hated anything that wasn't surrounded in asphalt and brick. But once I'd removed him from my life, I'd fled to the safety of its foot-thick timber walls and had never regretted my decision to leave the urban life. Like Aunt Aggie, I often found myself in the shelter of the verandah, rocking back and forth in her old rocker, in the early years with a tumbler of lemon vodka and then after Eric reformed me, a cup of coffee or tea, while I pondered the ever-changing lake view and life's persistent hiccups.

The sound of an approaching motorboat warned me that I was about to get a visitor. Although the trees and the cliffs of the pine-covered point hid the boat and my dock from view, I could tell by the increasing putt-putt that it was nearing the dock. I tensed at the thought that it might be Eric. I waited for his head to emerge above the cliff wall as he climbed up the steep dock stairs. But the motor didn't stop. Within seconds a white fibreglass boat with two trolling fishermen puttered into sight as it headed out into the middle of the lake. I relaxed.

Tired of snuffling after strange smells, Sergei nudged me, impatient to leave. I tried to persuade him to lie down, but he gave me that "No way, José" stubborn stare, so after spending a few more minutes breathing in the fresh forest air, I got up and started the trek back to the cottage. Sergei responded with a joyful toss of his head and bounded back down the trail. Although I couldn't really call it bounding, it was more like an easy lope. I'd noticed lately that he was slowing down. His broken leg of a few months ago was no doubt a contributing factor, but I felt he might have a touch of arthritis. At nine years, he was getting on for a standard poodle.

The descending was a lot easier than the climbing. By the time I reached the more level sections of the trail, I was feeling quite invigorated. I was even feeling energized enough to consider restarting Aunt Aggie's sugar bush operation. Many of her giant sap-producing maples still stood. As I recalled, she'd made a respectable amount of money from the operation, and I could always do with more money. The income from the investments I'd inherited from her was just enough to live modestly without any major purchases, such as a new vehicle. And my rusted-out Ford pick-up was in dire need of replacement. A spiffy new Jag like my sister's would be just the thing. But hey, who was I kidding. A prissy Jag would never survive the area's gravel roads. Still, another source of income would come in handy. After all, some of my investments hadn't done too well of late, and the income they produced was somewhat lower than a couple of years ago.

Eager to get home, Sergei didn't linger. Instead he trotted on ahead and was soon lost from view. My feet crunched through a clump of freshly fallen leaves, these ones a deep orange. In another few weeks the trail would be buried under this year's crop of dying leaves. But for now the surrounding maples still wore their green summer foliage, apart from the odd orange or red leaf.

A short while later the back of the woodshed loomed into view. At the same time, I caught the sound of a vehicle coming along my road, confirmed by Sergei's warning yelps. Someone was paying me a visit.

My heart stopped when I recognized the pale gold Grand Cherokee as it flashed past the gap between the woodshed and pump house.

Eric was here!

He'd come. He'd opened the door first.

But maybe that wasn't why he was here — maybe this was just a social call to tell me about something happening on the reserve that would affect me, like increasing the number of cabins at the Forgotten Bay Hunting and

Fishing Camp, something I'd been dreading for years. It would have to be something important, since he hadn't set foot on my land since the night he ran out of my house thirteen months and two days ago.

I took a deep breath and tried to rein in my galloping nerves and plaster an expression of indifference on my face. No way I wanted him to know how much this visit unnerved me. I heard the SUV door click open. Sergei stopped barking. He'd found a friend. But of course he had. He and Eric had always had a special bond.

Taking another deep breath, I emerged from behind the pump house. So certain was I of seeing Eric's burly shape that it took me several seconds to take in the long, satiny black hair flowing over the slim shoulders as the person bent over to give the dog a big hug.

"Teht'aa, I thought you were Eric." I glanced nervously around. "Where is he?" I blurted out before realizing I'd given myself away. I'd never confided in her how much I missed her father.

She straightened. "He never arrived. I guess something must've come up. But what does it matter to you?"

I felt disappointment wash over me as she eyed me suspiciously.

"Oh, it doesn't matter at all. I just thought it was him driving the Jeep. That's all."

"Nope. It's all mine until he gets home." She flashed an expanse of pearly white before turning serious. "I wanted to see how you were doing." She paused. "You had me very worried yesterday."

"As you can see, I'm okay. I guess I kind of went overboard yesterday, didn't I?"

But afraid she'd come to lecture me, I didn't wait for an answer. Instead I turned and tripped up the stairs to the front door, hoping she would take this as a sign that I wanted to be left alone. However, when I turned around and saw her standing forlornly by her father's vehicle, her beautiful face creased in concern, I felt so awful, I invited her in for a coffee.

CHAPTER TWELVE

"I see my dad was here recently," Teht'aa called out from the front of the house.

Certain I'd heard incorrectly, I shouted from the kitchen where I was making coffee, "What did you say?"

"I said, you must've seen my dad recently." Her shout was accompanied by the sound of approaching footsteps echoing along the hall's creaky wooden floors.

"Of course I haven't. You know that," I replied.

"How would I know? Neither of you ever tell me anything." Despite her tone, she was smiling as she stepped onto the kitchen's worn linoleum floor, which should probably be replaced one of these days.

Since moving in, I hadn't been in any hurry to replace much in the century-old house other than items that had reached the end of their lifespan. I liked the lived-in feel of Aunt Aggie's roomy country kitchen with its white wooden cupboards, their edges rounded from numerous coats of paint, the Arborite counters with the 1950s pink and fuchsia swirls adding a touch of brightness, and of course the antique wood cookstove standing stately in chrome and grey metal against the outside wall. I had replaced the 1970s refrigerator after it broke down last year, along with the equally old stove, with basic white models that had few frills. The latest gewgaws would've been totally wasted on me.

I poured hot coffee into two mugs. "I don't have any cream. Will milk do?"

"Yeah, it'll do. Lots of it along with some sugar. I need it. You do like your coffee strong, don't you?" She smiled. "Just like my father."

She tossed a small white object back and forth between her hands. It sparkled as it caught a shaft of sun streaming through the window. Tucking it into her pocket, she added copious amounts of milk and sugar to her mug.

"It gets me going. That wimpy stuffy you drink would put me to sleep."

I piled some chocolate chip cookies onto a plate. After my long walk, I figured I could reward myself with one or two of these calorific gems made by my mother's long-time cook. Mother had couriered them up last week from Toronto along with a few other items.

I found it amazing that in the few months following my trip to the Far North, we'd had more to do with each other than in the past five or more years since I'd fled the big city for the isolation of this northern paradise. Before, I would've sent the stuff back or slammed the phone down in annoyance. Now I quite enjoyed our frequent conversations and regretted the years it had taken us to step out of our roles of chastising mother and rebellious daughter.

"I noticed some terrific watercolours in the living room," Teht'aa said. "Are they new?"

"Mother sent them last week. My father painted them when I was a child. As you could probably tell, they're scenes from around here."

I collected the plate of cookies. "Let's go out onto the porch. I think it's warm enough to sit outside."

Sergei followed us into the screen porch and with a deep sigh plunked his long curly-coated body down beside Teht'aa's wicker chair. She gave him several vigorous pats, while he stretched and groaned contentedly.

I sank into the bentwood rocker, sipped my coffee and pretended to be engrossed in the happenings on Echo Lake while waiting for Teht'aa to speak. There was no point in asking her why she'd dropped by. She wanted to give me a sermon on yesterday's slip-up. Although I wasn't looking forward to it, I felt I should let her get it out of her system, then we could get on with our friendship. Besides, I deserved it.

The boat with the two fishermen had joined the other boat on the other side of the lake at the fishing hole near Whispers Island. My mouth watered at the thought of freshly caught bass sautéed lightly with fresh herbs, a meal Eric often prepared for us. I hadn't eaten any as good since. My one attempt had ended up tasting like dried-out, overcooked parchment. Cooking wasn't exactly one of my strengths.

I rocked back and forth, trying to absorb the calm, while I waited for Teht'aa to begin. But when she did, she took me completely by surprise.

"So if Dad didn't give this to you, where did you get it?"

She dropped the object she'd been tossing in her hands onto the round wicker table between us.

It took me a few seconds to recognize the jagged piece of quartz. "How do you know this belongs to Eric?"

The only time I'd studied his stone closely was when I compared it to the ones Aunt Aggie had found on Whispers Island eighty years earlier, but I couldn't tell whether this was the same stone or not. It could just as easily have belonged to Aunt Aggie.

Teht'aa pointed to a tiny speck of orange near the faint thread of gold. "He told me he'd found this where the mining company marked its claim on Whispers Island."

The speck did appear to be similar to the fluorescent paint the miners had used.

Teht'aa continued, "He'd kept it as a reminder of what could've happened if you guys hadn't stopped the mine. Are you sure he didn't give it to you?"

"No. I found it on the ground. He must've dropped it without knowing it." I thought of where I'd found the stone. "He must've lost it some time ago."

"Nope, I don't think so. I remember seeing it in mid-July at a smudging ceremony in the Council Hall, when he laid it out with the other sacred items from his medicine bundle."

Mid-July … about the time Fleur and Becky disappeared. I felt a chill of dread creep over me. Should I tell Teht'aa where I found it?

"Did he mention that he'd lost it?"

She shook her head.

"Maybe he gave it to someone and they lost it?" I thought of Fleur. But no, she'd left the reserve at the end of June, a good two weeks before the ceremony.

"I doubt it. It would have to be someone very special. And as far as I know, there is no special person in his life at the moment." Her ebony eyes bore into mine before turning back to the lake.

I squirmed. What was she trying to do?

She took a sip of coffee before continuing. "Maybe he came here when you were up north and it fell out without him knowing."

So … she thought I'd found it on my property. I hesitated about correcting her and then decided not to, not yet. There had to be a simple explanation for its presence in the parking lot close to where Becky's body was found. I'd like to be able to give her this explanation, rather than have her go through the dread of wondering what connection, if any, her father had to Becky's death.

CHAPTER THIRTEEN

I was so worried about Eric and the implications of the stone that I tossed and turned most of the night. And my nightmare of a man looking a lot like Eric being dragged to a noose hanging from the branch of a pine tree didn't help my sleep either. So by the time the grey light of dawn finally seeped through my bedroom windows, I felt as if I'd been trampled by a herd of moose.

No matter how hard I searched for a different answer, I couldn't come up with a logical explanation for Eric's stone ending up in the parking lot other than he was the one who'd lost it. But if he had, what was he doing there? The parking lot was intended for users of Gatineau Park, such as hikers, mountain bikers, and city dwellers wanting nature's relief from urban stress. I'd never known Eric to hike, and he certainly didn't ride a mountain bike, although he did love his Harley. And of course he had no need to go elsewhere to enjoy a forest. He spent his daily life living and breathing in one.

And as Teht'aa said, her father wouldn't give away an object he considered a gift from the Creator, from *kije manidu*. In fact, it was so special that he wore it around his neck, along with other sacred items, inside the beaded deerskin amulet his grandmother had made for his grandfather. Which raised another point. How did the stone get out of the amulet?

Eric wouldn't just throw it away, not without a very good reason, particularly in a place as meaningless to him as a parking lot. I could see him returning it to Whispers Island, but he would do that with a small ceremony, like sprinkling tobacco and chanting a few words to *kije manidu*.

The amulet was old, the deerskin paper-thin. I supposed it could've come apart and its contents fallen out. But surely Eric would've noticed. And he would've retrieved the items, all five of them, each with a special and sacred meaning to him, like his grandfather's tiny carving of a fisher, his family's namesake, for *odjik* means "fisher" in Algonquin.

As reluctant as I was to speak with him, I knew the only way I was going to learn how the stone had ended up in this isolated parking lot would be to ask him when he finally got home. And once I learned the truth, I would no doubt be shaking my head at my useless worrying. Clearly it would have nothing to do with Becky or her death.

I'd also lost sleep over Marie-Claude. Yesterday Teht'aa had remarked how terrible our friend had looked when she'd run into her at the Migiskan General Store. Apparently her hands shook so much, she could barely extract the money from her wallet at the checkout counter. Her hair looked as if it hadn't been combed since she'd gotten out of bed that morning, and her clothes were a crumpled mismatch of odd items. Although Marie-Claude generally looked unkempt, Teht'aa thought her appearance was scruffier than usual.

And when Teht'aa had asked if she was all right, Marie-Claude had barely acknowledged her presence, let alone responded to the question. Teht'aa had left her alone, but after seeing Marie-Claude's erratic driving as she left the parking lot, she'd followed her home to make sure she arrived safely.

Right after Teht'aa had left, I called Marie-Claude. Unfortunately, Jeff answered and said she was resting and couldn't be disturbed. In what I was learning was a typical response for him, he dismissed any suggestion that all might not be well with his wife. He was equally abrupt when I asked about the search. He merely said the police were doing all they could and hung up before I had a chance to ask anything else.

I was surprised by Jeff's behaviour. Although I'd only met him on social occasions, he'd always been friendly and quite willing to chat. Not now. I sensed this hostile abruptness was his way of dealing with his daughter's disappearance.

The day was turning out to be a dreary, rainy fall day, not the kind to spend outside, as I'd hoped to. Last night I'd decided to spend the morning surveying the maple forest. I figured before going further with the idea of resurrecting the sugar bush operation, I needed to get a good idea of the state of the trees. No doubt some had died over the past twenty years or so since Aunt Aggie had stopped the operation, while others would've grown large enough to be good sap producers. But I didn't feel up to slogging around in the rain. Given Sergei's sedentary state in front of the kitchen's hot woodstove, he didn't either.

I found myself at a loss for something to do. I could clean the house — it always needed it. But vacuuming and the like wasn't exactly my thing. Besides, it needed to be really dirty before I felt compelled to do something about it. And since I'd cleaned a week ago, I considered it still clean.

Many women baked on rainy days, but since this wasn't my thing either, I didn't even consider it. However, I did like painting. I enjoyed the mindless rhythm of running a paintbrush or roller up and down a wall. And the kitchen was in need of a fresh coat to cover the scrapes and marks I'd been pretending didn't exist. In fact, I had wallpaper I'd bought in a burst of energy in the spring but had as yet done nothing with it. All I needed was some matching paint for the wainscoting and trim, and my day was set.

I clipped a piece of the wallpaper with bright yellow lemons to take with me. I was tired of the basic white motif of the kitchen and thought a matching shade of yellow for the wainscoting would liven up the room nicely. But I would keep the cupboards and trim white. After letting Sergei out for one last pee, I headed off to the paint store in Somerset, the closest town, a good forty-five-minute drive away.

As I reached the section of the main road where the gravel changed to asphalt, I was passed by a grey van whose driver I recognized immediately. It was Jeff. And he was in a hurry to get somewhere. Probably Somerset. Possibly Ottawa. But either way, he would be gone for at least a couple of hours. I turned around and headed back, towards the Lightbody house.

CHAPTER
FOURTEEN

Marie-Claude's dark blue Honda with the familiar
dent in the front bumper was parked next to her
two-storey frame house. Although I didn't see light coming from any of the facing windows, I assumed she was
probably in the kitchen at the back of the house.

Bracing myself for the deluge, I flipped up the hood
of my rain jacket, hopped out of the truck, and splashed
through the puddles to the side door, not caring whether
my feet got soaked or not. I knocked on the cold metal
door, at first lightly, then more vigorously when she failed
to appear. I peered through the side windows, and seeing
no sign of her, I walked around to the back and checked
the kitchen windows. Though the overhead light was on
and breakfast dishes had not yet been cleared from the
table, the room was empty. I banged on the window, hoping the noise would get her attention, but after several
attempts, I gave up. I even shouted her name. Surely if
she was somewhere in this house, she would've heard the
ruckus by now.

I thought it unlikely that Marie-Claude would've gone
to visit a neighbour, given the distraught state Teht'aa had

found her in yesterday. Besides, she wasn't the most active person I knew. She would've taken her car.

There was one other possibility. She'd gone to the camp. By now my sopping pants were clinging to my legs and my feet were soaked, but I felt it was more important to ensure Marie-Claude was all right than to escape back into my truck. I splashed along the winding path through the woods to the birch grove, where I could just make out the Quonset-like outline of the birchbark wigwam through the trees. I checked for smoke rising through the hole in its roof, for surely on a cold, damp day like today a fire would be needed, but I didn't see any. Nor did I smell any, only the earthy dampness of the rain. There was also no smoke rising from the sweat lodge, which might have offered the healing peace she no doubt was seeking. And the workshop appeared equally unoccupied.

Nonetheless I checked inside each building. While several half-finished baskets from our attempts of a week ago remained on the worktable in the workshop, there was no other sign of recent activity. The wigwam was similarly cold and empty, as was the sweat lodge, although I was tempted to heat up the stones, remove my damp clothes and warm up in the swirling steam.

I was about to turn away and head back to the house when I heard a faint cry. I strained to see through the veil of rain and saw nothing other than drenched vegetation. Then I caught a slight movement from the other side of the beaver pond. Something was floundering in the water a short distance from the pond's edge. A sudden chill raced down my spine. This wasn't a beaver or a heron or any other water animal. Horrified at what this might portend,

I raced around the pond, praying I wouldn't be too late, and arrived just as Marie-Claude's head sank beneath the swampy water, leaving a radiating swirl of blonde hair.

Without another thought, I waded in after her and realized the minute I was over my head that I should've removed my shoes and jacket. I struggled to kick off the shoes and succeeded, but the cold water made the jacket too slippery to grasp hold of. And I knew I didn't have enough time to return to land to remove it. Taking a great gulp of air, I shoved my head beneath the surface in search of Marie-Claude.

The water was dank and murky. I could barely see my hand in front of my face, but at least it wasn't too deep. My feet quickly touched the soft, squishy bottom. Like a blind person, I spread my searching hands out in front of me. My heart raced as a dark object loomed into view, but when I touched the soft, gooey surface, I realized it was a sunken log. I don't know how many times I came up for air, but each time I ducked back down determined to find Marie-Claude.

Finally, after what seemed like hours, but was probably only a couple of minutes, my fingers became entangled in the floating tendrils of her hair, then I saw her face, eyes closed almost as if she were praying. But the minute I touched her, her eyes sprang open, and she began fighting me, struggling to get out of my grasp. Unprepared for her violent reaction, I felt her slip from my grasp. Out of air, I returned to the surface, gasped in another deep breath and swam down to the spot where I'd last seen her. By the time I found her, she had stopped thrashing and no longer fought when I grabbed her arm. In fact, she didn't respond at all. I frantically pulled her to the surface and struggled to get her ashore as fast as I could. Once I did, the lifeguard training I'd learned years ago as a teenager miraculously kicked in.

After ensuring there were no obstructions in her mouth, I placed her on the wet ground on her stomach with her arms raised and her head turned to the side. I began pushing into her back then releasing in the hope her lungs would give up the water they'd taken in. Thankfully, after a few pulsating pushes, water began to seep out of her mouth. Finally she coughed and began breathing. Thank God.

Exhausted, I collapsed beside her still body. I could feel the reassuring rise and fall of her breathing as we lay side by side in a puddle of water. The rain had stopped, but at this point it hardly mattered. Finally she began to stir.

"*Pourquoi vous m'avez sauvée?*" she whispered hoarsely. "Why did you save me?" she repeated several more times in French in a voice that was so low, I had to put my ear to her lips.

I began to shiver. "Come on," I said in French. "We've got to get out of these wet clothes and get warm. Can you get up?"

I rolled her over and tried to sit her up. She neither resisted nor helped.

"I want to die." She kept her eyes closed and spoke as if in a dream. "I deserve to die."

I tried to raise her to her feet, but it was like trying to raise a dead body. "Come on, Marie-Claude, you have to help me. We can't stay here."

I'd been planning on taking her to the house but realized there was no way I could carry or drag her the several hundred metres if she wasn't prepared to walk. I thought of the birchbark wigwam, but it would take too long for a fire to heat up the interior. Instead I would use the smaller sweat lodge.

I dragged her around the pond to the entrance of the low dome-shaped structure covered in sopping wet moose hides and plastic tarps. Again she neither resisted nor helped. I thrust aside the soggy moose hide covering the entrance, and ignoring the wolf skull guarding it, dragged her inside and set her down on a pile of freshly cut cedar boughs. Fortunately, apart from the rain that had come through the central opening, the surrounding platforms were dry.

Although most sweat lodges are temporary structures intended for limited use, Marie-Claude had built a semi-permanent one that could be put quickly into action. The fresh boughs suggested she'd been planning a sweat ceremony until her ultimate despair had taken over. Fortunately, dry firewood and kindling were stacked at one end of a platform. But I couldn't find matches.

Marie-Claude, lying where I'd left her, was now shaking. I had to act fast. I ran to the workshop and found a barbeque lighter resting beside an oil lamp. Grabbing it and some of the birchbark we'd used for our baskets, I hurried back to the sweat lodge, fearing I would no longer find her inside. Thankfully, she hadn't stirred. I hoped her desire to live was taking over. I placed some kindling along with the birchbark in the central fire pit. My hands trembled so much, it took me a several tries to flick the lighter into action. Once the blaze had taken hold, I added more kindling and a couple of logs.

I was shivering almost as much as Marie-Claude. We had to get out of our waterlogged clothes, but we needed something to warm us up until the fire was able to heat up the sweat lodge. Remembering the wolf skins the Lightbodys used for bedding, I raced back to the wigwam to retrieve some.

In all this time, Marie-Claude hadn't moved from the position I'd placed her in. And her eyes remained closed, although she kept whispering over and over again, "It's all my fault. It's all my fault...."

I extracted some boughs from the pile and placed one of the wolf skins over them, fur side up. Then I struggled to remove her drenched clothing, all of it, down to her bare skin. Although I'd had little experience undressing babies, I was sure they would offer more help than she did. I half-shoved, half-dragged her onto the warming fur. Her lips and her fingernails were blue. Her entire body shook. As I wrapped the rest of the wolf skins around her, her eyes briefly opened and regarded me with such over-whelming sadness that I wondered if I'd done the right thing by saving her. But no, I couldn't have left her to drown, the same way I couldn't let her die on me now.

I ran back to the lodge to get more furs. By the time I returned, I could feel the heat starting to fill the sweat lodge. Marie-Claude appeared to be asleep in her cocoon of warmth, while the furs' guard hairs quivered with a life of their own. I threw more logs onto the fire and won-dered if I could chance leaving her alone while I ran to the house to get dry clothes for both of us. But remembering the depth of despair in her eyes, I wasn't entirely certain that she had decided to live. I wouldn't chance it. Instead I laid her wet clothes out on the opposite platform as near as I could to the fire and did the same with mine. After throwing more wood onto the fire, I burrowed my naked, shivering body under the soft warming furs and waited.

What I was waiting for, I wasn't certain. But I dearly hoped that after a sound sleep Marie-Claude would wake up glad to have been given another chance at life.

CHAPTER
FIFTEEN

I awoke to a hissing sound and a low murmur. Exhaustion and the warmth of the furs had lulled me to sleep. Except now I was hot, very hot. My face was dripping with sweat, as was my body. At first I was confused, not sure of where I was or why. But when realization hit, I threw off the hot furs and crawled over to the pile covering Marie-Claude. Except she wasn't there.

I frantically scanned the dark interior and finally saw her opposite me through the clouds of steam rising from the central pit. She was kneeling on cedar boughs, rocking back and forth, chanting in Algonquin. While she rocked, she dipped a wooden ladle into a birchbark basket filled with water and tossed the liquid onto the hot stones at the bottom of the pit. Another cloud of steam billowed upwards.

Beside her, several items were laid out on the pinkish-orange underside of a length of birchbark, as if they were sacred items from a medicine bundle. They included a pink and green beaded necklace and a Barbie Doll dressed as an Indian, complete with fringed garments and a feather in her black hair. I wondered if these belonged to her missing daughter. Smudge from a bowl of burning cedar wafted over them. Its sweet burning smell mingled with the cleansing scent of the fresh cedar and the burning sensation of the steam.

I thought it best to not disturb her. I wasn't certain she realized I was sitting opposite her. With her eyes closed, she seemed to be performing a ceremony. Perhaps she was praying for the safe return of her daughter.

I let the hot steam fill every pore of my body as I swayed to the rhythm of her chanting. It felt good. The nervous tension I'd felt after saving her was draining from my body. My main concern now was to somehow convince her that life was worth living. This ceremony gave me reason to hope. I doubted she would perform it if she intended to go back outside and drown herself. But then again, she might be asking the Creator for forgiveness before doing just that.

I became so immersed in my own thoughts that I wasn't sure how much time had passed when she suddenly stopped chanting and starting speaking in French in a low, soft voice. She was praying. And I realized with a sinking feeling that she was praying for forgiveness for what she had done to her daughter.

Before I had a chance to digest the implications, she opened her eyes, and their pale blueness stared at me through the swirling steam. Damp tendrils of hair snaked over her bare shoulders and onto her sagging breasts. Her thinness was evident in the protruding ribs and hipbones.

"Meg, *je suis trés désolée*," she apologized, then switched to English. "I made you get wet in that filthy swamp." Her voice sounded stronger.

"Don't worry about me. I was already soaked from the rain. How are you feeling now?"

"*Merci bien pour me sauver.* Thank you for saving me. You have given me a second chance. What I tried to do was wrong. I have prayed to the Lord and to the Creator for forgiveness."

"Do I have your word that you won't try it again?"

She nodded. "It is against God's will. Dying was the easy way out. I must live so that each day I am reminded of what I have done to my daughter. It is my cross to bear."

I tensed, afraid to ask the obvious question.

She answered for me. "I killed my daughter."

What I'd feared. Fleur had been found dead. Was this the trigger for the mother's attempted suicide? "I'm so sorry, Marie-Claude. Where did they find her?"

"They haven't found her, yet. I only know she is dead. I feel it in my heart as only a mother can." She stabbed at the limp flesh covering her heart.

"But you can't give up hope. We didn't find any evidence that placed Fleur with Becky when she died. Fleur could still be alive."

She shook her head vehemently. "No, she is dead and I killed her."

"What are you saying? That you actually harmed her?"

"I sent her away."

"But you didn't shoot or kill her with a gun or other kind of weapon, did you?"

"I might as well have. If I hadn't thrown her out of the house, she would be here safe and sound with me."

"But I thought the reason for her leaving was to find a summer job in Ottawa."

"That's what Jeff wanted people to believe. He was very angry with me."

"Why did you throw her out of the house?"

"I found drugs in her dresser."

"What kind? Marijuana?" I couldn't see Fleur using anything stronger.

"No, it was some pills in a bottle. The label said they were Oxycontin. I'd read some place that they are a narcotic and only available via prescription. Fleur's a healthy girl. I knew no doctor had given them to her."

"Did she say where she got them?" Eric would be very upset to learn about this. For the last several years he and Will had been waging war against drugs on the reserve and thought they'd finally got the upper hand.

"No, she refused to. Just said a friend had given them to her to hold onto. But she wouldn't give me his name. She insisted that she hadn't taken any. And I believed her until I came across the nude photos of her on her computer. I was so angry, I told her to get out of the house. *Mon dieu*, can you imagine taking pictures of yourself naked then sending them to your friends, like a *putain*. I'd raised her to be better than that."

"But I think with today's teenagers, these nude photos are really intended as innocent fun. Sexting, they call it."

"I don't care what they call it. Good Catholic girls don't do such things."

"Was this when she went to Ottawa?"

"*Oui*, I was so angry I refused to take her to the bus." Her voice drifted off as she dropped her gaze. "I didn't even say goodbye." She whispered. "*Mon dieu*, my own daughter and I never said goodbye to her. What kind of a mother am I?"

I watched her shoulders convulse in silent weeping.

By now the outside coolness had begun to seep in. The distraught woman had become so absorbed in her guilt that she'd forgotten to pour more water onto the hot stones. But with the burning coals long since having died out, I had a feeling that the stones had cooled down too much to produce any more hot steam. I gathered some wolf skins and crawled over to Marie-Claude, careful not to bump my head on the low ceiling. I sat down beside her, wrapped a couple around her and some around me.

I tried to comfort her. "You're no different from any mother, who's upset and worried about the bad influences in her daughter's life."

"But I made no attempt to find out where she was going to stay in Ottawa. I just assumed she would stay with my brother. But I didn't call him to make sure she arrived. I didn't even try to contact her on her cell."

"But surely your husband would've called."

"He didn't. When he came to me wanting to know if she'd arrived safely, I pretended I'd already talked to her. I wanted to teach her a lesson. I wanted to let her know that because of her bad behaviour, her family no longer cared for her." The tears coursed down her cheeks. "*Mon dieu*, I am such a bad mother. I should be punished for leaving my child alone in the big city and not caring."

I draped my arm around her shoulders. "But I know you. You love your children very much and you're a good mother, a very good mother. You were just being human. Fleur hurt you badly. Besides you thought she was safely with your brother."

She murmured, "*Oui*. I never thought she wouldn't go there. So when Richard called me two weeks later and mentioned that she wasn't at his place, I became very worried. I tried calling her on her cell, left messages, but she never returned my call. That's when I told Jeff what I'd done."

"And what did he do?"

"He was very angry with me. Told me it was my fault. He called the Ottawa police, but he didn't tell them about the argument. Still, the police just said she was a runaway and would come home when she wanted to. This made Jeff even madder at me. He drove many times to Ottawa to look for her. But didn't find her."

"Did you go too?"

She shook her head. "No, Jeff wouldn't let me. Said she might run away if she saw me. *Mon dieu*, me, her own mother." She looked up at me beseechingly. "You see, it's all my fault. I've killed my own daughter."

Another flood of tears descended as her body shook with her grief and guilt.

I wanted to offer her a life raft, but I felt paralyzed by my own guilt, for I too had caused the death of a loved one and knew the agony of never being able to forgive myself. I also knew the terrible impact this could have on a family. No matter how hard they tried to pretend otherwise, they couldn't forgive you either. They might not tell you to your face, but it came through in the small slights, the forgotten birthdays and infrequent calls and the relentless criticism for even small misdemeanours. Even when they thought they were being nice to you, they couldn't quite remove the reproach that constantly lurked behind their gaze.

I suspected that this was behind Jeff's sudden change in behaviour. He was unable to forgive Marie-Claude, and he wanted to make her pay. It would explain why he wouldn't let others near her, why he seemed to want to keep her confined to their home.

But maybe there was something I could do to help the stricken woman. "Tell me, have the Ottawa police resumed their search for Fleur?"

"No. Jeff's gone into Ottawa today to see if he can convince them. They still say she's just a runaway and will come home when she's ready."

"And what do you think? Do you think she is angry enough to stay away?

"No, it's not like Fleur. I could see her being mad at me for a couple of weeks, but not for this long. She would miss her sisters, and even if she didn't want to talk to me, she would call them."

"Do you know if she has?"

"No, they say not."

"Are you sure they would tell you, if Fleur told them not to?"

"I don't know. I suppose they might want to protect her if they knew about our argument." A glint of hope suddenly appeared in her eyes. "Do … do you think you could ask them? They might tell you."

"I will try. They might not tell me, but perhaps with Summer Grass Woman's help they would."

For the first time in a long while, I saw her lips waver in a smile.

At that point, the moose hide covering was suddenly whipped aside, and Jeff stepped inside, startling us both.

CHAPTER
SIXTEEN

Jeff's scowl deepened as he confronted his wife. "I thought I told you to stay in the house."

I watched her shrink back into her wolf skins and knew her suicide attempt was best kept between the two of us.

"It's all my fault, Jeff," I said. "I thought Marie-Claude could benefit from a sweat bath. You know how much she values their healing properties, so I suggested we come here. As you can see, we're just finishing up."

His brow furrowed in suspicion, he glared first at me, then at his wife and back to me.

Although she seemed to cower even further into the furs, she did take my cue and said in a surprisingly strong voice, "*Oui*, I am much better."

She glanced in my direction and smiled wistfully before turning her gaze back to her husband. "Did you have success with the Ottawa police?"

Unable to stand fully upright under the low ceiling, Jeff moved to the other side of the barely warm fire pit, where he dropped down onto the cedar boughs and crossed his legs. His lips curled in distaste as he flicked a piece of cedar from his immaculate khakis.

His coal-black eyes flashed in anger. "No, those bastards gave me some mealy mouth crap about giving the case their full attention, but I could tell they didn't plan to do anything more than what they've already done."

"I thought Chief Decontie was going to talk to them," I said, pulling the wolfskins more tightly around me.

"He did and got the same response. He feels no more optimistic than I do."

"Surely Becky's death is incentive enough?"

"You'd think." He shrugged. "I'd say it's time to pull the media card. I doubt they'd want to see a headline that says, '*Ottawa police are racists.*' I'm waiting for Eric to get back. He's got some contacts at CBC and with the local papers."

Yes, Eric had been quite successful in his media campaign a couple of years ago, when it was discovered that a number of wells close to the Misanzi River that runs through the reserve had become contaminated by groundwater pollution from a mining operation further upriver. The company had refused to do anything about it until Eric turned the media attention onto them.

"Sounds like a good idea," I replied. "In the meantime, we could continue the search on our own."

"I've already tried that route. I turned Ottawa inside out searching for Fleur when we finally realized she wasn't at Richard's." He glowered at his wife, who shrank even further into the furs. "And it didn't get me anywhere. Ottawa's too big a town. You need the capabilities of a city police force to carry out a proper search."

"Yeah, but they're not doing their job," I countered. "So why don't I give it a go? I got to know the woman from the Welcome Centre who saw her with Becky. She might open up more to me than to the police." I was certain a bottle of vodka would do the trick quite nicely. "Maybe she can give us some good leads to help narrow the search."

He waved his hand dismissively. "Sure, whatever. I'm going to concentrate on siccing the media on the cops." He turned to his wife. "Come on, Marie-Claude, get dressed."

He gathered up her still-damp clothes and passed them to her. But instead of giving her privacy, he watched with his arms crossed against his chest while she struggled to get into them. There was no way I was going to dress in front of him, so I waited demurely encased in my wolf skins.

Not a single word passed between the married couple, although I did notice that Jeff's expression seemed to reflect a pensive sadness instead of anger. But he offered no help when her trembling hands made it impossible for her to do up the zipper of her jeans. I had to do it for her. As I did, I squeezed her hand and whispered that I would do all I could to find her daughter. Her eyes fluttered a brief thanks before returning to the haunted expression that had taken over with her husband's arrival.

Nor did he offer to help her stand up when she finished dressing. Instead he left it to me, and it wasn't easy, particularly when my fur pelts kept threatening to slide off. Clearly she was still traumatized by her near-death experience and barely had the energy to stand. It took all my strength and dexterity to raise her off the ground while attempting to maintain my modesty. In the end I had to reveal more naked flesh than I cared to in order to pull her into a half-upright position. She wobbled to such an extent, I wasn't sure how she was going to walk the distance to her house on her own, for it was obvious she wasn't going to get any help from her husband.

I was about to suggest that he wait until I dressed so I could help her. But he pre-empted me by passing her a long stick and ordering her to get moving. He then flung the moose hide to one side while she struggled out the entrance. The opening closed shut behind them without another word.

I frantically donned my own cold, damp clothes and raced along the narrow path after them as best I could in my bare feet, bare only because my trail shoes now lay on the bottom of the pond. But when I caught up, it looked as if my support was no longer necessary. Marie-Claude had found the inner strength to walk, if not spryly, at least determinedly with her head held higher.

I bade them as hearty a farewell as I could muster when we reached the house. While Jeff merely acknowledged with a grunt, Marie-Claude flung her arms around me and kissed me on both cheeks in Quebecois fashion.

She thanked me profusely in French for all I'd done and said without bothering to lower her voice that if I wanted to speak with her daughters, today was the best day. Every Monday they attended the Algonquin cultural school that Summer Grass Woman ran. I could meet them there.

I glanced nervously at Jeff to ascertain his reaction, but from his disinterested stance, I realized he'd never bothered to learn his wife's native language as she had his.

"Good," I answered in French. "I'll pick them up at their regular school and drive them."

"And bring your dog. He would help you gain their trust."

I left feeling a bit more confident that Marie-Claude might be able, if not to overcome, at least to live with her demoralizing guilt. But her husband's harsh treatment bothered me, particularly after I saw his reaction when she reached out for support after losing her balance. He recoiled as if bitten by a snake. I thought back to the few times I'd seen them together since their daughter's disappearance and realized he always held himself at a distance from his wife. He could no longer bear to touch her.

I thought back to my own long-dead marriage. Jeff was acting like Gareth had. Once Mother had told my then husband what I'd done, he couldn't bear to touch me either, and when he did, it was not without some infliction of pain.

I started worrying about Marie-Claude for another reason.

CHAPTER SEVENTEEN

I was waiting by the front door of the Migiskan School when the bell announced the end of the school day. Although Sergei was sitting calmly by my side as commanded, I knew he'd be running up to the first child that came out that door. He loved kids, loved to play with them. Sure enough, with the first rush, he bounded, albeit a bit creakily, from my side and romped amongst them amidst cries of "Nice dog," "Isn't he cute," "Want to play fetch?" and so on. I was hard pressed to keep track of him while watching out for Marie-Claude's daughters. Ajidamo came to the rescue.

Ever since a frigid winter day a couple of years ago, when Sergei had kept the unconscious Ajidamo warm while I skied for help, the two of them had become the best of buddies. I too had developed a fondness for the orphan boy, whose name meant Little Squirrel. Jid, his friends called him, as did I. Although he still retained the impish traits of a squirrel, he'd taken on a maturity beyond his young years, particularly after his beloved grandmother died. I'd wanted to adopt him, but the band had decreed that he live with his aunt, to maintain his

Algonquin heritage. Nonetheless, he often visited, and we'd become more than good friends.

With a yelp, Sergei bounded up to his buddy, who shouted with almost as much glee and buried his face in the dog's black curly fur. Jid, who was able to get Sergei to do things I never could, decided to put him through his paces. Soon there was a small audience of kids intently watching Jid make the dog lie down, roll over, and shake-a-paw. I noticed Neige, Marie-Claude's youngest daughter, among them. I waved, and she smiled back shyly. I didn't see the older daughter, but since they were both going to the Cultural Centre, she would probably arrive soon to fetch her sister.

As the other kids gradually moved off, Neige continued to watch. I could tell she wanted to pat Sergei but was afraid to. A word to Jid, and the boy grasped the dog by his collar, and with a broad smile, a twinkle in his eye and a swagger in his step, he walked Sergei over to the slim girl. Although Neige was a bit taller than Jid, I thought they must be close in age, around eleven, and might even be in the same class.

Jid made Sergei sit while Neige gingerly patted his head. When the dog nuzzled her for more, she was emboldened and used both hands. Soon she was smothering her face in his soft, curly locks. Jid stood back and beamed proudly at his protégé's good behaviour. But when his eyes kept resting on Neige, I began to wonder if the object of his admiring smile wasn't in fact his pretty schoolmate.

I wasn't certain if Marie-Claude had managed to tell her daughters that I would be taking them to their Algonquin lessons, so I wasn't quite sure how to approach them. Although we knew each other, I wasn't exactly a close family friend.

"You gonna take Neige and me to our Anishinabeg lessons?" Jid suddenly asked. "That way we get to spend more time with Sergy."

Problem solved. "Sure, if you want. We can take the truck or walk."

The sun had managed to push away the heavy rain clouds, warming up the afternoon quite comfortably for the kilometre or more walk to the Cultural Centre.

"Let's walk. It'll take more time." His face broke out into a shameless grin.

"Where's your sister, Neige? I think we should probably wait for her."

Neige continued to pat the dog, who was preening with the attention. Bringing him had clearly been a good idea.

"She's gone on ahead with Kathy," she said.

A minor glitch, but not a serious one. Perhaps it would make sense to question the sisters separately. Alone, they might more readily divulge the secrets they could be hiding about their missing sister.

The four of us started down the path that cut through the woods to the Cultural Centre. The sun filtered through the changing leaves on the trees, while our feet crunched through the freshly fallen leaves. Under Jid's direction, Sergei was walking obediently between the two children, who were chatting amiably together. I hated to interrupt their fun but felt with Jid and the dog making Neige feel more relaxed and comfortable, she might be more willing to open up. The trick would be how to broach the subject without being obvious.

Once again Jid came to my rescue. I was even beginning to wonder if he could read minds.

"Auntie, tell Neige that her sister is coming home. She says Fleur's never coming back."

One pair of eyes shone with hope. The other pair reflected only despair. I knew I had to be as upbeat as I could without glossing over the real situation.

"We don't know when, kids. All of us are hoping and praying she'll be found soon. The police are doing all they can."

"No, they aren't," Neige shot back. "My dad says they don't want to look for her because she's an Indian."

"I think it has more to do with the police thinking Fleur ran away from home and doesn't want to come back. What do you think, Neige? I know she and your mother had an argument." I saw her eyes flash in acknowledgement. "Do you think she's so angry with your mother that she never wants to come home again?"

Although the girl remained silent, she kept staring at me as if willing me to go on.

"We know she hasn't called your parents, but maybe she's called someone else to let them know she's okay."

I thought I saw a glimmer of admission in her amber eyes before she shifted her gaze onto the dog.

"Your parents are sick with worry, particularly your mother. It would really help her just to know that Fleur's all right. So if she has called someone, that person should let your mother know. It would make her feel so much better. And I know she won't be angry with that person for not telling her sooner. She just wants to know Fleur is safe."

Jid's eyes remained fixed on his friend, almost as if he knew or had guessed at something.

"Your mother's very sorry for what she did to your sister. She won't punish her. She only wants her home."

By this time the round, teepee-like wooden building of the Cultural Centre could be seen through the trees. Neige gave me one long last stare then ran off. Flinging a rushed "I'll talk to her," back at me, Jid chased after his friend, and unfortunately so did Sergei.

I followed at a more leisurely pace. I felt it best to leave them alone. I'd planted the seeds and there was nothing more I could say to the girl. By the time I arrived at the front door, the two children had disappeared inside. But Sergei, thankfully, was sitting on guard by the door, probably obeying Jid's command to stay. He wagged his tail eagerly but remained in position until I gave him his reward, a dried piece of venison liver, his favourite treat.

We had a leisurely walk back through the woods to the truck. At least I had a saunter, while Sergei, nose to the ground, pursued one smell after another. He did manage to rouse a tiny red squirrel who'd become too focused on some seeds on the ground. But luckily the squirrel realized the dog was almost upon him and made good his escape to a nearby maple. He scampered up to a safe branch, where he soundly scolded Sergei until I managed to drag the barking dog away from the tree.

On my way home I stopped at the Migiskan General Store to buy dinner, one of their delicious venison and cranberry pies that would go nicely with the bottle of cabernet I'd picked up the other day. These ready-made pies prepared by the reserve's best cooks were the brainchild of the store manager. After a recent trip to Montreal, she'd come back full of ideas to improve the store's products and to help provide another source of employment within the community. She used as the main ingredient, venison, duck, moose or any of the other wild game the community hunters had shot. Needless to say, I relied heavily on these tantalizing microwaveable specialties.

I headed home intending to enjoy my evening while I waited. There was no need to bring in the help of Summer Grass Woman, nor did I need to talk to Moineau. Her younger sister would do that for me. If anyone could convince the sisters to reveal what they knew, it was Jid. He could charm the quills off a porcupine. I just had to be patient and see what my seeds would yield.

In the end it came from a wholly unexpected source.

Around ten o'clock that night I was roused from my TV watching by the rumbling racket of a motorcycle at the front of the house. There was only one person I knew who drove a motorbike. *Eric*.

After several bracing gulps of wine, I walked as slowly as I could down the long hall to the pounding on my front door, which of course had elicited frenetic barking from Sergei. I was so certain that I would see Eric when I opened the door that it took me a few seconds to realize that the thin, wiry man with the threatening black eye-patch standing in front of me was Marie-Claude's biker brother, J.P.

CHAPTER EIGHTEEN

My immediate reaction was an overriding desire to slam the door in the biker's face, so fearful was I of being alone in the middle of the night miles from the nearest help with a full patch member of *Les Diables Noirs*. But my childhood etiquette training won out, as well as the realization that this one-eyed man likely didn't mean me any harm, so I kept the door open, but only enough to carry on a conversation, and asked him what he wanted. I didn't feel secure enough to invite him into my house. Sergei, however, felt no such need to be polite. He continued to bark and even bared a tooth or two. I let him.

"Moineau sent me," the biker rasped.

"I'm surprised. I thought her father told his kids to have nothing to do with you."

So black was the night that I could barely make out the faint gleam of his bike parked just beyond the range of the porch light.

"She's a girl, eh? Don't always do what her papa say."

"How do I know she sent you?"

"It's about the phone call Fleur make." He placed his hand on the door. "Let me in. I tell you."

So my planted seeds had born fruit. But I still didn't feel comfortable enough to let him inside my house. Too many of my great-aunt's valuable belongings would be in full view of his assessing eye. "Tell it to me here."

"*Tabernac*, you think I gonna rape ya? Fuck. You ain't my kinda woman."

Wearing a wry, wonky smile, he held up his arms as if to prove he was harmless, that he wasn't carrying any weapons. More importantly, I didn't have any either, other than Sergei, who fit the all-bark-and-no-bite adage a little too perfectly.

"If you don't wanna talk to me, I'm gonna leave. Marie-Claude say you care about Fleur. I see you don't." He turned on his boot heels and started tramping back down the stairs.

Damn. I'd made a promise to Marie-Claude that I would do all I could to help find her daughter. This could be a valuable clue. I was being a silly scaredy-cat....

Clutching a growling Sergei by his collar, I called out to the biker as he was strapping on his Nazi helmet. "I do care about Fleur."

I opened the door fully while he placed the helmet back on the seat. A faint animal cry, possibly an owl or even a wolf, drifted in on the rising wind. The roar of the surrounding pine trees filled the night air, while the sound of leaves skittering along the ground came to me through the darkness. The solitary blotches of light coming from a pole by the woodshed and from the house only served to remind me how utterly isolated I was.

He tramped back up the stairs into the full glare of the porch light. His solitary pale blue eye seemed to be laughing at me, but I didn't sense any threat or danger lurking behind the amusement. Sergei continued to emit a low, throaty growl, but he stopped when the biker offered him his hand to sniff, followed by several pats. Some watchdog, eh, when he could be bought off that easily. But I hadn't bought him as a guard dog. I'd bought him to keep me company during the waning days of my miserable marriage and to defy Gareth, who hated dogs and was in fact afraid of them, as I'd gleefully discovered.

J.P. whistled. "*Merde*, ya got a nice place here, that's for sure." His eye roved along the hall into the doorways of the living and dining rooms, where my Aunt Aggie's treasured antiques and paintings lurked in the darkened rooms.

I hastily led him to the brightly light kitchen. "I'm going to make myself some coffee, do you want some?" I reached into a cupboard for the coffee tin.

"Got any more of that?" He pointed to the empty bottle of wine standing on the counter.

Despite my good intention of having only a glass or two, I'd ended up drinking the whole bottle. I could still feel the buzz. Maybe that had fueled my overreaction to J.P.

"Sorry, just coffee ... or tea, if you'd prefer that," I suggested, although he didn't exactly fit my image of a tea drinker.

"Yeah, tea good. Coffee keep me awake."

I ended up making tea for both of us and added a plate of the cookies.

In the brilliance of the overhead lights, he didn't appear quite so threatening as he sat hunched over the kitchen table slurping his tea. Although he was supposed to be younger than Marie-Claude, the scars and the lines on his ravished face made him look twenty years older. Clearly a biker's life wasn't easy. I noticed the hand clutching the mug was missing the tip of a finger. I was beginning to feel a bit embarrassed about my treatment of him.

"So Fleur phoned Moineau, did she?" I asked.

"*Oui*," he mumbled between mouthfuls of chocolate chip cookie. The nasal "oway" sounded more like a duck quack than the refined "we" of Parisian French.

"Did she say when?"

"Yeah, when she was in Trois-Rivières. The girls visit with their *grandmère* in the summer, eh? It is something they do since they were *p'tites filles*."

"Do you know if this was after Fleur was reported missing?"

"*Oui*. It is why I come tell you."

"How long after?"

"Moineau say it was on her birthday. Fleur wanted to wish her *bon anniversaire*."

"And when's the birthday?"

"July 28. I always send her a card. Send all the girls cards on their *anniversaires*."

I grabbed the calendar off the wall and flipped back to July. "The police think Becky was killed about five weeks before her body was found, which would make it the third week in July. So this phone call suggests that Fleur was alive the week after Becky was murdered."

"*C'est bon ça.* Good news, eh?"

"Let's hope so. Did Moineau say whether her sister said anything else?"

"I think the call was pretty quick. But she tell Moineau to tell nobody. It is why she say nothing to Marie-Claude, eh?"

"And she didn't say where she was calling from?"

He shook his head.

"And she didn't give her a phone number or an address?"

"*'Sais pas.* Maybe it is better you talk to her."

"Do you know if she told her mother?"

"She's afraid. She don't want to make trouble between her mother and that bastard."

"You mean Jeff. You know Marie-Claude tried to kill herself again this morning?"

"*Tabernac!* I tell her leave the guy. He nothing but trouble. But she don't wanna."

"She's probably afraid to." The same way I was afraid to leave Gareth until fear for my safety finally took over.

"I fix that pretty quick. I get some of my brothers." He crammed another cookie into his mouth. "*Tien*, I take you to Moineau. Is better you talk to her, eh?"

"But what about her father?"

"No problem. She sleep at house of girlfriend."

I glanced at the clock. It was close to eleven. A bit late to go visiting.

As if reading my mind, he said, "I tell her you coming, okay?" He pulled out his cell.

"Use my phone. We don't have cell coverage here."

After he confirmed with Moineau, we set out, he on his Harley and I in my truck with Sergei. I didn't want this guy coming back to my place.

CHAPTER
NINETEEN

Throughout most of the drive to Moineau's friend's house, J.P.'s motorcycle was a wavering dot of red light. I tried to keep up with him, but my ancient rust bucket of a truck was no match for his Harley. At one point I thought I'd lost him when his light vanished into the pitch black as we wended our way along one of the more convoluted roads of the reserve, but on rounding the next curve I almost collided with his bike stopped in the middle of the road. With an impatient fling of his arm, we continued at a more leisurely pace until we stopped near the entrance to a driveway.

As I stepped onto the road, I spied the sudden glow of a cigarette and the pinprick of another coming out of the darkness. From the direction of the driveway, I could just make out the lights of a house twinkling through the gaps in the dense bush. But that was the only light penetrating the night along this stretch of road. If there were neighbouring houses, the residents had either gone to bed or were away.

"Moineau, that you?" J.P. shouted in French as he walked towards the glowing cigarettes.

Leaving the dog inside the truck, I followed. But I left the headlights on to provide us with a modicum of light. The slim height of Moineau and the shorter and plumper figure of another teenager with purple streaks in her spiked black hair stepped into the light. While her friend had put out her cigarette, Moineau sucked on hers with the aplomb of an accomplished smoker and the challenging attitude of a teenager intent on doing something forbidden, which it no doubt was. I knew Marie-Claude would be mortified if she could see her daughter now.

The girl and her uncle bantered in *joual* for a few seconds before she turned to me and said in English, "My sister told me you wanted to know if we'd heard from Fleur after she left home."

"That's right. Have you?"

She took another deep drag on her cigarette before answering, "Yeah, she called, but don't tell maman, okay? She'd get really mad at me for not telling her."

"At this point, I doubt she'd get mad. I think it would do her a lot of good knowing that your sister had called, but I won't tell her. I'll leave that up to you. I gather from your uncle that she called on your birthday during your visit to your grandmother."

"Yeah, we always have birthdays together. So this was the first time she wasn't there. She felt real bad she couldn't be with me."

"Did she say where she was calling from?"

Her long, satiny hair rippled as she shook her head. "Nope, but I could hardly hear her for the noise. It sounded like a lot of people laughing and talking."

"Any idea where this could be?"

"I figure she was at a party."

"Did she at least say if she was calling from Ottawa?"

"Nope, but I know she wasn't in Ottawa," Moineau said succinctly before taking another drag. "She was at the rez."

J.P.'s face bore the same startled expression mine no doubt did. "How do you know this?"

"From her telephone number. It had the same area code as the rez, 819."

I was about to ask her how she knew the number, when I realized. "You saw the number displayed on your cell, didn't you?"

"It was on grand-maman's phone. That's the number she called. When I picked up the phone, I didn't know who was calling. It wasn't her cell. And it wasn't my parent's number or any of my friends. So she kinda took me by surprise."

"Did the number look at all familiar?"

"Not really. It didn't have 986 like I'm used to seeing with the rez numbers."

"Unfortunately I think the 819 area code covers pretty well most of western Quebec, so the only thing we know is that she was in Quebec when she called. Can you remember what this second set of numbers was?"

"Not really. It mighta been 243, but I'm not sure. Sorry, I didn't pay much attention." She chewed nervously on a strand of hair.

"It's okay. You were just glad to be talking to your sister."

"Yeah. I miss her." She smiled wistfully. "Do you think she's ever coming home?"

"I sure hope so. Do you think she's staying away because she doesn't want to come home?"

"I know she was real mad at maman. That's why she went away. But I don't think she's mad any more."

"Why do you say that?"

"Well, when I was talking to her, I asked her when she was coming home. She said she wanted to, but for the moment she can't. Then she started to cry. Then I heard some man's voice and she hung up."

"What did the man say?"

"I couldn't hear that well with the noise and all, but I think he told her to get off the phone." She shrugged. "He kinda said 'Get the fuck off.' He didn't sound very nice."

Shit. I didn't like the sounds of this. I glanced at J.P. to see if he was also worried, but his face was mask of inscrutability.

"Moineau, I think it's crucial we let the police know about this phone call. They might be able to trace the number from your grandmother's phone records and find out where Fleur is or at least where she was."

She shook her head as the tears began to cascade down her cheeks. "I can't. Daddy will kill me."

I started to ask her whether it was more important to avoid punishment than to save her sister's life when her uncle cut in with a barrage of *joual*, which caused more tears. At the end, she turned to me and whispered. "I'll do it. But … but can you take me?" She bit her lower lip as she cast her gaze to the ground. "I don't want Daddy taking me."

Her eyes had taken on the same fright I'd seen in her mother's eyes, which made me wonder what this man was doing to his family.

"Okay, I'll take you. And I'll see if we can get Chief Decontie to agree not to tell your parents, all right?"

She crowded into the front seat of my truck, with Sergei crammed in between us. Fortunately, Will was still at the police station dealing with what looked to be a couple of drunks.

Before Moineau told her story, I got him to agree to keep the information confidential. He added the proviso, "As long as it wasn't needed as evidence in a legal proceeding," which prompted me to glance nervously at him. He shrugged as if to say "you've got to plan for the worst." Fortunately Moineau missed the implications of "legal proceedings" and responded with a smile of relief.

Will promised to do what he could to get the provincial police working on the trace as quickly as possible. Unfortunately, it was outside his jurisdiction, but he felt this call provided sufficient evidence to show that the missing woman had been in Quebec after her disappearance. Remembering the disdain of the SQ cops at the search, I didn't feel quite so confident.

After returning Moineau to her friend's house, I drove back to Three Deer Point. It was well past midnight, and I was tired, wanting only to go to bed. But the sight of J.P.'s motorcycle parked in my driveway dispelled all thought of sleep.

"What are you doing here?" I asked, not the least bit thrilled to see him sitting at the top of my stairs. As far as I was concerned, when we agreed that I would go alone to the police with his niece, he would be heading out of the area, back to wherever he came from.

"We gotta talk." He stomped down the stairs and stopped so close to me that I could smell the mint on his breath, which surprised me. I hadn't expected a biker to be concerned about the state of his breath.

Nonetheless, I backed out of range while Sergei nudged his thigh for a pat, which was promptly given. "I thought we'd done all our talking. I'm certainly thankful that you let me know about the phone call, but there is nothing more we can do. The police will handle it from here."

"*Tabernac* ... the cops, they do nothing."

"So why did you persuade your niece to go to Chief Decontie?

"It make her think everything gonna be okay. But Fleur probably dead before they get off their ass. You, me, we gotta do something."

"So you think she's in danger?"

"*Foque!*" He spat. "A pimp got her, that's for sure."

"That's who you think the guy on the phone was?"

"*Bien sûr*. A boyfriend don't talk to his girl like that."

"Maybe you're right. I'll mention this to Will. Maybe he can use it to get the SQ moving."

He spat. "Fuckin' cops think all Indian women are whores. They do nothing. We gotta do it."

"But what can we do?"

"I know some guys I can talk to. You talk to people in Ottawa." He paused. "Better you ask than me." His one eye winked as if laughing at his decidedly unapproachable appearance.

I didn't bother to query him further about his contacts, feeling certain it had to be within his biker community.

"I suppose I could start with the woman who saw Fleur with Becky," I suggested. "In fact she brought up the possibility of prostitution herself. Maybe she knows something."

"*Bon*." He strapped on his helmet. "I call."

He kicked his bike into an ear-shattering explosion of sound. Without another word he roared down my drive, leaving the night air vibrating.

CHAPTER
TWENTY

Two days later, as I was about to leave for Ottawa to meet Claire, Sergei ran off into the woods after a deer. When I'd put him out for one last pee, I'd seen a big buck at the salt lick at the bottom of the clearing. But since the dog hadn't been showing too much interest in chasing deer lately — I was blaming his slowing pace on arthritis — I figured Sergei would ignore him. He didn't. His creaky joints must not have been feeling so creaky this morning, for the minute he finished his long pee, he was off, barking and yelping, intent on the chase.

Normally he lost interest the minute the deer vanished into the confusion of the dense forest. But this morning it was not the case. Maybe he'd discovered another critter to hassle or perhaps some enticing smells. Whatever it was, he didn't return for a good thirty minutes. By then my voice was hoarse from calling, and I had begun to worry he'd had an accident.

When he finally stepped out of the trees, it was all I could do not to scream at him for being such a bad dog. Instead I gritted my teeth, held out his reward for returning, and waited for him to come to me. Although he was dragging his paws, his tongue flopped out of his mouth, and bits of bark and twigs decorated his fur, he was looking as pleased as punch with himself. There was even a slight spring in his exhausted step. I guessed a morning deer chase had gotten the old adrenaline running. At least he'd be tired enough not to fret about being left alone for most of the day.

Later, during the two-hour drive, I had another encounter with a deer, this one a little too close. As I rounded a curve, a doe jumped out in front of my truck. I slammed on the brakes, but the bumper caught her hindquarters, and down she went. I hopped out of the truck, terrified that I'd killed or badly injured her. But in a heartbeat, she was up and scrambling across the road, intent on getting as far from me as possible. Fortunately her gait showed no sign of serious injury. As I drove off, I noticed in my rearview mirror two small fauns gingerly crossing the road after her. Thank goodness I hadn't struck one of them, otherwise it might have been a far less happy ending.

But my hapless encounters didn't end with the deer. On the outskirts of Gatineau, two speeding motorcycles narrowly clipped my front bumper as they wove their way in and out of traffic. I slammed on the brakes, which ricocheted into the sound of brakes screeching behind me. I braced for the impact, but the car on my tail managed to swerve into the lane beside me.

Twenty minutes later, with my nerves still jangling from the near-miss, I found myself snarled in traffic as I approached the bridge that would take me across the Ottawa River into the city itself. Nothing moved. In front of me was a swarm of red lights. Behind, the lanes were equally jammed. I was too far over in the left hand lane to squeeze my way to an exit, so I couldn't escape the slow shuffle forward. It was stop and go with the lights of emergency and police vehicles blinking in the distance. Eventually vehicles began merging into my lane, and within another fifteen minutes I was inching past fire trucks, ambulances, and police cruisers surrounding a jack-knifed transport trailer, its front end smashed. It was stopped at a yawning gap in the bridge's twisted metal railing.

A cold shiver crept down my spine. I didn't want to look but couldn't help it. It was a long way down to the river below. On the far shore, men clad in canary yellow were clambering into a red rescue Zodiac. Another was just disappearing under the bridge. But I would hardly call this a rescue. Nobody could survive plunging a hundred feet or more to the swirling waters below.

The accident so distracted me that I could barely remember the directions to the restaurant where I was to meet Claire. Yesterday she'd been too busy, so we'd agreed to meet today around noon at the Dreamcatcher Bistro in the ByWard Market. And of course the accident had made me late. To avoid wasting time getting tangled up in the one-way streets that crisscross the Market, I parked my truck in the first parking lot I came across and hotfooted it to our meeting place. Although I managed to make up a few minutes, I was still a good twenty minutes late by the time I walked into the crowded restaurant. But I found no Claire waiting at a table.

She'd obviously become impatient and had left. But the waiter's negative response to my query and her unanswered phone suggested that she might be equally tardy, so I ordered a glass of white wine and waited. But by the time my wine was finished, she still hadn't arrived. It was now almost one o'clock and highly improbable that she would show up an hour late. After leaving a message with the waiter, in case Claire did arrive, I set out for the Anishinabeg Welcome Centre. Either she'd forgotten about our lunch or something had come up at work.

With the directions provided by the waiter, I easily found my way to the Centre, which was situated in an old yellow brick school building in one of the more run-down sections of east Ottawa. But given the number of native people I'd seen walking while I navigated the maze of roads, it looked to be an area where many lived, hence the Centre's location.

The Anishinabeg Welcome Centre was immediately recognizable from the large multi-coloured medicine wheel painted on the brick wall to the right of the front door. It added a spark of excitement to the otherwise drab façade. When I stepped onto the hard stone floor of the front lobby with its institutional green cement block walls, I felt like I'd returned to the faceless institution of my early school years.

Scribbled bits of paper posted by people wanting jobs or places to rent filled a billboard hanging to the right of the door. I noticed with a start several sheets with the words "Missing" or "Have you seen" blazed over a photo of the missing person, mostly girls in their teens or early twenties, but there were a couple of boys. It appeared that missing aboriginal youths weren't a rarity. No wonder the police expressed little interest in Fleur's case.

I found her poster partially covered by others in the upper right hand corner. The photo had been taken at the time of her crowning as Miss Algonquin Nation. With her dark braids and high, sculpted cheekbones, she seemed to epitomize the description "Indian princess." Of the three girls, she was the one who most took after their father. Though her brown eyes sparkled with the excitement of winning, I nonetheless caught a hint of the same wariness I'd noticed in her mother's eyes and wondered about the significance of its cause, if she was unable to forget it even in a moment of triumph.

To provide an unobstructed view of her poster, I repositioned the others, one of which offered modeling opportunities in bold red and purple lettering. Maybe, just maybe, someone seeing Fleur's photo would know where she was.

I approached a rather sour-faced woman with tiny dreamcatcher earrings, who appeared to be a receptionist. She was sitting behind a scratched metal desk, the kind of desk teachers used when I was in school. She seemed to be admonishing an old man and woman who were sitting on two collapsible metal chairs next to her desk. The receptionist's scowl relaxed into a welcoming smile at the sight of me. Unfortunately, she could only tell me that she had yet to see Claire today. But that didn't mean Claire hadn't come in before the receptionist was at her desk or while she was on lunch or in the can.

I followed the woman's directions to Claire's office, which took me past the gym, where the sound of kids' laughter filtered through the closed door, and up a flight of stairs to the next floor. While a number of people had been milling about on the main floor, on the second floor my footsteps echoed through an empty hallway, past equally silent offices, as I searched for Claire's. I finally found her name, Claire Terrance, written in large block letters on a piece of paper that was taped under the designation "Nanabush Youth Program." I knocked politely on the closed wooden door, but hearing no response, I opened it anyway. The narrow room contained two desks, one with scattered papers and a screen saver oscillating on the computer that suggested the person had just stepped away from her desk. The other desk looked as if it hadn't been disturbed in days. I assumed the messy desk was Claire's and that she'd probably gone to the washroom.

But after waiting impatiently for fifteen minutes or so, I went in search of someone in a neighbouring office who might know where the woman was. But the offices were still empty, and this at a quarter to two, which made me wonder about the work ethic at the Centre. However, as I started to descend to the first floor, I almost collided with a group of chattering men and women coming up the stairs. They were returning from celebrating someone's birthday at a nearby pub. And no, Claire had not been with them, although she had been at work early this morning, in fact, considerably earlier than normal.

"Do you know where she went or even when she left?" I asked.

One short, squat woman shook her grey-haired head and said, "Claire's frequently out. It's her job to follow up with her cases. The kids are sometimes afraid, eh? They don't like to come here, so she goes to them."

"So you have no idea where she's gone?"

"She wasn't here when we went out to lunch," answered a younger woman wearing a lovely shell necklace. "I thought she was coming with us. She said she was."

"She was supposed to have lunch with me," I replied and told them why I wanted to talk to Claire.

"Yeah, a lot of kids go missing these days," replied the grey-haired woman. "What did you say the girl's name was?"

"Fleur Lightbody. There's a poster of her at the front door."

She sighed. "We've got a lot of those. Look, I'm also involved in the Youth Program, maybe I can help you."

CHAPTER
TWENTY-ONE

I followed the woman's swaying gait down the hall to an office across from Claire's that identified itself as belonging to Paulette Coon Come, Nanabush Youth Program Co-ordinator. Like Claire's office, hers was long and narrow but with only one desk, which was cluttered with stacks of files and assorted papers. Museum posters of various aboriginal artifacts filled the white walls, while a myriad of flourishing plants crowded the deep sill of the sun-filled window. Unlike Claire's office, which had been cold and uninviting, Paulette's office spoke of warmth and sympathy, as she herself did.

Troubled youth should have no problems connecting with her, I thought as I sat down in a surprisingly comfortable captain-style wooden chair in a seating area next to the desk.

"Can I get you some tea or coffee?" she asked.

In the sunlight of her office, her unlined, beaming face suggested she was younger than her grey hair would indicate, while the jagged scar that pulled her smile into an awkward grin spoke of a life that had had its difficult moments.

I felt my stomach growl with hunger and thought a bit of food was what I really needed, but instead I answered,

"I'm fine, nothing, thank you. I don't want to take up too much of your time."

"No problem." Her black eyes twinkled. "It won't take a second, the kettle is right over there. Besides, my next appointment isn't until three. So we have a good hour for a chat."

Although I thought my business wouldn't take long, I acquiesced. "Tea would be perfect. Thank you."

She plugged in the electric kettle standing on the same narrow table as a jar containing tea bags, a bottle of instant coffee, a teapot, an assortment of souvenir mugs, and a box of Tim Hortons donuts.

She must've noticed my intense gaze on the box, for she immediately passed it to me. "Please, help yourself."

Muttering my thanks, I helped myself to my favourite, a cream-filled chocolate one, and plunged my teeth into the ecstasy. Just what my stomach needed.

After pouring the boiling water into the teapot, she eased her chunky frame into the chair beside me. In an attempt to hide her expanding stomach, she tugged at her red felt vest with its aboriginal renditions of killer whales in black appliqué, and failed.

Shaking her head, she sighed. "Too many donuts, but I love 'em and I see you do too." She grinned, then continued. "Like I said, we have a lot of missing kids, sadly, too many of them. They get bored with life on the rez. They see what they think is the good life on TV and come to Ottawa to find it. Only trouble is most of them don't. That's what the Nanabush Youth Program's all about. To help them adjust to life in the big city."

"Do you see many kids?"

"Enough to keep me plus two other counsellors busy. But we're short one at the moment." She got up to pour the tea. "Creamer? Sugar?"

"Just black," I said, preferring to have it black than polluted with whatever chemicals the creamer was made of.

I noticed a number of framed photos on a bookshelf beside her desk, one of a beaming bride resplendent in white, a couple of pictures of young women and men wearing graduation togs, and several with young children and their smiling mothers.

"Your children and grandchildren?" I asked.

She laughed and glanced at them fondly. "In a way, but I'm afraid they aren't of my blood. These are some of my successes, young people I was fortunate enough to help."

"That must make you feel good."

"It does, but it's the faces of the ones I couldn't help that haunt my dreams. My lost souls, I call them."

"Yes, that would be discouraging. Did you ever deal with Fleur Lightbody?"

"That's the girl you mentioned, eh? Isn't she's the one from Migiskan the police were looking for a few months back?"

"Yes, she disappeared in mid-July."

"What does she have to do with you, if you don't mind my asking?" She passed me the mug of tea and offered another donut.

"I'm doing this for her mother. We're friends. She couldn't come to town, so she asked me to see what I could do to try and find her."

"So I take it the girl hasn't been found?" She sat back down in the chair beside me.

"Nope, and more worrisome, the girl she was last seen with was found murdered a couple of weeks ago."

"That's gotta be Becky. Real tragedy that, though I'm not surprised."

"Why do you say that?"

"She was one angry girl. Mad at the world and at life. I started working with her not long after she came to Ottawa, fresh off her James Bay rez. I'm afraid her story is one we see far too often. Both parents drank. At fifteen, she was raped by a male relative and ended up having a kid who died when he wasn't quite three."

"I'm so sorry to hear this. Were you able to help her?"

She shook her head sadly. "I really tried. I thought we were connecting. She was doing well in her computer course. She even participated in a couple of healing ceremonies and seemed to be learning how to deal with her anger. Then one day she stopped coming. I thought maybe it was me, so I tried to get her to see another counselor, but she wanted nothing to do with that woman either."

"Was that Claire?"

"Yeah, how'd you know that?"

"Just a lucky guess. So what happened with Becky?"

"What I was trying to prevent. She started hanging around with the wrong crowd. Got into drugs and was soon hooking to pay for them. I'm afraid it happens to a lot of young native women who've got big dreams but aren't equipped to fulfill them."

"I'm sorry about Becky. I guess she was one of your lost souls."

She nodded sadly.

"Fleur, however, isn't from the same background," I continued. "She comes from a good home. As far as I know, she isn't into drugs and certainly is too well brought up to get into prostitution. She has no need to. Her family would give her money if she needed it. She even has an uncle in town she could stay with."

Except she didn't, I thought. Moreover, Claire had intimated that Fleur had become a prostitute.

"You sure she and Becky were friends?" Paulette asked before biting into a sugar-coated donut.

"That's what Claire told the police. It's why I want to talk to her. You don't happen to know her home number, do you?"

"I can give you her cell. But like I said, she's probably off seeing to one of her cases. I don't remember Fleur Lightbody being one of hers, but let me check just to make sure, okay?"

While she went through the files, I helped myself to another donut. Amongst the photos of her successful cases, I spied a photo of Paulette surrounded by several men decked out in their traditional chief's attire. All wore big smiles of congratulations. One of them I recognized with a start.

"I see you know Eric Odjik," I said.

She whirled around. "Why, yes I do. How do you … oh of course, the photo with me accepting the Turtle Island Award for contributions to the aboriginal community. I was so pleased to get it. Eric has been one of the Centre's biggest supporters. He was invaluable in helping us get extra funding." She raised her eyebrows in query. "Where do you know him from?"

I wasn't about to tell her that I was his former girl-friend, so instead I said, "My property borders the Migiskan Reserve. Eric and I have joined forces on a number of issues that have affected our area."

"A wonderful man, isn't he? You know there's talk of him being a real contender for National Chief of the Grand Council of First Nations when the current chief's term is up."

"Really. I didn't know he'd put his name forth for election." I was surprised his daughter hadn't mentioned it, but then perhaps she didn't know either. It would, however, explain the amount of travelling he'd been doing lately. "I'm sure he'd be very good in the job, although the reserve would hate to lose their band chief."

She nodded absentmindedly then said, "Nope, I don't see any file on Fleur, so she was never one of our clients."

"I really wasn't expecting it. She has a good future ahead of her. She was supposed to be starting a nursing program at a CEGEP in Montreal this fall, something she was very much looking forward to."

"Well, I'm sorry, dear, I can't help you. Here's Claire's number. Hopefully she can help you."

"Unfortunately, I don't have a cell, so do you mind if I use your phone? I'd like to see her before I leave Ottawa."

"Sure, go ahead."

But all I heard was Claire's voice mail greeting, so I left a message for her to call me at home.

However, I didn't want to leave Ottawa empty-handed. "Is there anyone else here at the Centre that might be able to help me?"

"Me and Claire are probably your best bets. But any-one could've seen her, if she came to the Centre. I'd start with Doris at the reception desk. If you've got a picture, I'd show that around."

Damn, I hadn't thought to bring a photo — but I could use the poster on the downstairs bulletin board. "Thanks, I will."

"You know, you mentioned Eric Odjik. I remember him asking about a girl from his reserve, probably the same one."

"Most likely. Do you know when he was asking about her?"

"It was a while back, sometime in July, I think, towards the end of the month. I believe I told him to ask Claire."

Another reason to speak to Claire.

"I gather Fleur was also seen at Becky's apartment. You don't happen to have her address, do you? I'd like to go there to see if I can find the witness who saw her."

"I guess now that she's dead, I won't be breaking any confidentiality rules, but the address I've got is at least a year old. Chances are she moved."

After writing the address down and thanking Paulette for all her help, I wandered back downstairs, where I extracted Fleur's missing person poster and ran it by a number of people while I waited for Doris to return to her reception desk. But apart from "pretty girl" comments, no one remembered seeing her at the Centre or anywhere else in Ottawa.

Doris, however, immediately raised my hopes when she said, "Sure, I remember Fleur. She helped out at last year's pow-wow. A great gal. Quite the looker. The young bucks couldn't keep their eyes off her." She laughed shrilly.

But when I asked whether she'd seen Fleur this past summer, her answer was a brusque "Nope," which made me wonder about Claire's statement placing her here at the Centre with Becky. But then again, Doris could've been off on a break when Becky and Fleur came through the front door.

As I turned to leave, a woman, tears streaming down her cheeks, came running up to the desk. "Oh Doris, the police have just called wanting to know where Claire is. Apparently her car went off the MacDonald/Cartier Bridge."

"Oh my God, was she in her car?"

"They haven't been able to look inside it yet, it's so far down. But the divers were able to identify the car from her licence plate. Dear God, I pray by some miracle she escaped," the woman replied.

I thought back to the gap in the bridge's railing and shivered. "I was supposed to meet Claire for lunch," I said. "But she didn't show up."

"Oh, are you the one who wants to know about Fleur Lightbody?"

"Yes, I am. Do you know anything about her?"

"She came to me looking for a job."

CHAPTER
TWENTY-TWO

"I know this is probably not a good time, but can you spare a few minutes? I'd like to ask you some questions about Fleur," I said to the woman.

Maybe I was being inconsiderate, but I felt finding the missing girl was just as important. Besides, there was nothing she or any of us could do about Claire. Either she'd been in her car when it plunged into the river or she hadn't.

The woman wavered.

I continued, "With Becky's murder, her parents are very worried she might be in trouble too. So anything you could tell me about your dealings with Fleur might help in finding her."

She firmed her lips and glanced at Doris, who was blotting her tears with a Kleenex. Finally she said, "Okay, as long as it doesn't take too long. Doris, do you mind calling around and seeing if you can locate Claire? Pray to the Creator we do."

"I should forewarn you," I said. "I wasn't able to reach her when I tried her cell about ten minutes ago."

The two women exchanged worried looks, which mirrored my own uneasy concerns.

"You might as well come to my office," the woman said as she started down the hall. But before she'd gone too far, she stopped and turned back to me.

Offering her hand, she said, "By the way, my name is Mary Eshkakogan. I'm the executive director of the Anishinabeg Welcome Centre."

Although her office was considerably more spacious than either Claire's or Paulette's, the furniture was comprised of the same dreary institutional castoffs, albeit with fewer scratches. One wall was filled with the flowing lines of Benjamin Chee Chee's flying geese. He was an artist I recognized from my mother's collection. While two of the framed pictures were definitely copies, I noticed an edition number at the bottom of one of a mother goose tending to her gosling, which suggested it might very well be an original print. According to my mother, who was interested in such things, a Chee Chee original was a valuable rarity, because the artist died before he'd had a chance to produce a sizable body of work.

The message light was blinking on Mary's phone. Her brow creased with concern as she glanced at it before turning her gaze back to me. Her short, dark auburn hair gave her a professional, no-nonsense look, as did her forest green suit, the tailored neatness of which was in sharp contrast to the considerably more casual attire of the Centre's other staff. The turquoise and bone choker and silver North-west Coast Indian bracelet and earrings did serve to tone down its businesslike severity.

She must've noticed my perusal, for she smoothed her skirt and said, "I'm meeting with one of our key sponsors this afternoon, hence the spruced up attire, but I tell you, these pantyhose are killing me. Give me a pair of slacks any day."

"I'll second that. I haven't worn a skirt in years, just to avoid the itchy things." I smiled. "Look, I'll be quick."

I remained standing to show I meant what I said, while she sat in the chair behind her desk.

"You said Fleur had come to you looking for a job. Do you mind telling me when this was?"

"Towards the end of June. She came to me highly recommended by her chief."

"You mean Eric Odjik?"

"Yes, do you know him?"

I nodded. "I live next to the Migiskan Reserve."

"Sadly, our two positions for summer help were already taken, otherwise I would've hired her. She seemed a very capable young woman."

"Do you know where she was living at the time?"

"Before I go any further, I should ask you what your relationship is to Fleur and why you want to know about her?"

I repeated what I'd told Paulette, and that seemed to satisfy Mary. "Poor child. Such a tragedy that she's missing. In my mind she didn't seem a typical runaway, so I can't help but think something has happened to her. That's what I told the police."

"That's our worry too. But the police refuse to believe us. They're treating her case as a runaway and doing nothing."

She shook her head. "I'm afraid Fleur is just a statistic. Did you know that there are more than five hundred and eighty missing aboriginal women in Canada, sixteen in our area alone. In most cases nothing is being done to find them. Tragically, when they are finally found, they are invariably dead, as happened recently to Becky Wapachee, who used to be a client at our Centre."

"Yes, I know about Becky. Apparently Fleur was last seen with her."

"Oh dear, I hadn't realized. But I doubt they would've been friends. They had absolutely nothing in common."

"So you don't know anything about Fleur living with Becky?"

"I find that hard to believe. Becky was living a rough lifestyle, hardly the kind that would attract a smart, well-educated, young woman like Fleur."

"Apparently this is what Claire told the police, that's why I wanted to talk to her."

She sighed but didn't voice what we were both thinking. Claire wouldn't be around for me to question.

"As I told the police, since we didn't have a job for her, I didn't have her fill out an application. So we have no record of her address."

"Do you know if anyone, besides the police, came around asking for Fleur when she went missing?"

"I remember Eric dropping by looking for her. But I hadn't realized she was missing at the time."

"And not her father?" I asked. "I understand he came to Ottawa to look for his daughter after he and his wife hadn't heard from her for some time. I would think the Centre would be a good place to start."

She nodded. "He certainly didn't speak to me, but ask Doris. If anyone knows if he was here, she would."

She glanced at her flashing message light.

"Just one more question and then I'll go. Can you remember when Eric came looking for her?"

"I think it was only a week or so after the job interview. He thought she'd got a job and had come to see how things were working out. As I recall, he was quite surprised to discover she wasn't here. I guess because he hadn't heard from her, he assumed she'd got a job."

Her phone started to ring. As she reached for it, I thanked her for her time and turned to leave.

As I headed out the door, I heard her answer the phone then the words, "Can you hold the line a minute, Paul?"

She called out, "Meg, go see George, the director of our Jobs Program. I sent Fleur to talk to him about possible job opportunities."

It took George a few minutes to resurrect his memories, but when he did, he was able to provide me with the names of two businesses to which he'd sent Fleur. One was the Dreamcatcher Bistro, the restaurant where I'd been to meet Claire, and the other was a spa. And no, he hadn't passed this information on to the police, because they'd never asked.

"Besides," he said, "I was away on vacation and didn't know Fleur was missing until I got back after Labour Day."

I groaned in exasperation. If the damn police had gotten off their butts and taken the time to discover what I'd easily learned in the past hour, Fleur could very well be sitting safe at home by now. Instead we were fearing the worst, and I was trying my best to uncover what should've been found out weeks ago.

Feeling somewhat discouraged, I headed back downstairs to Doris and found an empty reception desk instead. After waiting several long minutes for her return, I finally gave up and headed outside to my truck. I figured she probably wouldn't remember if Jeff had come to the Centre looking for his daughter. Besides, knowing whether he had or not wouldn't help find Fleur.

I climbed into my truck intending to drive straight back to the Dreamcatcher Bistro in the hope that they had hired Fleur. As I started to back up, a tap on the passenger window made me stop. Paulette's broad face peered through the pane.

"Good, I caught you," she said as I rolled down the window. "I just remembered something. You should speak to Becky's best friend Monique. If Fleur and Becky did become friends, she would know."

Apparently Monique had also been a one-time client of the Centre, and like Becky, she'd stopped coming. Paulette referred to her as another of her lost souls. Unfortunately, she couldn't provide me with an address. But she told me the most likely place to find Monique.

"She usually hangs out at the corner of Cumberland and Murray." She paused. "You'd probably find her there any time after nine p.m. And if she's not there, wait. She'll be back after servicing one of her johns. You see, it's her usual corner." She pursed her lips grimly. "I tried so hard to help her. I just don't understand why these girls prefer hooking to getting a decent job."

Then shaking her head sadly, she said, "I know it's the drugs, always the drugs."

She wished me good luck and promised to call if she remembered anything else that might be useful.

CHAPTER
TWENTY-THREE

The minute I climbed into my truck, I flicked on the radio, hoping to catch news about the car crash. I didn't have long to wait. "Car Plunges into Ottawa River" was the big story.

One eyewitness tearfully recounted seeing the car fly off the bridge and into the water with an enormous splash. Another was three cars away when she saw the green car climb the railing before tilting downward into the water. A third was convinced a transport trailer had crashed into the car, causing it to go over the bridge, while a fourth insisted that the car was already climbing the railing before the truck hit it.

Needless to say, the police weren't saying anything, other than they would be conducting a thorough investigation, while a spokesman for Public Works insisted that the bridge railings met all safety standards.

The newscast ended with a last-minute update. Police divers were loading a body into their Zodiac. The reporter, however, was unable to confirm whether it was male or female.

But I knew it was female. The person was Claire.

Since it wasn't a direct route from the Welcome Centre, she would've been returning from visiting a client on the Gatineau side of the river. I did wonder, though, if alcohol had been a contributing factor, for it was obvious from the moment we met that the woman had a thirst for liquor.

When I stepped into the Dreamcatcher Bistro, the staff was abuzz with news of the accident while setting up the tables for the evening meal. The grapevine had been busy. Word had already reached them that the car belonged to Claire.

"She was one of our best clients," the chef said, wiping her hands on a dishtowel as she strode out of the kitchen. She hadn't noticed that she was already referring to Claire in the past tense.

"I was supposed to meet her here for lunch today," I added.

"That's right, I remember you," piped up the young waiter who'd sold me the wine. His face creased into a sad, lopsided smile. "I guess this explains why she didn't arrive."

I nodded, wondering if her meeting with me had put her in the wrong place at the wrong time. "Is the manager in? I'd like to speak to him."

My nose twitched at the enticing smells drifting out from the kitchen, while to my embarrassment, my stomach let out a growl.

"Hungry, eh? You've come to the right place." The chef laughed as she tried to shove a tendril of escaping black hair back under her checkered chef's touque. Her white chef's coat was splattered with samplings from the day's menu.

"I'm the manager and owner," she said. "What can I do for you? But if you're looking for the assistant chef job, that's already filled."

"No, I'm looking for information about a possible employee, Fleur Lightbody. I'm not sure if she's working here now or perhaps did during the summer."

Her brown eyes lit up with recognition. "Sure, I remember Fleur. I would've loved to have hired her, but I'm afraid the job was already taken when she came to us. She would've made a great maître'd too. A lot better than the one I hired. In fact, if you see her, tell her the job's hers. I had to let the other gal go."

"She didn't happen to mention where she was staying, did she?"

The woman's eyes narrowed in suspicion. "Why do you want to know about Fleur, anyway? You sure ain't a relation." Her gaze shifted to my red hair as if to emphasize the point.

After I'd explained my relationship and the reason for asking, the woman shook her head. "Too many of us missing. I'm so sorry to hear this. Wish I could help, but she never said where she lived, and I didn't ask." She paused. "You know, you aren't the first to come by asking for her."

"Who was that?" I asked, wondering if it had been her father. But if he hadn't gone to the Welcome Centre first, he wouldn't have known to check here.

"It was her chief, Eric Odjik. You might know him."

I nodded. "Can you remember when he came around?"

"I think it wasn't long after she'd been here, either the first or second week in July."

He would've come after discovering she wasn't working

at the Welcome Centre. Was he worried about her even before she was declared missing? Or was he just doing his chiefly duty and ensuring a member of his band was getting along okay in the big city?

"What was his reaction when he discovered she wasn't here? Did he seem concerned?"

"Sorry, I don't remember. But I do remember him asking if I knew where else she might've gone for a job. I'm afraid I couldn't help him."

"I was going to ask you the same thing."

"Sorry, but give me your phone number. I'll ask around, and if I hear anything, I'll let you know."

"Did anyone else come by looking for her, like her father or the police?"

"Nope, Eric was the only one."

After thanking her, I headed out the door.

As I tripped down the stairs to the sidewalk, the young waiter called to me from the open door. "You're talking about Fleur Lightbody, eh?"

When I nodded, he said, "I used to see her at a pub I go to."

"When was this?" I asked, praying it was after Becky was killed.

"It was the beginning of the summer." He scratched his head. "Actually I can be more precise. It was the first couple of weeks in July when I was still playing soccer, before I wrecked my knee. I would go there with the guys after the games."

I let my breath out slowly. Nope, the timing was before Becky was killed, which was supposed to have been sometime during the third week in July.

"But not recently?"

He shook his head.

"How do you know it was her?"

"That's the name she gave me."

I showed him her poster just to make sure.

"Yeah, that's her. Great kid. She reminded me of my little sister. I bought her a beer a couple of times." He must've been older than his boyish looks reflected, for he didn't seem old enough to liken an eighteen-year-old to a kid sister.

"Was she alone or with somebody?"

"A girlfriend, except for the last time."

"Did you know her friend?"

He shook his head.

"Or even a name?"

Another shake of the head. "She wasn't native. Had frizzy blonde hair."

"Have you seen her since?"

"Nope. Last time I saw Fleur, she was with some guy. He didn't like her talking to me."

"Have you seen him since?"

"Yeah, he comes to the pub every once in a while, usually with some babe, but it isn't always the same one."

"Which pub?"

"O'Flaherty's up on Rideau."

I knew the place on the edge of the dead zone of Rideau Street. On some of my early trips to Ottawa, I had sometimes dropped in for a drink or two to get myself into the proper frame of mind for the long drive back to Three Deer Point. Although it was a good couple of years since my last visit, there might be a few familiar faces I could ask about Fleur. Or better yet. "What time do you get off work tonight?"

"I'm usually finished around ten thirty, eleven, depending on how long the last people stay."

"Do you mind going to the pub with me? Maybe the guy she was with might be there, or at least you could ask around to try to find out his name."

He ran his hand through his short curly brown hair. "Well, I was going to meet my girlfriend at another pub, but I guess I can change it. Fleur was a good kid. I'd like to help if I can."

So Sean agreed to meet me at O'Flaherty's at eleven, which would give me more than enough time to try to find Monique. However, since I hadn't planned on staying so late in Ottawa, I hadn't made any arrangements for Sergei. With a couple of quick phone calls from the restaurant — the chef was more than accommodating — I arranged for Teht'aa to pick up the dog, feed him, then take him over to Jid's aunt's place, where he would spend the night under the good care of his buddy. Although I didn't want to spend the night here, if I had to I could, knowing he would be in good hands.

My next stop was Fleur's other job possibility, the Black Orchid spa located on the other side of ByWard Market. I decided to leave my truck at the city parking lot and walk the four or five blocks through the Market to Rideau Street. People clogged the sidewalks. Some were trying to make last-minute purchases from the fruit, vegetable, and flower vendors who were more intent on packing up for the night than selling. Others were headed to the many restaurants and cafes lining the streets. And of course, there were the usual tourists, easily identified by their cameras and ambling gait. I tossed a couple of toonies into the case of a violinist serenading passersby with a fiery rendition of the "Flight of the Bumblebee."

I finally found the spa on the second floor of an office building, which seemed an odd location. But when the elevator doors opened onto its white marble lobby and strategically placed orchids, also white but for the black stylized orchid inscribed on the wall, there was no mistaking the cloying scent of perfume nor the heavily made-up, perfectly coiffed, stringbean-thin receptionist perched on a chrome stool behind the glass counter. She too was attired all in white, at least the part of her that was covered. The part which wasn't covered, which was considerable, was a rich chocolate brown.

Her nose wrinkled in disdain as I approached. I guess my expanding waistline didn't exactly conform to the dimensions of their usual clientele. Or maybe it was my clothes, country casual, although I had worn my best blue jeans and the beaded deerskin jacket Eric had given me.

She seemed relieved when I said I wasn't there for a spa service, but when I asked to speak to the manager, she quickly informed me of the need for an appointment. Nor did she relent when I explained the situation. In fact, she seemed to become more determined to keep me from placing one millimetre of the dusty tread of my trail shoes on the pristine white floor of the inner sanctum.

When she buzzed the door open for a returning staff member, I realized I couldn't exactly storm the ramparts, so to speak, without doing damage to myself and the glass door. The only way I could get in was following immediately behind the next person who entered the spa. She must've realized my intention, for she finally admitted that the manager had already left for the day and wouldn't be back until next Monday. She'd gone to New York to attend the annual spa convention.

She did grudgingly provide me with the manager's name and a phone number. I could probably learn what I needed to know over the phone anyway.

She seemed to hesitate when I showed her Fleur's picture but admitted that the woman she was thinking of was much older and a specialist in hot stone therapy with many years of experience. Besides, she said, she didn't know everyone, she'd only been working there for a couple of weeks.

CHAPTER
TWENTY-FOUR

I had several hours to kill before I could go in search of Monique. Although my stomach seemed to have resigned itself to its empty state, I figured I might as well fill it up. So I returned to the Market, to the Tex-Mex restaurant I'd passed on my way to the spa. I had a hankering for some chicken fajitas and maybe a margarita or two.

I tried to put sense to what I'd learned about Fleur's movements. I had leads that had led to other leads and hopefully would pan out tonight. But so far no one had seen the pretty girl after the beginning of July. At least I knew that she had endeavoured to get a job shortly after her arrival. And that Eric had been looking out for her. Likely her father had let him know that she'd gone to Ottawa. However, knowing how adverse Jeff was to revealing private family matters, he probably hadn't told Eric the real reason behind her leaving home.

I also wondered if Eric had passed on what he'd discovered to the Ottawa police, when it was finally established she was missing. I would expect so. But if that were the case, why hadn't they followed up with the people he'd talked to? The only ones they seemed to have bothered with were the executive director of the Welcome Centre and Claire. Although why they would seek out Claire and not Paulette, the head of the Youth Program, wasn't readily apparent, unless Claire had overheard them asking about Fleur and had volunteered the information. Regardless, whatever Claire knew about Fleur had died with her.

Little wonder Marie-Claude was so upset with them. If the cops had done their job when Fleur was first reported missing, she would in all probability be safe in Montreal enjoying the start of her nursing course.

I was also confused about something else I'd learned. Both Marie-Claude and Jeff had told me that he'd come to Ottawa several times to try to find their daughter. If so, why hadn't he talked to the people I'd so easily found? Unless Eric had told him the results of his effort, prompting Jeff to decide there was nothing more to learn from these people.

And I couldn't forget Eric's sacred stone found in the Gatineau Park parking lot. Was it in any way connected to Fleur? Had something he'd learned about the missing girl here in Ottawa led him across the river to that dark, lonely place? And, more importantly, when had he dropped it? Before Becky was murdered or afterward? I didn't want to consider the possibility of it being lost while she was being killed.

The two margaritas had gone down very smoothly, as had the fajitas. Although it had been many years since I'd had the tangy lime and tequila drink, my taste for it hadn't diminished. Another would do me very nicely. I couldn't think of a better way to kill the remaining hour I had before Monique was supposed to be at her corner. And since my stomach wasn't completely sated, I added a plate of all-dressed nachos.

A couple of hours later, I stumbled out of the restaurant, feeling somewhat woozy. I sure couldn't drink like I used to. A rather good-looking chap sitting at the bar — one of those tall, dark, handsome types — had offered me another margarita, and not wanting me to drink on my own, he had joined me. It had been more years than I cared to count since anyone had tried to pick me up, so I was feeling quite thrilled by the compliment, particularly since he appeared to be younger than me. I became so engrossed in our conversation and his admiring glances that I totally lost track of the time. It was ten past ten and another margarita before I glanced at my watch and realized with a sickening jolt where I was supposed to be. While I scrambled to pay my bill, I apologized profusely and hastened out of there, but not before exchanging email addresses. Who knew, maybe next time I was in Ottawa ...

Once outside, it took me a few minutes to get oriented. I'd forgotten exactly where I was and where I had to go. But the crisp, cold night air managed to clear my confusion, while a passerby set me in the direction of Cumberland and Murray, which turned out to be only a few blocks away. Hopefully, Monique would still be standing on her corner waiting for a client, and if she wasn't, I would do as Paulette had suggested and wait until she returned.

But it took me longer than anticipated. I took a wrong turn then several more minutes to realize my mistake. I'd also felt dizzy and had sat down on the curb until it passed. By the time I arrived at Monique's corner, it was after ten thirty.

The skinny bleached blonde with thigh-high leather boots and mini skirt that barely covered her scrawny bum turned out not to be Monique. Apparently Monique's station was the opposite corner, but she'd just left with a client and wouldn't be back for another thirty minutes or so.

"But you ain't gonna wait here, are ya?" The woman eyed me with suspicion. Under a streetlight's harsh light, I realized that though she stared at me through world-weary eyes, she couldn't be more than eighteen or nineteen. I couldn't help but wonder what could have gone so wrong in her short life to force her into such a demeaning and potentially dangerous business. No doubt drugs were part of it.

A passing car slowed and the male occupant gave this young woman a thorough once over before speeding up.

She cast me an angry glance. "These here are our corners, eh? Ya can't take 'em."

It took me a few seconds to realize what she was referring to. I laughed. "You don't have to worry about me. I won't provide you with any competition. I just want to talk to Monique, that's all."

"If ya gonna wait for her, ya can't stand here. Omar'll get mad."

"Whose he?"

"My pimp. He'll be coming around soon to check up on me."

Another car slowed down, but the man, this one bald with several double chins, rather than nodding in her direction, rolled down his window and leered at me.

Yikes, she was right. I vehemently shook my head and backed away from the curb. He sped up through the light and stopped further along the road, where a woman with more curves than Pamela Anderson hopped into the passenger seat.

"Get the fuck outta here. You're takin' away my business," the young prostitute hissed, scanning the passing parade of cars. She'd plastered an awkward come-hither smile on her face that looked more pitiful than sexy.

"Okay, I will, but before I go I just want to ask if you knew Becky Wapachee?"

"She the one that got killed, eh?"

"She's a friend of Monique's. Maybe you knew her too?"

A car glided to a stop beside us. A grey-haired man that appeared old enough to be my grandfather and her great-grandfather flicked his head for her to get into his vehicle without cracking a smile.

"Yeah, I knew Becky," she yelled as she ran behind the car to the passenger side. "She got what she deserved."

"Why do you say that?" I shouted back.

"She hung out with —" Her words were cut off by a sudden blast of a horn from across the street.

Before I had a chance to ask again, the door slammed shut and the car sped off.

I hoped Monique could finish the sentence. But after waiting more than a half-hour, most of that lurking as far out of the sightline of the trolling cars as possible — although I did have one unnerving encounter with a john who refused to take "no" for an answer — Monique failed to show up.

It was well after the time I was to meet the bistro waiter at O'Flaherty's. I could only hope that Monique would be here when I returned.

CHAPTER
TWENTY-FIVE

For several anxious minutes I thought I'd missed the waiter and his girlfriend. But after squeezing through the throng of drinkers, I finally found them tucked into a back corner of the dark pub, their heads bent towards each other, the one curly and dark-haired, the other willowy blonde, their eyes locked in dreamy-eyed courting mode. Feeling somewhat embarrassed at interrupting such love-struck communing, I hovered over their table, hoping they would notice me. But when they didn't, I was forced to intrude.

Neither showed the least annoyance at the interruption, and they graciously invited me to join them, though I did notice that their hands remained inter-locked. I quickly learned Sean's girlfriend was named Julienne and that Sean was in his last year of undergraduate biochemistry. In fact, this was his last week working at the Dreamcatcher Bistro. A week later, and I would've missed him. Julienne, on the other hand, would continue her summer job on a part-time basis, while she started her doctorate in child psychology.

"Have you seen the man Fleur was with?" I asked Sean.

R.J. HARLICK

Despite the dreamy glaze in his soft green eyes, his boyish eagerness shone through. Without his waiter togs, his
athletic build was more obvious.

"Not yet," he said, which did make me wonder how he
could be so certain, since his focus seemed to be entirely
on his girlfriend. He did, however, offer to do another
tour of the room.

While he was gone, Julienne and I attempted to con-
verse above the din of the crowded room and the Irish
music blaring out of nearby speakers. But first I ordered
a round of beer. I figured I'd fallen so far off the wagon,
there was no point in trying to climb back on.

I learned that Julienne had also seen Fleur with this man.

"She was so pretty," she said almost wistfully as she
shoved a wavy length of blonde hair behind her ear.
She was rather pretty herself, in a tall, lanky way, with
long-lashed grey eyes and a dimple that emerged when
she smiled.

"But I couldn't understand why she would be with
such a man," she continued.

"What was wrong with him?"

"He was old, too old for her."

"How old?"

"Late thirties, maybe forties." Then as if suddenly realizing what she'd said, she blushed. "Oh, I'm so sorry. I, ah …
didn't mean to …"

"Don't worry. At your age I thought anyone over thirty
had one foot in the grave."

She had a sweet, almost endearing smile that would
make any man fall in love with her.

"He didn't treat her very nicely," she added.

"What did he do?"

"He ignored her. Kept talking to his buddies. And when she got up to leave, he grabbed her arm and pulled her back into the chair, yelling at her to stay put."

"You're sure the girl was Fleur?"

"Yeah, when Sean saw that picture you showed him, he recognized her right away. You see, we were kind of worried about her. We were sitting with Sean's soccer pals a couple of tables away and noticed how unhappy she looked, never smiled, didn't say a word, even seemed kind of scared. When the guy grabbed her, Sean thought she might be in trouble, so he went over to see if he could help. But that guy, oh he was terrible, he told Sean to eff off and acted like he was going to hit him, so Sean backed off. He went to talk to the manager, but by the time they got back the guy and the girl were gone."

"Did you let the police know?"

"Sean wanted to, but the manager wouldn't let him. He said the guy was likely the girl's pimp, and he'd learned from experience that it was best not to get involved. Besides, he said there wasn't much the police could do anyways. If the girl is over sixteen and says she wants to be with the guy, there's nothing they can do. He said the girls usually say everything's okay."

But surely Fleur would've said otherwise. "Did you ever see her again, either here or in the Market, or anywhere else?"

"No. I'm sorry now we didn't let the police know. I guess she's been missing for some time, eh?"

"Since mid-July, about the time you saw her."

"Oh, that makes me feel terrible."

"Please don't feel that way. You did more than most people would."

At that point Sean returned. After giving his girl-friend a reassuring smile, he sat down and said, "The guy's not here, but I see some of his buddies. So he might come later."

"Why don't you point me in their direction and I'll ask them about Fleur."

He glanced at Julienne, who arched her brow in worry. Turning an equally worried glance back to me, he said, "I wouldn't advise it. They're a pretty rough bunch."

"I'm in a public place, what can they do to me?"

"It's not what they would do here, but afterwards. They're bikers."

When I walked over to their table, I could clearly see the biker patches affixed to the backs of the black leather vests of two of the men, a patch I immediately recognized. It was the same snarling red devil that Fleur's uncle wore on his T-shirt and vest, with the words "Black Devils" clearly written in French.

Although I'd quaffed a good measure of beer to bolster my courage, I didn't feel so brave now that I was standing before them. There were three of them sprawled at the table, unlit cigarettes dangling from their lips. They were a cliché dressed in their black leathers with their bulg-ing muscles and beer bellies. One even sported several-days-old stubble on his face while another had a full beard, more grey than brown. The third, the redhead, was clean-shaven. None of them smiled at me.

"Whaddaya want, mama?" the redhead rasped. "If you come for a fuck, you come to the right place."

His dead eyes surveyed me from head to toe and stopped a little too long at my breasts. I crossed my arms in embarrassment.

He guffawed. "*Câlisse,* you're fat and old, but I'm not fussy."

I almost chickened out but sensed Sean standing behind me.

I wasn't quite sure how to approach them, so I pulled out the poster of Fleur and asked, "I was wondering if you had seen this girl."

He yanked the piece of paper from my hand and scanned it without comment before passing it onto the other two. The beard whistled, "*Tabernac!* Sweet and tender, the way I like 'em," while the stubble merely shrugged and said, "Nope, I ain't seen this broad."

"I think one of your friends might know her."

"Who?" demanded the beard.

"I don't know his name, but he comes here sometimes with you guys."

"Who's the spy?" he growled back.

I didn't dare look behind at Sean but was saved from answering.

"Ain't one of us. We don't go for Injun meat," the redhead snarled back, cutting off all further dialogue.

But I persisted. "You may not like Indians, but she happens to be the niece of one of your gang members."

Redhead jutted out his chin. "Like who?"

"J.P. Lamonte."

"Never heard of 'im," came back the too-quick reply, although I thought his eye flickered with recognition.

"Now mama, you get out of our space, unless you want

a good fuck." His thin lips creased into a gap-filled leer.

Sean nudged me from behind and whispered, "Time to go."

In complete agreement, I turned on my heels and walked as calmly and confidently as I could away from them. I wasn't going to let them know they had achieved what they'd set out to do, scare me.

As I followed Sean, I suddenly realized that the din of conversation had all but stopped, with many eyes turned in my direction. The conversation only returned to normal once I joined Sean and Julienne at their table. My hands were shaking. I could barely lift the beer mug. But lift it I did and took a very long, slow quaff.

"Where are you going after here?" Sean asked. The boyish eagerness was now completely gone from his face.

"I need to speak to someone. I was going to go look for her."

"I suggest you go home. You really pissed them off."

"But I didn't do anything other than ask them about Fleur."

"Yeah, well, they didn't like it. I was watching the guy with the beard. He recognized her. In fact, I think they all did, they just didn't want to admit it."

"Shit, you sure? I'm afraid my nerves were jangling so much, I couldn't concentrate on anything."

"Yeah, I'm sure. Look, I think we should leave now. Where's your car? I'll walk you to it."

I tried to persuade him that it wasn't necessary, but he and Julienne were so insistent, I relented. As I walked past the cold stares of the three bikers on our way to the exit, I was very glad I wasn't alone. And even though my truck was parked on the other side of the Market, a good four blocks away, they escorted me the entire way. Fortunately, the streets were still filled with evening revellers and the odd cop out on patrol. Very thankful for what the two of them had done for a complete stranger, I drove them home.

Afterwards, I headed back across the river to home, but not immediately. Since I had to drive close to the corner, I took a short detour to Cumberland and Murray. For once luck was with me. Monique, a tall, big-breasted native woman with an engaging smile, was standing at her corner. She reluctantly agreed to talk to me until her next john arrived.

But she provided little new information. She'd never met Fleur, although Becky had talked about this new hottie she'd met at the Welcome Centre, which was at least consistent with what I'd learned from others. But the term "hottie" did little to quell my fears. It was hardly a term one would use to describe an innocent like Fleur, unless there was considerably more to the teenager than she cared to admit to her family, like the drugs her mother had found in her bedroom. And Claire had called her a prostitute. Still, I felt I was a good reader of people, and I'd never sensed anything tainted lurking beneath Fleur's sparkling girl-next-door demeanour.

When Monique told me that Becky's boyfriend was a biker, it confirmed the worst of my fears. It was likely that Fleur, probably through Becky, was involved with the Black Devils, possibly even being held against her will, otherwise she would've called home by now. Unless she really wasn't the girl we thought she was and wanted nothing to do with her former life. But I didn't believe that. Even Sean and Julienne had sensed her unhappiness and fear.

Monique, however, left me completely unnerved with her last question. "Does your girl like it rough? Becky liked it rough. I think that's what got her killed. Me, I stay away from those kinda johns."

I didn't bother to ask her what she meant. I had a good inkling. And once again I was left totally flummoxed by this apparent friendship between two girls who had absolutely nothing in common. In fact, I would've thought Becky was the kind of person Fleur would stay far away from.

I drove off feeling very despondent and very concerned. I would bring up what I'd learned with Will, but without anything firmer than a hooker's word and a long-ago sighting in a bar, I doubt he would get anywhere with either the Ottawa or Quebec police. I wasn't about to try to get more solid evidence of Black Devils' involvement myself, but I knew someone who could, her uncle J.P. — that is if he was as innocent of her disappearance as he made himself out to be.

CHAPTER
TWENTY-SIX

I had a terrible night's sleep. Thirty minutes into the two-hour drive home, I realized I would never make it when I almost drove my truck into a ditch after a near-miss with a porcupine. My hands were shaking so much, I could barely grip the wheel, while it took all my effort to keep my eyelids open. So I parked at a gas station closed for the night and attempted to stretch out on the bench seat of the cab. But the seat was too hard and too short, and I kept colliding with the gearshift and steering wheel. Plus it was cold, and I was only dressed for a warm fall day.

So despite being dead tired with probably less than a couple of hours of sleep and still feeling the effects of the evening's booze-up, I decided to continue my journey home at five o'clock in the morning. What helped me make up my mind was the cavalcade of motorcycles that had rumbled past five minutes earlier. Fortunately they were travelling in the opposite direction.

A streak of red dawn was lighting up my rear view mirror when I turned onto the Three Deer Point road. Despite knowing every twist and turn of the long, narrow drive to my cottage, I almost drove off the dirt track and into the surrounding forest a couple of times and narrowly missed one large maple that had seen its share of bumpers. I finally braked to a stop at the bottom of my front stairs and clambered up them, very glad to be home.

Too tired to take off my clothes, I crawled into bed and slept the sleep of the dead until the phone's shrill ring startled me out of a nightmare. Which was just as well. I was lying on a bed, naked, surrounded by the leering grins of a gang of bikers.

It took me a few seconds to orient myself enough to recognize Teht'aa's voice on the other end of the line.

"Why didn't you call me back?" she demanded. "I left you two messages last night."

"I didn't get back till early this morning. What's up? Has something happened to Sergei?"

"He's fine. It's about Dad. I don't know where he is."

"What do you mean? Isn't he supposed to be coming back from Vancouver sometime this week?"

"That's what I assumed after he missed the earlier flight. But I'm beginning to think he never went to Vancouver."

"Why do you say that?"

"National Chief Dan Blackbird called a couple of days ago wanting to speak to Dad, and when I told him he was still in Vancouver, he was really surprised. He hadn't seen Dad at any of the GCFN Annual General Assembly events."

"So many people probably attend the AGA that it would be difficult to see who all is there," I said hopefully.

"That's what I thought, so I called some of his friends, but they haven't seen him either. He never checked into the hotel where they were all staying."

"He could've checked into another hotel. Did he ever mention which hotel he was staying at?"

"Nope. I just assumed it was the AGA hotel."

"You're sure he was going to Vancouver?"

"That's what he told me. He said after the canoe trip that he'd be flying from Fort Smith to Calgary for a few days and from there to Vancouver to attend the AGA."

"Have you had any communication with him?"

"No, but I didn't really expect any. Whoops, just a sec, my coffee's ready." The receiver clattered.

A minute or so later she picked up it up. "Sorry, I need this." She took a long slurp before continuing. "Meg, I'm really worried. If he isn't in Vancouver, I have no idea where he is."

"Maybe he's doing a special GCFN project that needs to be kept secret. Remember the time he aligned himself with a number of chiefs to try to pressure the Mohawk Warriors into stopping the transborder trafficking of cigarettes and the like. I think they kept those discussions amongst themselves until they were ready to make it public. Could be he's involved in something like that?"

"Maybe, but he still would've told me he was involved in something. He just wouldn't give me the details. I don't know, Meg. I've never known him to keep secrets from me."

She was right. Eric had always been very open and up front with me, no matter how unpleasant the news or situation might be. Unless …

"What if he's having an affair?" Even as I posed the question, I felt an icy pit settling into my stomach.

"Why would he keep that a secret from me? I could care less who his girlfriends are." She paused. "Um, I …

ah … don't mean you, Meg. I was really sorry when the two of you broke up."

Me too. "What if the woman is married? Maybe he met her on the canoe trip and one thing led to another. It would help to explain why he didn't stay at the same hotel as the others and why he didn't attend the assembly." I tried to banish the image of him in bed with another woman and failed.

"I suppose anything's possible, but you know what a great supporter he is of the GCFN. He firmly believes that without it we'd break down into a bunch of bickering First Nations. So it would have to be something really important for him to miss the key assembly of the year. Besides, I think the canoe trip was mostly with Dad's old hockey buddies. I don't think there were supposed to be any women on the trip."

Relief washed over me. "I'm sure when he finally arrives, he'll have a perfectly valid explanation."

"I sure hope you're right. After the National Chief called, I went to the library to use their computer to send him an email message. I still haven't bought myself one. We'll see if he responds to that."

"What about calling him on his cell?"

"Funnily enough, he didn't take it with him. I guess he figured it would be useless baggage on the canoe trip. But he took his laptop, so go figure."

I could hear her sipping her coffee and realized I needed one desperately.

"But you know, Meg, you could be onto something. That flashy wife of George Tootootis was all over him at the Niitsitapi Pow-wow in Calgary last June. And he didn't exactly discourage her, either. And he was stopping off in Calgary after the canoe trip."

She actually had the nerve to laugh, while I felt like I was in freefall.

After agreeing to let me know the minute she heard from him, I hung up feeling as if the bottom had fallen out of my world. And the hangover hammering in my brain didn't help either. I crawled out of bed and down the stairs to the kitchen, where I made myself an extra strong pot of coffee and wished I had my stand-by remedy for a hangover, cognac, to add to it. Next time I was in Somerset I would pick up a bottle.

With a steaming mug in hand and a wool afghan, I crawled out to the screened porch, where I collapsed into my soul-soothing retreat, Aunt Aggie's bentwood rocker. After wrapping myself in the blanket to ward off the chilly morning air, I rocked back and forth, back and forth, while Sergei lay curled up, asleep at my feet. The bright morning sun sparkling off the lake did nothing to raise my spirits, nor did the emerging fall colours of the far shore.

Eric with another woman kept cycling through my brain, over and over again. But why should it bother me? It was bound to happen. He was, after all, a very attractive man. And even if this situation had nothing to do with a woman, one would eventually enter his life. For all I knew he could've been dating all this past winter, and Teht'aa, not wanting to upset me, had kept it from me.

It was time to get on with my life. Our relationship was over, finished, finito, dead. He was never coming back. I would have to accept that he had moved on, that another woman would enter his life, maybe had already done so. It was time I found myself another man.

I sipped the hot coffee, tucked the afghan closer around me and rocked back and forth, barely registering the two deer that had moved into my view. The wind rustling the white pine was soft and comforting. I retreated further. A squabble between a couple of red squirrels brought me out of my thoughts for a moment. Suddenly I was being shaken.

I awoke to find Teht'aa bending over me, her expression bleak. "Meg, I think Dad really is missing."

CHAPTER
TWENTY-SEVEN

Teht'aa dropped into the black wicker chair beside me. She didn't even attempt to admire the lake view, something she always did whenever she sat in the screened porch. Instead she directed her gaze at me, her features creased with worry.

"What makes you think Eric is missing?" I asked.

"Gerry called right after I talked to you this morning. He wanted to know where Dad was. Apparently Dad organized a special council meeting for this morning to discuss the new addition to the Health Centre, one of his pet projects. And he'd asked Gerry to bring in an architect all the way from Ottawa for the meeting. So when he learned Dad wasn't home yet, he got really angry, especially since Dad hadn't let him know he wouldn't be there."

"This isn't like Eric, is it?" I too was beginning to feel uneasy. "But maybe it was arranged at the last minute and he never received the notification. Did Gerry say when the meeting was set up?"

"Before Dad went on his canoe trip. Neither Dad nor the architect was available until mid-September. I gather this architect, who's done similar work for other reserves, was coming here with the expectation that the band would hire her to draw up some plans. But without Dad the council doesn't feel confident enough to go ahead. Unfortunately, the woman's going to be away on another job for a couple of months, so it means they either wait for her or look for another architect. Either way there'll be a delay. And I know Dad was really hoping digging could start next spring."

"So it isn't a meeting he would forget about, is it?"

"Nope. But much more worrisome, Meg, is that I called one of the men he was supposed to be on the canoe trip with. He never made it."

"Shit! How long ago was this?"

"Towards the end of July, the twenty-second to be exact. They were flying out of Fort Smith in the Northwest Territories for a six-week paddle along the Thelon River way up in The Barrens."

"Why didn't they let you know?"

"He said he called Dad's cell several times and the home number too but got no answer on either phone. He left a message on the cell, but since I don't know Dad's password, I couldn't check. The charter company was going to charge a hefty fee if they delayed the plane, so they had to take off without him. They just assumed something had come up."

"But surely they would've checked with him when they got back?"

"They did, in early September, and left another message on his cell."

"Shit, this means he's been gone almost two months. When was the last time you saw him?"

"We've barely seen each other over the summer between his travelling and my trying to find a job. I know he was home in mid-July, because he was the elder for the Kòkomis Ceremony to honour our grandmothers. You were there too, I think."

I nodded, remembering the beaming faces of the many grandmothers, some younger than me holding their tiny grandbabies, while the older ones were surrounded by grandchildren, even great-grandchildren of all ages as Eric walked around the sacred circle paying homage to them. "That was in mid-July, the fifteenth or sixteenth, wasn't it?

"The sixteenth. Next day he went off to Montreal for a GCFN meeting. I don't think I was here when he came back the following week, and then he was off to Fort Smith. Since he was going to be out of contact for such a long time, I didn't expect to hear from him until the beginning of September. I'll admit I was a bit surprised when he didn't call at the end of the trip, but I figured he was too busy. Besides, I wasn't around much myself. I was travelling back and forth between Montreal and Ottawa for job interviews."

"Almost two whole months and not a word from him." I felt the prick of fear trickle down my back. "I sure don't like the sound of this. Can you think of any place he might have gone and not wanted anyone knowing where he was?"

She shook her head. "No, it's not like him to take off like this without letting anyone know. Even his assistant, Jill, had no idea he wasn't where he was supposed to be." She cast worry sick eyes in my direction. "I'm afraid, Meg, really afraid that something terrible has happened to him."

"Me, too."

ooo

Fifteen minutes later, the two of us were in the police chief's cramped office sitting on the other side of his cluttered desk. We were hoping, more like praying, that Will knew where his best friend was.

When we finished telling him of our fears, Teht'aa asked, "Have you heard from him at all over the last couple of months?"

"Nope, and I didn't expect to either." Will ran his hand over his brush cut. "I can't for the life of me figure out why anyone would want to spend six weeks on the tundra battling blackflies and sleeping on the cold, hard ground, when we got such terrific paddling around here. Not for me, that's for sure."

He scratched his belly then lumbered out of his sagging leather chair and poured coffee into three mugs from an aluminum pot resting on a hot plate and passed them to us. He plunked a jar of creamer and another one of sugar onto the desk in front of us, threw in a couple of plastic spoons, and slumped back into his chair.

On the off chance, I said, "Maybe he's with a woman. Has he ever spoken to you about anyone?" Even though I didn't want it to be true, it nonetheless offered a ray of hope.

"Eric's not exactly the confiding type. But I'd say taking off on some secret rendezvous with a woman just ain't his style." Will glared at me as if to say I should know better. "And even if there was a women involved, he wouldn't take off for two months without telling anyone."

Still not wanting to admit to the increasingly obvious, I suggested, "Is it possible he could be involved in a secret project, like the time he tried to stop cross-border trafficking through the American and Canadian Mohawk reserves?"

"It's possible. I'll check with the folks at GCFN."

"But if he is working on some kind of project, I don't understand why he wouldn't at least tell me he was working on something," Teht'aa said.

"I'm with you on that," Will replied. "He kept me fully in the loop with his last negotiations, just in case something bad happened. He was going against some pretty hard-assed characters. This time around he hasn't mentioned anything."

His words merged into the silence as the three of us sat lost in our own separate worries, none wanting to voice what was uppermost in our minds.

Finally Will cleared his throat. "Now I don't want to alarm you gals, but I think we have to look at the possibility that something has happened to Eric. After all, two months is a long time without contact."

"You mean like he's dead," I shot back.

"Not necessarily. He might've been in an accident."

Teht'aa and I exchanged glances. She answered. "But surely if he had been, someone would've contacted me by now."

"Not if he's unconscious without ID. I'll get Sarah to start calling around at the various hospitals. Now Teht'aa, I'm assuming you've talked to a few people. Give me the list so I don't duplicate your efforts. I'll also get my staff to call around to see if by some chance one of his friends or acquaintances knows where he is. "

"Please God, let it be so," I said.

"I'll second that," Will said. "Teht'aa, starting with the Montreal trip, could you write down his schedule and give me any contact info you have." He turned to me. "Meg, anything you might know will help too."

"Well, as a matter of fact, I discovered yesterday that Eric was in Ottawa looking for Fleur in early July. I don't have the exact dates, but can get them for you if you need them."

Teht'aa stopped writing. I hadn't had a chance to tell her the results of yesterday's trip. After filling them in, I said, "I think he might've started to get worried about Fleur. Did he ever mention anything to you, Will?"

Will shook his head. "Nope, he didn't say anything to me. And I didn't learn she was missing until after the Lightbodys had talked to the Ottawa police. I think it was the third week in July, but I don't recall Eric being around then."

He directed his gaze to me. "Meg, before I forget, the Quebec police had no luck with the trace on the phone Fleur used to call her sister. It was a cell phone belonging to a numbered company."

"But can't they track down the owners?"

"Easier said than done. They said they'd do their best to try to unravel the ownership, but with their heavy caseload, it might take awhile." He shrugged. "Chances are, even if they do locate the company's owner, they won't be able to tie them to the actual usage of the phone."

"But surely they would know who was using the phone."

"Maybe, maybe not. They can say it was lost, stolen, whatever. Apparently, service was discontinued on the phone shortly after Fleur used it."

"For what it's worth, at least we know she was somewhere that had cell coverage, unlike around here."

"True, but she could've been using a satellite phone too. Some of them use regular numbers."

"Oh well, it was worth a try. You know, Will, there's something else I should mention." He looked at me expectantly. "I found something belonging to Eric in the parking lot close to where Becky was murdered."

His eyes narrowed.

"His sacred stone, the piece of quartz he found at Whispers Island and uses for ceremonies."

"When did you find it?"

"The day of the search."

"And why are you only telling me now?"

"I wanted to ask Eric about it first."

"Do you still have it?"

"It's at home. I can go get it, but I'm not sure how it can help you. There is no way of knowing when or how it got there."

"You're certain it's his?"

"Teht'aa recognized it from the dab of fluorescent paint that was put on it when the mining claim was staked on the island. And we know it was in his possession when he laid it out as part of his medicine bundle at the Grandmothers' Ceremony on July 16."

Teht'aa nodded.

Will stopped fiddling with a pen he'd been playing with. "There's something you two should know. It's just come up in the murder investigation. The Ottawa police have placed Eric with Becky about a week before she was killed. Apparently he was seen entering her apartment. They've contacted me about arranging an interview with him."

"Surely they don't think he killed her," I said.

"Nope, he's just a person of interest."

"I'm sure the only reason he went to see Becky was to try to locate Fleur."

"You're probably right, but it still doesn't explain how his sacred stone came to be in the parking lot close to where she was murdered."

"Surely, Will, you're not thinking Eric killed Becky. How could you? Her biker boyfriend is a much better candidate."

"I have no idea who they're looking at."

"When was Becky killed exactly?" I asked.

"The medical examiner has pinned it down to some-time around July twenty-first, give or take a day or two."

"Shit, about the time Eric appears to have gone missing."

CHAPTER
TWENTY-EIGHT

With Eric's investigation now in the hands of Will Decontie, there was nothing more Teht'aa and I could do, other than to get him the material he wanted. While I headed home to retrieve Eric's stone, she went to Eric's bungalow, promising to come to my place after she'd delivered her father's contact information to Will. Neither of us wanted to be alone.

Unfortunately, when I returned home after delivering the stone, I found a voice message from her. One of her Ottawa job possibilities had called to arrange a second interview and hoped she could make it that afternoon, since the interviewer would be out of town for the next couple of weeks. Needless to say, even though she didn't exactly feel chirpy, she felt she'd better go. She needed the job. But if it wasn't too late when she got back and she wasn't too tired, she would drop by.

This left me feeling more depressed. I really didn't want to be alone, but apart from Teht'aa, there was no one I could call on. For most of my time at Three Deer Point, Eric had been my friend. I hadn't needed anyone else. And when we'd parted, his daughter had become my friend, which was ironic, since she'd originally detested the sight of me, a white woman in a relationship with her father. I hadn't been exactly overjoyed by her presence either.

But we'd survived some unnerving experiences together and come to see and appreciate the real people beneath the veneer. Our friendship had grown. However, if she got the job, which with this second interview seemed likely, she would end up moving to Ottawa, and then I'd really be alone.

I still had Sergei, though as much as I hated to admit it, the grey on his muzzle and his stiff gait suggested his remaining years with me were numbered. Then I would have no one.

But for the time being, he was very much alive, even if he did spend most of his time flopped out on his favourite chesterfield. Regardless, he was another warm body in my big rambling cottage, which at the moment was feeling very empty.

Needing his company, I clambered into my truck and headed off to Jid's aunt's place on the outside chance that someone would be home, even though it was mid-afternoon. It was too early for Jid to be home from school, while his aunt and uncle would doubtless be at work. His two cousins could be anywhere, but since both boys had left school when they reached legal age and neither had a steady job, one of them might be home.

However, the squat clapboard bungalow, girded by a wasteland of dirt, weeds, and rusting equipment parts, appeared too quiet. All the facing windows were firmly shut and the doors closed, despite the afternoon's summer-like temperature. Plus there was no sign of Sergei, who was usually allowed to sleep outside when someone was home.

I heard his bark from inside the house the second I slammed the truck door. I waved at him through a window as I banged on the side door, then tried the knob. It was locked, which was unusual. Most people on the reserve kept their places unlocked, unless they planned to be away for more than a few days. The front door was also locked.

I tramped through the underbrush behind the house in search of an open window and found one, the bathroom. Although the narrow window was open just a slit, there was enough space for a hand to reach under the sash and push upwards. It was beyond my reach. Besides, it didn't feel right breaking into a house that wasn't mine, even if it was only to retrieve my dog. Figuring Jid would be home from school within half an hour, I waited.

But thirty minutes soon became forty, and I was getting antsy. Although Sergei had long since stopped barking, I knew he wasn't pleased with the situation either. Maybe Jid was tied up with an after-school soccer game or had gone to a friend's house. If so, it would be dinnertime before he arrived, about the same time as his aunt and uncle, two people I would rather not have to deal with. Ever since they'd done their utmost to prevent my adoption of their nephew, a boy they'd had nothing to do with until he became heir to his grandmother's bank account and house, they'd not exactly been at the top of my list of people to be nice to.

Although I'd done my best to keep dark thoughts of Eric at bay, I was quickly running out of distractions. I knew I couldn't wait much longer. I needed Sergei to help calm my fears, that and a bottle of lemon vodka, which I intended to buy the minute I had Sergei in the truck with me.

Fortunately, the large lot was for the most part heavily treed, with only a vague hint of neighbouring houses though the dense foliage, so there was little danger of anyone seeing me break into the house. Besides, the bathroom window was at the back, where the bush was thick and impenetrable.

I rolled an empty oil barrel around to the back and stood it upright against the wall beneath the window. It wobbled, but I managed to stabilize it enough with some rocks so I could climb onto it without fear of toppling. At this level I could easily place my fingers under the raised sash. Thankfully there was no obstructing screen to remove. I pushed upwards. At first it refused to move, but with a forceful shove accompanied by some banging to jog the window loose, it suddenly slid completely open with a grating screech, almost causing me to fall inside. The noise ignited Sergei to a new round of barking.

As I contemplated the best way to squeeze through the narrow opening, a voice suddenly spoke behind me. I jumped and only managed to avoid falling by clinging to the windowsill. But the movement had been too abrupt for the barrel, and it toppled over, forcing me to dangle for a few seconds before my hands let go of the sill and I crashed to the ground, narrowly missing the barrel. Fortunately, feathery balsam saplings helped cushion my fall.

"Child, why you do this?" Summer Grass Woman's creased moon face bent over me as I lay momentarily stunned. The tips of her grey, reed-thin braids tickled my nose.

I did a quick survey to ensure everything was intact then fought with the balsam to stand up.

"You okay, child?"

"Yeah, I think so." I felt a slight twinge in my right ankle, otherwise, apart from bruises that would no doubt show up tomorrow, I was whole. My face, though, was hot with embarrassment. I'd been caught in the act.

"Why you not come to me?" Her eyes, red-rimmed with age, peered up at me. I wasn't exactly tall myself, but beside her I felt a giant.

I relaxed when I sensed annoyance rather than rebuke behind her words.

"I got key." She showed it to me.

"I'm sorry, I didn't know. Jid was looking after Sergei while I was away, and I wanted to get him, but no one is home."

"They go Montreal."

"Oh, when did they leave?"

"This morning. Jid say he leave message on your phone. Say I have key."

"Oh dear, I forgot to check when I got home. I'm afraid I've got a lot on my mind."

"I can see, child. Go get dog." She passed me the key. "Come my house for tea. It good for you."

I knew from the steely glint in her eye that refusing was not an option. I meekly took the key and retrieved Sergei, who greeted me as if we'd been parted for days.

Even if his hindquarters were stiff with arthritis, he could still manage a mean wag of his tail.

After closing the bathroom window, I locked up the house, and the two of us followed Summer Grass Woman across the road to her log cabin.

CHAPTER TWENTY-NINE

Although I'd visited Summer Grass Woman a couple of times at her healing lodge on Whispers Island, this was the first time I'd come to her house. I hadn't realized how close she lived to Jid's aunt. But unlike their suburban bungalow and Eric's, in fact most houses on the reserve, which were built with man-made, store-bought materials, her cabin, a holdover from the reserve's early days, came from the land.

Round cedar logs of a size seldom found in today's logged-out forests formed the walls. Strips of peeling bark still clung from the odd log, while dried mud mixed with moss filled the gaps in between. The roof, partially covered by moss, was made of cedar shake that had weathered to a soft shade of grey. Attached to the back of the cabin was a lean-to addition also made of logs, but from younger, slimmer trees.

The two front windows, likely the only windows in the squat structure, were the one concession to modernity. Originally they'd probably been only one log high and without glass, but their height had since been extended to a second log with glass inserted into the openings. They didn't look openable.

A metal chimney was the other concession to modernity. Its glistening chrome newness seemed a betrayal of the earthiness of the dwelling. But in the interests of safety, it had probably replaced an older tin chimney that had become a fire hazard.

Over the planked door hung a strange animal carving barely recognizable after years of punishing weather, but I did make out a pair of very large teeth and two beady eyes that seemed to bore into me as I passed under.

"What's that?" I asked.

"My clan," the elder replied. "Amik. You call beaver."

I should've guessed. Amik was her last name.

As my eyes adjusted to the dark interior, my nose absorbed a cornucopia of aromas, from pine and balsam to tangy, sweet smells I couldn't identify. Finally the dimly lit room emerged into view. It wasn't large, about the size of the Three Deer Point dining room, which would make it about fifteen feet by twenty. I realized that apart from the lean-to addition visible through an open doorway, this was the only room.

Against the far wall was a simple kitchen recognized by the open shelving stacked with canned goods, bags of flour, and other food items. A couple of frying pans hung from nails hammered into the log wall, and underneath them stood a long wooden table with a clutter of utensils, several pots, a propane camp stove, and a metal basin.

These last two items made me realize that Summer Grass Woman didn't have electricity or water, which would have to be her choice, since directly across the road, Jid's aunt's house was fully equipped with both. In fact, the hydro lines ran across the front of Summer Grass Woman's property.

She ignited the propane stove, poured water from a metal urn into a dented copper kettle, and placed it onto the flaming burner.

"Sit," she ordered.

While Sergei had already decided that the worn wooden floor suited him perfectly, for me the choice was more difficult. I felt I shouldn't sit on her bed with its polished brass frame and fur coverings, but the only other possibility was a red velvet armchair with the plush almost completely gone from the arms and the seat. Clearly that was her chair, so I lowered myself onto a pile of furs on top of a low wooden platform near a cast iron stove.

This stove was the newest item in the room, along with the fireproof matting screwed into the wooden floor beneath it and the log wall behind. The wall mat, however, didn't completely hide the charred surface of the underlying logs. Rising from the stove was the shiny new chrome chimney. As with most old people set in their ways, it had probably required someone else to notice the danger the old stove presented. I wondered if it was Eric who'd had it replaced, since as far as I knew, Summer Grass Woman didn't have family of her own.

"You need special tea," she said as she passed through a doorway into the lean-to addition. I could see a variety of dried plants hanging from the ceiling and walls and several birchbark baskets on another long wooden table.

She returned with a small birchbark basket and her smudge bowl, which worried me. It was my intention to stay as long as politeness dictated then drive to Somerset to buy my evening's entertainment, a bottle of lemon vodka. But it looked as if Summer Grass Woman had other plans.

"I'm afraid I only have time for a quick cup of tea," I said, struggling to make myself comfortable on the furs.

"Tea good. You like." She threw some dried bits of plants from the basket into a porcelain teapot covered in pink rosebuds. "*Shingwàk*, pine you call. Bring harmony."

"I'm sure it will be very tasty, but I really can't stay long."

"Pfft." She waved her hand dismissively. "You not happy. You drink. Not good."

I'd been found out.

She sprinkled some dried cedar into the smudge bowl and lit it. "This better."

I made one more attempt, which was ignored, so I resigned myself to her tea. Besides, the liquor store didn't close until ten p.m. I had loads of time. I patted down the furs and tried to get comfortable again.

"Sit there." She pointed to the velvet chair.

I hesitated. She, with her arthritis, needed it more than I did.

"Better for you," she insisted.

So I sank gratefully into the chair, even if it sagged a bit in the seat, while she, after placing the tea pot, two porcelain cups and the smudge bowl on the floor between us, nestled herself into the furs with an ease that came from years of practice. I realized this was her regular seat. The chair was for visitors.

With her eyes closed, she began fanning the smudge with her eagle feather and chanting softly. Figuring I might as well get into the mood, I closed my eyes as well. The cedar smoke mingled with the other earthy aromas and seemed to transport me into the depths of a forest. I felt as if I was sitting in front of a campfire surrounded by the darkness of night. As I swayed with the rhythm of her chanting, I found myself humming. The sounds, the smells caressed my body, my mind. I felt the tension ease away. And then I realized she'd stopped chanting.

I opened my eyes slowly.

A broad smile spread across her face. "Good. Time for tea."

She poured the reddish liquid into the two cups and nodded for me to take mine. It tasted slightly bitter, but it wasn't unpleasant. I noticed a couple of pine needles resting on the bottom of the cup, along with what could've been part of a pine flower.

She said nothing, just watched me.

I didn't feel the need to talk either. Feeling this occasion no longer suited a chair, I moved down onto the floor and crossed my legs on the thick black bear pelt she'd passed me. The hot liquid flowed through me as the cedar smoke continued to swirl around us. I finished the tea, and she poured more. A woodpecker tapped on one of the outside walls. Through the open door I could hear the wind rustling the trees. It tickled my hair. I sat there absorbing the silence. I felt a calm.

Finally she said, "Tell me child, why not happy?"

So I told her about my fears for Eric, worried he was in some way be involved in Becky's murder and terrified he might be dead too. I told her how helpless I felt, wanting to do something to help find him, but not knowing how. And I even revealed how much I loved him, that he was my other half. If he were to die, I would die too.

"But not die. He come back. You marry. Live happy."

And for a moment I believed her, really wanted to believe her. Then I laughed bitterly and said, "It's ridiculous. It could never happen."

"Why not, child?"

"Because Eric won't want me." I braced myself with another cup of tea and told her what I'd never admitted to anyone before. "I killed my brother."

I told her the whole story, hiding nothing, with none of the half-truths I'd told my mother. It was time I owned up to what I'd done on that dreadful January day more than thirty years ago, when I was thirteen and Joey was seven.

A rare blizzard had descended on Toronto and left more than a foot of the white fluffy stuff. Perfect for tobogganing, I'd thought. But my mother forbade me, saying it would be too dangerous, and with Nanny on her day off, there would be no one to watch me. I kept arguing with her, insisting I was old enough to go on my own, until she finally sent me in a fit of tears to my room. As I headed upstairs, I could hear Joey in the kitchen whining about going tobogganing.

A short while later, I saw her car heading out of the driveway and figured she was off to some stupid ladies tea or her bridge club and wouldn't be back for hours. I snuck back downstairs, careful to avoid the housekeeper, who would no doubt squeal on me, and headed to the kitchen, where I knew the cook would be more sympathetic. Joey was sitting at the table drinking hot chocolate, while I could hear the cook in the pantry.

"Do you want to go tobogganing?" I whispered to my brother, who was small for his size and like me had the carrot red hair of our father, and his freckles too. He nodded vigorously. After yelling to Shelley that we were going outside to make a snowman, we headed to the garage where the toboggan was kept then raced away to the hill.

Now this wasn't just any hill — we lived near a ravine not far from a golf course. The older kids bragged about it having the steepest hill in town. But I'd never gone down it myself, since my mother wouldn't let me. So of course we went there and found lots of other kids, most of them older, zooming down the hill on their sleds and toboggans. I did feel a bit queasy at the sharp drop. Even Joey hesitated, but I figured if the big kids could do it, so could we.

We piled onto the toboggan and down we hurtled, screaming and yelling like everyone else at the rush of wind and speed. I had to keep my eyes closed most of the way, because the snow kept flying into my face. Joey almost fell off when we hit a big bump and the toboggan went flying into the air, but I grabbed him and we made it to the bottom, barely missing a big tree. There were a lot of trees at the bottom.

Then we huffed and puffed up the hill, dragging the toboggan behind. Boy, it was hard, but we made it to the top, and down we went again. We did it several more times, then Joey started whining that he was tired. He wanted to go home. But I wasn't ready to quit. I wanted to have one more run, but I couldn't leave him up on the top all alone, so I made him come with me, even though he started to cry. But he was a crybaby anyways — any little thing set him off.

Down we raced, really fast. All the kids going up and down the big hill had made the snow really smooth. It was even icy in spots. It felt like we were flying. Then I saw some kids coming up the hill, right in our path. I yelled at them to get out of the way while Joey shrieked at the top of his lungs. I could tell it wasn't from excitement. He was scared and I was too. I managed to swerve the toboggan around the kids, but the front caught on the edge of their sled and sent us sideways. We hit a big bump and went flying off the toboggan. I landed in a pile of snow with the toboggan on top of me. But Joey … Joey, he flew into a tree, a really big one.

For a moment I thought he was okay. I thought I saw him move, but when I got to him I realized he was too still. His head was at a funny angle. Then I started screaming.

"I don't remember much after that, Summer Grass Woman. I just remember the older kids coming to help, the men in the ambulance and the police, and most of all, my mother yelling and shaking me with all her hatred. Joey was the apple of her eye. He reminded her of our dead father.

"And I did one more terrible thing. I lied. I so wanted that hatred in her eyes to disappear that I pretended it was all my brother's fault. I told her that he was the one who'd insisted we go tobogganing, that he'd kept crying until I relented. I told her I'd planned to go to a smaller hill, but Joey had cried to go down the biggest. In fact, he was about to go down the hill on his own when I managed to jump on the back of the toboggan as it was starting down. And of course I told her that he was the one who'd wanted that one last run, not me."

I suddenly stopped speaking. The words were gone from me. Tears coursed down my cheeks. My whole body was shaking. I had to use two hands to try to keep the teacup steady as I brought it to my lips.

Summer Grass Woman continued to sit as she had throughout my confession, completely still and expressionless. I waited for the loathing, the accusation to appear in her eyes, the way it had continued to lurk behind my mother's eyes since that terrible day.

"Your mama, you tell her this true story?"

I slowly shook my head. "No, I've never told anyone what I've told you today."

"You gotta tell her, child. Bring you harmony. Stop drinking."

"But I'm afraid to. She'll disown me."

"What Creator want, it happen. But if she good mother, she say okay."

She reached over to pour herself another cup of pine tea, which was by now very cold. She refused my offer to make a fresh pot.

"You gotta tell Eric too."

"I can't. That's why I wouldn't marry him. My former husband turned against me after my mother told him her version. Can you imagine what Eric would do if I told him the truth? Any regard he has for me now would turn to hatred, and that I couldn't bear."

"No matter. He very important to you. No harmony until you tell him. But Eric, he good man."

203

Her face softened into a sympathetic smile. I saw no loathing, no accusation hidden in their dark depths. "Come child, sit by me."

She fanned the smudge around me in a cleansing wash as I collapsed onto the furs beside her.

"It okay. You good people too." She hugged me, which brought on more tears.

While she chanted, I laid my head on her lap and felt the soft caress of her hand as the rest of my guilt drained away.

CHAPTER
THIRTY

I returned home exhausted and emotionally drained. Driving into Somerset to buy vodka never even entered my head. I had only energy enough to feed Sergei and myself before crawling into bed, where I slept without dreams or nightmares and woke the next morning feeling as if it were the first day of the rest of my life.

But no, this was too easy. I shouldn't be able to get rid of my guilt by a simple confession. I should have to atone for what I'd done, for the lies I'd told, for killing my brother. I should be punished.

I thought of Marie-Claude and her way of trying to handle her guilt. I'd tried suicide too, when I was sixteen. I'd reached the point when I could no longer endure the thought of being my brother's killer, so I'd swallowed a bottle of Aspirin. Fortunately, although I hadn't thought so at the time, the bottle had been less than half full, and my sister Jean found me before the effect became irreversible.

After several months at a psychiatric institution and many years of therapy, I was declared fit to get on with my life. But strangely enough, at no time did I ever admit to the lies I'd just revealed to Summer Grass Woman. In fact, I now realized that I'd buried them so deep that only in the last few years had they gradually made themselves known.

Summer Grass Woman was right. I had to confess to my mother, but I was worried about the effect it would have on her precarious health. She'd had congestive heart failure. Although she'd survived a scare earlier in the summer, the doctors had warned my sister and me not to upset her. After living most of my life with my brother's death on my hands, I certainly didn't want to add my mother's.

I wasn't sure what to do. I knew I couldn't do it over the phone. I needed to do it face-to-face at her bedside in Toronto, but I should probably clear it with her doctors or even seek the guidance of her minister, and if they felt there was little danger, I would confess and accept the punishment she demanded. If they considered it too risky, I would still confess to my sister, for she'd been as much affected by our brother's death as my mother. Even if my mother didn't mete out a punishment, I would do it myself. I would give what would've been my brother's share of her sizable fortune to charity.

However, before I could go to Toronto, I needed to accomplish two things. One was to try to fulfill my promise to help find Marie-Claude's daughter. I prayed I would find her safe, so that her mother wouldn't have to live with the kind of guilt that I had.

The other thing was to confess to Eric then firmly shut the door on him, even move away from Three Deer Point if need be, for I wouldn't be able to bear the cold condemnation I would see in his eyes whenever we happened upon each other. But to admit my guilt, I needed him in front of me, alive and well. Although I knew I had to reveal the ugly truth, seeing him safe and unhurt would be paramount. Summer Grass Woman had said what the Creator wanted would happen. If Eric were found dead, I would know that the Creator had passed sentence on me.

Even though I felt confident that Will had set the police wheels in motion, I couldn't sit back and wait. I had to do what I could to find him. One thing I could do was to go back to the various people in Ottawa who'd seen Eric in July and determine precisely when they had. A couple had mentioned early July, but Paulette had said later in the month. I would start with her. If she'd seen him after Becky was killed, we could rest a little easier knowing that his disappearance wasn't linked to her death.

But Paulette's voice greeting stated she would be away for the next couple of days, so I left a message asking her to get back to me as soon as she could with the precise date of Eric's visit and anything else she remembered about it. To emphasize the urgency of my request, I added that he was missing, and apart from her no one had seen him since mid-July.

I had better luck reaching the executive director, Mary. Since she was a friend of Eric's, I thought there might be a chance he'd been in contact with her. But she hadn't seen him since that time in early July, around the fourth or fifth, she thought. She'd had no communication with him since.

"In fact," she continued, "he was supposed to come to the July twentieth board meeting and never made it. He didn't let me know either."

The day before Becky was killed, I thought with sudden dread. Will had said the coroner's date of July twenty-first could be plus or minus a day or two.

"We're very afraid something has happened to Eric." I brought her up to date on the situation and ended by asking, "Can you think of anyone who might know where he is?"

"Not offhand. I didn't really know him all that well. We only ever met over Centre business. But for him to miss meetings without prior notification is unheard of. I'm with you. Something is seriously wrong." She didn't bother to hide the alarm in her voice. "Have the police checked the hospitals yet?"

"They're working on it. Would you know if he was involved in any kind of a project or investigation that might be considered dangerous?"

She sighed. "Possibly. His main reason for coming to the July board meeting was to discuss the findings of his investigation into the high number of native woman that have gone missing in our area. I think I mentioned to you that the number is now at sixteen, which represents about two percent of the city's total aboriginal population, a very high percentage in contrast to the general population. So far, four have been found dead."

"You think this could've gotten him into trouble?"

"Possibly. For the past year he's been looking into the different cases to try to get a handle on the situation. Although he suspected a few disappearances were tied to domestic disputes, he felt that in the majority of the cases there was something more sinister at work."

"Such as?"

"He didn't say. But he did tell me that he'd begun to see a pattern. The women were young, in their late teens and early twenties. The disappearances happened in June or early July. And I think in all cases the girls were considered very pretty."

"Like Fleur."

"I'm afraid so. And like Fleur, they were alone in Ottawa without family. In all cases it had taken their families weeks, even months to realize their daughters were missing."

Just like Fleur. "So by the time the families contacted the police, the trail was too cold to follow," I suggested.

"I gather in one case it took almost five months for the mother to alert police."

"I guess these parents didn't really care what was happening to their daughters."

"I know it bothered Eric so much that he contacted some of the families. In some cases it had to do with parents caught up in their alcoholism, and in a couple the parents were dead and the remaining relatives were glad to be rid of the girls. A sad comment on our community, I know, but it happens. Here at the Welcome Centre, we try to help these girls and the boys too."

"Lost souls, Paulette called them."

"Yes, some of them are, but many of these kids go on to lead good lives. Please don't get me wrong, there are many more good and caring parents in our community than bad ones."

"I know. And don't think you've cornered the Market on bad parents. I find it curious, though, that all these girls came from family situations where communication was minimal if not nonexistent. I'm wondering if we couldn't read something into this."

"I'm sorry, I don't follow."

"Maybe they were targeted specifically because of this."

"Are you saying someone kidnapped these girls?"

"Well, it's a possibility, isn't it? They wouldn't be missed until long after they were taken. Maybe Eric had also come to the same conclusion."

"He didn't say, but I know what you mean. Young, pretty, alone, these girls are prime targets for the sex trade. And I have suspected that some of these missing girls probably disappeared into the drug/prostitution world, but voluntarily, if one could say becoming an addict was voluntary. But I think you're suggesting something more organized might be involved, like a prostitution ring."

"The fact that they all disappeared at about the same time of year might point to something organized. But what?"

Then I had a horrid thought. "What if a serial killer is at work?"

"Surely you don't believe that?"

"I sure hope not. But after what happened out in B.C., it's possible. Did Eric mention anything about the murders, whether he'd discovered any similarities?"

"No, no he didn't. As far as I know, he was just looking into the missing girls. He said he had a few more leads to pursue before he was prepared to make his results public. He also told me to keep it to myself."

"Do you know what those leads were?"

"No idea."

"When did he tell you this?"

"About a month before the July twentieth meeting."

"Why didn't you mention this when I talked to you the other day?"

"I assumed that Eric had already passed his findings on to Fleur's parents. But now you're telling me he couldn't have. That's why I'm mentioning it to you now."

"Do you know if Eric mentioned any of this to the Ottawa police?"

"I'm fairly certain he didn't. He said he would need something concrete before he could take it to the police. I do know that whatever he'd discovered troubled him greatly."

"But he gave you no hint of what it might be?"

"No."

"If you don't mind, I'm going to let the police chief at the Migiskan Reserve know about this. It could help with his investigation. I will probably have to give him your name in case he wants to talk to you. Is that okay with you?"

"I'm happy to do whatever it takes to find Eric. And by the way, we've just had sad news about Claire." She paused as if choking back tears. "They found her body. But more disturbing, the accident didn't kill her. A bullet did. The police believe she was shot just before it happened. In fact, they're saying the shooting caused the accident."

CHAPTER
THIRTY-ONE

I hung up feeling as if I'd been punched in the stomach. Although I'd only met Claire one time, I was stunned by the disturbing way she'd died. Murdered while driving her car, probably without warning or even knowing she'd been shot. For a few terrifying moments, she would've known something was dreadfully wrong. I hoped she was dead before her car made that horrifying dive into the river far below. I also couldn't help asking myself, would she be alive today if she hadn't been driving to the restaurant to see me?

Although Mary wasn't able to provide more details, the mid-morning radio newscast reported that the police were unable to say at this point in their investigation whether it was a random drive-by shooting or whether Claire had been specifically targeted. They were asking witnesses to contact them. The newscaster went on to say that there were several reports of motorcycles racing away at about the time her car swerved into the bridge, which immediately brought to mind the motorcycles that had almost driven me off the road a good fifteen minutes or so before I reached the bridge. But I'd been more intent on keeping my truck on the road than looking at them, so I would be useless as a witness.

Mary had also mentioned that though Claire's funeral would take place at her home reserve in the Yukon, the Welcome Centre was planning a circle of mourning, and I was more than welcome to attend. Although I could hardly be counted amongst Claire's friends, I took being invited as a compliment. It was Mary's way of saying I'd been accepted into Claire's broader aboriginal community.

I was in the process of dialing the police chief's number to let him know about Eric's missing women investigation when Teht'aa walked through the kitchen door. Too used to seeing her in the standard country garb of jeans and T-shirts, I was taken aback by her smart attire, her interview suit she called it, a sombre charcoal-grey jacket and knee-length skirt with a prim and proper white silk blouse. Hardly the kind of conservative attire I associated with Teht'aa.

"I'm just getting back from Ottawa," she said, pouring herself a steaming mug of coffee while Sergei nudged her thigh for a pat. "Any word on Dad?" The dark circles under her eyes spoke of a difficult night.

"I'm calling Will as we speak."

I got his voice mail, so I left a message.

"So, did you get the job?"

"You're looking at the new Ottawa reporter for APTN News."

"Wow, super congratulations!" I hugged her, glad that she finally had a job, even though it would take her away from Migiskan.

I just hoped it was the right job. She'd walked away from the last one after it became apparent the job wouldn't live up to its billing. She'd only been hired because she filled the aboriginal checkbox. They hadn't expected her to actually work. But since APTN was Canada's nationally based Aboriginal Peoples Television Network, she shouldn't encounter the problem there.

"But I didn't know you had TV reporting experience." I dropped down into a chair at the kitchen table and motioned for her to do the same.

"I don't. They're going to train me. Part of yesterday's interview was a screen test, which I passed with flying colours."

She flashed the kind of smile that would indeed light up TV screens.

"I'll be on probation for three months, reporting on what's happening in Ottawa in aboriginal affairs, and if all goes well, I might have a chance at my own show. Apparently in January they're starting up a weekly half-hour show on what's happening on the aboriginal scene in the nation's capital. The person they had in mind had to pull out, so they're looking at me. Ta … dah!"

She flung up her arms and flashed another pearly white smile.

I had no doubt that she would be a magnetic presence on screen, I just wasn't too sure about her reporting skills. But that probably didn't matter. Others would prepare the material. She would only have to read.

"So when do you start?"

"They wanted me to start this coming Monday, but when I told them about Dad, they delayed it a week. Only problem is once they learned he was missing, it immediately became a news item. I hope that's okay with Will."

"It couldn't hurt. In fact, it'll spread the word much broader and faster than the police can. If someone does know something about his disappearance, they'll get in touch with the police that much faster."

I didn't want to dwell on the obverse. If we received no response, would we have to assume he was dead?

"Teht'aa, I have a question for you. Did you know that just before he disappeared, your father was looking into the high number of cases of missing women in the Ottawa area?"

"Yes, I did. Do you think it's related?"

"I don't know, but the Executive Director of the Anishinabeg Welcome Centre told me Eric had uncovered a disturbing pattern in a number of those cases. I thought he might have mentioned something to you."

"I know they worried him, but I thought it had more to do with police inaction than anything to do with the actual cases. Did she say what it was?"

I told her about the similarities. "It could point to the same perpetrator, like a kidnapper for a prostitution ring, or much more scary, a serial killer. Did he talk about the ones who were murdered?"

"Surely you can't be thinking all those missing women have been killed, including Fleur?"

"I don't know what to think, but four, including Becky, have already been found dead and twelve are still missing. Something has happened to them. Maybe it's murder. We can't forget about the fifty or more missing women that ended up in bits and pieces at that pig farm out west."

"Meg, you're making my skin crawl." She winced. "But there are enough rednecks out there that consider Injuns good only for hunting and screwing, so I could see it happening. You think Dad might've uncovered something that's got him into trouble?"

"It's possible. Let's hope it's nothing worse than trouble. Do you know if any of the material he was working on is at your house? It might help us figure out what's going on."

"I think most of it's on his laptop, which is with him, but there might be some stuff on his desk. Let's go have a look."

She jumped up from the table, added her empty mug to the other dirty dishes in the sink, and headed out the back door with Sergei trotting behind.

I started to follow, but the phone rang. "You go on ahead," I shouted to her retreating back.

It was Will returning my call. After filling him in on what I knew about Eric's investigation, I asked him if he'd known about it.

"I know he was looking into something related to these cases. He asked me for some information, which I provided. But I didn't know what line he was following. He never discussed it."

"Given your knowledge of the cases, including the four murder victims, do you think it's possible that a serial killer is involved?"

"Hmm, as far as I know, no one's raised that supposition. And I doubt they would. The method of killing was different, unlike what you'd find if the same perp murdered all four. We find a killer generally sticks to the same method, be it a gun or knife, even strangulation. That's certainly the case with organized crime hit men, and of course with serial killers."

"But don't these guys sometimes leave their victims in similar locations? I seem to remember that the Mohawk woman killed last year was also found in a wooded area in West Quebec, near Highway 5, I think. Do you know where the other woman was killed?"

"Yeah, you have a point. The case you're talking about happened about ten or so kilometres from where Becky's body was found. And the other woman who was killed three years ago was also found on the Quebec side of the Ottawa River."

"But surely the fact that four young aboriginal women were killed in West Quebec should've raised red flags with the Sûreté. Isn't there some kind of a police computer system that looks for these types of similarities?"

"Yeah, it's called ViCLAS. A Canada-wide system run by the Mounties. I can check to see if these deaths were entered. Not all crimes are. Only violent ones."

"You can't get more violent than murder."

"You like to think so, but some cops figure murder ain't good enough for us." He sighed. "Don't mind me, Meg. I'm still fighting mad over the way the SQ treated Becky's crime scene. Besides, entering the info takes a lot of time, so not every cop does it."

"Do they have any suspects yet in Becky's murder?"

"Not that I know of. Mind you, they aren't exactly keeping me in the loop. But thanks for reminding me. I'll give them another call." He covered his phone as if speaking to somebody then came back on after a few long seconds.

"Meg, you still there? Sorry about that. You're asking some good questions. Ever think of becoming a cop?"

I laughed. "Not on your life. I hate guns. Besides, I'm not very good with authority, so I'd probably find myself constantly fighting with my superiors. What about Eric? Any word yet?"

"You don't happen to know where Teht'aa is, do you?" The warmth had suddenly vanished from his voice. "I've been trying to reach her this morning."

"Don't tell me he's dead?"

"Sorry, I didn't mean to alarm you, but the Ottawa cops have found some luggage. They're pretty sure the suitcase belongs to Eric, but I just need Teht'aa's say-so."

"Oh, shit. Where did they find it?"

"I gather some beat cop came across a homeless guy trying to break into it in the ByWard Market. He recognized the name on the tag from the APB that's been sent out about Eric. At least we got one cop who was on the ball."

My stomach clenched. "Does this mean he's dead?"

"It could mean a lot of things. He lost it. It was stolen. He could've even tossed it away and bought a new one."

"Not if his clothes were still in it?"

"Now, Meg, I don't want you to get all worried. I'm sure Eric's fine. He's pretty good at getting himself out of tricky situations. I'd better go. Got a lot of things on my plate."

I noticed he didn't say the suitcase was empty, nor did he give me a chance to question him on the meaning of a "tricky situation." With barely a perfunctory goodbye, he hung up, leaving me with sweaty palms and a pounding heart.

CHAPTER THIRTY-TWO

I could tell by the tears trickling down Teht'aa's cheeks that the police chief had told her about the suitcase. She hadn't answered when I'd called through the open side door of Eric's bungalow. I figured she was in her bedroom changing, so I went inside to wait in the kitchen. Instead I found her crumpled up on the leather sofa in the living room, still wearing her got-the-job suit, although the jacket was now draped over the back of a chair. Sergei, lying on the sofa beside her, rested his head in her lap as if trying to comfort her.

It had been many months since I'd been inside Eric's home. I'd avoided it. Instead, whenever Teht'aa and I had gotten together, I'd asked her if she wouldn't mind coming to Three Deer Point. I was afraid his house would speak too much of his presence, and it did. It damn well shouted it.

His red and black logger's shirt hanging beside the door smelled as only Eric could smell. The spice bottles on the kitchen counter were lined up as if he were about to cook one of his favourite meals. Even the pile of dirty dishes next to the sink could've been left by him, and his favourite sagging La-Z-Boy chair, complete with peeling duct tape, seemed to rock as if he'd just risen from it. Beside it on a table lay his much-thumbed copy of *Kiss of the Fur Queen*. It was almost too much for me. I would've turned tail and run if Teht'aa hadn't needed me.

In an attempt to convince both of us, I said, "The abandoned suitcase doesn't necessarily mean something terrible has happened to your dad."

"Of course it does. Especially with his clothes still inside," she shot back.

"Will confirmed they were?"

"Yeah, he recognized Dad's ceremonial deerskin jacket from the description," she sputtered.

Unfortunately, it was catching. I slumped onto the couch, hid my face in the dog's curly fur and let loose my own share of tears. Teht'aa reached across the dog and clasped my hands. I don't know how long we both sobbed out our fears and anguish.

I finally reached a point where I felt drained of emotion. I sat up and brushed away the last of the tears.

Feeling one of us had to remain strong, I said, "Okay, we've both had a good cry. But we just can't sit here waiting in terror of another phone call from Will. It's not going to help us or Eric."

Teht'aa raised her head. Her face, no doubt mirroring mine, was puffy-eyed and blotchy. Sergei started licking her tears away.

I continued, "Other than this suitcase, there is nothing to say Eric is dead. We have to continue to believe he is alive. So where are those papers you were talking about? Let's go through them now."

Teht'aa firmed her lips as she straightened up. She brushed away the hair plastered to her cheek. "You're right. The stuff's over there." She pointed to the dining room table. "You start while I change."

It looked as if Eric no longer bothered to have people in for one of his signature meals. Instead, the large maple table where we'd had many a memorable feast was stacked with papers and books. A couple of electrical cords snaked across the table to where he probably worked on his laptop. The brand new ergonomically designed office chair replacing a dining chair was a sure sign that his back was bothering him again. Little wonder, when he refused to stop using the sagging La-Z-Boy that had long since given up all pretense of providing good back support.

I sank into the chair and began sifting through the first stack of papers, but they appeared to be mostly GCFN-related and nothing to do with missing women. The next stack was about a business venture another reserve was considering. Eric appeared to be offering them advice.

I'd just uncovered files on five of the missing women when Teht'aa returned dressed in her usual garb of skin-tight blue jeans and equally tight T-shirt. I slid the files over as she pulled up a chair.

"I'm not sure what we should be looking for," I said, "but I guess anything that might have gotten your father into trouble, whatever that might be."

While she started going through the five files, I found files for six other missing women and the ones for three murdered women. I noted with surprise that there wasn't a file for Fleur until I realized he'd probably disappeared before she was declared officially missing. Nor was there one for Becky, no doubt for the same reason.

I searched through the murdered victims' files first. They contained mostly notes in Eric's handwriting about inquiries he'd made with the Ottawa police, Will, and one or two family members, plus some printouts, mostly news articles, from Internet searches. Each also contained an official-looking case summary, which had probably come from Will.

There was no mention of how the girls had been killed, nor was there any indication either officially or as part of Eric's musings that a serial killer was being considered. But I did notice that he had circled the West Quebec crime scene location for each girl in red. He'd also red-circled another location related to two of the young women.

"Teht'aa, it looks as if another common thread is the ByWard Market. One of the murdered victims was last seen at a bar in the Market and another lived in a rooming house on the edge. Have you seen any mention of it in your files?"

"Yeah, this girl, Kelly, an Ojibwa from northern Ontario. She disappeared four years ago. Apparently she did some hooking on the side, and her usual place was in the Market."

"Does it say where?"

"Yeah, Cumberland and Murray."

Monique's corner, where I'd stood two nights ago.

"And Dad circled this reference too," Teht'aa added.

"Any mention in the other files?"

"Not in the other one I've finished, but I'll check the last three."

By the time we finished going through all the files, we'd found five more with a ByWard Market connection, another prostitute who favoured a different corner, two residents, and two who worked there, one at O'Flaherty's and the other at the Dreamcatcher Bistro.

"That makes eight out of fourteen women with this connection," I said. "I'd say a rather high percentage can be dismissed as coincidental. I'm absolutely amazed that the Ottawa police didn't pick up on this."

Teht'aa merely shrugged, confirming her already low opinion of the Ottawa police. "I noticed Dad circled another common factor, although I only saw it in two of the files I was looking at. Maybe you saw it in yours. *Les Diables Noirs*. Didn't you say the guy Fleur was seen with was a member of that gang?"

I sat up. "I did, plus they were seen at O'Flaherty's. Monique also mentioned Becky had a biker boyfriend. I also saw a mention of the Black Devils in two of these files."

"Makes you wonder if the gang is somehow involved, doesn't it?"

"It does, doesn't it? Maybe if your father was trying to check into a possible connection, he might've asked one question too many." I didn't bother to finish the rest. Teht'aa's imagination was as good as mine. "Curiously enough, Marie-Claude's brother happens to be a member of this gang. I suggest we talk to him."

"But won't it be dangerous?"

"I don't think so. I believe he's genuinely worried and upset at his niece's disappearance. In fact, he was going to check with some of his biker buddies to see if they knew anything about it." I paused. "I'm beginning to wonder if he doesn't either know or suspect that members of his gang might've had a hand in their disappearance."

"Are you suggesting they kidnapped them? For what purpose?"

"Why do men usually kidnap women? For sex, what else. It certainly wouldn't be for money. These women wouldn't have any."

"So you're saying these women may be stashed away in a Black Devils clubhouse?" Teht'aa leaned back into her chair as she shoved the files away from her.

"I suppose so, for their own use or maybe as prostitutes. I could see a biker gang being involved in prostitution. They're not exactly known as upstanding citizens."

"But one of these girls has been missing for over five years." Teht'aa flipped open one of the files to show me a photo of a young woman, barely out of her teens, laughing at the camera. "Can you imagine the kind of shape she must be in now?"

I didn't want to think about it, and I certainly didn't want to envision the impact this kind of life could have on an innocent like Fleur.

"On the plus side, if one could say there is one, if bikers are involved, I think we can probably rule out a psycho serial killer," I hazarded.

"Maybe they're not serial killers, but they sure don't hesitate to kill. Look at all the headlines involving biker gang shootings."

"True, but I think they're more likely to kill rivals than non-threatening people like these women. So I think it's likely they, including Fleur, are still alive."

"Yes, but we know four of these women, including Becky, were murdered."

"Maybe something went wrong or their killings had nothing to do with the Black Devils."

"But what about Dad? Do you think he could still be alive, if the Black Devils do have him?"

"The only way we're going to find out is by asking Fleur's uncle."

CHAPTER
THIRTY-THREE

With Sergei crowding the bench seat between us, Teht'aa and I headed back in my truck to Three Deer Point to retrieve the cell number Fleur's uncle had given me. But the drive proved considerably slower than normal. Word had spread about the missing band chief, so we were constantly flagged down by worried passersby wanting to commiserate with Teht'aa. It did nothing to bolster Teht'aa's frame of mind, so by the time our footsteps were echoing along the hall of Three Deer Point, her tears were flowing once again. It was all I could do not to join her.

It took me a few minutes to locate J.P.'s number in the papers scattered by the kitchen phone, but when I did, it was only to discover that his phone was no longer working. I called Marie-Claude and fortunately reached Neige instead. Not being too adept at lying, I would've found myself stumbling over the half-truths I'd be forced to tell the distraught mother to avoid revealing the dark implications of Eric's findings. Thankfully, her daughter was able to provide me with her uncle's home number. That number was no longer in service, which I found curious, though it probably just meant he had recently moved.

Hoping that his cell was either switched off or he was temporarily out of range, I tried it every fifteen minutes or so. In the meantime we ate lunch, my usual standby of chicken noodle soup and grilled cheese sandwiches. My culinary skills might not come close to Eric's, but I thought I made a rather tasty grilled cheese, bacon, and tomato sandwich. Even Teht'aa agreed, although true to form, she only ate half of it.

Finally J.P.'s cell worked.

He gave a hurried "*Ouiais*," barely audible above the rumble of a motorcycle engine and the rushing sound of wind.

Worried he wouldn't hear me, I shouted out my name.

"No problem. I hear you okay. Gotta an earphone," he shouted. "Whaddya want?"

"I'm wondering if you've made any headway in your search for Fleur."

"Can't talk. Be in Ottawa soon. You come, eh?"

"You mean to Ottawa, now?"

"*Ouiais*. I tell you what I find out."

"Okay, but it'll take me a couple of hours. Where should I meet you?"

"Bar LaFayette in the Market."

"It's two o'clock now, but I won't be able to get there until after four thirty."

"I got to do something first. Six o'clock better for me, okay?"

A half-hour later I found myself sitting in Eric's Grand Cherokee heading down the road from Migiskan, with Teht'aa driving and Sergei sound asleep in the back seat. Since Jid was still away, I didn't want to leave the dog alone in the house in case my return was later than anticipated.

Teht'aa was coming because she'd noticed several references to three women at the Welcome Centre during her search through the missing women's files and felt we should follow up on those. Two of them were unavailable, namely Claire and Paulette, who wouldn't be back in her office for another couple of days. The third, Louise, agreed to talk to us if we got to the Centre by four thirty. She had to leave by five.

We were using Eric's car, not only because was it considerably faster than my turtle-speed truck, but Sergei could have the entire back seat to himself, leaving us to enjoy the spacious front seats.

And speedy the trip was. Despite a slowdown due to highway construction as we neared Gatineau, we arrived at the front door of the Anishinabeg Welcome Centre with ten minutes to spare, though I will admit that I couldn't prevent myself from shuddering as we drove past the fluttering police tape where Claire's car had plunged over the bridge.

Doris at the front desk gave us directions to Louise's office. "Louise's got that hair appointment of hers, so you'd better be quick."

We rushed up the stairs, along the hallway past Paulette's closed door, and stopped in front of Claire's old office door. "Louise LePage," read the new piece of paper taped under the Nanabush Youth Program sign.

A diminutive woman whose flyaway locks did suggest a new haircut was in order was talking intently into the phone. Without interrupting her conversation or even offering us a welcoming smile, she gestured at the chairs by her desk. The longer the exchange continued, the gloomier her expression became.

Even though the office had only been vacated two days ago, Louise had already stamped it with her style. While Claire had tried to create a more intimate, less threatening setting for client consultations by shoving her desk against the wall and placing chairs in the open space, Louise wanted you to know that she was in charge. She'd moved the desk into the middle of the long, narrow room and had re-established the boundary between caseworker and client by positioning the chairs in front. The second desk she'd made into a work table, now covered with stacks of case files and a large box of chocolates.

Finally she put down the phone. For several long moments she sat in silence, her eyes unseeing, her fingers fidgeting with a pair of wire-rim glasses lying on the desk in front of her. Clearly something was wrong. Teht'aa and I exchanged nervous glances, wondering if we should interrupt or leave quietly.

At last she looked up, startled. "Oh, I'd forgotten you were here. Please, I'm sorry. I've just heard some bad news."

"Would you like us to leave?" Teht'aa suggested.

"No, it's okay. I was expecting it anyways." Louise lapsed back into silence.

We waited. The seconds stretched into minutes. Feeling we had to do something, I was about to speak when the woman roused herself from her reverie and said, "It's no big secret. It'll be on the news soon enough. The police have just found the body of one of my girls."

"Oh dear, I'm so sorry to hear about your daughter. I think we should go," I said.

"No, no, she was no relation of mine, although I loved her as a daughter. She was one of my clients. A young woman I'd tried to help."

I went cold. "Not Fleur Lightbody?"

She put her glasses on. "No. Her name was Sandy White Owl. She disappeared over three years ago."

Girl number four in Eric's files.

"I'm afraid when Sandy went missing, I was worried there would only be one possible outcome. And sadly, today I've been proven right. Such a tragedy."

Teht'aa's voice broke through the ensuing silence. "Any death is a tragedy, none more so than that of a young person killed before they'd had a chance to live a full life."

Louise nodded, her eyes glittering with tears. "Such a waste. Unlike many of the girls that come seeking our help, she'd been given a much better start on life. Her father was band chief, her mother a teacher. After taking a year off after graduating from high school, she was registered for the fall semester at Carleton University when she had a falling out with her family."

I felt myself go cold. This was sounding too familiar.

"I'm not sure what happened," she continued. "Given her addiction, maybe it was drugs. I don't know. She never told me, but her father kicked her out of their house and off the reserve. She went first to Montreal and then a couple of years later came to Ottawa. When I first met her, she was in a bad way, but I worked carefully with her over a nine-month period, and in that time she made significant improvements. She'd gone onto a methadone program, had stopped hooking and got herself a job as a sales clerk. I felt she was finally turning her life around."

Had Fleur been heading in this direction?

I could hear Teht'aa fidgeting impatiently beside me. No doubt wanting to be polite, like me, she gave the woman time to tell her story. Unfortunately, our precious time was quickly being used up.

"And then one day she didn't show up for her appointment. After the second missed appointment, I went to her apartment and discovered that no one had seen her for over a month."

"Was that when you called the police?" Teht'aa glanced at her watch then showed it to me. We only had another fifteen minutes.

Louise shook her head. "Sadly, I didn't. I assumed heroin had once again taken over her life. It took a couple of her friends to convince me that she was missing."

She sighed and was about to resume when Teht'aa spoke up. "Sorry, I don't mean to interrupt, but you mentioned having to leave by five, so we don't have much time. As I mentioned on the phone, my dad has disappeared, and we think his investigation into these missing women, including Sandy, might have triggered it. I believe he talked to you about it."

"He's such a nice man. He has done so much for the Centre." Louise patted her hair down as if trying to tame it. "I'm so sorry. It must be very worrisome for you and your family."

"I'm afraid there's just me. When did you see him last? And was it about Sandy?"

"Let me see. I think it was before the May board meeting. The ED suggested he talk to me. Apparently he was doing some kind of an investigation into missing native girls. Did you know that sixteen are missing here in Ottawa? Four have been found dead and now there's a fifth victim. I wonder how many more of them are dead, waiting to be found in the bush."

"Was Sandy's body found in West Quebec?" I interjected.

"Yeah, about an hour's drive from here, not far from Lac aux Herons. Apparently some hikers found her. I gather given the state of the remains, she's been dead for some time."

"Do you know if it was close to where Becky's body was found?"

"Not sure, but I know that lake is sometimes used for floatplane training. My brother-in-law, who teaches flying, uses it for training in take-off and landing. I gather it's a pretty isolated lake with no cottages on it."

"We think Eric was working on a theory as to why these women disappeared or were murdered, and we're wondering if he might've shared it with you," I asked.

"He didn't mention anything at that first meeting, but when I bumped into him a few months ago, he mentioned the Welcome Centre, something about it being a common link to many of the murdered and missing women."

Teht'aa raised a quizzical eyebrow. We'd only noticed the reference to the Centre in three of his files.

"You're certain that the fourteen missing women my dad was investigating were all clients of the Centre?"

"Not all. I think Eric said there were ten. I only know about the four or five that participated in the Nanabush Program. The others were probably using the Centre's other services, like Job Placement."

"When did he tell you this?" she asked.

"Let me see. Sometime in mid-July ... I know, it was July nineteenth, the date of my niece's christening. I bumped into him on my way to the Bay to buy a gift. I was running late and —"

Teht'aa cut in again. "Did he tell you what significance, if any, the link might have?"

"No, he didn't. I mentioned it to Claire, but she just laughed, saying it was no big deal. Since we handle the majority of cases for troubled aboriginal girls in the city, she said that chances were high most of the missing women had used our services at some point in time. And I would agree. I've handled —"

"Did you talk to anyone else about it?" Teht'aa had completely given up on being polite.

It was now 4:55.

"No, I don't think so." Louise glanced at the clock on her desk. "Oh my, look at the time. I'm afraid —"

"I just have one more question," Tehta'aa said. "Did Dad mention if he'd been talking to anyone else or who he was going to see next?"

"I know he talked to Paulette. She mentioned it when I told her about your dad's idea about the Centre being in someway implicated in the disappearance of these women." She paused and patted her hair down. "That's right, I did mention it to her, didn't I?"

"So Eric had suggested that the Centre might be involved?"

"Yes, I guess he did, though I don't remember his exact words. But I thought it was a silly idea. In fact, I was a bit insulted that he thought we would harm our girls."

"And what was Paulette's reaction?"

"The same." She began putting away material on her desk and shutting down her computer. "Look, I've got to go."

I had one last question. "You didn't happen to have Fleur Lightbody as a client, did you?"

"She's missing too, isn't she?"

I nodded.

"When I bumped into Eric that time, he asked me the same question." She pulled her purse from a drawer.

I waited for her to continue while she locked up her desk. As we followed her out her office door, I finally gave up waiting and asked, "What did you tell him?"

"About what?"

Our footsteps clattered down the hall.

"About Fleur?"

"Oh yes, Fleur, such an unusual name." She stopped and turned to me. "She didn't come to me about helping her, rather it was for a friend of hers, Becky."

"The girl who was murdered?"

"You knew her, did you?"

"No, I didn't. Why did Fleur want help for Becky?"

"She was worried that Becky had gotten into serious trouble. She wanted to know if I could help her."

"Did she say what that trouble was?"

"No, she didn't, but I had the feeling Becky was being forced to do something she didn't want to."

"Like prostitution?"

"I've no idea, but I wouldn't be surprised." She frowned at her watch and resumed walking at a much faster pace. The empty hall echoed with our thudding footsteps.

"When did you see Fleur?" I asked, trying to keep up.

"July sometime."

She tripped down the stairs with Teht'aa and me endeavouring to stay within voice range. At the bottom, she suddenly stopped. We both narrowly missed colliding with her.

"I remember. It was before I bumped into Eric, maybe a week or so," she exclaimed. "Such an unusual name. Pretty girl too. I remembered her visit the minute Eric mentioned her name. Now I really must go."

She headed out the door to the waiting cab, leaving Teht'aa and me breathless and confused.

CHAPTER
THIRTY-FOUR

As we watched the black cab veer around the corner, I mused, "I'm surprised we didn't see any red circle reference to the Welcome Centre in your father's files. He seemed to have highlighted all the other common links."

"True, but most of his analysis will be on his laptop, which he took with him," Teht'aa replied. "At least she helped narrow down the date Dad was last seen. July nineteenth."

"Which happens to be the day before the Centre board meeting he missed. So it looks as if he disappeared sometime after bumping into Louise on July nineteenth and the meeting, which I think Mary said was in the evening of the twentieth."

I turned to go back through the glass doors of the Centre. "Let's see if Mary is still here. She might know more about the Centre's connection to these women."

"But is there enough time?" Teht'aa remained fixed to the sidewalk. "I don't want to miss Marie-Claude's brother. I have a feeling that if anyone knows what happened to Dad, he does."

"We've got about forty-five minutes, which should give us plenty of time to talk with her plus the ten or so minute drive to the Market. Okay?"

"Sure, as long as it's quick."

Since it was past quitting time, Doris had already vacated the reception desk. But I vaguely remembered the location of the Executive Director's second floor office and was able to navigate us there without getting lost. Luck was with us. The woman, this time dressed more casually in slacks and a sweater, was clearing her desk when I knocked on her door.

Although she seemed eager to leave, she graciously invited us in. "Nice to see you again, Meg. And you must be Eric's daughter," she said, turning to Teht'aa. "I can see him in your eyes and smile."

Funny. I'd never thought there was any family resemblance between the two of them. Her slim gazelle-like grace had always seemed at odds with Eric's bear-like build. And certainly the daughter's fiery black eyes were a distinct contrast to the father's soft grey ones. But Mary was right. The similarity was in their expressions. The way they looked at you, the way they smiled and laughed. Maybe subconsciously I'd recognized it, and that was why I'd turned to Teht'aa when Eric left my life.

"Any word on your father?" Mary asked Teht'aa.

"No, I'm afraid not. And to make matters worse, they've found his suitcase."

"Oh dear, I'm so sorry, where?"

After bringing her up to date, Teht'aa explained, "We're following up on the investigation Dad was doing into the missing women. We've just learned that ten of the women had a connection to the Anishinabeg Welcome Centre. Were you aware of this?"

"I was, but didn't think it important, since many First Nations people living in the area drop by from time to time, if not to take advantage of our services, at least to socialize with members of our community. In addition to our annual pow-wow, we have many evening events, including aboriginal film nights, art exhibits, and other cultural events."

"So you wouldn't read anything sinister into this connection," I said.

She didn't try to hide her outrage. "Surely you're not suggesting that the Centre had any involvement in the disappearance of these women?"

"I don't know what to think. But I do find it curious that apart from being aboriginal, young, with little or no family contact, the only other common thread that links most of these women, including the five that were murdered, is the Anishinabeg Welcome Centre. Did Eric suggest a possible involvement?"

"Of course not. There is no way the Centre could be responsible for the disappearance of these women. It would be a betrayal of all we believe in."

"I don't think Meg was suggesting that the Centre itself is responsible," Teht'aa said to ease the tension. "But it could be someone close to the Centre, like an employee or volunteer. Does anyone come to mind?"

Mary shook her head vehemently. "All our employees and volunteers are carefully vetted. As I said earlier, a connection to the Centre is not unusual. It could apply to most of our people living in the area." She paused.

"But I should tell you that your father did ask for a list of employees and volunteers."

"Did he indicate that he might have someone in mind?" I asked.

"No, he didn't," Mary replied brusquely before turning back to Teht'aa. "You mentioned five murdered women. I'm only aware of four."

"One of the Nanabush counsellors, Louise, told us about this latest death," Teht'aa replied. "I think her body was recently discovered. The woman's name was Sandy White Owl."

"Oh God, I hadn't heard." Mary paused. "I hate to think how many more will turn up dead."

I nodded grimly. "It also looks as if a biker gang might be connected. They're called *Les Diables Noirs*, or the Black Devils in English. Did Eric mention them to you? Or perhaps you might know if any of your employees are involved with this gang?"

She turned her unsmiling face back to me. Clearly she didn't like the thought of her organization being implicated. "No to both questions," she exclaimed. "But if a biker gang had something to do with their disappearance, it makes me even more worried about the fate of these poor girls. Now if you don't mind, I have to go. I have a hungry family to feed."

Switching her smile back on, she held out a hand to Teht'aa. "I must congratulate you on your new job."

"Oh, you know about it." Teht'aa seemed momentarily flustered. "I only just found out myself."

"Ours is a very small community in Ottawa, so word gets around quickly. But in your case I also have insider knowledge. My husband works at APTN. I think you'll be wonderful on the screen. You have quite a presence, you know. And I gather your screen tests were fantastic."

Teht'aa squirmed. "Thanks. I'm really looking forward to it. We won't keep you any longer. We've got to get going too."

She pointed at her watch and mouthed that we were going to be late.

I had one more question. "Mary, I hope you don't mind my asking, but I find it curious that even though ten of these missing women had connections to the Centre, you didn't do anything about it?"

"I did," she shot back. "I went to the police repeatedly. They refused to do anything more than they already were doing, which was nothing." She shoved papers into her desk drawer and slammed it shut with such force that the desk shook.

"You could have turned to the media?"

"I wanted to, but the board wouldn't let me. I was hoping Eric would be able to convince them. Now if you don't mind." She motioned for us to leave.

Teht'aa was beginning to walk down the hall when Mary called out, "I almost forgot. Please let me know the minute you hear any news on your father. I pray to the Creator that he is found safe and well."

"I pray too. Thanks for your wishes," Eric's daughter said and walked away.

I turned to follow, but as I did, I happened to notice several photos scattered on a table next to the door, one in particular. "I see you were at the same place as Paulette."

I pointed to the photo with a group of people sitting in Muskoka chairs spread out on the lawn in front of a timber building. Although I didn't recognize the people, I did recall the sprawling verandah, which reminded me of Three Deer Point's Victorian version. I'd noticed it in one of the group photos in Paulette's office. She had been sitting in these same chairs with several young women, who I assumed were some of her successes.

Mary's brow arched as she stared at the photo. "Sorry, I've never been there. Someone gave it to me."

She hustled me out of her office and locked her door with a firm click.

Teht'aa and I had exactly ten minutes to drive from the Welcome Centre in Vanier to the Market. Although I felt it was doable, unlike Teht'aa, I wasn't particularly worried that we would miss J.P. if we were late. I doubted he would be punctual himself, but if he was, he'd likely settle in to wait with a beer or two. After all, it was a bar. And I was sure J.P. wasn't exactly averse to drinking.

But I hadn't counted on us getting lost. Unlike most downtown Ottawa streets, Vanier's roads didn't follow a grid pattern. Instead they meandered with a will of their own. I thought I was directing Teht'aa on a shortcut to Beechwood, the most direct road to the Market. Instead we found ourselves going around in circles as we confronted one curved one-way street after another, none of them going in the desired direction. Finally, in exasperation, Teht'aa screeched the SUV to a halt to get directions from a pedestrian.

Unfortunately, we ended up on a less direct route, one clogged with traffic lights, all of which were either red or turning red as we approached. By the time we arrived in the Market, we were fifteen minutes late. It took us another ten minutes to find a parking spot and the bar itself, tucked away on one of the Market's less travelled streets. I tried to quell Teht'aa's spitting anger by insisting that J.P. would be well into his second beer. But when we walked through the scuffed wooden door, we were greeted by a mostly empty room with no sign of the one-eyed biker.

"Damn it, Meg, I told you I didn't want to miss him," she hissed as we stood on the threshold with the eyes of the bar's few clients focused on us.

"Relax, he's a biker. I doubt he's a clock-watcher. Besides, he said he had to do something first, so it's probably taken longer than expected. Let's have a beer and wait. I'm sure he'll be along shortly."

I walked over to an empty wooden table, its heavily shellacked surface marred by scratches, cigarette burns, and the ringed outline of the previous occupant's glass. I sat down.

LaFayette's wasn't exactly a sophisticated establishment like O'Flaherty's. More like a holdover from the sixties, when bars were never called pubs and men could be men without fear of female onlookers, who were relegated to closed-off areas for women and escorts only. Certainly the current clientele was all male, as in elderly male, which was why our sudden arrival had caused a stir. We were probably the highlight of their day. Even the barman was of a certain vintage. This all made me feel decidedly young and nubile. I expected this bar was a holdover from the days when the ByWard Market was simply an ordinary market and not the fashionable destination it was today.

The barman confirmed that J.P. hadn't arrived, though he did mention that the biker was a regular. He often came with some of his buddies. But as long as they behaved themselves, which they did, the barman was happy to have them as good paying customers. Besides, their presence had deterred a fight or two amongst the other patrons.

Over the hour Teht'aa and I waited, the empty room remained empty, the number of patrons static. Whenever an elderly gent left, another one replaced him. For the most part they sat in their loneliness sipping their pint and watching the football game on the overhead TV. They only acknowledged each other with brief nods.

I tried J.P.'s cell several times using the bar's pay phone, but after several unanswered rings, it went to voice mail. The first time, I left a message telling him we were waiting. I didn't bother with the later tries.

Finally, after finishing our meagre dinners, mine a soggy fish and chips and Teht'aa's a chicken salad sandwich, we decided there was no point in waiting any longer. He wasn't coming. After leaving a message with the barman, we headed out the door.

"I guess we might as well go back home," Teht'aa said despondently. "There's no point in hanging around Ottawa."

"I think Will said something about you having to identify your father's suitcase. We could do that before we leave and maybe drop back at the bar afterwards in case J.P. finally shows up."

"Yeah, let's do that. I'd totally forgotten about the suitcase. I think Will said it was at police headquarters."

It was now almost eight o'clock, and dusk was turning to night. Bar LaFayette was tucked away on a side street on the fringes of the bustling Market. I could hear crowd noise from the top of the street, but we were headed in the opposite direction, towards the car parked several blocks away.

I was a bit worried about Sergei. Although I knew he would've spent the time comfortably asleep in the back seat, he would be hungry by now. And he'd want to go to the bathroom. Although I'd let him out when we'd arrived in Ottawa, it was almost four hours ago. So we hurried along the almost empty street, past a couple of darkened stores and a number of houses, also dark but for the odd one with light filtering through curtained windows.

While we were crossing an intersection, I happened to glance down the cross street and noticed a motorcycle parked at a meter, its chrome gleaming under the streetlight. I ignored it, before realizing that there was something familiar about it.

"Teht'aa," I said. "I think that's J.P.'s bike." I walked towards it. "Yes, I'm positive it's his. I recognize that tooled leather saddle with the high back and those handlebar fringes."

The Harley was cold to the touch. "It's been here for a while."

"So where is he?" Teht'aa asked.

"Maybe he's in one of these buildings?" I skimmed my eyes past the darkened facades of nearby storefronts to a brightly lit apartment building halfway down the block that showed more promise. But short of banging on every door, there was no way of knowing if J.P. was inside.

The sudden blaring of country music startled us both. It came from the laneway behind us. It stopped for several seconds then started up again, repeating the same tune.

"That sounds like a cell phone ring to me," Teht'aa offered.

"Let's take a look."

I started down the dark alley with only the faint rays of a streetlight to guide me. The phone stopped then started back up again. It played a few bars of what I now recognized as a Johnny Cash song then stopped once more.

"Are you sure it's safe?" Teht'aa whispered from the sidewalk.

A low moan seemed to be coming from where I could see a black shape against the lighter grey of the ground. "Come here, Teht'aa. Someone's here."

A faint odour drifted in the closed air of the alley. A slightly metallic odour. The music rang out again. It came from the dark object. Light glinted off metal. A faint movement. Another groan.

"Teht'aa, I think they're hurt. See if you can flag down someone on the street to get help."

As my eyes adjusted to the darkness, the outline gradually emerged of a person sprawled on the ground. "Are you okay?" I asked, leaning over. Then, realizing it was a stupid thing to ask, I said, "Hang in there. We're getting help."

The person moaned and whispered something.

I knelt down to get closer. My hands touched a warm sticky liquid. Startled, I jerked them away. The darkish liquid dripped from my fingertips. Blood! And a lot of it, judging by the pool at my knees.

The man, for I knew by now he was male, whispered again.

I placed my ear over his face and recognized with a start the eye-patch and the scraggly goatee.

"*Oiseau vert*," J.P. rasped, then another word I couldn't quite make out, then he went still.

CHAPTER
THIRTY-FIVE

I was leaning over the motionless biker trying to detect signs of life when the alley was filled with brilliant white and flashing red light. J.P.'s single eye stared sightless through its paleness. Blood drenched his *Diables Noirs* T-shirt where his chest should be moving.

"Drop your weapon!" a female voice shouted from the street. "And move away from the body."

Weapon? Sirens approached. I started to get up.

"Drop your weapon immediately!" she shouted again. "And stay on the ground." I detected a nervous quaver in her voice.

"But I don't have one," I yelled back, wanting to turn around, but afraid to. I could almost feel the barrel of her gun pointed at the centre of my back.

"Put your hands up and lie face down on the ground."

On the body? No way. With my hands in the air, I shifted my weight away from J.P. and the blood and lay as directed on the filthy ground of the alley. It stank of oil, rotting garbage, and blood. Footsteps crunched over the gravel towards me. The sirens came to a stop.

"But she was just trying to help this person," Teht'aa called out as my arms were jerked behind my back and manacled together.

"Get up," the cop ordered.

I struggled to stand, but with no free hands it was difficult and the cop made no effort to offer a helping hand. By propping myself against a wall I managed to inch up onto my feet. While another uniformed officer watched over me, his hand on his open holster, the female officer patted me down. Fresh-faced and young, she was obviously nervous, almost as if this were her first crime scene.

"No weapon," she called out to her partner.

Paramedics brushed passed me with a stretcher to reach the dead biker.

"I told you I didn't have any," I said, trying to keep the anger from my voice. "Could you remove these handcuffs. I've done nothing wrong."

"What were you doing here?" she snapped as she pulled her police cap further down her forehead in an attempt to appear tougher.

"I heard a noise and went to check."

After performing a cursory examination, the two paramedics pronounced J.P. officially dead and walked away, taking their medical equipment with them. They didn't even bother to cover him up, just left him lying forgotten in his own blood against a brick wall that curiously was covered in a painted scene that seemed to mock the killing. Giant multi-coloured flowers and butterflies gyrated above his head and green grass rippled behind it.

"You're covered in blood. How do I know you didn't kill the guy?" the female cop demanded.

"I got covered trying to help J.P." The second I blurted out his name, I realized my mistake.

"So you know the dead man, do you?"

"As a matter of fact, I do. But when I came down this alley, I didn't know it was him."

"What's your connection to the Black Devils?"

"There isn't any. This man happens to be the brother of a friend of mine."

"We'd better take her to the station," her partner said.

"Wait, I was just trying to be a Good Samaritan," I insisted. "I've got nothing to do with his killing or his biker gang."

"I can vouch for her," Teht'aa said from close behind me. "We were just passing by when we heard his moans."

"And who are you?" the young cop demanded.

"I'm her friend. Neither of us have done anything wrong."

"We'll take her to the station, too," the male cop ordered.

"By what right?" Teht'aa demanded.

"By right of law. We are conducting a criminal investigation into this man's death, and you and your helpful friend here," his lip curled in a sneer, "are being brought in for questioning as material witnesses."

"I demand a lawyer," she shot back.

"You can make your call at the station. Looks like we got us a wild one here, Constable. Cuff her too."

And so we found ourselves crammed into the hard back seat of a police cruiser, unable to sit properly with our arms clamped behind our backs and a metal cage separating us from the two cops in the front seat. An entirely new and decidedly unwelcome experience for me, although not for Teht'aa.

ooo

By the time we'd managed to convince them we were telling the truth, we'd been harassed by a barrage of questions and innuendos. We'd been locked alone in separate windowless interview rooms with no other furniture than three metal chairs and a scratched metal table. If my chair hadn't been bolted to the ground, I would've thrown it at the two plainclothes cops, so frustrated was I by this charade of an interview.

Realizing co-operation would end this farce faster than hostility, I told them everything I knew about Marie-Claude's brother and our aborted meeting at Bar Lafayette. I even mentioned Fleur and the other fifteen missing aboriginal women, five of them dead. I voiced my fears that a serial killer might be at work and raised the possibility of a link to the Black Devils. But all I received from the two cops were noncommittal shrugs and blank stares.

I decided not to mention J.P.'s last words. I figured they were for me alone and not for police consumption. If at some later point I learned they were pertinent to solving his murder, then I would pass them on. But not now. I wanted first to find out what *green bird* meant.

However, the minute I mentioned Eric's name, the bald cop, who'd said very little thus far, muttered to his hirsute partner, who'd carried out most of the onslaught. "Yeah, he's supposed to be some fuckin' Indian bigwig. Upstairs is riding our ass to find him."

Turning to me, he fired his opening salvo. "What do you know about him, lady?"

"I know he is an upstanding citizen of his community, who commands considerably more respect that you would with your racist comments."

I thought he was going to hit me, but the other cop intervened. "Sorry, miss. He didn't mean it. Just got a little carried away. Now answer the question."

Swallowing my anger, I described Eric and his role in his community. I detailed his last known movements prior to his disappearance and itemized the places he'd failed to arrive at. Finally, I told them about his investigation into the missing women with the suggestion that it might be related to his disappearance. I didn't tell them about the Welcome Centre for fear of causing the Centre unwarranted grief, if the link was as innocuous as the women thought. The two cops were no more forthcoming on their thoughts about Eric and my theories than they were about the missing women.

At one point a nondescript man in a crumpled suit carrying an aura of authority opened the door and asked the bald interviewer to come outside. "Yes sir, Inspector Green," he said and hastened away.

A short while later I was released with the proviso that I must make myself available should they need to question me further. It was another hour before they let Teht'aa go, I later learned, because of her previous convictions for drug possession and aiding and abetting a jailbreak.

Behind her she dragged a wheeled black leather suitcase. "Dad's," she said. "Let's get the hell out of here. I can't stand the stink of pigs."

"Shshhh," I whispered, glancing frantically around

the lobby to see if anyone had overheard. By the time I turned my attention back to her, she was out the door. I scooted after.

CHAPTER
THIRTY-SIX

The cops might have brought us to the station in their government-issue limousine, but they weren't about to take us back to where Eric's Jeep was parked. That left Teht'aa and me to find our way in a city neither of us knew well. Before I'd had a chance to ask anyone about finding a cab, Teht'aa had charged out the door. I had no choice but to race after her. It took me two blocks of running to catch up. Propelled more by her outrage than any sense of direction, she'd headed along a street bordered by a raised highway, which I realized with a sinking feeling was the Queensway, a major highway that cuts through the middle of town.

"Slow down, Teht'aa," I shouted between gasps. "You're going in the wrong direction."

"I don't give a fuck," she flung back without a backward glance and continued walking rapidly as Eric's wheeled suitcase bumped along the pavement behind her.

"Well, I do. I've got to rescue Sergei. Throw me the keys."

The dog had been alone in the car for a good six hours. Though he'd probably been sleeping the entire time, his bladder would be close to bursting and his stomach very empty. Fortunately, with the night's cooler temperatures and the partially open windows, the interior would have been comfortable enough for him.

She raced on, ignoring my request.

"Stop, Teht'aa. I need the keys. Otherwise Sergei's going to pee all over the back seat of your father's car."

When she didn't respond to my threat, I stopped trying to catch up to her. Her mind was clearly elsewhere.

Still, I tried one last time. "If you don't give me the keys, I'll have to break a window."

At that point an empty cab drove by. I waved frantically. It came to a halt beside Teht'aa, who completely ignored the black sedan and strode onwards. I ran up to it and jumped inside. Before racing off to find the Jeep, I asked him to slow down beside the angry woman. I powered the window down.

"Teht'aa, jump in," I called out.

Her head never wavered a fraction in my direction and her eyes remained fixed ahead. From the glassiness of her gaze, I wasn't sure if she was paying attention to where she was going. Unfortunately, we were approaching an intersection, and the light was red. I feared she wouldn't stop.

"Sound the horn," I asked the cab driver.

She jumped at the sudden noise, then as if suddenly realizing where she was, she stopped just as she was about to step off the curb. She turned a dazed look in my direction.

"Meg, is that you?" She shook her head almost as if she was trying to clear it. She glanced around. "Where are we?"

The light turned green. A driver behind us blasted his horn.

"Quick, jump in."

As I slid over to the far side, she slung her father's suitcase into the middle of the backseat, climbed in beside it and banged the door shut. The car behind us honked again. The cab driver took off.

"I'm so sorry, Meg. I was so mad, I just had to get out of there."

"I know, no need to apologize." I could understand her anger, if they'd treated her with the same thinly disguised racism they'd revealed to me. "You didn't happen to notice the name of the street where you parked the car, did you?"

She shook her head. "Nope, I just know it's a couple of blocks from that bar."

"I find for you, ladies, no problem." A flash of white lit up the cabbie's dark face. The spiralling notes of a Middle Eastern singer trilled from his radio.

The lights sped by as we drove along the almost empty streets of the downtown core. Other than the odd dedicated worker or curious tourist, the closed office towers and darkened stores served more to keep people away than attract them during the night hours. People only began to appear as we neared the Market, where the pubs and some of the restaurants were still bursting with noise and light. I stiffened at the sight of a number of motorcycles parked near the central Market building but relaxed once I realized the bikes were predominantly recreational.

The cabbie was right. It took him no time to find Eric's Jeep on one of the nearby residential streets. In fact, it was the only car parked on that side of the tree-shrouded road. Sergei barked as we drew alongside and shoved his nose out the narrow window opening. Leaving Teht'aa to pay the cabbie, I leapt out and hastily opened the door.

Not taking the time to greet me, he bounded past to the nearest object, a mum-filled planter guarding the bottom of the wood stairs of a refurbished nineteenth-century triplex. It took several minutes for him to drain his bladder. Finally he turned back to me and clung to my side for reassurance, moaning. I guiltily showered him with hugs and pats as I filled a bowl with water and one with kibble. But other than a quick slurp, he was too upset to eat, so we snuggled until he calmed down. Meanwhile, Teht'aa was getting impatient.

"Come on, Meg," she persisted. "Get him in the car, and let's get the hell out of here."

"But it's one in the morning. Don't you think we should find a motel somewhere and get some sleep before driving back to Migiskan?"

"No way. I've gotta get out of here. I can't stand another minute in this fuckin' town. You stay if you want."

This was hardly an option, since she had the car, but I wasn't about to let her drive a hundred and fifty kilometres on her own in the dark, particularly given her mood. In her present state, she would speed faster than usual and end up wrapping Eric's SUV around a tree. So after Sergei drank more water and ate a handful of kibble, I persuaded Teht'aa to let me drive while she kept Sergei company in the back seat. I was hoping his need for comfort might help settle her down.

And it did work, for she fell asleep, something I was doing my damnedest to avoid. But finally the dead silence of the car became too much for me, and after catching my eyes shutting one time too many, I tuned the radio to a station guaranteed to be playing loud rock and blasted it. So deep was Teht'aa's sleep that she promptly returned to it, after muttering "Where are we?"

She did fully awaken when I stopped at the twenty-four-hour Tim Hortons on the highway before the turnoff to Somerset. I'd reached the point where a stiff jolt of caffeine was the only thing that would keep me awake for the last fifty kilometres. While Sergei continued to sleep in the back seat of the Jeep, Teht'aa came in with me to use the washroom and get a couple of Timbits to go with her tea. I'd ordered two cream-filled chocolate donuts along with a splash of French vanilla in my coffee.

For the next several kilometres we maintained our separate reveries as we munched our sugary treats and quaffed the caffeine.

Finally Teht'aa spoke up. "I'm sorry, Meg, if I got a little carried away back there, but those cops made me so angry. They were accusing me of being a prostitute and kept insisting that J.P. was my pimp."

"Why on earth would they think that?" I asked. There'd been no similar accusation against me during my interrogation. I didn't know whether to feel shocked or insulted.

"Only one reason. They think all squaws are whores."

"I hope you threatened to go to the Human Rights Commission."

"Yeah, I guess you know me, don't you?" she chortled. "They kept saying that if I told them what I knew about the Black Devils, they wouldn't charge me with prostitution."

"Does this mean they think J.P.'s murder is linked to prostitution?"

"I don't know. But they certainly gave me the impression that the Black Devils are heavily involved in the sex trade. Apparently, they're linked to a couple of escort services in Ottawa and a massage parlour in Gatineau."

"Did they think J.P.'s death was related?"

"Didn't say. But, you know, Meg, I can't help thinking that J.P.'s murder is linked to his inquiries about Fleur."

"I know. I've been having the same thought. He must've learned something he wasn't supposed to. I sure hope it doesn't mean that Fleur has been coerced into being a prostitute."

"I hope not either, but better that than being dead," she replied succinctly.

"Yes, but if she's still alive, how much longer will she be, now that they've killed her uncle?"

Unable to provide an answer, she lapsed into silence as the dark miles passed in a blur of illuminated foliage and yawning black holes. A pair of tiny headlights flared and disappeared into the underbrush.

Finally she voiced what I'd been wondering myself. "Do you think we could be in danger?"

"I suppose. It depends on whether J.P. mentioned us to anyone."

I glanced out the rear window to double check for following headlights, something I'd been doing frequently since fleeing Ottawa. But since we'd turned off the main road onto the dirt road to Migiskan, only vacuous blackness filled the rearview mirror.

"Teht'aa, does *oiseau vert* or *green bird* mean anything to you?"

"No, it doesn't. Why?"

"They were the last words J.P. said, plus another word I couldn't quite make out. I'm convinced he was trying to tell me something."

"If he's referring to a real bird, I don't know of any green birds that live around here, but you're the bird expert."

"I only know of the ruby-throated hummingbird, which is a luminescent green, and I suppose you could call some of the warblers green, although their feathers tend to be more a yellowy olive colour than a true green."

At that point, my headlights lit up the fluorescent numbers on my mailbox. I slowed to turn into my road. "Do you want to go home or stay at my place?"

"I think I'd better get home in case there's any news or messages from Dad. Why don't you spend the night with me?"

Neither of us wanted to be alone.

Exhausted, I slept the sleep of the dead in Eric's guest bedroom with Sergei hunkered down beside me, which brought back a host of memories, except it wasn't Sergei who was sleeping beside me. Guns could've blazed around me, and I wouldn't have heard them. In the morning I awoke to Teht'aa shaking me.

"Wake up, Meg. You've got to see this. I found it in Dad's suitcase." She held what looked to be a small box of wooden matches in front of my face. There appeared to be something green on the cover. I pushed her hand back to get a better view.

A saucy-eyed parrot stared back at me. He was a magnificent metallic green, and beside him were printed the words, also in metallic green, "*Le Bar de l'Oiseau vert.*"

CHAPTER
THIRTY-SEVEN

Although the matchbox had no contact information for *Le Bar de l'Oiseau vert* printed on its cover, Teht'aa and I figured it could be readily found in the online phone directory. So without bothering with breakfast or even our morning coffee, we headed off to use the computer at the Migiskan Library, it being considerably closer than mine at Three Deer Point. But we were wrong. After failing to find the bar in Gatineau or even the province of Quebec, we tried Ottawa, then spread the search wider to Ontario. We even searched for "Green Bird Bar," but without success. So we googled it and again came up empty, although we did come across The Green Parrot Bar in Dubai and another in Kuala Lumpur. We figured they were too far away to be linked to J.P. and Eric.

Since the library was in the same block as the police station, we decided to head over and bring Will Decontie into the loop in the hope that he could bring more sophisticated resources into play. Unfortunately, he was away for the day, but Sarah Smith, the young cop who'd brought the unwelcome news about Becky's death to the

Grandmother Moon ceremony, was sitting at the duty desk pounding away on the keyboard.

Patrolman Smith jumped as Teht'aa approached her. "Whoops, sorry. I didn't hear you." She scrambled up. "Gosh, Teht'aa, I'm so sorry about your dad. The Chief's in Ottawa right now talking to the cops there about the case."

Teht'aa tensed with hope. "Have they found something?"

"I think they have a witness who might've seen your dad." Sarah bit her lower lip. "I ... ah ... I'm not sure if I'm supposed to tell you this."

"Do you know who it is or where they saw him?"

Sarah shook her head. "I don't really know anything other than the Chief drove to the Ottawa early this morning to talk to the guy."

"Do you know where in Ottawa?"

"I'm sorry, Teht'aa, I wish I could help you, but I know as much as you do right now."

As if she hadn't heard the entreaty in Sarah's voice, Teht'aa persisted. "Do you at least know if the guy saw him recently?"

The young cop glanced at me helplessly.

I interjected, "Teht'aa, I know you're as anxious as I am to find your father alive and safe, but we'll have to wait for Will before we can learn more. Meanwhile, maybe Sarah can help us in locating this bar."

I told the young policewoman about J.P.'s dying words and the matchbox found in Eric's suitcase. "Although I've suspected there was a link between Fleur's disappearance and Eric's, I think this common reference to the Green Bird proves it. I'm hoping if we follow this lead, we'll find both of them."

Sarah shrugged. "Makes sense to me. But what do you want me to do? The Chief wants me to follow up on the outstanding fines file today."

"We've had no luck searching the Internet, but maybe you have other resources you can check?"

"I don't know. I'm not sure."

"Teht'aa, did you bring the matchbox with you? Maybe someone will recognize the parrot logo."

Sarah scanned the small box carefully. "He's kinda cute, isn't he? I suppose I could fax a copy of this to other police stations." Then she peered at the box cover again. "You know, sometimes bars in hotels aren't listed separately in the telephone directory. Maybe this bar is in a hotel?"

Teht'aa and I exchanged hopeful glances.

"I think you might be onto something, Sarah," I replied. "It could also be in a private club or other type of social establishment. I would think the local police in any town would pretty well know the names of all the bars and lounges in their area. So why don't you send it out?"

She walked over to the copier and placed the box cover-down on the glass. As the machine whirred, she said, "I'll check the online police files for any reference to *Le Bar de l'Oiseau vert*. Could be it figured in another case."

"Sounds good to me. Do whatever you can to locate this bar. I'm convinced it's tied into Eric and Fleur's disappearance."

As Sarah passed the matchbox back to Teht'aa, she studied the copy. "You know, I could swear I've seen that bird before."

"Where?" Teht'aa snapped.

263

"That's what I'm trying to remember. I don't know whether it was tied into another case or not. But he sure looks familiar. Except I don't think he was on a matchbox. It was something else, larger ... and I think it was from around here." She tugged at her Kevlar vest. "Sorry."

"Maybe you could ask around the community to see if anyone recognizes it?"

"Yeah, I suppose ... after I send this out." She glanced at the outstanding fines file she'd been working on.

"Please, Sarah, the information could save a life, two lives. Please give it your top priority."

"Yeah, sure, of course. I want Chief Eric and Fleur to be found as much as you do."

"Great, thanks. And I'm sure the Chief will forgive you for not working on the outstanding fines."

She smiled. "Yeah, you're right. It's just tough knowing where to put your effort. I'll let you know if anyone gets back to me. But this might take awhile, so please don't expect an answer today, okay?"

We left her writing out a message for the other police forces and headed back onto the main street of Migiskan. A brisk wind was pushing low clouds across the sky, promising rain at any moment. Neither Teht'aa nor I were wearing rain jackets, but that didn't prevent us from asking anyone we passed on our walk back to Eric's bungalow if they recognized the saucy green parrot on the matchbox. All commiserated with Teht'aa on the disappearance of her father, but none recognized the bird or the name of the bar.

Drops began to fall. We continued asking but to no avail, until we ran into a neighbour of Eric's. By then we were drenched.

"Yeah, sure I remember that crazy bird," Al said between puffs on the cigarette dangling out of the corner of his mouth. Although not dressed for rain either, he didn't seem to mind being soaked. "I seen it on a beer glass."

"Where? Was it here on the rez?" Teht'aa asked.

"Yeah, it was. I'm pretty sure it was in your daddy's house." He blew out a stream of smoke.

CHAPTER
THIRTY-EIGHT

"How stupid can I be." Teht'aa stomped up the wooden stairs of her father's house, shaking her head. "Of course, he has those damn beer glasses with the stupid parrot on them. I've drunk out of them a hundred times."

She flung open the ochre door, almost tearing it off the hinges, and squelched through the living room to the kitchen, leaving a trail of muddy tracks behind her. Even though Eric wasn't exactly a paragon of neatness, I knew he valued his pine flooring, so I left my wet shoes at the door.

I was trying to remember the glasses but couldn't. He must've obtained them after we'd gone our separate ways.

She slapped four tall, slender glasses onto the counter, followed by two more. Each had a perfect rendition of the matchbox parrot painted in emerald green at the top of the glass. It was bordered on either side by a thin line encircling the rim of the glass. But that was all. The words *Le Bar de l'Oiseau vert* or even *Green Bird* or *Parrot Bar* didn't appear anywhere on the glass.

"I don't think I've seen these before," I said. "Where did he get them?"

"That's just it. I don't remember."

Damn. "Do you know how long he's had them?"

"Sometime last fall. I think he brought them back from a fishing trip."

She brushed a soggy strand of hair from her face. I could feel my own drenched curls plastered against my head, and drops dribbling down my face. I grabbed a dishtowel.

"Do you now where he went?"

"Nope. I don't think I ever knew the name. It was some stupid fishing camp way the hell up north that he'd gone to for a week's fishing." She paced back and forth over the tiled kitchen floor, while I dried myself as best I could. "Damn, I should've asked him, but I was so ticked off that he'd taken off without telling me, I ignored him."

"Do you know if anyone went with him? We could ask them."

"I don't know. If so, it wasn't anyone from the rez."

"Maybe his office will know."

Her onyx eyes gleamed with hope. "I'll call Jill at the band office."

However, after a brief conversation, she slammed the phone back down. "Nope, she doesn't know. She just remembers him being away fishing. Apparently, he brought her back a nice lake trout, which was more than he did for us. I guess he felt we needed the glasses more than we needed fish."

"He might've told Will. We'll get Sarah to have him call us from Ottawa. I don't think we should wait until he gets home."

"I agree. I'll call her after I get out of these wet clothes. You should change too. I have some old sweats that should fit you."

Yeah, ones that had probably bagged well beyond their original slim shape. No thanks. "I'm fine. These pants are synthetic, so they'll dry quickly."

I removed my wet fleece jacket and hung it over the back of a kitchen chair. Underneath, my light wool top was barely damp.

"Help yourself to coffee and toast or whatever you want for breakfast," she called from the back of the house.

I glanced at Eric's espresso machine and thought a latte would be just the thing to warm us both up. While I waited for the machine to power up, I decided to call Sarah myself. There was no point in waiting for Teht'aa to finish changing.

"I'm glad you called," Sarah answered breathlessly, as if she'd been running to get the phone. "I was about to call you. I've remembered where I've seen that parrot. It was on some glasses."

"We know about the glasses. They belong to Eric. Unfortunately, Teht'aa doesn't know where he got them from. That's why I'm calling. We're hoping Will might know."

"But I didn't see the parrot glasses at Chief Eric's house."

"Oh, there's another set? Where?"

"I saw them a couple of months ago, when I was over at Wendy's place for one of her Mary Kay evenings. You know, she's become one of their sales reps."

Yes, I knew. I had several pink tubes of anti-aging moisturizer and the like sitting unopened in my bathroom cabinet. "Great. Do you know where she got them from?"

"Not yet. Her phone's on the fritz, so I was going to drive over there shortly."

Forget the latte. "Teht'aa and I will meet you there."

I hung up before she had a chance to say we couldn't.

ooo

We splashed into the Whiteducks' puddle-filled driveway just as the Migiskan First Nations Police Department SUV was turning onto their road. Teht'aa parked Eric's Jeep beside a snowmobile with the track missing. Rain slithered over a couple of overturned canoes and drummed a staccato on the aluminum motorboat sitting on a trailer.

Wendy bounced out of her side door, a broad smile creasing her pudgy cheeks. "Hi. Great to see you guys. What brings you here?"

The smile vanished when she saw the police vehicle coming to a stop behind us. "Oh, no. Has something happened to George?"

"No, no," I hastily interjected. "It's a completely different matter. I'll let Sarah tell you about it."

The smile returned, but not showing the confidence with which she had welcomed us. "Why don't you come in for some coffee then? I have some freshly made bannock."

We traipsed into Wendy's storey-and-half house, still a work in progress. While the front of the building was completely covered in dove-grey aluminum siding, the sidewall facing the drive had only been partially finished. Above the metre or so of siding, weathered plywood peeked through gaps in the protective covering.

More effort had been made to finish the interior. Wendy led us into a rambling country kitchen, complete with pristine white melamine cupboards, faux marble counter tops, and steel appliances, gleaming with recent polishing. My mouth watered at the sight and aroma of the bannock cooling on the counter.

The three of us sat around the birch table while Wendy poured each of us a mug of coffee. Not exactly latte, but very tasty all the same.

After a few minutes of chatting about Wendy's winnings at last night's bingo game, Teht'aa and I encouraged the young policewoman to begin her questioning.

"Mrs. Whiteduck, I believe you have some beer glasses with a green parrot on them."

As Wendy squeezed her eyes in bewilderment, Teht'aa set the one she'd brought with us on the table in front of the chunky woman.

"Oh, those. Yeah, we have a couple like that." She picked up the glass and ran her finger over the parrot. "Kinda cute, ain't he?" She got up to retrieve two from a cupboard and set them beside Eric's. They were an exact match, except for a nick in the rim of one of hers.

"Do you know where you got them from?" Sarah continued.

"I think George brought them home." Wendy cast the cop an anxious look. "He didn't steal them, did he?"

Sarah laughed. "Maybe he did, but I don't care. We believe they came from a bar your husband might have frequented. There appears to be a link between this bar and the disappearance of Chief Eric and Fleur Lightbody. Unfortunately, we don't know where it is."

"Oh, such a terrible thing." Wendy turned her amber-eyed sympathy to Eric's daughter. "I'm so sorry, Teht'aa. Gloria told me about your dad last night. And you have no idea where he is?"

Teht'aa shook her head. "We're hoping this bar will lead us to him. We think the bar is in a fishing camp, but we don't know which one. Now I know George is a guide at a couple of remote camps. Is he around so we can ask him?"

"Oh, I'm afraid he's off on one of his trips. He took a client in a week ago to one of his secret lakes no one else knows about. A rich American, I think. They're the only ones that can afford the float plane charter."

"You wouldn't happen to know the names of the fishing camps or their locations?" Teht'aa asked.

"Oh, gosh. I'm really sorry. I don't know. I'm afraid I'm not very good with names. They kinda go in one ear and out the other. I just know they're way up north. He has to fly in."

"How many camps does he work at?" Sarah asked.

"Just the two of them, although he likes one better than the other. He doesn't like all the young girls at the one camp. He thinks more is going on than just fishing."

A dropped penny wouldn't have disturbed the tense silence that followed.

Sarah sat up straighter and pulled out her notebook. "Did George say what he thought was happening?"

"Well, you know … I guess it's mostly men that go there, rich men, and well … you know men…."

"So George thinks these women are being used for unlawful purposes?"

Wendy screwed up her eyes. "If you mean are they being screwed, whoops sorry, I mean being used for sex, yeah. George couldn't see any other reason for having so many pretty girls on staff. He also didn't like it that many were native."

More silence except for the scratching of Sarah's pen.

Wendy suddenly lifted her hand to her mouth. "Oh … my God … you don't mean that's where Fleur is?"

"And you're sure that you don't know the name of this camp or its location," Sarah asked.

When we had entered the kitchen, I'd noticed bits of paper stuck to the fridge door. Most were lists, but two were photographs. In one photo I'd recognized the verandah in front of which George and a beaming client were standing. The client was clutching a very large and obviously heavy fish.

I retrieved the photo from the fridge and placed it in the centre of the table. "Is this one of the camps George works at?"

She nodded. "He says it's a lovely old log building, probably over a hundred years old and has that terrific verandah." She glanced over at me. "Kind of like yours, eh?"

"That's what I thought when I first saw it in another photo." I turned to Sarah. "A woman at the Anishinabeg Welcome Centre in Ottawa had a photo with this same verandah. She should be able to tell us where this camp is. Only problem is she's away from work at the moment. But you could probably get a hold of her or have the Ottawa police do it."

"Yeah, I'll call the Chief the minute I get back to the station. Wendy, is this the camp where the girls are?"

"I dunno. It might be."

While we talked, Teht'aa brought the photo closer and was leaning over it, peering intently. "Is that what I think it is?"

She pointed to a greenish smudge half-hidden by one of the verandah pillars. There seemed to be something yellowish protruding from it. The more I stared at it, the more the smudge took shape. I could even make out the wooden bar it was sitting on.

I sat back. "Yup, you're right. It's a parrot, a very green parrot."

"I'd say so too," added Sarah. "It's got to be the place. Canadian woods aren't exactly filled with parrots. Can I take this photo, Wendy?"

Before Wendy nodded, she'd already slipped it into her notebook. "We need to speak to George. Can he be reached?"

"He'll have his satellite phone with him. But I don't think he'll have it on. It's too expensive. He only turns it on when he has to make a call. But he's supposed to be back tonight. You can talk to him then."

I had a better idea. "Give me the name of the charter airline he uses to fly into the fishing camp. They can tell us its location."

She shook her head. "He uses the camp's plane to get there."

CHAPTER
THIRTY-NINE

After Wendy promised to contact the policewoman as soon as she heard from her husband, we three went our separate ways. Sarah returned to the police station to follow up with her chief while Teht'aa drove me back to Eric's to pick up Sergei and then on to my house, where she left me to my own devices.

We both felt there was nothing more that could be done until the fishing guide provided the name and location of the camp and Will was fully in the loop. We were confident that once the police chief knew its location, a contingent of police would be flown in to investigate, and if our suspicions proved correct, rescue Eric and Fleur, hopefully both very much alive.

But we hadn't counted on the slow machinations of the law and on Marie-Claude.

She arrived at my front door not long after Teht'aa dropped me off. I was rocking back and forth in the screened porch with Sergei fast asleep at my feet. While the rain had stopped, it continued to drip from the trees. I was sipping another mug of coffee while trying to decide how best to distract myself to keep from being overwhelmed by my worry over Eric, when I heard a car crunch to a stop in front of the house. I knew the minute I saw the tears streaking down her face that Marie-Claude had been told about her brother's death. I also noticed that the right side of her face was puffy with the beginnings of a bruise.

"He's dead," she cried out. "My little brother is dead."

"I know. I found him. I'm so sorry." The Lightbodys' van, not her Honda Civic, was parked behind my truck. Normally her husband wouldn't let her drive the bigger vehicle.

I tried to explain how I'd come to find him, but the distressed woman was too upset to listen.

"What am I going to do?" she wailed. "First Fleur and now J.P. Who else will die because of me?"

"You don't know that Fleur is dead. And you had nothing to do with J.P.'s death."

"But I did. I told him to find Fleur. And Fleur might as well be dead, given what she is going through."

Uh-oh. J.P. must've told her.

"Come inside. I'll get you some coffee," I said, wishing I had bought some vodka in Somerset. She needed it. "By the way, where's your car?"

"Jeff took away the keys. But I knew where he kept a duplicate set for the van. Besides, I've left him."

A double uh-oh.

"He said if Fleur has become *une putain*, he wasn't going to let her back in his house."

Marie-Claude's hands were trembling so much, I had to carry her mug outside to the porch. I wasn't sure how she was going to get it up to her mouth without spilling half the steaming liquid onto herself, but there wasn't much I could do short of holding the mug for her. I didn't think she'd want me to do that. But she surprised me and only dribbled a small amount onto her crumpled blouse.

I waited for her to settle down before asking my questions. Sergei, recognizing her pain, placed his muzzle on her lap. Patting him seemed to calm her.

Finally I asked, "What did J.P. tell you about your daughter?"

"He said Fleur had been taken by some men he knew."

"Were they members of his biker gang?"

"I don't know if they were *Les Diables Noirs*. He just called them other bikers. He was really mad at them. Said he was going to kill them once he rescued Fleur."

"Did he mention where Fleur had been taken?"

"No, just that it was some place far away. A place that can only be reached by plane. He called it … he called it *un bordel*. I think it is brothel in English. He said Fleur had been forced to be *une putain* for rich men …" Her voice faded to a whisper as her tears overflowed.

I waited for her to quiet down before asking, "Did he mention the words *oiseau vert* in connection with this brothel?"

"*Non*, no I don't think so. What does a green bird have to do with this place?"

I told her about our suspicions of a remote fishing camp with a bar by that name and finished by saying, "We think this might be where Fleur has also been taken."

She grabbed my hands. "Oh *mon dieu*, you give me hope she will be saved."

"Did your brother mention anything else?"

"I thought I heard him say she was *une esclave*. But when I asked him what he meant, he told me I hadn't heard right. But I'm sure he said *une esclave*. What do you think it means?"

Esclave. Yes, that could be the other word I'd heard on his dying breath. "He probably meant that Fleur is being held as a slave against her will."

"*Mon dieu, ma pauvre petite chérie*. What are they doing to you?" She buried her face in her hands.

Rubbing my hand up and down her shaking back, I tried to give her as much reassurance as I could, not entirely believing it myself. "I'm sure she's okay. It's probably just an expression your brother was using."

After a few minutes, she sat up. Brushing the tears from her face, she said, "I was so upset, I told Jeff. I thought he would get angry and call the police. I did not think …" She stopped talking as emotion overwhelmed her once again.

I pulled her out of the chair and hugged her. For several long minutes she poured out her anguish onto my shoulder, while I mumbled comforting words.

Finally, she raised her head and stepped back. "He said she was no longer his daughter. He called her a dirty whore and said she can never come home again. How can he do this? He's her father."

His response so infuriated me, I spat out without thinking, "Because he's probably one those bastards that thinks they own us and can dictate who we can and can't have sex with. And when we're raped, they consider it our fault and disown us."

"But this *isn't* Fleur's fault. Surely he can understand that?"

"Is this why you're leaving him?"

"I don't know if I will ever see Fleur again, but if she is rescued from this *bordel*, this camp with *l'oiseau vert*, she will need me. For once I am going to be a mother, something I haven't been very good at."

"Don't even think that way. Of course you've been a good mother."

She smiled wanly. "*Cher amie*, you don't know how bad I've been."

Figuring she wasn't in the right frame of mind to be convinced otherwise, I said instead, "You're welcome to stay here until you find a place on your own."

"*Merci*, but my brother in Ottawa said he'd look after us."

"Us?"

"Yes, Neige and Moineau. I'm going to pick them up after school."

Her husband was going to be one very angry man. "Where is Jeff now?"

"At work. He doesn't know I've left."

"I'm wondering if you shouldn't pick up the girls now, in case he does find out. He might prevent you from taking them."

"But he can't. I won't let him." She stared at me in horror. "They are my girls. I would never leave them alone with him."

"Why don't I go with you?"

She touched the redness of her face. "Sometimes he gets angry. But it's not his fault. I've usually done something wrong."

"Marie-Claude, you haven't done anything wrong. You have every right to leave him. Does he hit the girls too?"

She raised startled eyes to me then dropped them again. "But only when we've done something wrong. He's so forgiving and loving afterwards."

This endless cycle of abuse and paternalistic love was sounding far too familiar. I'd been there myself, before I'd been jolted into leaving Gareth. It might also help explain the wariness I'd seen in the two older girls' eyes.

"Let's go now. We'll take my truck, in case he spots the van. Better yet, why don't I go alone and get the girls. You can write a note to the principal giving me permission to take them out of school."

Ten minutes later, I was heading down my drive with Marie-Claude's note in hand, praying that her resolve wouldn't leave her. The principal didn't hesitate in accepting the note, although both girls eyed me curiously as they approached me in the school hallway. I felt it best that their mother explain what was happening. I only told them that something had come up and that they would be joining their mother at my place.

Neither made any comment. Neige only asked if it was about Fleur, to which I could honestly respond, "Yes."

Perhaps the two girls had guessed, for they both ran into their mother's arms and hugged her longer than a casual greeting would warrant. I gave Marie-Claude several minutes alone with her daughters then interrupted. "I think you should go now."

Moineau stepped back, her lips firm with determination. "Yes, maman. We should go. Papa might come and stop us." She certainly had the measure of her father.

We were filing out my front door when Marie-Claude's blue car slid to a stop behind the van.

Jeff, his face twisted in rage, jumped out and yelled, "Get in the car!"

I shoved the three of them back into my house and closed the door. "Lock it," I ordered, then turned to Jeff. "They aren't going with you."

I stood in front of the door with Sergei standing threateningly beside me.

"Who the hell do you think you are? Stay out of my affairs!" He walked towards me, fists balled. Sergei growled.

Behind me I could hear Moineau pleading with her mother not to open the door.

"If you come any nearer, I'm going to call the police."

I pretended I had a cell phone in my pocket. I was hoping that in his fury he would lose sight of the fact that we had no cell coverage in the area.

"It'll take them an hour to get here. By then we're gone," he spat out.

He continued advancing towards the stairs as Sergei's low guttural growl turned to a snarl. My dog might be a coward at heart, but he sure could put on a good act.

"Maybe, but I can destroy your standing in the band, and you would lose your cushy job. You know what Eric thinks about wife and kid beaters. In fact, I bet you're the reason Fleur left home."

The second the guilt flashed over his face, I knew I'd hit the bullseye. That bastard! He'd let his wife think she was to blame.

"So what," he yelled back. "I can get another job else-where."

"Not with another First Nations community. And without a reference from Eric, I doubt you'd get a decent job anywhere else."

"Marie-Claude," he shouted. "It's okay. I forgive you. Just come home with me and the girls, and everything will be fine. I'll let Fleur come back home."

I tensed, expecting to hear the door open and see Marie-Claude rush out into his deceitful arms, her tears filled with apologies for causing so much trouble. But she didn't. There was only silence.

Jeff tried again and again, becoming smarmier each time, but the door remained firmly closed.

Finally he spat on the ground. "Okay, if this is how you want it, don't expect a cent from me. And if you take that van, I'm going to have you charged with stealing."

He stomped back to the Civic, slammed the door shut and sped back down the road, swerving from side to side. I hoped he'd slam into a tree.

After the sound of the car faded, I let out a deep sigh. The door opened behind me, and the three came crowding out onto the verandah. We held each other in a long, tearful collective hug.

Finally I extricated myself. "I don't think we should hang around here any longer. I don't trust him. I'll drive you into town."

"There's no need to," Marie-Claude said, wiping the tears from her face. Some of the tension had gone. She seemed more at peace than she'd been in a very long while. "My brother's coming to get us. Moineau called."

"I'd just as soon not wait the two hours. How about we meet him in Somerset?"

A smiling Moineau rushed back inside to call, while Neige remained glued to her mother's side. She seemed less certain about this sudden change in her life.

"I'm also going to get the Migiskan police to come and pick up the van. I don't want him accusing me of theft."

Although her lower lip quivered ever so slightly, she smiled. "*Merci, merci beaucoup* for your strength. I couldn't have done it without you."

CHAPTER
FORTY

That bastard! When I called the Migiskan police station to have them remove the Lightbody van from my driveway, I discovered that he'd already reported it stolen. He was counting on his fleeing family being stopped by the police and returned to him. I fully expected him to come zooming up behind us and bouncing my bumper to stop us, but thankfully, if he was following us, he remained out of sight. Unless, of course, he was waiting in Somerset, which was why we'd agreed to meet Marie-Claude's brother at an abandoned drive-in cinema on the outskirts of town. A good distance off the main road, it wouldn't require either of us to travel through the middle of town and risk being seen.

Thankfully, her brother was waiting for us by the time we arrived. It had been a tense drive, and although I could feel Marie-Claude desperately trying to bolster her courage, it was slipping away as the miles ticked by. From the moment the professor climbed out of his ancient BMW and embraced his sister and nieces, I could tell he fully supported her decision. Thank God. Worried Jeff might still track us down, we spent little time in exchanging words, other than offers of thanks and encouragement.

I did, however, suggest they consider hiding out at a shelter until Jeff's fury had abated, since he probably knew where Richard lived. While Marie-Claude seemed reluctant, I could see the suggestion resonate with her brother. Another person who wasn't fooled by his brother-in-law's outwardly respectful demeanour.

As I was about to climb back into my truck, Marie-Claude called out and came running back to me.

"I am so busy thinking about my own problems, I forget *ma cher* Fleur," she said, gripping my hands. "Please save her. Now that my dear brother J.P. can no longer help, you are my only hope."

"Don't worry. The Migiskan police are working on it. Once they pinpoint the location of this fishing camp, they'll launch a rescue. By this time tomorrow, she'll be safely with you," I said, crossing my fingers and praying it would be true and that Eric would also be found alive and well at the camp.

"How I wish this will happen. But sadly, I see that Will has no power. The Sûrété du Quebec, like the Ottawa police, will do nothing. No, you must find this place yourself and rescue her."

"You're wrong. I hate to say it, but your brother's murder will force the police to ramp up their search for Fleur. After all, he was probably killed for what he'd learned about her."

"You are so trusting, *ma cher amie*. J.P. was *Les Diables Noirs*, one of the toughest gangs in Quebec. They are involved in many criminal activities. The police will see his death as one less gang member and will do nothing about finding his killer."

"You'll be in Ottawa shortly," I persisted. "Go to the police station and tell them what J.P. told you. Surely that will force them to do something. In fact, Will Decontie is there right now working with them on Eric's disappearance. Speak to him and the police involved in Eric's case. I'm convinced his disappearance is tied in with Fleur's."

By this time, Richard had come up behind her and had been listening to our conversation for the past several minutes.

"I think this is a very good idea," he said in French. Although taller than his sister and with darker hair, he had the family's pale blue eyes and slim build. "And you can file a restraining order against your husband at the same time."

The haunted look in her eyes returned. "Oh, I couldn't do that. He would be very angry with me." Her eyes began to tear. "If only *ma petite* Fleur hadn't gone looking for a job, she would be here safe with me."

I started. "What do you mean?"

"J.P. said that a place where she went to looking for a job put her in this danger."

"Did he tell you where or what this job was?"

"I didn't ask him. I thought it didn't matter. He said he was going to rescue her, and I believed him. And now he can't." More tears fell. "That's why, Meg, you have to do it. I have no one else."

"Please, *ma petit soeur*, do not worry," her brother said. "The police will find her. I will speak to them personally when we arrive in Ottawa." He nodded at me then pulled her gently around. "Now we must leave."

With her head against his chest, his arm around her shoulder, they walked back to his car, from which her daughters peered worriedly out the back window.

A knot tightened in my stomach as I watched their car turn onto the empty road and disappear from view. I was worried the terrified woman would lose her resolve and go back to her husband. And I was beginning to worry that she was right. That despite her brother's efforts or Will Decontie's, the Ottawa police and the SQ would do little about rescuing her daughter or Eric, for that matter, even though they supposedly had made his case a priority.

But what could I do? I could hardly commandeer a plane and rescue them myself.

However, before I got too wound up, I decided I should check with Sarah. Hopefully luck was with us and Will had managed to mount a rescue.

Unfortunately, when I reached the policewoman on a payphone at a gas station, I learned that the rescue would be delayed by at least a day. George had notified the charter plane company to delay pick-up until tomorrow. His client was enjoying himself too much. Wendy had only found this out when the plane company called her to let her know the change in plans. When she'd tried to call her husband on his satellite phone, he'd already turned it off.

"But the charter company knows the location of the lake where George is. Why don't you send a plane in to ask him about the fishing camp?" I asked.

"I don't think we can do that. It's outside our jurisdiction, besides the Chief says he's not convinced Chief Eric is at this fishing camp."

"What about the matchbox found in his luggage?"

"The Chief figures Chief Eric picked it up at the same time he got the beer glasses."

Possibly, but ... "What about the fact Marie-Claude's brother mentioned this same bar in his dying breath? Surely that counts for something."

"Yeah, but it doesn't place Chief Eric there. Besides the Chief says the Ottawa police are following up on other leads."

"What about Fleur? Her uncle places her there."

"How do you know that?"

"He told his sister before he died. Called the camp a brothel, which is hardly legal. Surely that's enough evidence to launch a rescue."

"I'll pass it onto the Chief. I'm afraid I've got to go now. There's been B&E at the Rec Centre."

"Do you have a number I can reach Will at?"

"He's on his way home. You can try his cell."

After hastily scribbling down the number on a corner of a page from the phone book, I scrounged through my wallet for more change, but not finding any, had to run across to the gas station to get some. When I finally managed to place the call, I heard his voice mail instead. Figuring there was no point in leaving a message, I tried the number again without success.

I reached him on the third try.

"Look, Sarah, can't it wait until I get back to the station?" He sounded exasperated. I could hear wind blowing through an open window with the sound of a car passing by.

"Will, it's me, Meg."

"Sorry." He chuckled. "I'm afraid this is the first time my young gal has been manning the office on her own, and she's a bit nervous. What can I do for you?"

"I gather from Sarah that you don't think Eric's at that Green Parrot fishing camp."

"To tell you the truth, Meg, I have no idea whether he is or not. Just the matchbox isn't sufficient evidence to place him there. Besides, the Ottawa police have a couple of much stronger leads they are pursuing."

"Like what?"

"Now you know, Meg, I can't discuss an ongoing investigation with you."

"Come on, Will. You know how much Eric means to me. I have to know you guys are doing all you can to find him."

"You can be assured that we are."

"Good. Did Sarah tell you that before he died, Marie-Claude's brother told his sister that her daughter was being held at the camp as a prostitute?"

"She just told me."

"Isn't that sufficient evidence to fly into the camp and check it out?"

"I'm afraid we just can't go on the word of a known felon. We need more hard evidence from more reputable sources. Besides, we don't know if it's the same place."

"Oh, come on, Will. How many remote locations can there be with green birds?"

"Look, I want to find Eric and Fleur as much as you do, but to mount a proper investigation takes time and money."

"Christ, you're sounding like a bureaucrat."

"Look, my hands are tied. If it were up to me, I'd send a plane in now, but it's not. The SQ is the only police force with the authority to fly into that camp, and they need considerably more solid information before they are prepared to commit their men and their resources. Mounting a plane operation isn't cheap."

"What do they need to know?"

"Now, Meg, I don't want you running around half cocked, trying to collect more information. It could be dangerous. The Ottawa police think there might be a link between the shooting death of the woman who went over the bridge in her car and Marie-Claude's brother-in-law."

"Why do they say that?"

"Sorry, I can't tell you, but lets just say the Black Devils appear to be involved in both cases."

"Didn't I hear mention of witnesses seeing motorcycles speeding away from the accident? Were they identified as Black Devils?"

"Now, Meg, I can't say any more."

At that point the pay phone operator asked me to insert more money. Deciding that if the police were going to be cash conscious, I would be too, I hung up.

Marie-Claude was right. We couldn't count on the police.

CHAPTER
FORTY-ONE

It was well past lunchtime, and I was starving, so I headed off to a traditional Quebec cafe on Somerset's only main street, where I devoured a *croque monsieur*, merely a fancy name for a grilled ham and cheese sandwich, and *poutine*, Quebec's answer to a calorie bomb, French fries smothered in gravy and cheese curds. I was hoping this bit of sustenance would help me figure out what to do next.

Even though the police chief thought it likely Eric had picked up the matches during his earlier visit, I wasn't convinced. Sure, he could've left them accidentally in his suitcase, but given his recent travels, I thought it likely he would've found and removed them. No, I believed that he'd come across the matchbox elsewhere, and recognizing the green parrot logo, he'd figured out its origin. Because it was significant, he'd kept them. Since Eric wasn't a smoker, there was no other reason for keeping the matches. I figured the matchbox had to be related to his investigation into the missing women. He'd told Mary that he'd uncovered something disturbing but needed more evidence before making his findings public. And then he'd disappeared.

With J.P. confirming that Fleur had been taken away to a remote brothel with this strange *oiseau vert*, I could only conclude that Eric had uncovered this same nasty business. He must have come across the matchbox during his investigation, and having recognized it, he knew where the girls were being taken. Someone had realized this and set about to have him silenced. But did they kidnap him ... or kill him?

I couldn't bear the thought of Eric gone forever, so I had to believe that he was still alive. In fact, I was convinced he was. We'd been so close. Surely I would feel an emptiness if he were dead, but I didn't. But I was terrified that his time was running out. Eric would be a liability to the criminals behind the trafficking. If the police delayed much longer, they might very well find him dead.

In my mind, the most likely place to hold him was this isolated fishing camp accessible only by plane. It was supposed to lie somewhere in the vast empty forests of northern Quebec, hundreds of kilometres from any habitations, which would make escaping alive all but impossible.

But how to convince Will Decontie of this?

He said he needed evidence, concrete, irrefutable evidence. But how could I obtain that short of flying into the camp myself? I wasn't about to do that, even if I did know its location. For one, I didn't know how to fly, nor did I have access to a plane, and for another it would be pure madness to try to mount my own rescue operation.

I supposed I could pretend to be a client and do some sniffing around while I was meant to be fishing and hope I would come across Fleur or Eric or both. But since I imagined the clientele was mostly male, my solitary female presence would be suspect. Moreover, this could take time to arrange, and time was what I believed Eric didn't have.

On the other hand I didn't believe Fleur's life was threatened, unless of course she did something to get her captors angry like trying to escape or refusing to service the men she was required to. Still, Becky had been killed, as were four others. But I didn't know if their deaths were linked to the prostitution ring Fleur was trapped in. They had, after all, been killed not far from where they'd gone missing and not hundreds of miles away at the camp of the green parrot.

And where did the biker connection come in? I couldn't see a biker gang running a fishing camp-cum-brothel, but I could see them being behind the trafficking of the women. And Eric had noted a Black Devils connection to some of the missing women. Fleur had also been seen with a gang member. Still, if the Black Devils were in the business, one would think that J.P. would've been aware of it. Unless it was a secret operation run by only a few members, one the broader membership didn't know about. But J.P. had found out and paid the price.

Will said that Claire's murder was also linked to bikers and to J.P.'s killing. But where did she fit in? She'd told the police that she'd seen Fleur with Becky. In fact, she was probably the last person to see both girls before they disappeared. Had she seen something she shouldn't have? After Becky's body was found, had she begun to suspect someone and asked one question too many?

I found it curious that all these missing girls were estranged from their families. It was if they had not been randomly snatched, but rather had been specifically targeted by a perpetrator who knew their absence wouldn't be noticed. It suggested maybe they had been followed, even wooed by someone who already knew their history. Hadn't I read somewhere that human traffickers often used a job as the incentive to lure unsuspecting young women into their trap?

And Fleur *had* gone in search of a job. In fact, J.P. had said this search had led to her entrapment. Perhaps I *could* find the evidence Decontie needed to convince the SQ to fly into the fishing camp. I knew of three places where the young woman had gone looking for a job: the Welcome Centre, the Dreamcatcher Bistro, and the Black Orchid Spa.

I also knew that most of the missing women, except Fleur, had at one time been clients of the Welcome Centre, which had worried Eric. But surely an organization that was in the business of helping its own people wouldn't be instrumental in causing them harm. But they would've kept detailed family histories of their clients. Either someone outside the organization could be illegally accessing its files or someone from within had turned on his or her own people.

It looked as if I should return to these establishments to see what more I could learn. Although I hadn't seen anything to spark my suspicions on my first visits, now that I knew what I was looking for, I could follow up with more discerning questions and a more critical eye. But I wouldn't do this on my own.

I found some more change, went to another pay phone, and called Teht'aa, who promptly agreed to join me at the cafe. She would also bring Eric's files, along with photos of each of the women.

My plan was to try to determine if any of these women had gone to the spa or the restaurant, either in search of a job or as a client, and if so, whether we could home in on one place where the majority had gone. I was also hoping we could link their visit back to a specific person or leak of information at the Welcome Centre.

I felt there was no point in going back to the Centre itself. I'd already spoken to a number of people, all of whom knew some, if not most of the missing women, and who would have had access to their client information. None of them had acted particularly suspicious to me, although I'd only been asking about Fleur, unless Paulette's possession of the photo of the camp with the green parrot made her a likely suspect. Besides, if one of them were indeed guilty in providing information to the traffickers, I wouldn't want to tip them off to my suspicions. And if the Black Devils were behind it, it put Teht'aa and myself in danger.

CHAPTER
FORTY-TWO

Worried we were running out of time, Teht'aa and I decided to split up. I would go to the Black Orchid Spa while she went to the Dreamcatcher Bistro. Since the owner at the restaurant had been more than open with me, I doubted she was involved in any kind of nefarious dealings. Still, she would probably be quite familiar with the native scene in Ottawa, so she might be able to pass on places frequented by native women that could be possible conduits for trafficking.

The spa, on the other hand, with its haughty receptionist who'd been less than helpful on my first visit, seemed a better candidate. I could see a job at a fancy spa easily attracting pretty young women, and once lured behind its locked glass doors, they could be spirited away elsewhere. I'd called the manager three times, and she had yet to return my call.

The minute Teht'aa arrived at the café with copies of the photos of the missing women, we took off in our separate vehicles. Our plan was to meet at O'Flaherty's at six to compare notes. On her way to Somerset, Teht'aa had dropped by Three Deer Point to feed Sergei and to let him outside to do his business. He should then be set for several more hours on his own, no doubt blissfully flopped out on his favourite chesterfield until I got home later in the evening.

With Eric's Jeep long since out of view, I reached the bridge into Ottawa in time to join the thick rush hour traffic. However, even though the pace was barely above a crawl, it did move, and within a short time I found myself searching for a parking spot close to the Black Orchid Spa. Fortunately, it was early for the ByWard Market's evening action, so I easily found a place on the same block as the spa.

Once again the elevator doors opened onto its sparkling white marble and glass lobby. Perched behind the glass counter on her chrome stool sat the same skinny, almost naked, receptionist under the stylized black orchid logo on the wall behind her. At the sight of me she wrinkled her nose, just as she'd done last time. Maybe Teht'aa should've come. This girl wouldn't have wrinkled her nose at her.

This time, however, I had much better luck in gaining access to the manager. A svelte yet big-breasted amazon was just breezing out of the elevator when I asked if I could speak with the manager. I knew when I saw the receptionist's eyes flicker to this imposing woman sheathed, like the receptionist, all in white, that she was the person I sought, so I introduced myself and held out my hand.

But rather than being cold and standoffish, as I had been led to expect, the woman was all apologies for not returning my call. Without hesitation she invited me into the inner sanctum. Though I was sorely tempted to stick out my tongue, I instead smiled broadly at the frowning receptionist as I floated through the glass doors.

She led me into a spacious glass-walled office. It too followed the all-white motif with white leather furniture, including a desk with a glass tabletop, white broadloom, and of course the white orchids, except for one, which was such a dark purple, it was almost black. Clearly business was good.

"Please, how can I help you?" She revealed a row of gleaming white teeth that had obviously been straightened, whitened, and polished to movie star effect.

"As I said in my message, I am looking for a missing young native woman by the name of Fleur Lightbody. I believe she might have come here in search of a job."

She tucked herself into the white desk chair, elegantly arranging her legs beneath it, and motioning me to sit down on the sofa. I hesitated for fear of dirtying the soft, buttery white leather with my less than pristine jeans, but she insisted.

"Yes, I remember her. Quite a pretty girl. She would've been an asset to my establishment, but I'd already hired a girl to fill the position."

"Can you remember when she came?"

"I believe it was in early July. I don't have the exact date, but I can look it up if you wish. I've already told all this to that man who came looking for her."

So Eric had been here too. "When did he come?"

"Shortly after I sent her away. I was quite surprised when he asked about her. I hadn't thought she was the type of girl who would associate with that sort of man."

"Sort? What do you mean by 'that sort'?"

"The kind who like it rough."

"I'm sorry, you've lost me."

"She was such a sweet thing, hardly the type to like the kind of brute that can be hard on women."

This was hardly a description one would ever give Eric. "Did he give you his name?"

"No, but he looked as if he belonged to a motorcycle club. The Black Devils, I think. When I saw him, I was just as glad I hadn't hired her. I can't have my girls associating with men like that. It could harm the reputation of my establishment."

Was he the so-called boyfriend? "Did he give any indication as to his relationship with Fleur?"

"I assumed he was her boyfriend. He thought she had gotten a job here and was surprised to find that she hadn't."

I didn't know how to interpret this. Had he really been her boyfriend, or was he checking her out as future merchandise? "Did anyone else come looking for the girl?"

"Yes, a couple of weeks later, an Eric somebody. I think he said he was her band chief."

"Was this about mid-July?"

"Yes, I think so."

"Did you tell him about the biker?"

"I can't remember." The woman paused. "Wait, I think I did."

This would've happened shortly before he disappeared. Had he gone in search of this Black Devil "boyfriend" and gone one step too far?

"I remember now. He seemed quite upset when I mentioned the biker," she said. "He asked me a number of questions about the man, but I couldn't tell him anything more than I've already told you."

Thus far I felt the woman had been open and honest with me. I didn't sense any underlying attempt to hide illicit activity. Nonetheless, I decided to show her the photos of the other missing women. "I am wondering if you have ever seen any of these women, either here at your spa or elsewhere in the Market. I'm helping the Anishinabeg Welcome Centre in trying to trace their last known steps, and the Market seems to be a common thread."

"The director must've sent you. Mary's one of my oldest clients."

I mumbled something without committing myself one way or the other and placed the photos of all sixteen women on her desktop. I included Fleur's to confirm she had actually met the girl.

She picked out her photo right away. "Such a pretty girl. I hope you find her."

She was either a very good actress or indeed had nothing to do with the prostitution ring. She glossed over most of the photos but did home in on four of them. Two she thought had come to the spa as clients, and one, the woman who'd been missing for five years, she'd actually hired six years ago but had fired her for pouring scalding water over a client. The fourth woman she remembered seeing at a nearby native craft store. In fact, this woman had served her when she was buying a bear-claw necklace for her boyfriend. Unfortunately, this was Sandy, the woman whose body had just been found, but I kept it to myself.

When we'd finished, she said, "You might want to check out Auntie's Place. I see a lot of aboriginal women going there. I might even have seen some of these women. Several of their faces do look familiar, but I'm not sure from where."

No one had mentioned this place. "Is it a cafe?"

"I believe it's a drop-in centre, a place for aboriginals living in Ottawa to hang out." She raised herself from her desk and began to walk towards the door. "I'm afraid I have an appointment. I hope I've been of some help to you."

"You have. Thanks for your time." I followed her out the door. "Do you know if this Auntie's Place is it associated with the Anishinabeg Welcome Centre?"

"I don't know. I believe a local minister runs it. An article appeared in the paper not long ago and mentioned that he started this drop-in centre to serve as a gathering place for natives who were having a difficult time dealing with urban living. I believe they also have a job placement program."

"Where is it?"

"A few doors down the street from me."

As she escorted me to the reception area, she said, "I remember seeing Fleur coming out of it not long after she came to see me."

As the elevator doors started to close between us, she added, "In fact, I believe I mentioned this to Eric when he asked me about other places in the Market that Fleur might've approached about a job."

CHAPTER
FORTY-THREE

With an hour to spare before I had to meet Teht'aa, I felt I had enough time to check out the drop-in centre. Auntie's Place was three doors down from the entrance to the spa. Even if I hadn't known it was a gathering place for aboriginals, I would've recognized it by the symbol above the name. The sign outside the Migiskan Recreation Centre used these same concentric circles with radiating straight lines to designate it as a meeting place for the community's teenagers.

I pushed my way through a group of smokers congregated at the entrance and headed up a narrow flight of stairs to the second floor. The stairwell's scuffed walls and worn steps foreshadowed the equally downtrodden room at the top. If it hadn't been for the vibrantly coloured native art on the dull grey walls, the dreary atmosphere of the room would've been enough to turn anyone's optimistic hopes into gloomy dejection. Several people lounged on mismatched chairs and sagging sofas that were haphazardly arranged along the walls. Some flipped through magazines while others chatted amongst themselves. In the corner stood a coffee machine, a cooler containing cans of pop, and a large box of picked-over donuts. I noticed a billboard on a nearby wall crammed with various announcements, much like the one I'd seen at the Welcome Centre. I even recognized several of the ads, including the flashy one offering a chance-of-a-lifetime modeling opportunity for young aboriginal women between the ages of sixteen and twenty-six.

Only a few people paid attention to me as I scanned the room for someone to speak to. Finally a young woman with an acne-scarred face and greasy hair pointed to an open door at the beginning of a hallway.

You could imagine my surprise when I encountered Doris, the receptionist from the Welcome Centre, her dreamcatcher earrings fluttering, sitting at a desk sorting mail. She was equally startled to see me, and I thought, none too happy.

"Is this place connected to the Welcome Centre?" I asked.

"Nope. I'm a volunteer. What are you doing here?" Gone was the friendly smile with which she'd greeted me at the Centre. With the muddy sallowness of her complexion and her limp, straggly hair, she appeared even plainer under the harsh office light than I remembered from the Welcome Centre.

"I'd like to speak with the minister that runs this place."

"No can do. He's not here." She stared back at me as if challenging me to accuse her of lying.

"Then I'd like to speak to whoever is in charge tonight."

"If it's about that girl, Fleur, I can tell you she never came here."

"That's not what I heard. I have a witness who saw her coming out of here."

"Who?"

"I'd just as soon not say."

Although Doris was the only one in this room, I could hear voices coming from another room at the end of the hall, along with a faint smell of burning sweetgrass. I headed towards it.

"Hey, you can't go in there," Doris shouted from behind me.

I ignored her and walked through the open doorway only to realize that I'd interrupted a ceremony. A number of people were sitting cross-legged on the floor in a circle. All stared back at me.

Before I had a chance to excuse myself, a man sitting at the far end spoke up. "Please, you are very welcome to join us. Janice here was just telling us about her sister. Perhaps you have a story you can share." In front of him rested a smudge bowl. The spiralling smoke tickled my nostrils.

This sounded more like a counselling session than a ceremony.

"No, I'm good." Despite his casual hippie demeanour, he had an air of authority. "I'm wondering if I could speak to you when you're finished."

"I'd be happy to. We'll be taking a break shortly. You can wait for me out front."

"Thanks, I will."

On my way back to the front, I noticed the sign for the ladies washroom, so I decided to take advantage of it. Settling into one of the cubicles, I could hear murmuring coming from the cubicle next to me. Although the woman was speaking in a very low voice, I easily recognized Doris's droning tone. It sounded as if she was talking on her phone. I placed my ear against the metal wall.

"I tell you she's here," she whispered.

Three guesses who *she* was, and the first two didn't count.

"I don't know if she suspects anything, but I can't keep the girl any longer. We've gotta move her tonight."

A long pause while the other person spoke. I rustled the toilet paper to convince her I wasn't eavesdropping.

"And she knows that Eric guy. I tell you I'm getting scared. I don't know how much longer I can do this."

I'd heard enough. I had to get out of there before she discovered me. I flushed the toilet and fled the washroom, not daring to look back in case she was behind me. I didn't know what to do, whether to wait in the front area as if nothing had happened or to leave. But one thing I knew for sure, I had to find out who was on the other end of Doris's phone call. And I had to find out if "the girl" was Fleur. The only way was to follow the woman. Deciding it was probably best for her to think I'd left, I headed back out to the street.

I did notice on my way out that the flashy ad seeking aboriginal models no longer hung on the bulletin board. I almost stopped in mid-step with the sudden realization that this ad could've been the method used to lure the missing women. Few young, pretty, and unemployed women would be able to resist such an alluring opportunity.

"Did you see who removed an ad looking for models?" I asked a young man sitting next to the board.

"I don't know what it was, but the lady who works here took something down."

It had to be Doris. And its hasty removal had to mean I was getting close. If only I'd paid attention to the contact information.

Fortunately, my truck was parked with a good view of the entrance. But first, I had to let Teht'aa know what was happening in case I missed our six o'clock meeting time. I found a payphone in a fast food restaurant around the corner and called her cell phone, which I'd insisted she bring with her. The line was busy, so I left a detailed message telling her my plans. I thought of asking her to join me, but I worried that Teht'aa's arrival might coincide with Doris's departure and alert her to our presence. I did, however, finish the message with a suggestion that she call the police if she didn't hear from me by nine. I figured I couldn't be too careful.

Within fifteen minutes of my setting up watch, Doris scurried out the front door and hastened along the street in the opposite direction. Fortunately, she didn't give my truck a second glance. I'd started to manoeuvre my truck out of the parking spot when I noticed that she'd stopped at the bus stop in the next block.

I waited for the bus to arrive and when satisfied she had gotten on, I slowly followed behind, keeping at least a couple of cars between us. I was terrified I would miss seeing her leave the bus, but when she did, I recognized her immediately by her bustling gait and fluttering earrings. She was obviously in a hurry. She transferred to another bus. Occasionally, when it stopped for passengers, I was forced to pass. A little further along I would stop at the side of the road until it overtook me then continue my pursuit.

After about twenty minutes the bus turned into the labyrinth of Vanier, not far from the Welcome Centre. I followed it through every twist and turn of the haphazardly placed residential streets until Doris finally stepped out onto the sidewalk. I slowed to a stop. I ducked when I saw her walking down the street towards me and sighed with relief when I saw her walk on without any hesitation in her step. She turned at the next corner.

I quickly did a U-turn and turned down the road in time to see her tramp up the concrete stairs of a brick triplex, its faded vinyl awnings in drastic need of repair. I turned onto the next street and parked out of sight. Fortunately, the corner house had a nice thick two-metre-high cedar hedge. I positioned myself behind it with a good view of her front yard, and waited.

Five minutes later, the front door opened and Doris stuck her head out. She glanced up and down the street before stepping outside with another woman. Although this woman's face was not the least familiar to me, I realized she fit the profile, pretty with a luxurious fall of black hair and pouting lips, in her early twenties and native. Half supporting her, Doris dragged her down the stairs toward a tiny red Focus. She continued to prop up the young woman as they walked to the car. When the girl turned a dreamy smile in my direction, I realized she was drugged.

I hoped to god this wasn't how Fleur had been treated.

If I'd had a cell phone, I would've called the police. Instead I did the next best thing; I followed the red car. Doris was delivering this young woman to someone. Chances were this person would be more important to the police than Doris, for they could be a direct link to those responsible for the trafficking, if not the ringleader themselves.

CHAPTER
FORTY-FOUR

I was surprised to discover that Doris was the traitor at the Welcome Centre. My suspicions had focused on Paulette, not only because of the photo of the fishing camp in her office, but also because she seemed to be doing her best to remain out of sight just as things were heating up. Nonetheless, I wondered what would prompt a woman like Doris, who appeared to be well-liked at the Centre, to betray her own people.

I had little difficulty following her tiny red car, easily recognized by the stylized medicine wheel in the back window and damage to the back bumper. I tried to keep at least two vehicles behind her, which was easy to do as long as she remained on the busier streets.

This she did for the first several kilometres as I followed her onto the main road, where she turned west into the vermillion of a setting sun and headed across the Rideau River in the direction of the ByWard Market. Remembering the significance the Market had played in Eric's analysis, I began to suspect this was her destination until she turned right onto the road that I'd travelled on less than two hours ago and drove across the now infamous bridge into Quebec.

I wondered if Doris dared glance at the water far below to where her colleague had fallen to her death. Had she had a hand in her murder? Perhaps Claire had started to suspect Doris's involvement in the disappearance of the Centre's clients. Perhaps in one drunken moment, the woman had said too much, giving Doris little choice but to kill her?

And yet I couldn't envision Doris a killer. Perhaps she'd mentioned her suspicions to others involved in the trafficking, and they'd made the decision to kill Claire. I wondered with a vague sense of disquiet if it was the person Doris was leading me towards, the one who would be taking possession of the drugged girl.

When she reached the other side of the river, she continued driving straight ahead along the four-lane highway that winds north into the Gatineau Hills and beyond. By now the cars were thinning out and the setting sun was almost gone, which made the pursuit trickier. With the growing darkness I had to follow closer to ensure I could identify her car. At the same time, with fewer vehicles on the road, it was all but impossible to keep two or more between us. I compromised by driving directly behind her but as far back as I could without losing sight of her taillights. Fortunately, there were few exits.

We quickly lost the lights of Gatineau and headed into the heavily forested Gatineau Hills, with only the occasional flicker of light through the trees from an isolated building. I started to worry about how much further her destination would be when a quick check of my gas gauge told me I was getting short on fuel. I hadn't exactly planned on this pursuit. And the way she was speeding determinedly onwards made me think that she wouldn't be turning off this highway any time soon.

Then, suddenly, without warning, without even a flicker of a turn indicator, she swerved onto an exit. I slowed and carefully trailed her onto a secondary road with almost no traffic. I was nervous that she would start suspecting my following headlights, so I sighed with relief when a sports car loomed up on my bumper and passed. He zoomed up behind her but was prevented from passing for several winding kilometres.

Just as the road straightened out and he drew closer to pass, she moved into a left turning lane and turned. Although I slowed, I continued driving past to remain innocuous. A hundred metres down the empty road, I did a U-turn and headed back. I clicked off my headlights and turned onto the same dirt road. Her taillights vanished into the darkness. I picked up speed but kept my headlights off. Without benefit of moonlight and with dense forest crowding in on either side, the roadway was dark, making it difficult to pick my way along it with any speed. The area, however, seemed vaguely familiar, although why it should I didn't know, since one forest looks pretty much like another. The occasional flicker of red before her taillights vanished beyond the next bend kept me going.

The trees parted and a dirt road appeared on the left. I stopped but didn't see any taillights travelling down this road. But I did see a sign I recognized with foreboding. A Gatineau Park sign for parking lot P48, the lot close to where Becky had been killed and the one where I'd found Eric's sacred stone.

I hesitated. Should I continue, or was I getting into deeper trouble than I wanted to find myself in? If only I had a gun, or any kind of weapon. But I didn't. I could always turn back, find a payphone, call Will and let the police take it from there. But if I stopped now, I wouldn't know where Doris was delivering the girl, and I needed this hard evidence to convince the police that the prostitution ring existed.

When I approached the next parking lot, I realized Doris's car was coming to a stop at the far end. I drove past. Within a short distance I came across the start of a hiking trail, where I could safely park my truck without it being easily visible. As I walked back along the edge of the road to the parking lot, bright beams suddenly lit up the road ahead of me. I managed to jump behind some trees before the lights shone on me. A dark van clattered along the road into the parking lot.

Rather than continuing walking along the road, I decided to make my way through the woods to the far end of the parking lot, where the van's brake lights were stopping next to Doris's car. The night was still, too still. I worried that the slightest sound could warn them of my presence. I tried to walk as silently as I could through the dense underbrush, but a rustle here, a crunch there, and the startled flight of a bird had me cringing. Fortunately, both occupants were still in their vehicles by the time I found myself behind a clump of cedar with a clear view.

Loud rock music suddenly cut the stillness, as the van door opened, then abruptly stopped as the door was slammed shut. The dark shape of a man lumbered over to Doris's car and opened her door.

Light spilled out of the car and onto the man's face. I tensed with the cold dread of recognition. He was the biker with the red hair I'd confronted at O'Flaherty's, the one who'd treated me like a slab of meat.

Doris climbed out of her car but kept the door open. Inside, the girl didn't budge from her slumped position in the passenger seat.

"Where are you taking her?" Doris asked.

"Better you don't know," he answered gruffly.

"To the Parrot?"

My ears pricked up.

"Nope, too late in the season. It'll be closing soon. We have a couple of Caribbean clients. We'll move her there along with the other girls from the Parrot."

Shit. Fleur could be gone by the time the police got their act together.

"And what about that Eric guy? Surely you're not going to ship him south too?"

He emitted a cold, brittle laugh, which wasn't really a laugh at all. "Hardly."

I went cold.

They walked around to the other side of the car and pulled the girl to her feet. They half walked, half carried her to the passenger side of the van and shoved her inside as the rock music once again shattered the stillness.

Then much to my amazement, the two of them embraced, a long, lingering, passionate embrace, perhaps more on her side than his. I'd never thought love would be behind this nasty business.

Releasing his grip, he said, "Don't worry, *chérie*, you

gonna be okay. One of my buddies gonna take care of the spy business."

I slunk further behind my suddenly flimsy screen. I didn't need a name to know the identity of the spy, me.

"Fran, this is the last time, eh? I can't do this no more."

"Yeah, of course, babe." He shrugged then turned and got into his van.

"Fran, you'll call tomorrow, eh?" she shouted above the music.

"Yeah, babe." He clicked the van into gear and drove off in a sputter of gravel.

She continued standing, watching the taillights of her lover's van fade. At that moment she seemed very alone and afraid, afraid he might not return, afraid her usefulness had run its course, even afraid for her life.

For a moment I almost felt sorry for her, until I remembered that her actions had destroyed the lives of sixteen young women.

CHAPTER
FORTY-FIVE

I waited until Doris had driven away before returning to my pick-up. As much as I wanted to know where her lover was taking the girl, with barely a whiff of gas in the tank, it would be impossible for me to follow. Besides, he might very well be taking her to a place that was just a little too dangerous for my liking, like a gang clubhouse. Still, I did have the van's licence plate number, and once I gave it to the police, they could go after him and rescue the girl.

I'd hated leaving her in the hands of such a brute, but I figured there was no way I could rescue her without both of us getting hurt or worse. I felt her life wasn't in any immediate danger, and she would soon be freed by the police.

I drove back out to the main highway, praying I wouldn't run out of gas before I found a station. Thankfully the next exit led me to one, which I swear I reached on fumes alone. The station also had a phone booth tucked away at the far end of the lot.

I reached the Migiskan police chief on the first ring. "What do you mean by calling collect?" Will growled. "You think we've got a big budget?"

"I'm afraid I've run out of cash, and I need you to get the Sûreté du Quebec to go after a van."

"Don't tell me you've been snooping again," he growled, which was so unlike Will. I hoped this didn't signify that Eric's case wasn't going well.

"I have solid evidence for you that this prostitution ring exists. I just saw a man kidnap another native girl in this van."

I told him about following Doris, watching the exchange, and finished by giving him the van's licence number. "Now you have proof to give to the SQ to get their butts moving. But if they don't act right now, this girl will be forced into prostitution, Fleur and the other missing girls will be gone from the fishing camp to some place in the Caribbean, and Eric will be dead."

"Did you take any pictures? Record any of the conversations?"

"No, I didn't. I never thought. But all the Ottawa police have to do is arrest Doris and they'll get all the evidence they need, including the name and location of this fishing camp. She can even tell them what she knows about Eric."

"I'm afraid what you witnessed probably isn't enough to raise an arrest warrant, but they can take this woman in for questioning. Though chances are she won't know much."

"She knows about the Parrot, as she called it."

"Yeah, but she probably has no idea where the camp is. She's just small fry. The people behind the trafficking would've kept key information from her. Still, she'll know something."

"Is there any way they can protect her? I'm sure if her biker friends find out she's talked, they'll want to kill her."

"If they don't get to her beforehand. Hold the line a moment while I call the sergeant in charge of the case."

I could hear him talking on another phone. Meanwhile, a dusty Harley rumbled into the gas station and stopped beside a pump. As the rider hopped off, I slunk back into the phone booth.

Will interrupted his conversation and returned to me. "What's her address again?"

I told him in a hushed voice, afraid the biker might overhear and finished by saying, "I'm hoping she went home."

"This apartment could also be just a holding place for the girls before they ship them off. So she might not have gone back there."

I hadn't thought of that.

The biker, wearing the now too familiar *Les Diables Noirs* patch, glanced in my direction. I held my breath and cowered even further into the phone booth.

"Do you know Doris's last name?"

"Nope," I whispered, anxiously watching the biker from behind the phone equipment. "But the police can get it and her home address from the Anishinabeg Welcome Centre, where she works as the receptionist."

"Can you speak louder? I didn't catch what you said."

As the biker turned his attention back to filling his gas tank, I raised my voice slightly and repeated what I'd just said. At least I had a policeman on the other end of the line.

"Good, be back to you in a minute," Will said.

The biker, who wasn't Fran or any of the other bikers I'd seen at O'Flaherty's, flipped open his cell and started talking while holding the gas nozzle with his other hand.

After several more minutes of muted talking, Will returned to the phone. "A squad car's on the way. Since the action took place in Quebec, I also want you to leave a statement with the SQ telling them what you saw."

I relaxed slightly as the biker swaggered into the gas station with his ear still clamped to his cell.

Will continued talking. "Christ, I hate these cases that cross provincial boundaries. It causes me no end of grief."

"I guess this means the two police forces aren't working together, eh?"

"Christ, you can say that again. They both refuse to treat Becky's murder, Eric's disappearance and Fleur's, along with the other missing women, as a single all-encompassing case."

"And don't forget J.P.'s murder and Claire's. They're tied in too."

"Yeah, right. Christ, Ottawa has four different teams working on the separate cases, and none of them are talking to each other. And to make matters worse, they're still continuing to treat the missing women cases as unrelated. I don't see how we're going to get anywhere solving this mess."

"Please don't tell me that. The longer they delay mounting a rescue of Eric and Fleur, the more likely it'll be we'll never see them again."

"Believe me, Meg, I'm doing all I can to get them moving."

I ducked again as the biker sauntered back out and returned to his bike. But without another glance in my direction, he kicked it into action and was gone with a squeal of tires. As I watched him speed down the road, I wondered if their clubhouse was close by and if Fran had taken the girl there. But even if it was, I wasn't about to go looking for it. I would, however, pass this info on to the Quebec police.

"Where should I go to give the SQ my statement?"

"The main Gatineau station on Jean-Proulx Street and speak to Sergeant Tremblay. I'll let him know you're coming."

"You mentioned something earlier about the Ottawa police having a couple of leads in Eric's case. Did they get anywhere with them?"

"Nope, they didn't pan out. But they did find a witness that saw a man fitting Eric's description being shoved into a van on Clarence Street in the Market on July nineteenth, which seems to be the last time anyone saw Eric. But that's as far as it goes. No licence plate number other than it was a Quebec plate."

"The van I saw also has a Quebec plate. Maybe it's the same one. Did the witness say what make or colour the van was?"

"He couldn't remember, other than it was a dark colour and he thought it was an old van."

"It could fit. Although I couldn't see it that well in the dark, it rattled enough to be old. Where on Clarence Street did he see it? It could be around the corner from Auntie's Place."

"I'll check."

"By the way, I saw an ad at Auntie's Place that might've been used to recruit the women. The same one is hanging on the billboard at the Welcome Centre. Maybe Eric saw it too and realized what it meant."

"Describe it for me and I'll pass it on to Ottawa."

After taking down the information, Will hung up, leaving me feeling very disheartened and very worried for Eric and Fleur.

My spirits weren't improved with my visit to the Gatineau police station. Although Sergeant Tremblay did pour on his Gallic charm, when I recounted my story, he gave no hint that a follow-up was imminent, not even when I pointed out that the parking lot where another native girl had been murdered was in the same area as the parking lot where I saw the exchange.

"In fact," I continued, "maybe a similar exchange was taking place when Becky was killed. Maybe she tried to run away."

He merely nodded but did continue writing in his notebook.

"And by the way, the parking lot where the murder occurred is also the same one where I found an item that belongs to Eric Odjik, who is also missing. Maybe he witnessed an exchange and was caught."

He lifted his gaze. "I did not know this, madame. Perhaps you could tell me more."

Hoping that this would help spark some action, I told him how I'd found Eric's sacred stone the day we conducted the search of Becky's crime scene. I also mentioned that the last time this stone was seen was only a few days before a witness in Ottawa saw him being shoved into a van with Quebec licence plates.

But at the end of my story, he just nodded again.

Worried that nothing was going to be done, I asked, "Can you tell me if you are going to mount a rescue of Eric and Fleur from this fishing camp?"

"You know, madame, that I cannot talk about an ongoing investigation, but I can tell you that at this point in our investigation there is no evidence that suggests that this man Eric Odjick is being held at this mysterious fishing camp."

"No, I suppose there isn't any direct evidence, but what I've just told you points to these kidnapped women being forced into prostitution at this camp. And I'm convinced that Eric's disappearance is linked to this prostitution ring. It makes sense that if they didn't kill him, then they would take him there."

He shrugged. "*C'est possible*, but I understand that the Ottawa police are pursuing other leads." He leaned back in his chair and placed his arms around the back of his head. "Madame, you must understand that this Eric Odjik case is currently not an active case with us. There is no evidence that currently places this man in the province of Quebec."

I ground my teeth. "But I've just told you that a sacred stone belonging to him was found in the Gatineau Park parking lot. I doubt it walked there on its own. Plus the van that took him had Quebec plates. Why can't you just fly into the camp and check it out before it's too late?"

"Madame, you must understand that it takes much coordination to mount such an exercise. Besides, our float-planes are currently occupied on another case."

"Can't you rent some?"

"Madame, please be assured that should the assistance of the Sûreté du Québéc be required, we will do all we can to locate this missing man." He stood up and held out his hand. "I thank you for coming in and providing us with this most valuable information. We will do our best to locate this young woman."

I felt like saying, yada, yada, yada, but didn't.

CHAPTER
FORTY-SIX

It took considerable effort to keep my foot from plunging the gas pedal to the floor and burning rubber out of the police station parking lot. I felt frustration, outrage, and a flurry of other emotions at the smugness of this penny-pinching, by-the-rule-book bureaucratic cop, who probably wouldn't protect his grandmother unless his orders were signed in triplicate.

And it took me several kilometres to cool down enough to remember that I was supposed to be meeting Teht'aa. Of course, I was headed in the wrong direction, which I quickly discovered when I stopped to ask at a *depanneur*. Before going to the station, I'd arranged to meet her at a Tim Hortons a few blocks down the street from the station. It was now many blocks and a labyrinth of streets behind me.

After another stop for more directions, I finally arrived at the busy coffee shop. I sighed with relief when I saw Eric's Jeep in the parking lot but groaned in frustration when I realized that most of the other vehicles were cop cars. Of course, cops, donuts, coffee would be a guaranteed mix at a Tim Hortons less than three blocks away from the station. We should've thought that one through.

Since there was no way I was going to spend any more time in their company, I ran inside, plucked Teht'aa from the midst of the shop full of cops and ran back out with her clutching her uncapped coffee cup.

"Jeez, what's got into you?" Teht'aa shook her hand free of my grasp and began brushing off the dark liquid trickling down the front of her jeans. "You made me spill half my coffee."

"I'll tell you later. Right now I need something stronger than coffee and to be a long way from cops. Plus I'm famished. Got any ideas?"

Teht'aa knew of a restaurant in the middle of what used to be the old town of Hull before it was merged with the much larger municipal entity of Gatineau. I followed close on her bumper through the twisting streets to the downtown core of low nineteenth-century buildings overshadowed by sky-high twentieth-century office towers. We managed to find a couple of parking spots on a side street not far from the sprawl of a national museum and walked along another side street to a restaurant tucked inside a gabled two-storey house with a large side verandah. Despite the late hour, the restaurant was still full, although several tables were in the process of being vacated. Five or so minutes later, we were ushered into the stylish dining room to one of the freshly reset tables. The waiter, however, didn't appear to be particularly pleased with our arrival, which had probably back set his departure by a good hour and a half.

Even though Teht'aa wanted me to immediately launch into what had me all fired up, I was in no fit state to talk. I needed sustenance above all else. Plus, I was flinging emotional daggers and knew my recounting would be fraught with more passion than sober second thought. Only after the soothing warmth of the cream of asparagus soup did I feel sufficiently calm to recount all that I'd encountered since we'd parted. I had wanted wine, but a warning glance from Teht'aa dissuaded me.

I watched her face run a gamut of emotions, from elation at learning that we finally had proof of the prostitution ring's existence, to chagrin at knowing yet another of her sisters was being trafficked, and finally to the same rage that I'd felt at listening to the self-serving cop say that the SQ couldn't mount an expensive rescue operation without firmer evidence that Eric and the kidnapped women were at the fishing camp with the green parrot.

"So what do the stupid pigs want?" she spat out when I'd finished. "A YouTube video of him being tortured at the camp or his cut-off finger with a map showing where to find the rest of his body?"

There was no point in answering. I felt the same way.

"Did you learn anything we can use, either for Fleur or your father?" I asked.

Her beaded earrings danced as she shook her head. "Not really, but Charley, the owner of the Dreamcatcher Bistro, knew about the missing women and knew a couple of them. In fact, one who disappeared about four years ago had been a good friend." She pulled out a photo of a young woman in her early twenties with laughing eyes and a bright smile. "But she hadn't employed any of them, and Fleur was the only one who'd ever come to her restaurant looking for a job."

"Well, we didn't really think the restaurant was involved, did we?"

"She did mention the drop-in centre you talked about, Auntie's Place. Apparently her friend had been all excited about an ad she'd seen there. In fact, she even had an interview set up before she disappeared."

Teht'aa smiled her thanks up at the waiter as he placed a dish of veal kidneys smothered in mustard sauce in front of her.

"Do you know what the job was?" I nibbled on a french fry while I sliced through my tender steak. *Steak et frites*, one of my favourite meals.

"Modeling for a magazine."

"I think that ad was used to lure these women. I saw a similar ad at the Welcome Centre. Did she tell you the name of the magazine or the name of the person this friend was meeting?"

"Sorry, I didn't ask. I didn't know it was important."

"That's okay. I've already told Will about the ads. But we should probably let him know that we have proof that it was used to entrap at least one of the missing women, in case the Ottawa police want to follow up. But let's face it, it won't happen."

"You can say that again. Ignorant bastards." Teht'aa dropped her utensils onto her empty plate to emphasize her disgust, then ordered a double espresso.

"Make that two," I said to the waiter. "Anything to keep me from falling asleep on the long drive home."

Teht'aa continued. "I did learn something important from the bistro owner, even though there isn't much we can do with the information. Before she started up her restaurant, she was the chef at the green parrot fishing camp for a couple of summers. The camp, by the way, is actually called *L'Auberge du Soleil Couchant.*"

I laughed ironically. "Fitting name, isn't it? It may mean Inn of the Setting Sun in English, but the direct translation of *couchant,* meaning 'sleeping,' seems more appropriate."

"And the green parrot does exist. He has a perch on the verandah and in the lounge."

"Did she tell you where the camp's located?"

"She doesn't know exactly. She said it was about a three-hour flight from Gatineau to somewhere in northern Quebec. Unfortunately, the lake's name is White Fish Lake. And as you well know, if there's one lake by that name in Quebec, there must be a hundred."

"At least we have the lodge's name. Did Charley mention anything about prostitutes?"

"Nope, she said there were very few female staff members, only herself and a couple of older women from a nearby reserve who did the cleaning."

"How long ago was she there?"

"She was last there about nine years ago. She said the main lodge is a gorgeous timber building with a spectacular two-storey stone fireplace in the great room. It also has a number of outlying cabins and is on a rocky point overlooking the lake." She smiled. "Sound familiar?"

Except for the outlying cabins, she could've easily been describing Three Deer Point.

"Charley also said it was very isolated, accessible only by plane or canoe. I gather the reserve the two other women were from was at least a two-day paddle away. It's also the kind of fishing camp that only the wealthy can afford. She said during her time there were a number of prominent guests, mostly men."

"Did she say who owned it?"

"A man from Montreal, who was the owner of the parrot. But she'd heard he died about six or seven years ago. His brother-in-law took it over and sold it to some foreign company. She didn't think it was American, but it might have been Arabian or from another oil-rich state."

"For what it's worth, we should pass this info on to Will."

"She did mention that there were a couple of tragic accidents while she was there. Apparently one of the female guests, a young woman who'd come with one of the male guests, disappeared into the bush and despite an extensive search, she was never found. The people at the lodge suspected that she'd probably wondered too far from the lodge, became lost, and either died from exposure or was killed by a bear or wolves."

"Well, as we both know, it can easily happen, particularly with someone who isn't familiar with the wilderness. And the second accident?"

"It happened with another young woman also accompanying a guest. I don't believe either woman was married to these men. This time it was a drowning. Charley apparently found the woman's body drifting close to shore. There was a police investigation, but it was determined that the woman had taken a canoe out on her own and had been dumped in the middle of the lake. I gather despite being unable to swim, the drowned woman hadn't worn a life jacket."

"Another accident that can easily happen, but two accidental deaths within a short time must not have done the reputation of the fishing camp much good."

Teht'aa nodded. "It unnerved Charley so much that she decided not to return to the camp. In fact, she wasn't entirely sure the drowning death was accidental. The night before the woman drowned, she'd approached Charley, quite upset and wanting to leave the lodge. Before Charley had a chance to tell her that a plane would be coming the next day, the woman's escort arrived and took her away. She remembered noticing strange bruises on the woman's arms and neck."

"Did she think the man had beaten her?"

"She did and thought maybe this man had had a hand in her death. Apparently he was quite abusive to the woman when he dragged her away from Charley. But when she mentioned this episode to the cops, they said they'd been told the woman had been drinking all day, was acting erratically, which was supported by other guests, and had apparently fallen and hurt herself." She paused. "By the way, I gather this young woman was native. Charley thinks that's why she approached her, a kindred sister."

"It looks as if funny business has been going on at the Fishing Camp for some time, doesn't it? It makes me wonder why the SQ don't have it on their radar screen."

She waved her hand dismissively. "You know what I think of cops."

We both lapsed into silence. While she played with her empty espresso cup, I fidgeted with my empty plate. A kernel of an idea was beginning to form.

Suddenly she banged her fist on the table, startling not only me but also the couple at the only other occupied table in the dining room. "We've got to do something, Meg. If we don't, Dad's going to die, if he isn't already dead. But, jeez, I don't have a clue what we can do."

"How would you like to go on a trip?" I answered.

She arched her eyebrows.

"It's something I've been thinking about once I realized the police weren't going to move." I paused, thinking this was too much of a harebrained idea. But why not? It was worth a try. "Why don't we fly in to this camp ourselves?"

CHAPTER
FORTY-SEVEN

"You've got to be kidding." Shocked disbelief spread across Teht'aa's face.

"Why not?" I said as I fished out my credit card and passed it to the waiter hovering at my elbow. He scurried away and returned within seconds with the slip ready for my signature.

"I figure if we could get some pictures or other hard evidence of illegal activity, like revealing it's a brothel and not a fishing camp, it would be enough to send the police in."

I'd been mulling over this idea since the Migiskan police chief first warned me of the difficulty in convincing the Quebec police to fly into the camp.

"I'm hoping we'll come across Fleur or one of the other missing women."

"And if we do, will we take them with us?"

"Only if it doesn't endanger the other women. I don't know how many there will be, but I doubt we can fit more than a couple of extra people inside a small float plane. I'm worried that the owners would harm them when they discover Fleur is missing."

"But surely they'll be suspicious of us?"

"I've been thinking we could go undercover, so to speak. We could pretend to be clients ... or upset wives looking for our wayward husbands." Chuckling, I followed Teht'aa out of the dining room.

She laughed. "Yeah, I bet there are a number of wives dying to know what their husbands are really doing on their fishing trips."

The skepticism on her face had turned to acceptance. "It's probably the kind of place you need to book weeks in advance. What about going as travel writers or better yet, reviewers? That way we can drop in unexpectedly without arousing suspicion."

"It would also help explain our snooping around. I like that idea."

Without so much as a thank-you for our business, the waiter clicked the door lock into place the second we walked out onto the street.

"But what about Dad? If he's there, we can't leave him."

"I know. It's something I've been struggling with. But I worry that if we take him, it will spell the end of the women. Perhaps it would be safer for everyone if we leave the rescue up to the police."

"Meg, you dreamer you. You honestly think the police will change their minds. No way. They're going to continue to sit on their fat asses. Nope, if we find Dad, we take him with us. That's the only reason I'll agree to this crazy idea."

"You're right. I wouldn't be able to leave him behind either, or Fleur for that matter. But we're going to have to come up with a plan to protect the women."

The night had turned cool. The streets were empty but for a ginger cat sitting by a front door. His eyes followed us as we headed around the corner to our parked vehicles.

"Damn. I hadn't thought of the danger. We'll have to think of something." She clicked the remote of Eric's Jeep, which responded with a flash of lights and a beep. "Now where do you plan to get this plane? Steal it?"

"I figure we can charter one."

"But, Meg, that'll cost a fortune."

"That's a fortune I'm prepared to pay. I have some bonds coming due. I'll use money from one of those."

"And where are we going to find this plane? I don't know any airlines that charter."

"I don't either, but Wendy's husband uses a floatplane charter service. I figure we can use his. And I'm also hoping that one of the company's pilots might know where this Sunset Lodge is located."

"I'll call Wendy now and see if she knows the name." Teht'aa dug her cell phone from her purse.

Although Wendy didn't recognize the name "Sunset Lodge" or its French equivalent, she did know the name and phone number of the airline. Air de l'Orignal, otherwise known as Moose Air, operated out of a town a little over an hour's drive from Somerset, but she said the plane picked up George and his clients on Echo Lake at the Forgotten Bay Fishing and Hunting Camp. That would be very convenient for us too, since it was around the corner from Three Deer Point at the bottom of a deep narrow bay. But Wendy had no idea whether the airline would know the location of George's fishing camp. As far as she knew, her husband always used the camp's private plane to get there.

Since neither of us wanted to spend the night at this camp, hundreds of kilometres from the nearest help, we would have to do the trip in one day. I doubted a float-plane could land in darkness, so given the three-hour trip Charley had mentioned, we would need to leave first thing tomorrow morning to ensure we could land in daylight on our return to Echo Lake.

But I was fooling myself if I thought we could charter a plane this quickly. The airline office was predictably closed when I tried calling before Teht'aa and I set off for home. And the next day the owner didn't return my message, nor the other ones left during the course of the morning, until it was almost noon. By then I'd convinced myself that chartering a plane wasn't going to happen.

Thankfully, business was slow and his Beaver, which could accommodate six people including the pilot, would be available the following day. So after haggling over the price, which meant I would have to put off replacing my decrepit truck for at least another year, and agreeing to giving him a hefty deposit, Bernie, the owner and pilot, agreed to pick us up at eight in the morning at the Forgotten Bay Hunting and Fishing Camp. Although he could've landed near my dock, he said the beach at the camp would make loading easier. He also wanted to use the Fishing Camp's gas pump to ensure he had a full tank.

Fortunately, he knew the exact location of Sunset Lodge. Over the years, he'd flown in numerous clients.

He hesitated. "You know, it's not exactly a place for women. But I guess no reason why women can't fish." He paused. "Just I don't think I've ever taken in a female client on her own."

Now was the time to try out our cover. "We're travel reviewers. We've been contracted by one of the big travel magazines to do a review for an upcoming issue on North American fishing lodges."

"I guess ... though I would've thought it wasn't exactly the kind of place people reviewed. Oh well, see you tomorrow."

He hung up leaving me convinced that we needed to learn a lot more about this fishing lodge before we arrived unannounced. So I left a message with Wendy saying I wanted to speak to George when he got home later in the afternoon.

While I waited, I called Will to bring him up to date on my disastrous meeting with Sergeant Tremblay. He was just as annoyed as I by the SQ cop's noncommittal response and vowed to go up the chain of command.

However, when I asked about Doris and how much the Ottawa police had managed to learn about the trafficking operation, I discovered that they hadn't been able to apprehend her. Apparently, she hadn't returned home, nor had she shown up for work today. But the apartment where I'd seen her did indeed appear to be a holding place for these women. It was furnished with the bare basics, no personal items and little food in the fridge. The bathroom cabinet contained a number of female cosmetic products and hygiene items, while the bedroom closet held a variety of scanty female clothing.

"Oh dear, what does this mean for Doris?" I asked.

"Hate to say it, but it's likely she'll turn up dead. An All Points Bulletin has been issued for her car."

Although we talked for a couple more minutes, I didn't

tell him about our planned trip. I figured he would try to stop us. He might even go as far as calling the airline and telling them not to fly us. I did, however, plan to tell him shortly before we took off. If we didn't return as planned, he would know where to send in the rescue. Surely that would be enough to fire the SQ into action.

CHAPTER
FORTY-EIGHT

Unable to sit still while I waited for George to return my call, I kept myself busy puttering around the yard under the watchful eye of Sergei, who preferred to stretch out on the wooden floor of the verandah rather than the cold damp ground. Occasionally he'd lift his head at a squirrel's chattering, but that's as far as he would move. Once he roused himself enough to shamble down the stairs for a pee, but after coming to me for a reassuring pat, he lumbered back up again to his resting spot. Gone were the days when he tore around the property in a fit of canine exuberance.

Although the wind carried the coolness of fall, the day was sunny, a good day for working outside. I clipped the perennials in the flowerbeds and pulled spent plants from the vegetable garden, dumping everything into the compost. I weeded, racked, and churned the soil, readying it for next spring's planting. Afterwards, I walked back and forth with armloads of firewood between the wood-shed and back porch. During the cold months I wanted a handy supply of wood without having to traipse through the snow to the woodshed.

Wherever I went I kept the portable phone within easy reach for George's call. He didn't call until after five. By then I was getting anxious that he'd been delayed another day.

"Sorry I couldn't get to you sooner," he said in his gravelly smoker's voice. "But I had to drive my client into Somerset. Wendy says you been asking about the fishing camp with the green parrot, the one called Sunset Lodge."

"You work there, don't you?"

"I guide there, off and on. Used to do more a few years back. I hear you think that's where Fleur is?"

"And Eric."

"Eric? What's he doing there?"

Apparently, Wendy hadn't had a chance to tell him about his chief's disappearance, so I filled him in.

At the end he said, "That crazy guy. Why can't he just leave things alone, instead of always trying to save the world?" He chuckled. "But, jeez, if he hadn't kept at us to clean up our act, we'd be just another broken down rez."

I had to agree. In the close to ten years since Eric was first elected band chief, he'd coaxed and cajoled the band into buying into more improvements to the community than had been implemented in the hundred and fifty years since it had been made a reserve.

George continued, "You know, I'm not surprised about the hookers. I knew funny things were going on up there. Ten years ago it was a great place to guide, plenty of fish, a lot of keen fisherman and top-of-the-line gear. Nowadays, the gear ain't in good shape. They've overfished the lakes and haven't bothered to restock them. And the few guys I take out don't know a hell of a lot about fishing."

"I understand it was bought out."

"Yeah, Pierre sold out about five or six years ago."

"Do you know the new owners?"

"Nope. Some foreign company, that's all I know. Only guy I know is the manager. He used to work for Pierre, but I never cottoned on to him. Smooth as silk on the surface, but underneath a mean son of a bitch. He's really why I don't do much guiding for them now."

"What's his name?"

"Etienne, Etienne Frazer. Comes from around Val d'Or."

"Is he the kind of person that would run a brothel, even kidnap girls for it?"

"Yeah, I could see him doing it. Before he worked for Pierre, he was in jail for stealing from old ladies. Pierre took him on because he was going out with the guy's sister. I think his brother's a member of that biker gang, *Les Diables Noirs*."

Bingo.

"You don't happen to know the brother's name, do you?"

"Yeah, François. They call him Fran."

Another bingo. I doubted there would be many Black Devils by the name of Fran.

"He's another mean son of bitch, just like his brother. He came out fishing with me once. Couldn't fish worth a damn. I kicked him off my boat after he hooked me one time too many with his godawful casting. He was so mad he almost dumped the boat. He liked to play it rough with the ladies too. Pierre had to evacuate one of the staff girls, a young Cree from the local reserve, after he beat her up. Pierre wouldn't let him back at the camp after that."

And this was the man with whom Doris had fallen in love.

"Can you give me an idea of the layout of the lodge?"

"What do ya want to know that for?"

I felt there was no point in pretending otherwise, so I told him about our plan to fly in tomorrow.

"That's a job for the police. What do ya want to do that for?"

"They haven't exactly been rushing off their feet to mount a rescue." I told him about the brick wall of inaction Will and I were running into.

"Figures, damn cops can't see beyond their stuck-up white noses." He paused. "Sorry there, Meg. I don't mean no disrespect. Tell me again how you plan to do this craziness."

This time I provided more detail, including going undercover as travel reviewers.

The moment I finished, he shot back, "It ain't gonna work."

"Why not?"

"Women don't go there on their own. It's just not that kind of place."

"But as I said, we're going to pretend we're travel reviewers."

"This kind of place don't get reviewed. Etienne'd be suspicious the minute you landed."

My heart sank.

"I got a better idea."

"Good. Tell me."

"It'd be better I come over to your place. I'll be there in fifteen."

"Can you pick up Teht'aa on your way? She should be a part of this discussion."

Within twenty minutes I could hear the two of them tramping up my front stairs. Teht'aa's model height might have overshadowed George's wiry thinness, but the look of determination on his face would be enough to cow anyone.

"But it's not your problem," Teht'aa was saying as they joined me in the screened porch.

"Damn right it is. It's our people you're talking about."

I intervened. "Okay, what's going on?"

They both spoke at once, garbling whatever they were trying to say.

"Please, one at a time. Teht'aa, you first."

"George says he's coming with us, but he can't. It's too —"

I cut her off and turned to the guide, his bronzed face bristling with stubble from his recent fishing trip. "Is that right, George? You want to come with us?"

"Yeah. You gals don't know the place. I do. You'd get yourselves in a shitload of trouble for sure."

"But you coming with us would put us in greater danger," Teht'aa retorted. "Alone we can pretend we're travel reviewers. But if we're with you, they'd never believe it."

"But I told ya, the reviewer story ain't gonna work. Etienne wouldn't believe ya for a minute." George's voice had risen a decibel or two.

"Sit, both of you, and let's discuss this calmly."

I motioned them to take two of the wicker chairs, while I sat down in my usual spot, the old bentwood rocker. The sudden roar of a plane coming in for a landing on the lake froze the three of us into silence, while we watched it bump along the surface, safely land, and plough through the water in the direction of the Forgotten Bay Camp.

"Okay, George. You mentioned you had a better idea. You might as well tell it to us."

"Like I says to Teht'aa, I'm comin' with you. It's the only way we're gonna save Eric and Fleur."

Teht'aa was about to interrupt. I raised my hand to silence her. "Go on, George."

"Etienne's gonna suspect you no matter what story you give him. We're gonna have to sneak into the place at night."

"But the plane can't land at night, and besides, the noise it makes would wake up a hibernating bear," I said.

"We're gonna go in by canoe. I know of a lake a half day's travel away where a plane can land. There's a connecting river. It's got some rapids, but I figure you gals can handle them."

Teht'aa cast questioning eyes in my direction. Last time we'd been together in a canoe, we'd battled not only rapids but also a forest fire. Although I was no great lover of whitewater, having survived that terrifying trip, I'd at least gained a degree of confidence and a certain dexterity in the art of whitewater paddling. "Sure, no problem. But won't it be trickier searching the grounds at night?"

"I have some ideas on where they could be holding our people. There's an old staff quarters behind the main lodge that was empty for a long time. I noticed they're using it again. I seen some of these young girls coming outta there. But I figure they can't be holding Eric there or close to where people could see or hear him. There's a huntin' cabin further along the shore, around a point. I figured that'd be a good place to hide the Chief."

"What if they have guards?"

"As far as I know, they only have one guy on at night. He makes the rounds a couple of times during the night, but since they're so far from anywhere, they don't worry about people coming in to steal. Just the bears they worry about."

I turned to Teht'aa. "Okay, I think it's doable. What do you think?"

She nodded. "Yeah, I think it'll work. But we'll need at least two canoes to hold the five of us."

"I have an eighteen-footer that'll hold three easy. Plus you guys can take my sixteen-footer."

"Or we can take Dad's."

"Whatever you feel comfortable paddling." George turned to me. "Hope you got the Beaver coming in for you tomorrow and not the Cessna."

"Bernie said he was bringing the Beaver."

"Good, that'll hold the two canoes and the five of us easy. And it's good you got Bernie. He knows that area better 'n any bush pilot I know and can fly in any kind of weather."

"George, I just realized I only have the plane booked for tomorrow. Since you're talking about doing this at night, then I guess I'd better make sure Moose Air can pick us up next day. And do we still need to leave early in the morning?"

"Yeah, it'll take us most of the afternoon to paddle upriver. Current's pretty strong in parts and we'll have to line the canoes around two sets of rapids with a long portage around a falls," George replied.

The two of them continued planning while I called Moose Air. Bernie was able to adjust his schedule to handle the pick-up on the following day, but the earliest he could fly in would be around three. We would need to leave almost immediately if we were going to get back to Echo Lake before dark. Although he had no difficulty with the change in destination, he would need to make a gas stop at a cache on another lake. He'd been planning on gassing up at Sunset Lodge. He was considerably more optimistic with our change in plans, and upon learning the real reason for our visit to the lodge, fully supported the fishing guide joining us.

"George is one top-notch guide. Not only can he find fish where they're not supposed to be, but he's very handy with a rifle. I suggest you take one along. You just might need it."

I returned to the porch to find Teht'aa compiling a list of required gear. When I suggested a rifle, neither blinked as Teht'aa pointed to it on the list.

It was all right for them to treat a rifle with such indifference. I knew Teht'aa had been hunting since she was a child living on a reserve in the Northwest Territories. And using a rifle was probably second nature to George. But I'd never held a rifle in my entire life, let alone fired one, and I wasn't about to change that. So if things did reach a point where a rifle was needed, I would just have to rely on their expertise. I prayed I wouldn't need to.

CHAPTER
FORTY-NINE

Rays from the rising sun were streaking over the cliffs of Forgotten Bay when I stopped my truck in front of the main lodge of the fishing camp. George had already unloaded his gear and canoe onto the camp's narrow beach, the sand damp with overnight dew. While he helped Teht'aa remove Eric's red canoe from atop the Jeep, John-Joe, a staff member and a friend I'd once helped out of a tricky situation, carried her pack and rifle case down to the beach.

My morning greetings were drowned out by the sudden howl of a white floatplane swooping over the ridge. "L'Air de l'Orignal," with a cartoon of a laughing moose with wings, was stamped in red along its sides. The plane circled overhead then zoomed in low for a landing, barely missing the lodge's cedar shake roof. It shattered the reflected mirror of the fall palette of the surrounding forest and splashed along the smooth surface to where Three Deer Point lay hidden from view, then it turned around and motored back to the lodge. By the time Bernie had run the plane's pontoons onto the beach, I, with the help of John-Joe, had my pack, paddle, and PFD propped against George's green canoe.

I'd been worried I would be late. Dropping off Sergei at Jidamo's aunt's place had taken longer than expected. Because the two of them hadn't seen each other since Jid had gone to Montreal, which was all of three days ago, there was a certain amount of boisterous play that had to take place before they settled down enough for me to pass on instructions.

After refueling the plane, Bernie, George, and John-Joe loaded the gear into the back of the cabin and were now strapping the two canoes, the smaller one nestled inside the larger, onto a pontoon. I was standing on the other pontoon, waiting for Teht'aa to climb into the plane, when I heard a crunch of gravel and the rumble of a truck engine. I turned around to see a muddy extended cab truck pulling alongside mine, one I recognized with foreboding.

Will Decontie had come to stop us.

After parking my truck in the camp's parking lot, I'd left a message on his voice mail telling him our plans and asking him to send the SQ to Sunset Lodge should we not be back in two days. I'd added an extra day in case the rescue didn't go as speedily as planned.

The speed with which Will had responded surprised me, since I'd left the message barely ten minutes ago. Moreover, I hadn't provided a departure location. But since the fishing camp handled most of the local float-plane traffic, I supposed it wasn't difficult to guess.

I nudged Teht'aa.

"Oh shit," she said. "No way. He can't stop us."

I agreed. Since I was paying for this plane, I had every right to fly it wherever we wanted it to go. But when he stepped out of the cab clad in hunting camouflage instead of his uniform and pulled a pack, a life jacket, and a rifle case from the back of his truck, I wondered.

And when neither George nor Bernie seemed the least surprised at his sudden appearance, my suspicions were confirmed.

"Morning, ladies." Will dropped his gear on the sand by the plane. "I'm coming with you."

"Who squealed on us? George, Bernie?"

"Both, actually." Decontie grinned.

I heard several confirming grunts behind me.

Bernie spoke. "I was worried about you gals. And when George here told me about the danger, I thought Will should know about your plans. I don't want you gals getting hurt."

George added, "I figured Will needed to know."

"Don't get angry with them," Will cautioned. "They had every right to tell me. You could be flying into a hornet's nest. I can't have you doing that on your own."

"So why come with us rather than stopping us?" I asked.

"I'm just as concerned about Eric and Fleur as you two and just as disgusted by the heel dragging of the SQ. I'm glad you're doing this. I wished I'd thought of it myself."

"So I gather this isn't in an official capacity."

"I'm on vacation, guys, off to join my friends for a bit of hunting, eh?" He passed John-Joe his gear before continuing. "There's something you should know."

If the mood had been tense before, it was now rigid with anticipation.

"I got a call late yesterday afternoon from the manager of our bank in Somerset. As you know, that's the bank that handles the reserve's financial affairs. Anyways, Xavier called wanting to know about Eric. Apparently he'd just received a strange call from a man claiming to be Eric, asking that money be transferred from one of our accounts to an account at a foreign bank. He was —"

Teht'aa cut-in, "Oh my God, was it really Dad?"

Will nodded grimly. "Xavier thinks so. Although the line wasn't all that clear, but he was fairly certain it was his voice, and he knew things that only Eric would know, like account numbers and the —"

"But what does this mean?" Teht'aa cut in again. "Is he not really missing?"

"Calm down and hear me out. From the news reports, Xavier knew your father was missing, so he was very surprised by the call. Apparently, Eric's answer to his question was to say that he'd been out of contact while on a northern Quebec canoe trip for the past couple of months. But Xavier didn't entirely believe him. He thinks he was being coerced into making —"

It was my turn to interrupt. "They want money. That's what this is all about, access to band funds."

Will removed his cap and ran his hand over his bristly hair. "It looks that way. Eric tried to alert Xavier by giving the wrong password. But more importantly, Eric knows full well that any transfer of funds requires two approvals, his and Jeff Lightbody's. So Xavier was suspicious from the get-go."

"But if these guys wanted the money, why wait until now?"

"Easy. The quarterly deposit from the feds for health care and education was deposited yesterday. It's over two million."

So this was all about money and had nothing to do with his investigation into a prostitution ring. "Does this mean he wasn't kidnapped by the Black Devils? And he's not at Sunset Lodge?"

"Not so fast. I'm interpreting his mention of a northern Quebec canoe trip as a hint to his current location. Besides, he happened to let slip something to Xavier about matches. I interpret this to mean the ones with the green parrot found in his suitcase."

"So what are you doing here? Surely this is enough evidence for the Quebec police to finally mount a rescue operation?"

"They're already working on it. But they're gonna be too slow. I'm worried about Eric. Xavier gave him some excuse about having to verify a few things before he could transfer the money over. Eric's supposed to call him back this afternoon. Once these guys learn that they're not getting the money, Eric becomes a liability. If we want to get him out of there alive, it has to be today. So let's get this sucker loaded up and we're outta here." He hopped onto the pontoon.

Although I was filled with relief that Eric was alive, the enormity of what we were about to do suddenly overwhelmed me. "Are you sure we can carry this off, Will, without anyone getting killed?"

"I don't like doing it this way any more than you do, Meg. But I don't think we have any other choice. The rescue has to be launched now and we're the only ones ready. Besides, we'll have surprise on our side. They won't be expecting anyone coming at them from the bush. All their attention will be directed at planes landing on the lake. I'm hoping we'll be able to spirit Eric and Fleur away without any of them knowing. And if we do get into trouble, you have two very good shots in George and me."

"And me," Teht'aa interjected. "I can shoot as well as the two of you."

"Yes, and you Teht'aa." He gave her a sidelong glance then turned to me. "Now Meg, if you want to stay behind, I can understand."

"No way you're leaving me behind. I'm coming. But we're now five in this plane. I thought it only held six. With Fleur and Eric we'll be seven, which means one of us will have to stay behind and wait for Bernie to come back."

"I've already thought of that," Bernie answered. "I've managed to free up my Cessna for tomorrow. It'll take one passenger."

Knowing I would absorb the additional cost even if it meant using up another bond, I'd decided not to ask about the price, but Bernie brought it up.

"Don't worry about the cost," he said. "Eric's my friend as much as yours. I owe him a lot considering all the business he's sent me over the years. I'm prepared to eat some of the cost. Once this rescue mission is over, we can discuss it, okay?"

"And I've got some money left in my budget," Will added as he tossed John-Joe his rifle case. The young man shoved it in with the rest of the gear. "Let's quit standing around. Teht'aa, into the plane with you."

I will admit that I felt considerably more at ease as we sped along the lake with Will's comforting bulk sitting across from me. I'd spent a sleepless night worrying that this mission might get some of us hurt, if not killed. With his added skill as a rifleman and his experience as a policeman, I felt the danger was greatly reduced.

As we sped past I waved at my cottage perched on its rocky point and prayed that I would be returning to it tomorrow with Eric safely by my side. I could no longer pretend that Eric wasn't a part of my life. I loved him. He was my other half. I would confess to him how I'd let my brother slide to his death and the terrible lies I'd told to cover it up. And I would leave it to the gods to decide my fate. If Eric no longer wanted any part of me, so be it. I would live with it, even though I would ache inside for the rest of my life. But if he chose to forgive me, I would accept whatever relationship he wanted us to have. And if he still wanted to marry me, I would gladly become his wife. I was no longer terrified of the idea.

I watched the red and orange splattered trees slide under us as the plane swooped over the forest and up into the cloudless sky. For the next two and a half hours we flew almost due north over a labyrinth of endless forest and meandering rivers and lakes. Only occasionally was this tableau sliced by a road or hydroelectric transmission corridor. At no time did we see the sprawl of towns; they were well to the south of us.

During the first hour I noticed the occasional cottage, sometimes a string of them, on the shore of a lake with the thin ribbon of a dirt road leading to it. But once we were beyond the main highway that threads its way to northern Quebec, the roads vanished, as did the dwellings. I did, however, notice with disgust the checkered ravages of several clear-cut logging operations.

With the noise of the plane's engines making conversation impossible, my fellow passengers were equally absorbed in the passing scene and their own thoughts. It was only as the plane began its slow descent that we started taking notice one another.

We circled over the flat blue expanse of an empty lake then zeroed in for the landing. The plane bounced once, twice, then skimmed across the surface and finally settled into the water as the engines slowed. Bernie drove the pontoons onto a golden sandy beach close to a number of oil drums.

The crystal clear waters of the lake sparkled under the noonday sun, while the tantalizing scent of northern woods floated on the light breeze. Dark green coniferous trees carpeted the surrounding hills, with only the occasional splash of yellow to mark a birch or poplar. Fall had advanced considerably further in these northern woods than at home, where the colours were just emerging. The hills were low and undulating, unlike the much higher hills, almost low mountains, and steep cliffs that surrounded Echo Lake. But it gave off the same serenity and calm, which did wonders to help settle my nerves.

With no time to spare, we set about unloading the plane, and within fifteen minutes all our gear plus the canoes were lined up along the beach. After Bernie had refueled his plane from a couple of the oil drums, he prepared to take off.

"There's rain in the forecast for tomorrow," he said. "But don't worry, I'll be here, at three sharp as planned. If you're not here I'll hang around for an hour, and if you still haven't come, I'll come back the next day at the same time, okay?"

"Sounds good, Bernie," Will answered. By unspoken consensus, he'd become our leader. "George and I both have our satellite phones, so one of us will be in touch. You also have the SQ emergency number, so if you don't hear from either of us by Tuesday morning, notify them. But, hell, they should already be here by then. Surely it can't take more than two days for them to mount a rescue operation."

Teht'aa and I clutched each other's hand as we watched the plane skim across the water and climb up and over the far shore. Even when we could no longer hear the drone, we both watched the tiny speck before it vanished into a jumble of frothy clouds.

It left behind a deadening silence.

We were alone, very alone.

What the hell had I gotten us into?

CHAPTER
FIFTY

Worried by the threat of rain and unsure of Eric and Fleur's state of health, we decided it would be better to have shelter ready upon our return. So we set up the tents, one George's, the other Eric's, in a clearing hidden from the lake. Eric's was the three-man tent Teht'aa and I had used on our ill-fated paddle down the DeMontigny River. The outer covering still bore a few tiny burn holes where hot ash from the forest fire had dropped onto the nylon fabric. After eating our lunch, we stowed the rest of our gear, plus the food in the tents, taking only what we needed for our venture.

Although Teht'aa and I had wanted to share the same canoe, George insisted that we split up. With Will giving us little choice but to agree, he argued that we wouldn't have the strength to maintain a good paddling pace against the strong upriver current. So I, sitting in the bow of Eric's canoe, was joined by Will, with his rifle case tied securely to the thwart. Teht'aa joined George along with their two rifles in George's twenty-foot canoe. With the addition of Will to our rescue team, George had brought the longer canoe to ensure sufficient room for both Eric and Fleur. Even though Teht'aa was a highly competent stern paddler, she bowed to George's superior expertise and sat in the bow.

It felt surreal as we set out shortly after noon under the brilliant sun of a crisp fall day. With only the whiff of a breeze, it was a perfect day for a paddle. Apart from a ridge of cloud forming in the western sky, there was no foreboding of the danger to come. I even found myself enjoying the canoeing as we sliced through the flat water, until I remembered the real purpose of our trip.

We rounded a point and followed George's canoe towards the distant mouth of a river. This was the river that would take us twenty or so kilometres northwards to the lake where Sunset Lodge was situated. According to George it followed a meandering course that included two sets of rapids and two waterfalls. We would only encounter one waterfall on our journey that we would portage around. The rapids we would line in order to save on time. He figured darkness would be starting to fall when we finally reached our take-out destination.

In a matter of minutes our canoe began to feel the force of the river's current flowing into the lake. For a moment we seemed to stand still before we dug in and paddled harder. When we finally reached the mouth of the river, we momentarily drifted backwards, such was the force of the current. Then Will dug in with even greater strength and we moved forward, which made me very glad that I had his hefty bulk to power the canoe. George was right. Teht'aa and I would never have been able to paddle up this river. As it was, I soon tired, and judging by Will's heavy breathing, he was tiring too. It was almost a welcome break when we had to stop and get out of the canoe to line the first set of rapids.

Fortunately, the rapids were relatively benign and the shoreline, although rocky, was walkable, which made lining easy. With the bowline gripped in his hands, Will pulled the canoe forward, keeping the bow as close to the shore as possible. I walked behind and used the stern line to keep the canoe from drifting too far into the swirling whitewater. Thirty minutes and a couple of wet feet later, we settled back into the canoe to continue our paddle along the next stretch of river before we reached the start of the portage around the falls.

Although my feet were feeling the water's cold, they were starting to warm up inside my woollen socks. When we finally began our hike in to the lodge, I planned to replace my wet footwear with fresh socks and a dry pair of trail shoes. These I'd put in a daypack, along with supper, a headlamp, and other items I might need, including a can of bear spray.

Worried by the possible need to defend myself, I'd brought the only weapon I was prepared to use, pepper spray that had worked wonders on my one close bear encounter. I'd never known that a bear could move so fast when he scurried away, desperately trying to remove the burning sensation from his eyes and nose.

Following George's example, we paddled as close to the shore as possible, where the current was not so strong. Will and I had developed a rhythm that made the paddling less tiring, so by the time we made it to the portage, we were feeling almost energetic. With his light pack strapped to his back, Will hefted the upside-down canoe onto his shoulders, while I wore my daypack and carried his rifle case. Since two people were required to carry the twenty-foot canoe, I also carried the gear Teht'aa and George couldn't handle, namely their rifles.

I laughed to myself as I slung the straps of the three rifle cases over my shoulders. Here I was, the one person of the group who wasn't a fan of bullet power, weighed down by three that, although intended for killing deer and moose, might end up killing a man.

An up-and-down, rock-strewn, sometimes muddy kilometre later I was very glad to see the end of the portage. My shoulders ached from the weight of the rifles. I'd had to put them down twice to ease the pain. Teht'aa, rubbing her shoulders as well, was just as glad to see the end, as was Will. The only one who looked as if he could've continued for several more kilometres was the slightest of us all, George.

We set our canoes back in the water, loaded them up, and continued on to the next rapid. By this time the sun had settled lower into the sky with two hours or more of daylight still remaining. The bank of clouds, however, had risen higher. Bernie had said rain was in tomorrow's forecast. This growing ridge suggested it might be sooner. Hopefully it would hold off until we had Eric and Fleur safely secured in our tents.

I frequently scanned the shore for signs that our passage was being watched, but didn't see any. And nor was I likely to. According to George, even though the river was filled with fish, people from the lodge never came this far downriver because of the falls a short distance downstream from where the camp's lake flowed into the river.

People fished only at the start of the river and rarely, if ever, close to the falls for fear of drifting over the precipice. We would be off the river well before there was any danger of being seen.

The sun had disappeared behind the cloudbank and twilight was settling in by the time we reached the take-out, a short distance from the bottom of the falls. Although the tumbling white was but a faint glow in the fading light, the forest reverberated with its power. We pulled the canoes out of the water and hauled them inland, where we hid them in a cedar grove. To provide greater camouflage, we spread several layers of freshly cut boughs over them. Then sitting down on boulders, we ate our dinner and discussed our next steps.

According to George the lodge was about two kilometres away as the crow flies. Walking, however, would add another kilometre or so, because of the need to skirt around two large marshes. Although the density of the bush discouraged people from coming this way, there was a barely discernable, ancient hunting trail that would take us close to the lodge. George had learned of this trail from a Cree trapper whose ancestors had used it in the days when they lived and hunted along these waterways of their traditional territory.

Although George said it normally took him no longer than thirty minutes to reach the lodge, he figured it would take us about an hour because — he looked at Teht'aa and me — some of us didn't know the terrain. He suggested if we wanted to we could start with our headlamps turned on, but when we closed in on the lodge we would have to turn them off in case the light alerted people to our presence. In fact, he preferred that we not use them at all to allow our eyes to become fully accustomed to the dark by the time we got there.

While Teht'aa and I groaned at the thought of stumbling blindly through the blackness, Will brought out his infrared goggles and proposed that he go first to ensure that we didn't lose the trail. George strongly disagreed. He said he could see as good as day in the dark, and since he was the only one who could interpret the trail signs, he had to go first. After a few more minutes of arguing, it was agreed that George would go first, followed by us two women, with Will bringing up the rear. Should either of us accidentally leave the trail, Will, wearing his fancy night vision goggles, would be able to redirect us.

We discussed whether we should remain together or split up into two pairs, one pair seeking out Fleur and the other Eric. In the end Will's opinion prevailed. He thought that we should stay together until we had fully assessed the situation. We had no idea how much opposition or firepower we would be facing or how difficult it would be to locate and then free our two friends. Once we had a better handle on the situation, we could decide about splitting into two groups.

"And gals, one more thing," Will added. "I don't want you getting killed on me, so if there's any shooting, I want you both to take cover immediately, okay?"

While I readily agreed, Teht'aa started to protest, but he cut her off. "Look, I know, you can shoot a rifle as well as any man, but getting caught up in a gunfight isn't like shooting at moose or deer. It'll be just too damn dangerous for you. And I sure don't want your death on my hands, so as your friend, I'm asking you to hide if shooting breaks out, okay?"

Teht'aa glared at him. "Okay. But I'm still taking my rifle with me."

"Fine, but only use it if your life is in danger, okay?"

The full realization of the risk we were taking took hold, and a yawning icy pit opened up at the bottom of my stomach. But this fear was something I would just have to deal with. Not for one second did I consider staying with the canoes. I wanted to be there when we found Eric. He would need me.

CHAPTER
FIFTY-ONE

It was dark, very dark as we crept along the trail. And quiet, almost too quiet, our footsteps the only sound in the impenetrable blackness. I could sense more than see the hovering forest, while the narrow band of starless sky suggested the clouds had arrived. But not the rain, not yet.

Barely able to discern Teht'aa walking in front of me, I hung onto her pack as it bobbed up and down. Where she went, so would I. While I could hear her light step and behind me Will's lumbering gait, George, at the front, walked as silently as a ghost. Vegetation brushed against my legs, leaves against my face. I tripped over a rock and was only saved from falling by Will's steady hand. A sudden noise close by made me jump. My heart raced.

"Just a grouse," Will whispered.

I felt as if every nerve ending was straining to see, to hear.

But the further we crept along the trail, the better-defined trees, rocks, and my companions became and the more recognizable forest sounds. As my eyes grew used to the dark, my nerves settled down, until I felt a steely calm. My pace became firmer and brisker, no longer a drag on the others.

When we reached the clearing of the first beaver pond, I felt as if daylight had descended despite the cloud-filled sky. I could make out the darker hump of the beaver lodge in the middle of the pond and spied the spreading wake of the beaver making its way through the water on its nightly forage.

Not long after we skirted the second marsh, George stopped. We'd reached an intersection with another trail.

"We're almost there," he whispered. "You can see lights over there." He pointed in the direction of the new trail to where I thought I could make out a faint twinkle through the trees. "That's one of the outbuildings. The main lodge is about a hundred metres to the left of it."

Will said, "George and I are going in to take a closer look. I want you gals to stay here."

I quickly acquiesced while Teht'aa reluctantly grunted her assent.

"Wait by that rock." He pointed to a flat boulder about a metre or so off the trail. "We'll be back within fifteen, twenty minutes, and then we'll continue on to the cabin where George thinks Eric's being held."

My watch said 8:14. At this hour most people would be finished dinner. Too early for bed, they could be any-where. And the night was warm enough for them to still be wandering around outside.

"Be careful," I said, although I knew it wasn't neces-sary. They were both hunters, conditioned to remaining invisible and silent.

Will continued, "And if we don't come back say, within an hour, or you hear gunfire or other unusual noise, call in the SQ and then hightail it back to where the canoes are."

He passed me his satellite phone. "Their emergency number is speed dial 4 and the lodge co-ordinates are on this." He passed me a piece of paper, which I zipped into my pocket.

Without another word, the two men headed towards the flickering light while Teht'aa and I waited at the rock. Apart from a few whispered words, we kept silent, fearful our voices would carry.

The wait, however, proved to be short. We'd barely had a chance to settle in when the two men returned as silently as they'd left. Only Will's heavy breathing warned us of their imminent arrival.

"Seems pretty quiet," he said. "Apart from a couple of guys smoking on the dock, everyone else seems to be inside."

"And we didn't see no guards," George added. "Let's go."

"Wait, George," Will said. "Before we set off, I just want to remind everyone that we might not find Eric tonight. Remember, we don't know if he's here for sure. So if we don't find him, don't get upset. It will mean they're holding him elsewhere."

Or he's dead, I said to myself, finishing the thought Will didn't want to voice. From the intense squeeze Teht'aa gave my hand, she was thinking the same thing.

We soon lost the flickering lights as the trail veered away from the lodge. Regardless, we tried to walk as quietly as possible. Apart from Will's breathing and the occasional rustle of vegetation, we made no sound. But I could hear night animals rummaging through the underbrush. A barred owl called out from his distant perch, while overhead the night sky momentarily filled with the honking of a flock of geese heading south on their fall migration.

At one point I caught the sound of a motorboat, which suggested the lake was nearby. The sound passed close to us, then faded. For a second I thought I saw a pinprick of red light, but it vanished before I could be certain. Shortly after, I heard waves splashing against the shore. Without a word, we stopped and remained frozen in silence while it passed.

"Bit late to be fishing, isn't it?" Will asked George.

George replied, "I think it was coming from the cabin, so we'd better be careful. Might be someone about outside."

We resumed walking. A short while later George stopped.

"The cabin ain't far from here. You gals wait here while Will and I go check it out. I'll make the sound of an owl when it's safe for you to come, okay?"

Without waiting for a response, the two men vanished into the darkness.

But this time, we didn't obey. We were too close to a beloved father and a sorely missed lover to remain behind. Without exchanging a word, we both noiselessly advanced along the path the two men had taken. Within a short distance we were standing on a small embankment overlooking the black expanse of the lake. Below our feet, waves lapped against rocks.

While night permeated the distant shore in front of us, in the direction we'd come from a faint glow defined a tree-fringed point that blocked the view of the lodge itself. In the opposite direction, at the end of a short bay, I could make out the dark shape of a small building with a narrow dock jutting into the water. There were no lights coming from that structure and there was no movement, either along the path or at the building itself. Will and George must be inside.

As Teht'aa and I starting walking towards it, I heard her cock her rifle. "To be on the safe side," she whispered.

The light from a headlamp suddenly glared from inside the building. We watched it move from one window to the next. Then we heard the clear hooting of an owl coming from the front of the cabin.

We glanced at each other and giggled somewhat sheepishly.

I almost called out before remembering that sound can carry a fair distance over water, particularly when the wind was so calm.

We stumbled over each other in our haste to get to the cabin. But when we reached the front steps, we stopped at the sight of Will leaning over the porch railing, shaking his head, his goggles replaced by a headlamp.

"Sorry, there's no one here," he said. "Although there are signs of recent occupancy."

"Do you think it was Eric?"

"Hard to tell. You might as well come inside and see if you notice anything that might belong to him."

We climbed up onto a narrow porch, switched on our headlamps, and stepped into the rustic log building. Our lights lit up a modestly furnished room. Curiously, I felt warmth coming from a woodstove. Against the opposite wall was shoved an overstuffed sofa bookended by two similarly overstuffed chairs. In the other half of the room stood a large wooden table surrounded by a number of straight-back chairs.

My hopes were raised when I noticed a single place setting on the table in front of one of the chairs. But worry set in when I realized the remains of a partially eaten meal lay on the plate.

"It looks as if someone left in a hurry," I said. "Do you think it was Eric?"

"Hard to tell." Will sniffed the plate. "The stew's still warm, which suggests they left recently."

"They must've been in that boat."

"Possibly."

"They've probably taken him to the lodge, then."

Will nodded. "Most likely."

"Will, come here a minute. I got something you should see," George called out from another room.

Teht'aa and I followed the police chief into a small back room lined with two sets of bunk beds. Rumpled sheets were clumped at the end of one of the lower bunks. A dark green windbreaker had been tossed onto the pillow. Teht'aa snatched it up and examined it.

"Nope, it's not Dad's." She shook her head dejectedly and let the jacket fall back onto the bed.

George and Will were peering at some dark splotches on the worn wooden floor near the other bunk.

"It looks like blood to me," said George.

Will took a bag of Q-tips from his pocket and removed one. He dipped it into the red smear and examined it carefully. "Yup, and fresh too." He placed this inside a Ziploc bag.

My heart skipped. "Does this mean Eric's been hurt?"

"It could mean anything. The person could've cut himself. We just don't know and we don't know if it's Eric."

My eye caught sight of an object wedged between the wall and the bunk bed. I reached down and picked it up. "But we know Eric was here." I held a tiny hand-carved wooden animal in my palm. "This is Eric's fisher, the one he keeps in his amulet, along with the sacred stone I found earlier."

Teht'aa turned it upside down. "Yes, it's his. See, here's the name of the carver, Odjik, his grandfather."

I remembered the first time Eric had shown me the thumb-size carving of his namesake. He'd proudly pointed out how well his grandfather had captured the ferocious spirit of a fisher through the tiny carving's threatening stance and snarling grin. The old man had given his grandson this keepsake to commemorate the younger man's return to the Migiskan Reserve after an absence of many years.

Will carefully turned the carving over in his hand. "Yes, it's his all right. We're going to have to assume they've taken him back to the main lodge. But this half-eaten meal worries me ... so does the blood."

"There's more blood." I pointed to several largish drops on the floor close to the doorframe.

"And more here," Teht'aa called out from the front room.

We followed an intermittent line of splotches onto the porch, down the stairs, and along the dock until they stopped, where he had no doubt climbed into the boat.

"With this much blood, he has to be badly hurt," I said.

Will, no longer bothering to pretend everything was going to be okay, grimly agreed. "Maybe they took him back to the main lodge to fix him up."

"Or maybe they took him there to do something worse. Remember what Fran said about not sending him south with the women."

Will turned to George. "Do you have any idea where they might be holding him at the lodge?"

George shrugged. "It's a big place. He could be anywhere, but I suppose he could be in one of the cabins. And there's a couple of outbuildings, plus the old staff quarters."

"George, we need to get to the lodge fast."

"We'll take those canoes." The guide pointed to three canoes overturned on the ground next to the dock.

CHAPTER
FIFTY-TWO

With one canoe following close on the stern of the other, we hugged the shoreline in an attempt to remain in the shadow of the trees and out of the glare of the lodge's outdoor lights. But as we drew nearer, it was clear that our fears were groundless. On such a still night we should be hearing sounds of a lodge in full swing, such as people talking, glasses clinking, footsteps echoing on the verandah. Instead, we heard only the quiet splash of our paddles dipping into the water and a distant wolf howl. From the lodge, nothing.

When we finally hauled the canoes up onto shore and peered through a barrier of low bushes, we saw no one, not even a bartender waiting for business in the empty bar clearly visible through the large windows overlooking the expansive verandah. We did see the parrot, his green feathers luminescent under the overhead lights. He was asleep on a stand next to the window, with his head tucked under a wing.

From our vantage point, I could make out the end of a dock where an aluminum boat was tied up under the glare of a dock light.

"I bet that's the boat we heard," I ventured.

"Could be," Will said. "George, is it always this quiet?"

"No, I never seen it this empty. Billy, that's the bartender, is usually behind the bar. He might be gettin' something from the kitchen."

We waited several more minutes to see if he would appear, and when he didn't, Will said, "I have a feeling there aren't any guests staying here at the moment. Look at all the dark windows."

Several tiny log cabins stretched away from us along the shore on the other side of the main building. Not a single ray of light glowed from their windows or from the second-floor windows overlooking the verandah roof. The lodge seemed eerily empty.

"When does the lodge normally close for the winter, George?" Will asked.

"Usually not till the middle of October, when it gets too cold to heat up the main building. They just have a couple of fireplaces, one in the lobby and another in the bar, and I think one or two of the guest rooms have them too."

"Got any ideas on why the place is empty a good month or so early?"

"Nope."

"I'm wondering if things haven't gotten a little too hot for them," Will hazarded. "And they've decided to close the place down before the SQ finally get their act together and come flying in."

"I did overhear that biker talking about moving the girls out when the place closes," I interjected. "Maybe they've already sent them south, which means we're too late."

But a shrill female laugh from somewhere on the other side of the lodge put the lie to my speculation.

"Sounds like some of them are still here," Will said. "George, how many staff usually work here?"

"Hmm, let's see. There's Billy, the chef, and a couple of helpers, the three ladies who clean the place. That's ah … seven. Then there's Etienne and the couple of people that work in the office and man the front desk. And Hal, the night guard. What's that get us up to?"

"Eleven," Teht'aa answered.

"I think there's a couple of people who look after the girls, but I don't know for sure. And of course the guides. They usually have two or three, depending on the number of guests."

"So we're looking at about fifteen people. But something tells me they aren't all here," Will said. "Either way, in a place this size, we should be able to keep out of their way. I'm gonna —"

He stopped talking as a door opened and a man stepped out onto the verandah. We froze. He walked over to the railing and lit a cigarette with the flick of a gleaming gold lighter. His bald head glowed under the overhead light as he sucked on his cigarette then spewed the smoke out in a forceful stream. He was dressed for the outdoors, in heavy jeans, a black leather Canadiens hockey jacket, and cowboy boots. His glasses flashed in the light as he passed his eyes over the grounds. He peered in our direction for what seemed like a very long minute. None of us dared breath. And then his gaze drifted back to the lake.

When two men joined him, we slunk back further, but not before I recognized one with a wrenching churn of my stomach. Though we could hear the sound of their voices, we were too far away to make out their words. A few minutes later the conversation abruptly stopped with the slam of a door. The stillness returned. Will waited until he deemed it safe before poking his head back through the branches of our cover.

"It's okay. They've gone inside to the bar," he said. "George, do you know who they were?"

"The bald guy's Etienne, the manager. The red-haired guy could be his brother, but I'm not sure. Been a long time since I seen him. I don't know the other guy."

"Yup, that's Fran, the biker," I confirmed. "Although the other guy isn't wearing his leathers either, I bet he's a Black Devil too."

Will shook his head. "Well, guys and gals, it looks like we've got our work cut out for us. I'd say they're settling in for a drink in the bar, so it gives us an opportunity to check out the outbuildings and those cabins over there. George, lead the way."

"We're gonna have to go 'round back, but we gotta watch out for the dogs. Etienne keeps 'em in a pen right by where we gotta go."

Maintaining the same order, with George in front, Teht'aa and I in between, and Will taking up the rear, we followed another narrow track through the trees away from the lake towards the back of the lodge. Once again we kept our headlamps off, although the light filtering through the trees made our passage easier. I could hear rock music coming from somewhere in front of us, but not from the lodge. And more laughter. Surely if the girls were being held hostage, they wouldn't be laughing.

The darker shape of a shed loomed into view. We stopped while Will checked it out with his infrared goggles. After he declared it empty, we continued onwards. A short while later, I heard a deep growl before I saw the chain link fence and then another growl from a different part of the pen. George called out in a low voice and threw a couple of items over the fencing. The two Rottweilers pounced.

"Moose bones," George whispered. "I always bring them. Never know when I might need these dogs to be friendly. Etienne lets 'em roam around the grounds after everyone's gone to bed. Says he does it to keep away the bears."

"Or to prevent the girls from running away," I suggested.

"Yeah, that too."

We continued until we were behind the main lodge, where the lighting was more spaced out. Although the vegetation at the front of the lodge had been tamed, back here the trees and shrubs had been allowed to grow wild. Off to the right, music, laughter, and light streamed from a building partially hidden by the dense bush.

"That's the staff quarters down there," George said pointing towards the noise. "There's another building back there." He pointed to where I could see a path leading away from the lodge and staff quarters.

"What's in that building?" Will asked.

"Don't know, never been in it, but I have my suspicions." He gave Will the kind of look men pass to each other when they're sharing a secret they think only men understand.

"Okay, we'll split up," Will said. "George, you and Teht'aa check out the staff quarters. Try to see what you can through the windows without being seen and then meet back here in fifteen. Meg and I'll check out this other building. Right now I just want us to determine where Fleur and Eric are and how well they're guarded. Once we know, we can plan the rescue operation, okay?"

Teht'aa and George nodded briskly before trotting off towards the staff quarters. I followed the police chief down the dark path towards the squat black shape of a building huddled under the trees. Before we reached it, he signalled for me to stay behind while he went ahead to check it out. I tensed when I heard him call out Eric's name in a low voice, and I waited anxiously for a response. But the only reply was the sound of an animal scurrying through the underbrush. Within minutes he whistled for me to join him. As an extra precaution I approached stealthily with the bear spray, ready for action.

Will was standing at the front of a single-storey structure with his rifle hanging loosely at his side. I clipped the bear spray back onto my belt. I had the impression that the building stretched far back into the woods, but without light it was difficult to tell.

"There are doors on either side," he whispered. "You take one side, I'll try the other. Check what's behind each door. I suspect single rooms. And Meg, don't be surprised at what you might see, okay?"

"I'll need to put on my headlamp."

"Yeah, sure, go ahead, but don't shine it in the direction of the lodge, eh?"

"What is this place?"

"You'll find out."

"Do you think they might be holding Eric here?"

"Hard to say. It's pretty quiet. I thought if they were holding Eric in this building, there would be a guard. But there's no sign of one. I think we should check it anyways to make sure he isn't here."

Will disappeared down a covered walkway attached to the right side of the building. I flicked on my headlamp and found a similar walkway on the left side. I stepped onto the wooden planks, careful to walk as lightly as possible. There were four doors, spread out equally along the length of the building, like a motel. Beside each hung a lantern style light fixture, but none were lit. My headlamp lit up colourful images painted on the top middle of each of the doors.

At first I thought they were numbers, but when the light shone on the closest door, I was taken aback. The image was of two white trilliums, but they were far from ordinary trilliums. In fact they were more human in their stance. The one flower was inserting its highly suggestive elongated stamen into the centre of the other flower in a manner that would make a proper lady blush. If I'd had any lingering doubts about this fishing camp masquerading as a brothel, I certainly didn't now.

Underneath these flowers was a peephole, but it was dark, suggesting the room behind was unoccupied. I tapped gently on the door, and hearing no answering sound, tried to open it. It was locked. I had, however, noticed a cupboard similar to a medicine cabinet attached to the front of the building. I walked back. Inside, hanging from hooks, were keys, each identified by a piece of wood upon which was painted a wildflower. I grabbed the one that bore the trillium and two with the same colours as the markings I'd seen on the other doors, purple and orange. One turned out to be a violet and the other a daylily. I didn't see any with a blue flower, the colour of the marking on the last door.

I returned to the trillium door, inserted the key, and carefully pushed it open. I chuckled. If I had ever imagined the interior of a brothel, this would be it. The walls were covered in red velvet and sported bejewelled light fixtures. Fringes dangled from the lampshades. In the centre of the medium-sized room was a red porcelain Jacuzzi large enough to hold two people. It was surrounded by white tile flooring and white shag carpeting. At the far end, layers of fluffy white towels and what looked to be white terrycloth kimonos filled several shelves, while on another set of shelves lay what I was fairly certain were sex toys.

I continued on to the next room, the one designated by violets also depicted in a state of sexual arousal. It was about the same size as the other room, and it too was dark and empty. But it held even more curious items. In addition to the queen bed filling the middle of the room, it contained a closet filled with outfits, ranging from little girl outfits to maid's dresses and uniforms. There were also a couple of Indian princess outfits, complete with feathers and fluttering fringe. All had extremely short skirts and ridiculously low necklines. Most seemed to be an average woman's size. There were, however, several outfits in a much larger size, a size that would fit a man. I even came across some giant diapers that no doubt went with the adult-size playpen filled with kid's toys shoved into the far corner.

I shook my head at the thought of what some men would do to get their kicks out of sex and was very glad that none of the men in my life had ever asked me to wear such attire.

Then I stepped inside the room with the fornicating daylilies. In fact, I almost didn't step inside, so disgusted was I by what it contained; chains, whips, handcuffs, hoods, and slinky black clothing. The entire theme of the room was black; black walls, black floor, and black sheets on the bed, where handcuffs were still attached to the posts at either end. The enormity of J.P.'s dying words now hit me. This was no doubt what he'd meant when he'd used the term "slave." I had to stop myself from slamming the door in my haste to leave, while all I could think was heaven help poor innocent Fleur.

Until this point, I hadn't been paying attention to what was going on around me, so absorbed had I been in the contents of these rooms. But now I realized the quiet of the night had been broken by loud voices, more like shouting coming from the direction of the staff quarters.

Will ran up to me holding his rifle. "Stay here. It looks like George and Teht'aa have run into some trouble."

CHAPTER
FIFTY-THREE

I didn't know whether to obey the police chief's orders and stay where I was or race after him to the staff quarters to try to help out. With one more room to check, I wasn't yet finished with this snake pit, but so far the other three rooms had revealed nothing to suggest that Eric had ever been inside. And while Fleur had likely been forced to prostitute herself in one of these rooms, she certainly wasn't here now.

The shouting intensified and was now joined by ferocious barking coming from the dog pen. From the direction of the lodge, a door crashed open. Three men sprinted past an opening in the forest. One was Fran, the other Etienne. The third I didn't recognize, but he held a rifle. I snapped off my headlamp and slunk further into the shadows.

With no means of defending myself other than the bear spray, I would be useless. I would only be a distraction for my friends; plus it would be better if the bikers remained ignorant of my presence. Besides, someone had to keep searching for Eric and Fleur.

I crept along the walkway to the last door, the one with the copulating irises. Since there had been no key for this door, I was hoping that it was unlocked. I had almost reached the door when I realized that a pinprick of bright-ness was coming from the peephole. The room must be in use, which would explain the missing key. But with no guests in the lodge, who could be using it? Was this where they were keeping Eric?

I'd started to put my eye up to the peephole when I heard rustling in the trees behind me. I pivoted around, almost knocking over a shovel propped against the wall. I managed to grab it before it went clattering to the ground. I flicked on my headlamp and scanned the foliage but saw nothing. Meanwhile, the rustling stopped. Probably just an animal foraging through the underbrush.

I returned my eye to the peephole. Like most security peepholes, I figured I wouldn't be able to see anything inside the room, instead I found myself looking through a fisheye lens that brought much of the room's interior into focus. However, the low light made it difficult to make sense of the jumble of equipment filling most of the room.

"Now what do we have here?" a voice snarled from behind me in French.

I whirled around to find myself facing the third man I'd seen on the porch, the one I suspected was also a biker. Tall, with arms as thick as stovepipes, he hadn't bothered to cover up his disfigurement with long hair. Instead his bristling blond brush cut seemed to accentuate the scar-ring where his ear should've been.

"Where have you come from, mademoiselle? You're too old to be one of ours." His protruding lips creased into a mocking grin.

Perhaps it was instinct that dictated my next action, for I didn't consciously remember making a decision. It was certainly fear, I know that much. The butt end of a gun had no sooner begun emerging from his pocket than I unclipped my bear spray and gave him a full blast in the face.

He dropped the gun and jammed his hands into his eyes. He clawed at the fiery pepper stinging them and shook his head so much he almost lost his balance.

He howled, "*Câlisse!* What have you done to me, bitch?"

Although his gun lay at my feet, I knew I couldn't use it. Instead, I reached for the shovel and walloped him hard on the head. He dropped like a felled tree. For a second I feared I'd killed him, but when I saw the rise and fall of his chest, I knew he was still alive. Even though I knew he wouldn't have hesitated to kill me, I couldn't bear to have his death on my conscience.

But he would eventually regain consciousness, so I needed to ensure he remained out of action.

I ran to the Daylily room with its restraining equipment and grabbed several unlocked handcuffs and some chains. I dragged his dead weight a short distance to where a couple of birch trees stood a few feet apart. I propped him against one, placed his arms around the trunk behind him, and snapped one pair of the handcuffs around his wrists. Then I stretched out his legs and secured his feet to the other birch by circling the chain around his ankles and around the tree. I snapped the two ends tightly together with another set of handcuffs.

I glanced at his partially open mouth and realized I would have to silence him too, so I ran back to the Violet room, where I'd seen several silk scarves. I wrapped one of these around his mouth as a gag. Only then did I feel safe enough to return to the Iris room to find out if anyone was inside.

But the door was securely locked with no sign of the key, either in the lock or hanging on a nearby hook. Hoping that this guy had been coming to check out the room, I raced back to where he sprawled still unconscious between the two trees. I waited a minute to ensure he was not faking before searching his clothing for the key. I found it, clearly marked with its iris tag, in the outer pocket of his frayed jean jacket. I muttered "Ah, ha!" when I saw the grinning image of a red devil on the front of his black T-shirt. And then I spied a hunting knife clipped to his belt. I slipped it out of the leather sheath and stashed it away in my pack.

I confiscated one more item. It had fallen out of the pocket that held the key. It was a small, paper-thin deer-skin pouch with the beaded image of a fisher embroi-dered on one side. Eric's treasured amulet. Final proof he was at the lodge and not of his own free will, for he would never have given this up willingly. I prayed I wasn't too late.

My heart racing, I sped back to the Iris room. Unable to still my trembling fingers, I dropped the key several times before managing to hold it steady enough to insert it into the lock and unlock the door.

At that precise moment, a shot rang out from the direction of the staff quarters, then another.

I slammed the door shut behind me and relocked it as my ear caught the almost inaudible sound of someone moaning. I turned around and gasped. This room, about twice the size of the other rooms, was a torture chamber with all the medieval paraphernalia of a B movie. Thick, heavy chains and massive iron hooks hung from the ceiling and walls, along with various lengths of leather straps with loops. In a corner of the room a black pillar rose from floor to ceiling, and in another a strange metal contraption. Protruding from both their surfaces hung more leather straps and chains. I tried not to think of the horrific use made of such hellish instruments.

The single lit bulb on a wall didn't provide sufficient light for me to see where the moaning was coming from, so I flicked on my headlamp and shone it towards the sound. From behind a large metal container with strangely positioned openings, a naked foot came into view. Around the ankle was clamped a thick leather strap.

I walked around the box and froze in horror. Along the back wall stood what could best be described as a medieval torture rack, and spreadeagle along its wooden frame lay a naked man, his head covered by a black hood. His arms, gripped by leather thongs around the wrists, were yanked painfully above his head, while his legs, almost rigid, were attached to a roller placed at the bottom of the rack by taut leather straps tied around his ankles. I couldn't bear to look at what they'd done with an electrode.

Oh my God. I felt the shudder start in my legs and arms as my entire body convulsed. The man's stocky, bear-like physique and the squiggly scar near his groin where a hockey skate had sliced him could only belong to one person.

"Eric, it's me, Meg," I cried out.

No response. No movement.

I rushed to remove the hood. His eyes were closed, but I felt a soft whisper of breath coming from his nose and a faint murmur of a pulse in his neck.

He was alive.

But oh, his face was so thin, almost gaunt, and the side of his head was crusted with blood where he'd been hit. Several amoeba-like red splotches soaked the wooden frame beside his head. He no longer appeared to be bleeding, but he was shivering.

It was only then that I realized my cheeks were wet with tears. "Eric, I'm going to get you out of this."

The first thing to remove was the electrical cord, in case it was emitting a shock. I followed the line to a metal box with a number of switches including a timer. I unplugged it. His body twitched when I carefully unwound the cord.

"Sorry, Eric. I didn't mean to hurt you."

His body relaxed.

"Can you hear me?"

Still no response.

I released the tension on the roller used to tighten the ankle straps, which released the pressure on his arms. I carefully removed the straps from his legs and arms, placed his limp arms by his side, and brought his legs together. The straps I threw in disgust on the floor. He remained unconscious.

While the faint red marks circling his wrists appeared to be new, the raw redness and bruising around his ankles suggested that he'd been wearing manacles for a long time. Where a soft cushion of flesh had once comfortably filled out his abdomen, ribs and hipbones poked through. And there were bruises liberally sprinkled over his body.

Some bore the yellowish colour of older beatings, while others were the angry purple of more recent ones. But his knuckles were scraped and bruised, as if he'd given as good as he'd got.

"Oh dear God, what did they do to you?" I leaned down and hugged him as best I could.

He continued to shiver.

"You're cold. I need to find something to warm you up." I looked around the room but saw nothing that would work.

"Eric, there's some towels and kimonos in another room. I'm going to get those. I won't be long, okay?"

I thought my talking might help him find his way back to this world, and if it didn't, at least help soothe him.

I unlocked the door and quietly opened it. The night's quiet had returned. I heard no shouts or gunfire, not even barking dogs. In their stead was an unsettling calm.

What if Teht'aa, Will, and George were hurt? What if they were dead?

But I needed to make sure Eric was safe before I could investigate. I ran back to the first room with the Jacuzzi and grabbed several towels and a couple of kimonos. Then remembering the bed in the room with the weird clothes, I picked up the duvet and half-dragged it behind me as I headed back to Eric.

He lay on the rack in the same position I'd left him in. I would've loved to remove him from this horrific piece of equipment, but it kept him off the cold floor. I wrapped him tightly with the towels, shoving them underneath him as best I could. After slipping one under his head, I draped the duvet over his body and tucked it under. Still he didn't move.

"Oh, my sweet dear love, I'm here and I'll never leave you again."

I brushed my lips against his, hoping for a response, but received none.

I caressed his much-loved face and felt the prickle of a beard that had not seen a razor for many days. I ran my fingers fondly over the scar beneath his eye, the one caused by an errant hockey puck. His people had named him Angry Scar Man because it turned white when he was mad. I smoothed out his long, thick mane of hair, careful not to dislodge the thick crust of blood on his scalp, and brushed away wayward strands. I wiped my tears from his face. I ached to lie with him to pass on my strength and warmth, but I didn't dare. I had to get help.

Having no idea how long he'd been unconscious, I worried that he might have a serious brain injury. Without immediate medical attention, it could grow worse. But the earliest medical help could arrive was tomorrow morning, when it would be light enough for the plane to land. Still they might be able to give me advice over the phone.

I reached into my pocket for the sat phone and felt Eric's amulet. His source of spiritual strength. Knowing it no longer contained at least two of his sacred items, I wondered how many more were missing.

The only item I found inside was the faded red petals of a dried cardinal flower. I smiled. I hadn't realized he'd kept it. I was certain it was the flower I'd laughingly placed in his hair one day several summers ago while we lay beside a burbling stream deep within the woods, making love on a carpet of moss. That was when he'd first called me *Miskowàbigonens*, "my little red flower."

I added his grandfather's fisher to the amulet and placed it on his bare chest under the duvet. I couldn't tie it around his neck, for the leather thong was broken, leaving behind noticeable marks where it had been yanked.

"May this bring you strength, my love."

As I started to walk outside to use the satellite phone, a voice whispered, "Help me … please."

CHAPTER
FIFTY-FOUR

I should've realized there was another person in this den of iniquity. After all, it was moaning that first alerted me to Eric's presence. But he couldn't have made the sound, not while he was unconscious.

"Where are you?" I cried out.

"Over ... over here." The voice, which I now realized was a woman's, was barely above a whisper. "I'm ... I'm tied up."

If I hadn't been so focused on Eric, I would've noticed this woman, also naked, with the smooth, unblemished skin of youth. Although a black hood also covered her face, I didn't need to remove it to know her.

Fleur.

Sweet, young Fleur, tied up like a sacrificial offering, her back arched in a revoltingly obscene position over a barrel-like structure and her arms and legs shackled as Eric's had been. At least the monsters had given her support for her head and not let it flop loosely over the end of the barrel.

I shuddered at the depths of depravity to which men could go to treat a young woman so despicably, anyone for that matter.

I hastily removed the hood. Amber eyes, wide with shock, stared back at me, while tears trickled over a face tinged with a light dusting of bronze. Long tendrils of silky dark hair clung to her wet cheeks and neck.

There was no hint of recognition in those beautiful eyes. "Fleur, it's me, Meg Harris. I'm gonna get you out of this mess."

I untied the straps holding her ankles and wrists. She remained arched over the barrel as if not realizing she was free. I raised her carefully upright and wrapped one of the kimonos I'd brought around her shoulders. Her body trembled, either from the cold or fear or both.

"Fleur, are you okay?"

She continued to ignore me, although she had closed her eyes and had begun to sing softly to herself as she rocked back and forth.

"She's seeking strength from Grandmother Moon," a voice rang out from behind me.

I whirled around to see Eric half-raised on his elbows, before he sank back down with a groan.

"Oh my God, you're okay."

I ran to him. I brushed my fingers gently over his face, his eyes, his cheeks, his lips, and his scar to convince myself that he really was okay. He reached for my hand and brought it to his lips.

"My little Red Flower," he murmured. I leaned down and kissed him on those soft, full lips and felt an invigorating warmth in his answering response.

Then he chuckled. "What took you so long?" He grinned, and the dimples I adored erupted on either cheek.

I helped him sit up and watched as the expression on his face changed to one of horror as he took in his surroundings. "Christ, I didn't know such places existed."

His silvery grey eyes looked up at me questioningly. "How in the hell did I get here?" Then he shook his head. "No, you can't answer that."

He raised his hand and gingerly felt the injury on his head. He winced. "Ouch. I think I know what happened. I was eating dinner in the cabin where they'd been holding me when a couple of guys I hadn't seen before came in and began dragging me towards the door. They didn't even bother to remove the chains around my ankles. I know I put up a fight. In fact, I can remember hitting one guy squarely on the jaw."

He grinned as he eyed the bruises and cuts on his knuckles. "Next thing I know I'm hearing your voice, your sweet, angelic voice, my *Miskowàbigonens*."

I blushed. "I think they brought you by boat to the main lodge. We heard it as we were approaching the hunting cabin."

Just then a shout from outside rang through the torture chamber.

We froze.

"Don't worry, I've locked the door. And I have the key." I held up the dangling iris keychain. Nonetheless, I could feel my body start to tremble with fear. What the hell were we going to do now?

"Meg, Meg, where are you?" someone called.

"That sounds like Will," Eric said. "Is he here too?"

"We're in here," I yelled back, hastening to unlock the door.

I opened it onto a dishevelled Will, his baseball cap gone, a jagged red cut across his cheek, his arm clenched to his side and a revolver jammed into the waist of his pants. A broad grin spread from cheek to cheek.

"You're hurt! What happened?" I asked.

"A bloody gun fight, that's what." He laughed. "But as you can see, we won. Three of the bad guys are trussed up in a shed and are being guarded by George. One has a gunshot wound to his leg, while the fourth guy is dead. I think he's the one you said was the manager's brother."

"You mean Fran."

"Yup. He was a shifty bastard, tried to sneak up on Teht'aa."

"Oh no, did he hurt her?"

"Nope, I caught him just as he was raising his gun. But we haven't been able to find Eric or Fleur."

"I have." I opened the door wide.

"That you, Will?" Eric called out. "I tell ya, you two are the best things I've seen in two months." He was now sitting with his legs dangling over the side of the rack and the duvet tightly wrapped around his body.

Fleur, however, remained where I'd left her sitting awkwardly on the barrel with her kimono hanging open. I ran to hide her nakedness. Still chanting, she paid no attention to me or to the others and limply submitted to the kimono being tied around her.

"She's been through a very rough time," Eric said. "If you can get her out of this room and into a safer place, her healing will begin."

"We'd better do the same with you," I said. "Will, here's the sat phone to call for rescue."

"Already done," he answered. "I used George's phone. But the planes can't land until daylight, so let's put them in one of the hotel rooms."

"Hey, man, you look like shit." Will walked up to his friend. "But Christ, it's sure good to see you alive and kicking."

He gripped the other man with the intensity of an enduring friendship.

With Will supporting a wobbly Eric and me guiding Fleur, we left the hellhole and firmly shut the door on the nightmare. We surprised Teht'aa in the lobby of the lodge, where she'd been checking the rooms to ensure they were empty.

"Dad, you're alive!"

Tears flowed from her eyes as she ran and flung her arms around her father with such force that he almost fell.

I beamed as the love I felt for both of them overwhelmed me. After giving them a few moments, I joined them in a communal hug and in turn was joined by Will. Finally we broke apart, laughing and crying at the same time. Even Will had wet cheeks.

But I'd forgotten about Fleur. She wasn't standing where I'd left her.

"Where's Fleur gone?" I cried out.

"What, you've got Fleur too? Thank God," Teht'aa said.

"But she's not in good shape. Come on, we'd better go look for her." I headed into the adjoining room filled with overstuffed leather chairs and chesterfields and a dying fire in a stone fireplace, a room that would've made a comfortable and warming retreat, but clearly not for her.

Instead I found her in the bar, talking quietly to the parrot, who glanced at her suspiciously out of one eye. She didn't turn or make any acknowledgement of my presence.

"Fleur, it's me, Meg."

She continued talking to the green parrot.

"Everything's going to be okay. Those men can't hurt you any more. They're locked up."

I saw her body go rigid, but that was the only indication that she was listening.

I continued, "The police will be here in the morning. You'll soon be going home to your mother, your father, and your sisters."

She jerked around, her eyes wide with fear. "No, I can't."

Before I could catch her, she sprinted out of the room, onto the verandah, and down the stairs.

I raced after her. "Fleur, come back! You're safe. You don't need to run. No one is going to hurt you."

She sped across the front grounds, the white kimono flapping in the glare of the floodlights. Even in her bare feet, she could outrun me. By the time she disappeared into the blackness of the forest, the distance between us had stretched.

"Fleur, please stop. You might hurt yourself."

"Who cares," came the response.

I stopped at the forest edge and flicked on my headlamp. I could hear her footsteps, still running. A path cut its way through the trees. I followed it, stopping every few minutes to listen to her running footsteps to ensure that she was still in front of me. Despite the blackness of the night, she never faltered, never stopped. She ran relentlessly onward, getting further and further away. So far she seemed to be staying on the trail. I followed at a slower pace until I could no longer hear her footsteps. By now I was convinced she'd travelled this path many times before, so I kept walking. She had a destination in mind. I would find her there.

The night had turned cold, but thankfully the rain still held off. My breath sent swirls of steam into the light of my headlamp. I zipped up my jacket, wishing I'd brought something warm with me to give to the girl. Once she cooled down from her running, she would need it.

I entered a copse of birch, and believing this might be her destination, I shone my headlight around their silvery trunks. She wasn't there. I continued onwards and upwards. The path was starting to climb, not sharply, but in a slow, steady rise. It had also changed in texture. Until this point the path had been predominantly bare ground with scatterings of dead leaves and pine needles. Now it was covered in soft, cushiony moss. Tall, feathery ferns defined its borders.

I could hear a low rumble coming from the direction I was headed. It made me nervous. I followed the trail upward until it suddenly opened onto a broad carpet of moss. The path stopped. The noise had become the roar of rushing water. My light shone out into a yawning, mist-filled blackness. Below glimmered water tumbling over rock. I had little doubt that I was looking down at the dangerous falls that lay upriver from where we'd left the canoes.

Terrified Fleur might have slipped over the edge, I scanned the rocks below but saw nothing but foaming white. Then I heard the sound of singing.

The young woman stood at the edge, her arms outstretched as if she was about to fly. Her long hair swirled in the breeze rising from the river.

"Fleur, don't!" I cried out. "You have too much to live for."

"No, I don't," she said. "I'm filth, I'm dirt. No one will want to come near me."

"But none of what's happened to you is your fault. Your mother loves you very much. She sent me to find you."

"I don't believe you. She kicked me out of the house."

"She's very sorry. She knows she was wrong and only wants you to return home. Here, I've got a satellite phone, call her, talk to her."

But she ignored my offer. Instead, she continued to stand with her toes curled over the mossy edge and her arms outstretched.

"Please, Fleur, come away from the edge so we can talk better."

"What's there to talk about? Sure I can tell you about the forty-one different ways I learned to fuck or the number of times I sucked the cocks of old men dressed in diapers, while I wore a nurse's uniform with my boobs hanging out. But I don't think you want to hear about that."

"Fleur, you can put all that behind you. You have your whole life ahead of you."

"No, I don't. It's over."

While we talked, I'd inched closer, hoping to reach her before she made up her mind to jump.

"Please, Fleur, there are people that can help you. Summer Grass Woman and others."

I was almost within touching distance when she turned her tear-stained face towards me and cried out, "You don't understand. You see, I enjoyed the filth. In fact, I liked the chains and the rack the best." She gave a high, almost hysterical laugh. "My father was a good teacher. Because of that I can't live with myself."

With those last words, she jumped. I flung out my arms and screamed, "Don't!" Our fingertips touched as her arms spread into a swan dive, and over she went into the mad water below.

CHAPTER
FIFTY-FIVE

After frantically scrambling along the rocky shore hoping to catch sight of Fleur, I eventually gave up and headed back to the lodge to get more help. By then it had started to pour and visibility had been reduced to zero. Nonetheless, Will and Teht'aa took up the search, intending to use our canoes to check the shoreline downriver from the falls. We prayed that the desperate girl had survived against all odds and had managed to make it to shore.

I stayed behind with Eric to make sure his condition didn't worsen. We huddled together under the warmth of a thick, fluffy duvet in the lodge's only guestroom with a fireplace. I had scrounged firewood from the bar, enough to stoke it into an acceptable blaze, and had been adding the occasional log.

On the advice of emergency personnel over the satellite phone, I'd carefully cleansed Eric's wound, bandaged it with gauze from Will's first aid kit then applied several treatments with an ice pack to minimize the swelling. Apart from being unconscious for an hour or more, he so far hadn't displayed any other symptoms of possible brain injury.

Aside from whispered endearments, we said little to each other. He wasn't ready to share his ordeal nor did I want to tell him about Fleur for fear that it would hinder his recovery. Instead we clung to each other, overjoyed to be in each other's arms once again.

He was tired, very tired, so when he drifted off to sleep, I relaxed. I'd been told that sleep would begin the healing process. But just in case, I remained firmly tucked in beside him, watchful for signs that all was not well. Every once in a while I would give him a gentle nudge, and when he would respond with a caress or a grunt, I'd smile. He was going to be okay.

But I didn't sleep. I couldn't. While the rain tapped a staccato on the window, my mind tapped its own. My thoughts and emotions were a conflicting whirl of jubilation and guilt. Jubilation that my friend, my lover was alive, that he was going to be all right. But these joyful thoughts were overshadowed by guilt that I had let Marie-Claude's daughter fall to her death. I held out little hope that she'd be found alive. The rocks under the falls were just too treacherous to survive.

I should've realized that Fleur would be so stressed by her forced prostitution that she would hate herself enough to want to end it. I should've tried harder to talk her out of jumping. I should've been close enough to get a firm grip on her when she dove off the edge.

I'd promised Marie-Claude that I would save her daughter. Instead I'd let her eldest die. I had no idea what I was going to tell her when I finally got home, but tell her something I must.

Fleur's words about her father also deeply troubled me.

Had more than physical abuse occurred in her family? Was this the underlying cause of Marie-Claude's paralyzing guilt? Had she turned a blind eye to the situation? And if Fleur had been sexually abused, what about the other two daughters? Did their father abuse them too? Perhaps this was the real reason behind Marie-Claude leaving the man.

At some point during the night, the rain stopped, and we awoke to the delight of morning sun spilling onto the bed. Eric no doubt was expecting to read bliss on my face. Instead, he must have read anguish, for he immediately asked, "What's wrong, my little red flower?" And he kissed me gently on the forehead.

Although I'd only wanted to give him comfort, to shield him from further pain, all my worry, all my guilt came spilling out.

I told him about Fleur fleeing into the forest, about her horrific dive into the raging river. I told him about my role and how I should've done more to prevent it. His response was to wrap me in his arms, saying it was the will of the Creator.

"She visited me several times on the sly, while I was detained in a cabin," he said. "She'd overheard one of the men talking about me, so she came to see if she could set me free. But we both realized even if she could unlock the chains around my legs, my chances of survival so far from any habitation were even worse than remaining in the cabin. So when no one was watching either of us, she would come to visit and to talk. At first she was reluctant to tell me how she was being used, but eventually she opened up. I tell you, Meg, I've seen and heard of some pretty sordid things in my life, but what she was forced to do topped them all."

As he said this, I thought of his own situation, chained to the rack, and hoped he'd been unconscious the entire time. Apart from the men who put him there, I was the only one who knew of the degrading position in which he'd been placed, and I would never divulge this to anyone.

"She was just a kid, a good kid, who'd never caused anyone trouble," he continued. "The despicable acts they forced her to do shattered her. I could tell by the desperation in her eyes. I'm not surprised she wanted to end her life. Some people can overcome demoralizing trauma to their bodies and minds. They are able to lock it away and continue on with living. Fleur was too open, too innocent, too young. It truly destroyed her, so please don't blame yourself, Meg."

Clearly Eric didn't suspect that any sexual abuse had happened in the Lightbody family. I felt that until I learned if it was true, it was best to keep my suspicions from Eric. He, after all, was the man's boss. A false accusation could lead Eric to do something he would later regret.

"Meg, even if you had stopped her from killing herself this time, she would have kept trying until she finally succeeded. You can put your mind at ease knowing that Fleur has returned to the protection of Mother Earth, where she will never again have to suffer at the hands of men nor relive the experience over and over again."

I kissed him for these comforting words and snuggled further into his warmth, while his hands gently brushed the tears from my face. I felt as if I had come home after a long absence in the frozen wasteland of estrangement.

Then, without realizing it, I found myself telling him about another person whose death I wore on my conscience, my one and only brother. I told him about the snowstorm, about how I'd defied my mother and taken Joey tobogganing, and how I'd made him fly down the hill to his death. I admitted to the cowardly lies I'd told my mother to move the blame from myself and onto Joey.

And I confessed to something I'd never divulged to anyone, not even Summer Grass Woman. I'd been jealous of Joey. Much celebration had taken place at his birth when I was six. My father finally had a male heir to carry on the Harris name. Though Father had done his best to give me and my sister equal attention, I could see that he preferred Joey, his only son, named after a favoured family member, Great-grandpa Joe. Even after Father's disappearance, Joey remained the special child in Mother's eyes. So when my little brother went flying down that steep snowy hill to his death, I'd felt a tiny quiver of satisfaction.

When I finished my confession, I waited in the deafening silence. I waited for the revulsion to harden the softness in his eyes, the same revulsion that had appeared in Gareth's. I waited for the damning judgment that still lurked in my mother's. I waited for him to say, "Go. Get out of my life. You are not worthy."

The room's coldness washed my face. The fire was almost out, but I dared not get out of bed to restart it, for fear of triggering a response. I wanted him to respond in his own way and in his own time.

And then I heard the rhythmic pattern of his breathing and turned around to see his eyes lightly closed in sleep.

I groaned. Had he heard any part of my confession? Was I going to have to repeat it all over again?

I carefully slipped out from under the duvet and coaxed the dying fire back to life. Once I felt the warmth of its blaze, I crawled back in beside him, careful not to wake him. But his arms reached around and drew me closer.

"Life goes on, my *Miskowàbigonens*," he murmured. "We all do things we're not proud of, things we wished we hadn't done. And as the years pass, we live with the guilt boring ever deeper into our soul. But there comes a time when we must relinquish this guilt. Toss it out for the gods to judge. And whatever they decide we must live with.

"You've been dealing with this guilt ever since you were a girl. It's time for you to free yourself of it. Toss it up to the Great Spirit and let him carry it.

"So please, my little red flower. Rest easy. I will not judge you. You've suffered enough. Besides, wait until you hear about some of the things I've done. I can outmatch you any old day." He chuckled.

Exasperated, I punched him on the chest, but with more play in the touch than force. However, when I pulled my hand away, he encircled it and placed it over the amulet hanging again around his neck, courtesy of a shoelace taken from my boot.

"You found my *odjik*, didn't you?" he said.

"Yes, in the cabin where you'd left it."

"And you put it back where it belongs with the red flower." His voice carried uncertainty. His brows were arched in query.

I leaned on my elbow and stared into the soft grey depths of his eyes. I hesitated before girding up my nerve. "More than anything, I want us to belong together ... but ... but only if you want to."

"I do. Life wasn't worth living without you. You are my one and only love, my *Miskowàbigonens*. I missed you."

I smiled into his beaming face. "I missed you too. I promise I'll never turn away from you again."

I collapsed back into his arms. We were whole again.

CHAPTER
FIFTY-SIX

Eric struggled to sit up in bed. "Whoa, I'm weaker than I thought."

"Do you feel dizzy?" I asked, suddenly worried as I placed another pillow behind his back.

"No. Just weak. But nothing a few days in bed with you wouldn't cure." His dimples beckoned.

"Just a few? I think it should be for at least a week." I tucked the duvet firmly around him.

"More like a month, I'd say. It's going to take a lot of TLC for me to recover."

I laughed. A month would suit me very nicely, even longer.

He winced as he gingerly touched the bandage on his head. "Boy, they sure walloped me, didn't they? It feels like the size of an egg."

"Not quite, but you have a good bump. Maybe some sense was finally knocked into you." I placed a hot mug of tea on the night table beside him. "I ran into Will on my way back from the kitchen. He wants to know if you're up to a visit."

"I know I'll have to talk to him soon, but for the moment I'd like it to be just us. What about my daughter? Is she around?"

"Will said she's gone back to the river to look for Fleur in the daylight. The rain last night made it too difficult to do a proper search. He's staying behind to deal with the women. I gather some of them need reassurance."

"I don't doubt they'll need time to adjust. They've been through a lot, but now thanks to you guys they are free and their healing can begin."

"I gather from Will that only two of the women were part of that group of missing Ottawa women you were investigating."

"Yeah, so I discovered. The other six were nabbed in Montreal. To tell you the truth, I never did hold out much hope that many of them would be found. These trafficked women get shunted from brothel to brothel, so the trail gets lost pretty quickly, and besides, this kind of business isn't exactly good for one's health."

"Will has started grilling the manager. Hopefully he can extract enough information to trace them."

"I'd sure like to hope so. But I tell you, Meg, after what I've been through and what I've seen, I've lost a lot of faith in my fellow man. I think it will be a miracle if any of those women are ever found."

"But at least the traffickers have been stopped, so no more women will be entrapped."

"True, but I don't doubt another group of traffickers will soon take their place. There's too much money to be made in prostitution."

"My, we are feeling gloomy, aren't we? You need a hug."

I wrapped my arms around him and held him tightly before letting go.

I passed him the steaming tea. "Here, this will make you feel better."

"Yes, Mother." He grinned and grabbed the mug. "Everything still feels so surreal, from the kidnapping to the rescue. After I made that call to the bank, I really believed I was a goner, so when I saw you standing in front of me, I was convinced I was dreaming. Even now, I still can't quite believe the ordeal is over."

"It's not a dream, my love. I'm here and will never leave your side again." I kissed him.

"The kidnapping happened so quickly. There wasn't much I could do. All I could think was of the need to leave a trail for someone to follow, like the kids do in one of your people's fairy tales."

"You mean Hansel and Gretel."

"Yes, that's it."

"I found your sacred rock too."

"In the parking lot?"

I nodded.

"Amazing, I was worried that it wouldn't stand out amongst all the other stones."

"The sparkle of the gold caught my attention. By the way, the body of a friend of Fleur's was found close to that parking lot."

"You're talking about Becky Wapachee, aren't you? I watched her die. She tried to run away while they were switching us from one vehicle to another. They couldn't catch her, so he dropped her with a knife then took out his anger on her. It was terrible to watch. Since she'd been used to recruit some of the young women, she knew what was in store. I guess forced prostitution was okay for her victims, but not for her." He paused to drink some tea. "And to set the record straight, Becky was no friend of Fleur's. She was the one who got her into this terrible situation."

"What about the woman at the Welcome Centre, Doris?"

"She and Becky worked as a team. Doris would identify potential candidates and Becky would befriend them. They used a modeling ad to reel in these poor unsuspecting women."

"Was there another woman involved? I ask because a woman who also worked at the Welcome Centre was killed. Claire was her name."

"I had my suspicions about her, but I was never able to prove them. I began to suspect that Doris was identifying potential candidates from information gathered at the Centre. Since she didn't have ready access to the files, she would need someone who did, and Claire, because of her role as a counsellor, could've been that person. But I think Claire was starting to regret her role. She left several anxious messages on my cell phone, but before I had a chance to return her calls, I was kidnapped."

"Maybe she was the one that got you kidnapped?"

"Maybe, but I have a feeling it was Doris. I could tell she was pretty upset when I turned up at Auntie's Place. She pretended she didn't know what I was talking about, but I was fairly certain she was lying. At one point she left the room. I think that's when she placed the call to the gang running this trafficking operation. When I stepped out of the building, they were waiting for me."

"I know. The Ottawa police have a witness who saw your kidnapping."

"So why the hell didn't they do anything about it?"

"Although getting the police to move has been a major challenge, in this instance they're not at fault. It took us a couple of months to realize you were missing, so they've only been working on trying to find you for the past week."

"But surely when Teht'aa didn't hear from me after the canoe trip, she should've known something was wrong?"

"She just assumed you were too busy to call her. It was only when Dan Blackbird called that she realized you never made it to Vancouver. She then called up one of your canoeing buddies and discovered you hadn't been on the canoeing trip either. That's when we knew something was terribly wrong."

"I thought the guy was going to kill me after he killed Becky. Instead they shoved me into the trunk of a car. There were two of them, bikers wearing Black Devils patches. I don't think they drove very far before stopping next to a lake and forcing me onto a floatplane. I left another of my crumbs on the beach, the miniature hockey stick given to me by a friend." He grinned. "I don't suppose you found that one?"

"Nope, I didn't know there was a lake. But perhaps the police will see it when they eventually learn of this lake and we can put it back where it belongs." I squeezed his hand and kissed it. "Wait a minute, I think the latest murder victim was found by a lake, Lac aux Herons, maybe that's the one. Do you know who the guy was that killed Becky?"

"Yes, a coldblooded bastard by the name of Fran."

"You will be relieved to know that he's the one Will killed last night."

His eyes brightened. "I don't think I've ever been so happy to hear of someone being dead. He was ruthless. Treated the girls as if they were his personal harem. He liked chaining his women up, particularly native women. I gather from Fleur he called them his squaw meat and treated them accordingly. He was the first to use Fleur so despicably. I'm glad he's dead.

"But you know, Meg, I owe Fleur my life. Once they stopped trying to beat out of me all I knew about their operations and who I'd told, I figured my days were numbered. But it didn't happen. Hoping to stall drastic action, Fleur told them about September's money transfer into the reserve's accounts, which she knew about from her father. She told them I was the only one with authority to access the account, so they needed to keep me alive. And they bought it. They pretty much left me alone after that. I thought for sure we'd be rescued before I had to make the phone call to the bank manager. That was two days ago."

"I know. Once Will heard about your call, he knew your life was in immediate danger. "

"I'd made my peace with the Creator before I made the call, knowing the minute those guys learned they weren't getting the money, that would be the end of me. The money belongs to our people. There was no way I was going to let them have it."

"You are very lucky they decided not to kill you right away."

"Once again I have Fleur to thank for that. God, it makes me sick to think that she is the one that didn't survive."

"She was a very brave young woman." I squeezed his hands and kissed him gently on the forehead. "And I will be eternally grateful to her."

"She concocted a story about me being a powerful medicine man and that if they killed me, the wrath of the spirits would descend and they would die a very painful and mysterious death. So I —"

His words were drowned out by the reverberating echo of a helicopter. I raced to the window in time to see a white helicopter with the words AirMédic stamped on its side land on the front lawn. Two floatplanes circled over the lake for a landing. Both bore the insignia of the Sûreté du Québéc along with the word "Police."

The police had finally paid attention.

At the same moment, Will burst into the room. "Teht'aa's found Fleur. She's alive!"

CHAPTER
FIFTY-SEVEN

Echo Lake was aglow with reflected oranges, yellows, and reds of the surrounding hills. With the colours at their peak, it was the kind of quintessential fall day that only seems to happen in Canadian Shield country; a sparkling sun that brings everything into sharp relief, an electric blue sky, cool, crisp air, and flat, still water, so still that you could cut a knife through it and barely ripple the mirror. I was basking in its glory, relaxing in a Muskoka chair on the dock with Sergei asleep at my feet. I was waiting for Eric to return from the Fishing Camp. He'd paddled down Forgotten Bay shortly after lunch on some secret mission he refused to divulge, despite my amorous entreaties. He'd promised a surprise for dinner and I was getting hungry.

Since our return over three weeks ago from the northern Quebec forests, this was the first time we had been parted, except for the three days Eric had spent in the hospital in Montreal. But even then, I had been at his bedside from the moment visiting hours started in the morning until they ended at night. If the nurses had chosen to turn a blind eye, I would've slept in my sleeping bag on the floor beside him. But rules were rules and they whisked me out of his room the moment the clock struck nine.

It had been a tense few days, while the doctors poked, prodded, and scanned his head searching for signs of brain damage. Fortunately, he hadn't sustained a skull fracture, and although there had been some intracranial bleeding, it had been minor and hadn't led to any brain swelling. So after laughingly declaring that Eric had one very hard head, the doctor had said he was well enough to return home, but he was to take it easy and avoid any activity that could cause another knock to the head. This latest concussion, together with the four he'd received playing hockey, had increased his risk for possible long-term effects. Another could tip him over the edge.

So we'd taken advantage of the solitude and isolation of Three Deer Point, keeping anyone other than close family and friends at bay, while Eric healed. His ribs were beginning to fill out and the redness around his wrists and ankles had almost disappeared, as had the soreness in his shoulder and hip joints. As for what he had unknowingly endured while lying stretched out, unconscious on the rack, there had been no detrimental effect … thank goodness.

Since the band's affairs had run so smoothly under the acting chief during Eric's long absence, he'd seen no need to dive back into its operations. Instead he'd decided it was time to retire. He'd achieved what he'd set out to do when he'd been first elected band chief almost ten years ago. He was confident that there were enough like-minded councillors and other band members to continue the course he had set in striving for greater self-sufficiency. Besides, last night, Dan Blackbird had called wanting to know if Eric was ready to become involved on a more full-time basis with the Grand Council of First Nations. He'd promptly said yes. Tomorrow he was submitting his resignation as band chief of the Migiskan Anishinabeg.

Yesterday we'd driven Fleur to Ottawa. Although much was being done to help her, I wasn't sure whether she would fully overcome her horrifying ordeal at Sunset Lodge.

After finding Fleur several kilometres downriver from the falls, Teht'aa had taken the half-drowned, shivering woman upriver to where we had set up the tents. There she had done her best to care for her. Fortunately, apart from hypothermia, the worst Fleur had suffered was a broken arm, from crashing into a rock.

I later learned from Eric about her recounting of her suicide attempt. As she was plunging head first into the falls, her will to live took over, and she arched her body as far from the rocks below as she could. Luckily, she'd overreached her dive, so found herself far enough away from the cascading water to avoid serious injury. But she became caught up in the powerful rotating currents below the falls. She was certain she was going to drown, when the river suddenly released its hold and thrust her upwards to the surface. "It was not your time to die," Eric told her. "The Creator has other plans for you." But rather than accepting his comforting words, she chose to scorn them with a few choice swear words. Still, she did later agree to spend a couple of weeks with Summer Grass Woman.

When we arrived in Montreal, her father was waiting by the ambulance. She refused to have anything to do with him. Instead she shouted at him to leave and denounced him as her father. Rather than protesting, he merely shrugged and replied derisively that she was damaged goods and wasn't worthy of being his daughter. He walked off without a backward glance, much to the astonishment of us and the paramedics. I later revealed my suspicions of sexual abuse to Eric. He had already started to form his own.

Fleur was no more forthcoming with her mother. I'd found Marie-Claude in tears in Eric's hospital room, after being turned away by her daughter. Once again she was consumed with guilt, insisting that she deserved this punishment for refusing to acknowledge, let alone try to stop her husband's abuse of her two oldest daughters. Eric managed to placate her by pointing out that she was now doing the right thing in leaving her husband. He also said Fleur needed time on her own to heal, but he believed that when she was ready she would seek out her mother. In the meantime, it was their job, his and Marie-Claude's, to do all they could to help Fleur, and a first step would be for Fleur to begin her healing under the care of Summer Grass Woman. So for the past two and a half weeks, the young woman had been staying with the elder at her healing lodge on Whispers Island.

Yesterday, after seeing her for the first time since I'd driven her back with us from Montreal, I knew Eric had given the right advice. The young woman no longer hid behind a mask of hostility and distrust. Instead she greeted me with a tentative smile and thanked me for having saved her, something she hadn't done until that moment. But she stiffened and backed away when I tried to hug her, so I knew it would take more time before she would allow anyone to come near her. With Sergei, on the other hand, she had no qualms about burying her face in his thick, curly coat and wrapping her arms around him.

We'd driven her to a farm just outside Ottawa, where she'd be staying for the next couple of months. The owner, a friend of Mary Eshkakogan, had a way with wounded creatures and ran a wildlife rescue operation that always needed helpers. The woman's grandmother, an Ojibway elder, lived with her. These two women had made great inroads in the healing of other abused women Mary had sent to the bucolic acreage.

Since Fleur wasn't yet able to forgive her mother, no consideration was given to her living with her family at her uncle's apartment. But she was still close to her sisters, so they would be visiting her at the farm. In fact, the two of them had been waiting expectantly when we arrived at the farm. As we drove off, the view through the back window of three of them wrapped in one anothers' arms made me feel considerably more optimistic about Fleur's recovery.

Apart from weekends, we had seen little of Teht'aa. Once her new employers learned that her father was safe, they'd insisted that she come to Ottawa to start her new job. She was enjoying it immensely. Watching the evening APTN news in the hopes of catching a glimpse of her as the Ottawa reporter had become a part of our evening routine. I quite enjoyed watching Eric preen as his beautiful daughter's face filled the TV screen. She had spent time with us on the last two weekends, but had forewarned us that she would be tied up this coming one, no doubt something that would happen more frequently as she got on with her new life.

Will had become a regular dinner visitor. As the sun's dying rays sank behind the far hills, he would arrive with a wine bottle in hand, ready to tackle whatever sumptuous meal Eric had prepared that night. In exchange he regaled us with the latest happenings in the broader world, including keeping us up to date on the case. The two bikers and the lodge manager had been charged with a number of things, including kidnapping and human trafficking. Although the police hadn't been able yet to prove the involvement of other members of *Les Diables Noirs*, they strongly suspected the gang's hierarchy was fully aware of the operation and was probably receiving of some of the proceeds. The difficulty was in proving it.

The owner of the lodge, a princeling from an oil-rich Middle Eastern state, was hiding behind a flank of lawyers, protestations of ignorance, and no extradition treaty. The police had, however, discovered that he was also the owner of the Caribbean resort where the girls were sent after Sunset Lodge closed for the winter. Apparently, he owned a couple of other similarly isolated resorts, one in the Seychelles and the other on a small South Seas island. So things might start heating up for the princeling. However, Will warned us that proving that these establishments were recipients of trafficked women would probably be impossible, for by the time the paperwork was finalized between the various governments and police organizations, the girls would be long gone.

As for the unaccounted missing Ottawa women, now reduced to eight, Will doubted we would ever know what happened to them. Only two men had known. One was dead, Fran, and the other, his brother-in-law Etienne, was not talking. And if and when he eventually did, it was hardly likely the missing women would be at the resort where the traffickers had sent them. The two had run the trafficking operation pretty much on their own, with some assistance from the other two bikers. At least that was the story so far. The police, however, were still working on them. Regardless, we had managed to stop the trafficking, so the streets of Ottawa were once again safe for aboriginal women. And the next time one did go missing, we would make sure that the police paid attention.

Sergei stood up, wagging his tail, as Eric's red canoe sliced through the water towards the dock. He carried a passenger, Will, grinning from ear to ear. Both men stopped paddling. Eric, looking somewhat sheepish, held up a large bass, still dripping. I smiled. One of my favourite meals. I could already taste the delicate white fish sautéed lightly in butter with some fresh tarragon from my herb garden.

And Will was holding up his usual wine bottle, except in this case, it looked to be a bottle of champagne with a bright orange label, which, if I remembered correctly was that of Veuve Clicquot. Once a favourite ... from another life. Although I'd had nothing to drink since we'd come home, not even Will's wine, I would make tonight an exception.

"What's the celebration?" I called out.

"You'll see," answered Will, laughing, pointing at the bulge in Eric's lumber shirt pocket. It looked to be that of a small jewellery box.

Oh my.

ACKNOWLEDGEMENTS

As I tossed around themes for the fifth Meg Harris mystery, my mind kept returning to one that resonates throughout the First Nations communities of Canada, that of missing aboriginal women. Currently there are over 580 women missing across the country. Sisters in Spirit, an organization of the Native Women's Association of Canada, has taken as its mandate the task of raising awareness of this alarmingly high number and of the high rates of violence against aboriginal women and girls. Every year since 2006, Sisters in Spirit have held vigils on October 4 in many cities across the country to honour the lives of the missing and murdered women. If one happens to take place near you, you may want to consider showing you haven't forgotten these women either.

I felt that perhaps I could help raise the awareness in my own small way, by making missing native women a central theme of *A Green Place for Dying*. But I do want to emphasize that the fictional story and characters within are not based on any true situation. If perchance they do mirror a particular situation, it is purely happenstance.

As with all my books, I rely on the advice and expertise of others. I want to give a special thank you to my dedicated readers, Alex Brett, Barbara Fradkin, and Judith Nasby for their valuable comments. And a thank you to those that lent their expertise, namely Alex Hall, Marie Tobin, Sylvie Blais and Bernard Crepeau.

I also want to thank my editor, Allister Thompson, my former publisher, Sylvia McConnell, and my new publisher, Dundurn, for helping to make this book happen.

As ever, I couldn't pursue my writing adventure without the enduring support of my husband, Jim. And I must not forget to mention the two who probably spend the most time with me while I am writing, Sterling and Gryphon, my standard poodles, who usually spend it sound asleep on the couch, when they are not barking at the squirrels attacking the bird feeders.

MORE MEG HARRIS MYSTERIES BY R.J. HARLICK

Arctic Blue Death
978-1894917872
$16.95

The sparsely populated Arctic is no stranger to murder...

The fourth in the Meg Harris series follows Meg's adventures in the Canadian Arctic as she searches for the truth about the disappearance of her father when she was a child. Many years earlier, her father's plane had gone missing in the Arctic and he was never seen again. What happened on that fateful flight?

Thirty-six years later, her mother receives some strange Inuit drawings that suggest he might have survived. Intent on discovering the answers, no matter how painful, Meg travels to Iqaluit to find the artist and is sucked into the world of Inuit art forgery. *Arctic Blue Death* is not only a journey into Meg's past and the events that helped shape the person she is today, but it's also a journey into the land of the Inuit and the culture that has sustained them for thousands of years. Finalist for the Arthur Ellis Award for best crime novel.

The River Runs Orange
978-1894917629
$15.95

Meg Harris is always determined to fight against injustice, but sometimes the line between right and wrong is fuzzy. During a wild whitewater paddle down a wilderness river, Meg discovers the skull and bones of a woman whose very existence takes the archeological world by storm. But when her neighbours, the Migiskan Algonquin, declare their rights to the ancient remains, Meg becomes embroiled in a fight that pits ancient beliefs against modern ones and can only lead to murder.

As Meg races to catch the killer, she finds herself once more daring the river's fury, this time with the added horror of a raging forest fire.

Available at your favourite bookseller.

9 781926 607245